1369

1369

H. Lee Bell

Halo Press, Inc.

WARNING!

THIS BOOK CONTAINS A PRE-RAPTURE BRIEFING.
MESSENGERS ARE ABOUT (*Hebrews 13:2*).
If you believe not, prepare to Code Blue.
IF YOU BELIEVE, THE LIGHT SHALL AGAIN SHINE.

Library of Congress Catalog Card No. 92-081201

ISBN: 0-9632869-0-0

Disclaimer: This book is fiction. No person, place or event herein pertains in whole or in part to any person, living or deceased, and any similarity is purely coincidental.

Cover Design by CNB & Co.; Artwork by Alford Treadway

First Printing, July, 1992

Published by: Halo Press, Inc.
902 West Second Street
Little Rock, AR 72201

Printed in the United States of America

CONTENTS

THE BRIEFING . . .

1   In the third year of the reign of Cash, King of Capitalism, there came forth visions with great laughter among nightmares of stark terror to the pious flock of the Church of the Marine Korps.

2   And one dollar begat five dollars;

3   And five dollars begat ten dollars;

4   And ten dollars begat twenty dollars;

5   And twenty dollars begat fifty dollars;

6   And fifty dollars begat one hundred dollars;

7   And one hundred dollars begat five hundred dollars;

8   And five hundred dollars begat one thousand dollars;

9   And one thousand dollars begat five thousand dollars;

10   And five thousand dollars begat ten thousand dollars.

11   And money gave great sustenance in the minds of men who knew not the way of the Lord.

12   The city counselman became mayor; and the mayor took to the statehouse; and the man of the statehouse took to the halls of the Fatherland; and round about there were many years and many brown bags of money needed to help the man succeed while consorting with the unwashed and unholy of the land,

13   And thus he became known as the King of Cash.

14   It was that the King of Cash delighted himself with a Queen of Loot, for in the gathering of money crops, there was need of trusted field hands.

15   And an Emperor of greed, vanity, and selfish thought pleased the King, and he proclaimed him the Prince of Money.

16   And the encircled High Sheriffs of Hubris envisioned unnecessary war as an economic necessity,

17   For cash crops are harvested from business plants.

18   Then the King commanded his chief eunuchs to bring forth youths without blemish, handsome and skillful in all wisdom, endowed with knowledge, understanding, learning, and competent to serve in the King's callings,

1

19   And it came to be that those of lesser pocket book were sent forth to nurture money from the fields of the Enterprise of War;
20   For the merchants were the great men of the earth,
21   And all nations were deceived by the sorcery.

The Word According to
TWODOGS

(Know Your Men and
Look Out for Their
Welfare)

CHAPTER 1

1   Now it came to pass on the seventh day of the seventh month of the seventh year, as the new souls were cast among the captives by the river of Perfume in the land of Nam Bo, that the heavens were opened, and there began visions of the deities implanted in their minds and of their religion, The Korps.

2   "To Die Marine is to live forever," the words of the Irish bantam Sergeant at the seminary school echoed through the stone-faced Injun's thoughts.

3   The military truck bounced from the hole-infested streets as it headed in the night for the helicopter base.

4   The Corporal driver had emphasized to the newly arrived pilots that they would have to pass through several unfriendly villages to get to double-seven (77), the name of the Diocese which oversees all the helo squadrons;

5   He had instructed the new peter pilots who arrived in Nam Bo only two hours ago to hit the deck if they heard any fire, then he had conspicuously chambered a round in his rifle.

6   The Corporal succeeded in his explanations—the pilots were scared, and fine-tuned to respond to the Corporal's orders.

7   All eyes stared into the night from the back of the canvas-

covered truck listening and watching for any attack warning signal.

8 Weaponless, except for the Corporal's rifle, the young pilots knew they could die;

9 No one wanted to die—especially in the first two hours of war.

10 The Corporal grinned to himself as he flickered the truck headlight signal down the palm tree-lined beach road to be seen by the artillery battery.

11 As the truck came adjacent to the big guns hidden from the view of the passengers, the artillery let loose a pre-arranged high explosive salvo—Boom! shaking the truck, lighting the sky, and scaring the new pilots into an instant leap to the truck floor, frozen with fear.

12 The Corporal shifted down, then raised the canvas flap behind the driver's seat, trying not to laugh openly at the mass of entangled flight officers kissing the sandy deck of the truck bed, "That's outgoing, . . . gentlemen," he said.

13 They were embarrassed; pilots don't panic—pilots don't get spoofed by Corporals.

14 The truck stopped between two long rows of the rusty, tin-roofed, plywood-sided houses called hootches.

15 And it was that the new souls of war were given welcome by other pilots.

16 Then it came to pass that the gaggle of comrades headed to the tabernacle of alcohol called the "O" Club.

17 As they entered the hallowed ground, the room of pilots as a choir began singing a song, which erupted in volume.

We are the men, . . . of Double seven
Fight'n in hell, goin' to heaven
From way down south, we came this way
Don't give a shit, about the Green Beret.

We fly in choppers—are real meanies
Don't need no chutes, or green beanies
And while they jump, we drink and fuck
We do believe, the Green Berets suck.

With these hard hats, upon our heads
We'd rather fly, than end up dead
One hundred men, were hauled today
Not a fuckin' one, had a green beret.

We too have wings, upon our chests
And can compete, for America's best
Our wings are gold, our caps are green
Rather than a beret, I'll be a Marine.

Back in Okinawa, a Ne'san waits
Pulls down her pants, jacks up her rates
She's added up, . . . oh eight months pay
And don't put out, for the Green Beret.

I know this song, won't be no hit
But a good Marine, don't give a shit
And when it comes, to glory and fame
We'll kick your ass, and take your name.

18   And it came to pass that the new pilots gave fresh meat smiles to other members of the aerial congregational church and joined in the drinking ceremony.
19   A drunken Lay-major held his glass high and proposed that he be allowed to buy everyone a drink;
20   "I am going back home to the land of the big PX tomorrow," he yelled, then recognized he could be heard by only a few, so he stepped up into the seat of his chair.
21   And it came to pass that as he got his balance and raised up that his bald forehead intermeshed with the spinning ceiling fan blades — Whack! Whack! and Thunk! he fell to a table.
22   The congregation roared with laughter; someone yelled "MedEvac" as the fan-wounded pilot's friends administered him with a bandage quickly taken from a flight survival jacket.
23   The Lay-major felt no pain; and as they carried him, he happily slurred, "If you ain't got no people, you ain't got no war."
24   Injun smelled the aroma of sweaty flight suits, salty beach air, and beer;

25   And the rising full moon sparkled through the lapping white froth of the sea's surf;

26   And Injun listened to the combat flying stories dramatized by the "old salts" at the table who had been "in country" for only a couple of months.

27   Injun learned which helo squadrons did what, which squadrons were assigned what area, and that he might be able to request a particular flying assignment.

28   And it was told that the Viet Cong were commonly referred to as V.C., Charlie, Victor Charlie, and respectfully, as Charles or Sir Charles;

29   That the Nam Bo Army was normally ineffective;

30   That diarrhea was a common ailment, giving meaning to the saying that "happiness is a dry fart."

31   With last call, the liturgy ended and the church service was over.

32   The boom of outgoing artillery fire in the distance reminded Injun what had slipped away in the alcohol, comradery, laughter, and singing—this beast called "war" was in process.

CHAPTER 2

1   Now it came to pass that the new pilots checked into the 77 Diocese Headquarters and waited for a conference with the Vicar-major who was empowered by the Bishop of the 77 Diocese to administer assignments to the flight squadrons spread out among the various parishes in the land of Nam Bo.

2   The reverent, deep voice of the man of the church of the Marine Korps who dispensed risk of life or death through his words spoke forth, "Gunny", he paused, "what have you got this morning?"

3   "Thirteen sixty-nines," the Gunny responded.

4   The field grade cleric appeared, and spoke, "Welcome to war gentlemen," the Vicar-major motioned the gaggle of new pilots into his vestibule next to the antechamber sealed so that the High Priest-colonel could reside in air-conditioning while administering helicopter warfare in comfort from his cottage by the sea.

5   "Any of you know what a 1369 military job number is," the Vicar-major clerically inquired?

6   Hearing no response, he said, "Thirteen sixty-nine means

'unlucky cocksucker'; any soldier fightin' in this war is just a plain unlucky cocksucker." Laughter in cautious respect came forth.
7   Injun and PennyWorth were assigned to Helicopter Squadron 777 at a place called Tru Lai in the Tekoa Wilderness.
8   "Well, PennyWorth," remarked Injun to his long-time friend as they picked up their belongings, "let's go get on our faithful pony and ride."

CHAPTER 3

1   And it came to pass that Injun and ShareCrop walked in the steamy sun to the big helicopter scheduled to carry passengers to the Wilderness to a place called Tru Lai.
2   The big antique helicopter used for transport was a strange looking machine, for it had two big round engines which stuck outward on its sides like two big grasshopper eyes; and the child men affectionately called it "Deuce."
3   The flight crew had humorously painted white, blood-shot eye-balls with black pupils on the front of each round engine cowling;
4   And from the front middle thereof, there protruded a guppy-looking nose in the form of green oval doors which opened wide like a clam's mouth, big enough to load jeeps and passengers inside the helo.
5   This flying relic quietly depicted the lack of political bid for monies by the Korps as compared to the Army in modern helicopter warfare;
6   If any helicopter looked like a grasshopper, the Deuce did; if any helicopter was cheap, it was.
7   Only the Nam Bo War shortage kept the Deuce from the graveyard; it was noisy, leaked oil, and it was temperamental.
8   Combat flying in the heat or thin mountain air frequently required helicopters to fly at critical engine power and high performance levels where simple error would cause a crash;
9   So the Deuce transport was stripped of all non-essential weight items, including a large flat metal sheet panel that fit squarely underneath the transmission in the ceiling above the passengers' heads;
10   And less weight allowed helos to carry more cargo;

11   Deuce passengers rode in two long rows facing each other with their backs against the windows and fuselage walls.

12   The missing cover underneath the transmission allowed the passengers to watch the spinning rotor blades turn at the center hub and to see the blue sky flicker through the open ceiling hole above their heads.

13   And it came to pass that the deafening roar of the Deuce engines sounded forth and it departed unto Tru Lai.

14   The child men Marine passengers being shuttled to Seventh Division near Tru Lai Air Field in the wilderness of Tekoa Province were like human livestock going to war's market,

15   But the earth below had a peaceful, green look; the sea harbor's beauty below was magnificent for the deep blue water was marked by interspersed gliding sampans like the cover of a romantic novel.

16   And then there came a small enclave strategically placed on a hill above the only highway running north toward the warring nation of Bac Bo,

17   Then there appeared rows of the brown holes of the artillery and bomb craters which dotted on the green terrain, evidencing war's dermatological traces on the earth's face. "War's zits," thought Injun.

18   And it came to pass that Injun was startled by the screams of a child man grunt passenger yelling and pointing his finger at the floor.

19   Instantly, Injun leapt outward as he saw large steel bolts and nuts falling from the rotor-blade transmission ceiling area onto the helicopter floor between the passengers' feet.

20   Injun was terrified!

21   The passengers were frozen with fear in their seats.

22   Injun's pilot training flashed the danger signal that the old helicopter's transmission was coming apart in flight, or tearing away from the airframe mounts;

23   Injun knew that a safe auto rotational landing was normal with the mere loss of an engine, but a transmission failure would be fatal, and would kill them!

24   Injun ran up the short ladder climbing into the cockpit, yelling to the pilots at his lungs' greatest scream that the transmission was failing.

25   The pilots broke into laughter, seeing Injun's large, black eyes and hearing Injun's death screams.

26 And one of the pilots grabbed him by the arm, pulled him close and yelled in his ear, "It's okay, just a joke the Crew Chief plays on the grunts."

27 Injun's death pulse calmed; he returned to his seat in time to watch the antics of the Flight Sergeant.

28 And it came to be that the Crew Chief's prank consisted of concentrating his vision on the transmission area pretending to look for the source of the instant death problem.

29 And the crew chief tweaked his bushy mustache, and then used his hand to scratch the top of his flight helmet like he was scratching his head, coolly seeing if they were about to die.

30 Soon, the crewman looked into the young faces anticipating imminent death and gave them a thumbs up signaling things were "ok."

31 Instantly, an obvious expression of relief could be seen on their panicked faces.

32 And the knuckles of the hands of the young Marines had turned white from squeezing their seat racks with fear, but now regained blood-flow.

33 Then the Crew Chief stepped to the electronics compartment and brought forth a broom with the handle sawed short so as to fit in the small compartment.

34 And the Crew Chief swept the bolts and nuts on the floor into a pile, then swept the pile of bolts and nuts to the back door of the helicopter, and holding the rear door cracked, he swept the pile out of the flying helicopter into the passing air.

35 Injun thought that this prank topped all others he had heard or seen used to scare passengers;

36 He had thrown empty beer cans from the cockpit to make the passengers believe the pilots were drinking;

37 He had cut engine power making the passengers believe the engines had quit;

38 And he had rolled with climbs and dives into unusual flight attitudes, but this trick took the cake.

39 And it all came to pass without the knowledge of Penny-Worth, for he slept.

CHAPTER 4

1   Tru Lai came into view.

2   And there were visions of rice paddies round about the land eastwardly that followed the sea coast like a strip of green rice plant ribbon with varying miles of width that ran north and south between the sea coast and the high purple mountains.

3   And there was one highway that wormed its way north and south like a black wiggly snake, mostly along the inland high ground, close to the Tru Lai Airfield;

4   And there was a railroad track that clattered itself along with and near the highway, but had fallen bridges from the bombings.

5   And it came to be that the passengers gladly and quickly escaped from the unfit helicopter after it landed and shut down its spinning rotor blades;

6   For the momentary encounter with immediate aerial death made Mother Earth a less frightening threat to the child men Marines who preferred dirt to air when it came to risking death.

7   Then Injun questioned the Crew Chief about how he had gotten nuts and bolts to fall to the floor in front of the passengers.

8   The salty flying Sergeant showed Injun and PennyWorth a cable hidden from view in the helo's ceiling;

9   And the cable was connected to a swivelled can full of old bolts, cleverly hidden in the ceiling transmission area above the passengers' heads.

10   Injun witnessed that a simple tug of the cable by the crewman at the rear door tilted the can thereby spilling nuts and bolts out of the ceiling onto the floor terrifying the passengers with flashes of instant death of the helicopter coming apart in mid-air.

11   And it came to pass that the two new pilots picked up their flight bags and walked to the tin-roofed building with the emblem of Helo Flight Squadron 777, the face of a lion.

12   It came to be that T.D. Tolmai and Philip Pennyworth were joined into Triple Seven as new pilots while a fine sandy dust blew through the screen wire windows surrounding the top half of the walls of the plywood building;

13   For the taxiing helicopters with their spinning rotors generated a thick, sandy, dust cloud downwind of the turning blades.

14   And Injun smelled the dirt-ridden air, and felt the gritty soil build between his teeth,

15   And Injun wiped his perspiring brow, and noticed the brown sandy residue on the green military handkerchief, and spat the grit.

16   It was that the Sergeant of Paperwork said, "Don't worry, sir, you'll cotton to the heat in a week."

17   And it was that in the Church of the Korps that Gunnery Sergeants talk turkey, for Injun was all ears in listening to the Gunny's answers to his questions.

18   Injun learned "Triple Seven" was the only helicopter unit in the Tekoa Wilderness and permanently assigned as the aerial workhorse.

19   And it was that Triple Seven pilots flew in all the battles fought from the sea across the flat rice field terrain and into the high mountains leading into the many jungles, all the way from the river Kishon to the Plain of Megiddo.

20   And Injun learned the leader of the 777 parish church was a Curate-colonel known as Artemis N. Temple, a devout, career Marine who volunteered his pilots for any mission he thought would place him in good graces of his Bishop,

21   For it was that the Temple man knew the sacraments of promotion and vowed piously that his cup would runneth over.

22   Injun learned that Triple Seven sprinkled its helicopters and crews throughout the Tekoa Wilderness, including at the Ada Sam Airfield built high in the Gilboa mountains at the edge of the wilderness soliciting the tribesmen of Bac Bo to come forth and make war for the souls at Ada Sam were used as flesh bait dangled vulnerably about.

23   Triple Seven flew the old lovable and reliable passenger helicopters called "Sea Dogs" or "Dogs", which were used for medical rescue, cargo hauling, and troop movement.

24   The pilots were nicknamed "Dog Drivers" by the pilots who flew the new jet engine powered helos.

25   And it came to pass that Injun and PennyWorth met Rusty Stoner, who told them of combat flying.

26   Then Injun learned of shortages of pilots,

27   And how simple errors issued forth death.

28   And it came to pass that Injun was scheduled to fly the next day and was provided with maps, a new bullet-proof vest, a pistol, and a survival jacket which contained one of the new radios to beep signals to help locate a pilot who had crashed.

29   Then it was that Injun said unto PennyWorth, "No wonder

the white man won, bullets bounce off, and you can order pizza when you crash with this radio."

30 And it came to pass that a small brown man called OverBoost came to the entrance way of the plywood hootch home where the big indian sat on his cot.

31 It was the meeting of a Mexican and an Indian.

32 The new friendship began, and Injun's knowledge about the war progressed, and in the chow line Injun met pilots called Bird-Man, TailWind, RedLine, and SmegMa.

33 The baby-faced cook serving food behind the table was busily shooing numerous flies that were caressing the round slices of mystery meat food that had been cut from a long, round tube.

34 "Horsecock again," quipped SmegMa.

35 "No, Sir," the kid cook said with a makeshift French accent, "youse guys is pilots, this here meat is Penis de' Stal'yone."

36 And the pilots laughed, and TailWind farted openly without changing facial expression, but the line behind him momentarily adjusted away from the invisible aroma of the human vapor trail.

37 And the token food offering was uglified with a huge vat of aging, deep-green drink, unaffectionately known as "bug juice," which left the taste, smell, and color of commode lime in the mouth.

38 And BirdMan griped, "Third day in a row we have had this crap and we've been drinkin' that green pea shit near two weeks. Seventh Ground's Mess only has orange glue-water—you'd drink it 'cause it's the only thing that kills the taste of the water."

39 And SmegMa said, "Seems they would swap out some of the green for orange, but the Navy supply blokes order orange douche water by the ship load."

40 And SmegMa said further, "Makes it easier for swabbies to load and unload a ship if they don't have to think."

41 Then TailWind grinned, "One of them damn Navy boats sink and the whole Nam Bo Sea will turn orange."

42 And the pilots laughed, sticking out and wagging their green stained tongues at each other.

CHAPTER 5

1   And it came to pass in the first evening of war that Injun attended drinking chapel at the Tru Lai "O" Club, a small, tin-roofed building at the end of the row of pilots' hootches.

2   Injun sat at the home-made bar and watched the beautiful red sun set over the violet streaked mountains while the Seventh Marine Division artillery banged deadly canon fire further west-ward into the free fire zones.

3   And Injun learned in the pilot's war that alcohol flowed cheaply—one could not afford not to drink.

4   The pilots befriended Injun and PennyWorth into the combat flying drinking fraternity.

5   And the new guys listened, not understanding the sadness of useless killing of child men Marines in useless battles for the sake of having battles, and the killing of Nam Bo peasants—zipperheads.

6   And they learned that death had an odor,

7   For a pilot could sometimes smell by the blowing odor emitted from the wounded when a passenger would die.

8   TailWind described the over-loaded flying schedule created because of the critical shortage of pilots;

9   And RedLine cursed the Bishop-general of the Seventh Ground who coldly sent Marines and helo crews as bait to lure out the unseen enemy.

10   And as the night progressed, the helo pilots sang forth several songs to vent mental pains from the hated war, one song of which cast vision of Tru Lai;

11   The pilots in unison sang,

As I go a wandering,
Around ole Tru Lai Base,
I love to go and laugh and sing,
I hate this fucking place.

Fuck Tru Lai, Fuck Tru Lai,
Fuck, fuck, fuck, fuck, fuck
Fuck Tru Lai, I hate this fucking place.

Oh, we may go a wandering,
And soon go far away;
Oh may we cross the Nam Bo sea,
And there forever stay.

Fuck Tru Lai, Fuck Tru Lai,
Fuck, fuck, fuck, fuck, fuck
Fuck Tru Lai, I hate this fucking place.

Someday we'll get to sleep at night
And with a lovely lass,
We'll tell them all to take Tru Lai,
And shove it up their ass.

Fuck Tru Lai, Fuck Tru Lai,
Fuck, fuck, fuck, fuck, fuck
Fuck Tru Lai, I hate this fucking place.

12   And Injun and PennyWorth began to feel the pain in these souls and witness in profanities the frustrations of death to retake the same hill over and over.
13   A Lay-leader-major at the bar sarcastically yelled that this was the best war we got.
14   And RedLine quickly began the next tune bringing laughter.

Oh Tru Lai, oh Tru Lai is a wonderful base;
There's nothing to do all over the place.
There's captains and majors and light colonels, too,
Hands in their pockets with nothing to do.

They stand by the runway,
They scream and they shout
About various things they know nothin' about.
For all good reason they may as well be
Shove-a-lin shit in the Nam Bo Sea.

15   And the room all joined in a loud, boisterous, almost screaming singing,

You'll wonder where the yellow went
When the "A" bomb hits the Or iE nt'

Nuke-em! Nuke-em! Nuke-em!

16   And it came to pass that Injun drank little and watched as the alcohol blossomed in others.
17   Injun witnessed that his new-found friends sought, and in alcohol, temporarily found relief and escape.
18   They referred to commander Temple as a curate priest of the low church of the Korps;
19   And they called him "Kiwi" and "Poncho Pilot," and told Injun that the commander was more dangerous than flying night MedEvac.
20   But Injun understood not, but Injun savored his new pilot friends and he was anxious to engage in combat flying.
21   And it came to pass that near midnight, a light rain commenced and dribbled its pitter-pat tune on the drinking temple's tin roof.
22   It was RedLine's idea—he made the telephone call.
23   And it came to be witnessed that he rotated the crank of the field phone, and he patched with call sign words through the awkward military telephone system until he connected with the Seventh Marine Division duty officer.
24   And the duty officer listened at attention,
25   "This is Ahimelech at Holy Sea Headquarters," RedLine said pretending to be a Chemarim High Priest of war, "I have a coded message—standby to copy," he instructed.
26   The young staff duty officer of non-wisdom immediately grabbed his combat note pad and copied the message with Naval Academy proficiency and ecclesiastical blindness.
27   RedLine stated the message, "The Moon is Low Over India."
28   Then he added, "Now read it back," for which the duty captain obeyed.
29   And he continued, "Now give me your full name and serial number for my report," and the captain obeyed.
30   And RedLine ordered, "Seventh Ground should take immediate action. Over and out."
31   And with that, he hung up.

32   Then he laughed, shook his head and said, "Now let's see what the crazy bastards do."

33   And it came to pass that in about ten minutes, artillery began shooting, and silver-white flashes could be seen from the big guns before the noise came.

34   And in a few minutes more, the loud diesel engine noise of numerous tanks could be heard in the misty, cold, night air.

35   And it came to pass in about forty-five minutes that the small night lights of tanks and trucks could be seen moving out of the mountainside Seventh Division area onto the highway.

36   And lights began to flicker from the troop tent area along the western hillside.

37   Then the lights of Division Headquarters and Operations buildings sprung forth like newly-lit rows of street lights in the chilly and wet night.

38   The pilots went to bed but were kept awake by the noises of war preparation.

39   And it came to pass that in the morn that the Division Sergeant-major walked into the flight operations ready room to request a flight and OverBoost asked of him what all the noise was about last night.

40   And the old salt Marine said, "Oh, hell, I don't know," as he withdrew a cigar stump from his lips. "All I know is round mid-night the pimple-faced duty officer got a coded message and didn't know what it meant, so he put the artillery and perimeter units on alert and woke up the senior duty officer and read him the message: 'The moon is low over India.' "

41   "And the senior duty officer didn't know what it meant, so he told the duty officer to wake up the reaction company and put the tank battalion on alert while he woke up the G-2 (intelligence officer) to decipher the message.

42   "And the division intelligence officer couldn't find the message in his code book so he decided that only the Bishop-general and the Deputy-commander knew what it meant;

43   "But in the meantime, the senior duty officer ordered the remaining troops of the reaction company, two of the tank platoons and the reserve battalion to be moved into position on both ends of the highway to be instantly ready.

44   "And they woke the Deputy-commander who didn't know what 'The moon is low over India' meant, either, and then they woke up the Bishop-general, and said, 'The moon is low over

India, Sir,' and he screamed when he found no one in his command knew what the code words meant," and the Sergeant-major grinned.

45 "And they found that no such coded message existed in all the secret code books, but the Bishop-general wasn't sure."

46 "And the Bishop-general screamed at the intelligence officer, and then the general himself called the Deputy-priest Ahimelech at Holy Sea headquarters to check."

47 "And Ahimelech refused to talk to the Bishop-general about the code on the field telephone because the telephone line wasn't secure."

48 Then the Sergeant-major continued as he inhaled a drag of the cigar,

49 "So the Bishop-general sent a secret message to Holy Sea on the scrambler net and, in the return coded message, Ahimelech denied that he had sent a coded message to Seventh Division."

50 "The whole thing's got 'em nut'zo over there," then the Sergeant-major again grinned, then continued exhaling cigar smoke, "I sorta figure one of you throttle jockeys instigated the whole thing;"

51 "Makes no never mind though Gooks moved into the DMZ last night and hit Aceldama OutPost. We got a war to fight."

52 And Injun grinned as he listened to the division Sergeant-major's tale of lack of leadership woe;

53 For RedLine's simple message had sent the Division's principal staff into pandemonium.

54 And Injun wondered if he had entered a war, or joined a deadly comedy in progress.

CHAPTER 6

1 Then it came to pass that Injun went unto the "Dog" helicopter while waiting for TailWind.

2 Injun inspected the old "Dog" helo's four main rotor blades, and the droopy nose which housed the big round engine;

3 And the two pilots' seats were high above the ground — up and behind the top of the engine compartment.

4 The passenger and crew compartment was directly behind the engine with space to carry nine people.

5 Injun saw that the oblong plexiglass side windows were

removed for there were two crewman with machine guns, one at the door and one opposite the door at the window side.
6   And the emblem of Triple Seven, a lion's face, was painted in the middle of the helo's nose;
7   The crewmen had painted the face of an eagle on the side door.
8   Then it came to pass that four helicopters were started in clockwork fashion and, following radio contact to confirm each was ready to fly, the four helos taxied one behind the other tilting with rolling take-off and prompt airborne join-up for a four helo formation—destination: Aceldama Airfield near the OutPost.
9   TailWind pointed out terrain features, and let Injun fly the helicopter.
10   Tru Lai City was a touching sight to Injun, particularly the old castle with its outer walls and inner garrison, and the lone white cathedral church shining among the primitive village houses.
11   Then it was that Injun saw the new Army turbine-powered helicopters parked at the Garrison airfield, home of the Nam Bo High Priests.
12   TailWind pointed out to Injun the helo pad used for landing to deliver wounded Nam Bo soldiers located next to the hospital with the big red cross.
13   And high above the earth, Injun could see that there were five long lakes looking like watery fingers across the rice fields of green near the only highway, which was many miles up the horizon.
14   And Injun remembered that soldiers of a past war called the road "la rue sans joie," or "street without joy."
15   TailWind shared with Injun brotherly thoughts from months of teaching fledgling pilots into combat flying.
16   It came to pass that Injun became in awe at Aceldama Airfield for TailWind shut the engine throttle back to idle taking the mighty horsepower away from the spinning rotor blades just like the engine would act if it had quit running when stopped instantly by a bullet;
17   Then TailWind commenced an autorotational glide to a perfect powerless landing, with the other three helos landing in line behind them.
18   Injun realized the magnificent flying abilities of these new found friends.

19   Now in those days, the Diocese 77 command post consisted of a sand bag bunker, a gasoline generator, and several radios.

20   It was the law that Marine ground units would seek to kill the enemy between Aceldama OutPost and the wilderness mountains through the rice fields and jungle hills.

21   And it was that helicopters and crews were on standby to deliver food, ammunition, and rescue the wounded, and return the dead.

22   Now in those times, the 77 Bishop-colonel had sent his deputy to personally command the helicopter assignments.

23   And the Marine Korps' shortage of helicopter gunships meant Injun and his fellow pilots would have to fly combat rescue missions without gunship protection to shoot at the enemy while the Dog drivers had to land as an easy out-in-the open target on the ground in the battle zone.

24   But it came to pass that two Army attack helicopter gunships landed, and the Army pilots came forth to help the Church of the Marine Korps.

25   And the men of the Army other church spoke that they heard that the Marines were short of gunship support for MedEvac helicopters and their Bishop-general had sent them to help the Marines,

26   For the Army would provide its own fuel, rockets, and ammunition; And fly to protect Marine MedEvac helos.

27   It was that the Marine Deputy-commander reacted with arrogant indignation.

28   The Marine Bishop-colonel with High Church blindness and disregard for the lives of the child men Marines said, "You can tell your general that this is an all-Marine operation."

29   And the High Priest of non-leadership turned his back, ignoring the Army captain's professional courtesies, and ignoring that Marines would die for such blindness.

30   Injun could not accept what he had heard, for the Bishop-colonel's orders issued death warrants;

31   Injun believed not, but said unto TailWind, "The Marine Korps is supposed to look out for the welfare of its men; those gunships could save lives, my life. What's this all-Marine operation crap! Our ass is the one in the sling."

32   And Injun became instantly angry at this life and death dispensing Ass Hole who would let Marines die for inter-service rivalry.

33   Then Injun said further unto TailWind, "What to hell difference does it make if the Marine Korps is short gunship support to accept help from the Army?"

34   And TailWind bitterly responded, "Look, Deputy Dog there is a Headquarters Marine Korps desk pilot. He ain't got no medals. This is his first war, and all he knows is the 'school solution.' Ya know that after every war the Army mounts an attack on the Marine Korps saying we don't need a second land Army. You're just seeing how the shit politics filters down to killing a few good Marines."

35   Injun argued back at his brotherly source, "It's our ass, it's a troop's ass!"

36   And TailWind, still not accepting what he had heard this High Priest say, told unto Injun, "You're right, kimo-sabe, but right ain't might."

37   And it came to pass that TailWind, StoneMan, BirdMan and a white haired pilot introduced to Injun as "SnowWhite," made comradeship with the Army pilots.

38   Then it came to be also that TailWind and Injun flew a leaflet mission near the beginning of the land of enemy Bac Bo.

39   And there came a flight of giant bombers called "Arc Light," which dropped rows and rows of big bombs to the earth.

40   TailWind and Injun watched the bombs explode, making half-mile expanding compressed air ghostly donut rings with big chunks of dirt and debris being hurled hundreds of feet into the air from the center of the explosion.

41   And TailWind commented to Injun, "It's a poor bastard that gets shredded in that nightmare, and they ain't got time for read'n no give-up leaflets."

42   And the bombs ate every living thing in the explosive path and discerned not good from evil in the killing frenzy, nor age, sex, religion, race, color or creed.

43   And the bombs raptured body parts of men, women, and children, and animals, with instant indifference.

44   And Satan was pleased, for acts of men give great disgrace to the word of the Lord.

CHAPTER 7

1   Now it came to pass that wounded Marines required medical evacuation along the river Chebar.
2   Sunset! Morphine eased the horrendous pain in the Corporal's gut wound. The platoon was pinned in the tree line.
3   And he looked, and behold, a chopper came out of the north, a great cloud, and a fire infolding itself, and a brightness was about it, and out of the midst thereof as the colour of amber, out of the midst of the fire.
4   Also out of the midst thereof came the likeness of four living creatures.
5   And this was their appearance; they had the likeness of a man.
6   And everyone had four faces, and every chopper had four rotor blade wings.
7   And their feet were straight feet; and the sole of their feet was like the sole of a calf's foot; and they sparkled like the colour of burnished brass.
8   The wounded Corporal knew they were airdales, he saw their flight boots with the brass zippers.
9   And he saw the four rotor blade wings were joined one to another; he saw the lion, the crewman's eagle; he saw the clear night helmet visors pulled down over the crews' faces, stretched forth over their faces like a crystal.
10   The engine roared, like the noise of great waters, and the chopper lifted and went straight forward.
11   The Corporal did not hear the tatter of machine guns, nor the whoosh of rockets, together with the small canon explosions fired from TailWind's new found Army helo gunship friends who attacked the enemy lines one at a time in a rotating tight race-track flight circle.
12   And the Corporal did not know that the white haired pilot called SnowWhite pretended to be landing nearby, soliciting the enemy's fire in SnowWhite's direction to buy time to answer his prayers.
13   And SnowWhite's tactic allowed TailWind to streak across the jungle canopy at tree top and dive into the landing zone at high speed accomplished by the artful and swift closing of the engine throttle, then kicking the tail rotor rudder pedal causing

the helo to momentarily fly sideways for an airborne quick-stop, settling immediately to the ground rescue spot.

14   And the sideward flight deceived the enemy; for the enemy would shoot in front of the flying helo's nose, thereby tricking the enemy into firing in the wrong direction.

15   And TailWind had landed behind trees—as cover to protect his crew and the Marines loading the wounded.

16   The living creatures ran and returned as the appearance of a flash of lightning.

17   Whithersoever the spirit was to go, they went, thither was their spirit to go; and the wheels were lifted up over against them: for the spirit of the living creature was in the wheels.

18   The wounded Corporal tweaked an expression of gratitude up from the stretcher to TailWind as he was delivered to waiting medics at the field hospital.

19   TailWind and Injun felt over-paid.

20   Twenty minutes from wound to the operating table; Injun felt godly; a life had been rescued from the grim reaper.

21   "TailWind was the best—he'd made Deputy Dog's wrong a right. This was a Sam Bo operation!"

22   "Fuck Deputy Dog," Injun thought. "He should be drumhead court-martialed."

23   Injun mentally paused, "Yeah, the kids are right, Eat the Apple, . . . and Fuck the Korps."

24   Injun felt himself growing to hate the High Priests of war who blindly failed to protect the child men Marines.

CHAPTER 8

1   And it came to pass when Injun returned to Tru Lai, he was instructed to see 777 Commander, Artemis N. Temple.

2   Injun had flown fifteen hours of combat flying; he was one of the chopper crew that had rescued eight wounded, one of whom had been yanked from the jaws of death and had to be extracted under heavy fire and the most magnificent flying he had ever seen.

3   But Injun had also witnessed the ugly of the ugly, the green rubber bags covering the dead . . . the 1369s of war.

4   Injun stepped into Curate-colonel Temple's command temple, anxious to meet the Command Priest.

5   Then the round face wearing a pointed nose visibly explained to Injun why he was called Kiwi, although TailWind called him Poncho Pilot.

6   Vicar-major Berry, the next-in-line low command priest, was also at his desk in the shared, tin-roofed synagogue.

7   And the short, overweight squadron commander said to Injun after the formalities of the shaking of the two command priest's hands, "Be seated."

8   And the Curate-colonel pretended to review Injun's pilot file, randomly asking unnecessary questions.

9   And Injun noticed the Korps' Litany on the wall behind the squawking commander.

13 COMMANDMENTS OF LEADERSHIP

I.   TAKE RESPONSIBILITY FOR YOUR ACTIONS AND THE ACTIONS OF YOUR MARINES.
II. KNOW YOURSELF AND SEEK SELF-IMPROVEMENT.
III. SET THE EXAMPLE.
IV. DEVELOP YOUR SUBORDINATES.
V.   INSURE THAT A JOB IS UNDERSTOOD, THEN SUPERVISE IT AND CARRY IT THROUGH TO COMPLETION.
VI. KNOW YOUR MEN.
VII. EVERY MAN SHOULD BE KEPT INFORMED.
VIII. SET GOALS YOU CAN REACH.
IX. MAKE SOUND AND TIMELY DECISIONS.
X.   KNOW YOUR JOB.
XI. TEAMWORK.
XII. LOOK AFTER THE WELFARE OF YOUR MEN.
XIII. SEMPER FIDELIS.

10 Injun thought to himself, "Yeah, the Aceldama Deputy Dog hadn't learned he was to look after the welfare of his Marines."

11 And Poncho Pilot learned that Tolmai was an Osage Indian from Salisaw, Oklahoma, that his father and his grandfathers were each tribal chiefs, and that in 1808 the Osage sold all their land in Arkansas to the Government and were removed to Okla-

homa, where, in the 1900's, oil was discovered on the one and one-half million acre Osage reservation.

12   Injun had graduated with a double major in civil engineering and political science; Injun would be a chief someday and was concerned for his people's future.

13   And the round faced commander of the 777 parish church continued, as he leaned back in his chair, "We're the best damn squadron in the 77 Diocese;

14   "We've got good maintenance—had only one engine quit. We've got thirty-eight pilots on board and twenty-four aircraft."

15   "We still fully support the entire Seventh Division, though we are short of people."

16   "We'll fly your ass off! Expect to get a hundred to a hundred plus flying hours every month you're here."

17   "Now every pilot ought to go home with a Distinguished Flying Cross and a Silver Star . . . or two. You can look in the ready room at our awards board. Every pilot's name, his missions, and his awards are listed. Dingle, got any comments?"

18   Vicar-major Berry stood as if he thought standing were necessary to communicate to the new pilot.

19   And Vicar-major Berry also stood because his short height had tortured his soul into believing he could have been a higher-ranking priest had God not given him a dwarf for a father; his rubber boots to mid-knee, his beer belly, and his mechanical grin sculptured under a hooked nose identified him with a penguin—except a penguin looks both handsome and dignified.

20   "Listen, Buddy-Buddy," the talking penguin began, "Takes lots of things to make a combat squadron go in addition to flying. We'll see that you get good maintenance support, intelligence information, chow, and that your medals get quickly processed. If you're going to make the Korps a career, now's the time to lock your future in—take it from me, I know. You got the chance to get your personnel jacket full, to show 'em you're a good combat pilot. Best little war we got now."

21   Injun instantly disliked the sawed-off excuse for a pilot, and a second-place commander.

22   "Now on policies," Vicar-major DingleBerry instructed Injun, "We keep wet and dry pilots around here."

23   "That means you don't drink much when you're scheduled dry," and he winked at Injun.

24   "We want at least half the pilots sober if we have to fly out of here some night. Keep your nose clean."

25   "Since you're the newest guy in the squadron, Friday at happy hour you'll be the new caretaker of the silver bullet."

26   "You get this silver bullet to keep with you at all times so's you can blow your brains out if you can't take it anymore, being you have more time left of the thirteen month tour in-country than any other pilot in the squadron."

27   And he said "Any question, Buddy-Buddy?"

28   Injun left the Commander's hootch wondering about leadership; a Curate-colonel nicknamed "Poncho Pilot" who couldn't waddle a hundred yards to escape if he crashed, and a career has-been Vicar-major that looks like a penguin, and had a stuttering problem — Buddy-Buddy.

29   Injun entered the ready room shaking his Osage soul at Marine chiefdom.

30   The flight operations clerk had added Injun's name to the bottom line of Temple's temple (the awards board), as it had become unaffectionately known, according to the clerk.

31   Injun's two days' missions had been posted; twenty missions were needed for one Air Medal; if you were shot at, you were given two missions credit.

32   Injun witnessed most of the career-priest pilots had several career makers and several had been given lesser hero medals.

33   Vicar-major DingleBerry had two DFCs, and Temple, one.

34   "We are doing our part," Injun thought, but he observed that from the number of hours flown, much of the flying was done by the junior pilots who the clerk called "meat pilots."

35   Injun also noticed that Temple didn't have many flight hours or missions, but seemed to get the awards.

CHAPTER 9

1   It came to be Friday, and the squadron happy-hour at the make-shift Tru Lai "O" Club drinking temple.

2   There came twenty-nine pilots, and many passers-by to the alcoholic prayer meeting.

3   And one pilot called Cumulofuckus was a field grade "jet" pilot who had been ruthlessly transitioned to fly helicopters in four short weeks;

4   And Cumulofuckus was promptly shipped to the land of Nam Bo, but would mope and not associate with the other helicopter pilots, and sat alone in the corner.
5   Cumulofuckus was angry with the Korps for taking him out of jet aircraft and putting him in the old oil-slinging Dogs,
6   For he hated helos.
7   Cumulofuckus missed the Mach 2 Club, the membership in which was proudly displayed by a "Mach Two" patch on his flight jacket.
8   And most of all, Cumulofuckus missed his wife.
9   The Nam Bo war was the first time this lay-major had ever been away from her for over thirty days.
10   Cumulofuckus had been both a meteorology teacher and jet pilot instructor in his first life.
11   "Cumulofuckus" was the name he cleverly coined to describe a type of cloud that eats airplanes,
12   For such occurred because the pilot had committed the unforgivable error of flying his aircraft into a cloud with a mountain hidden inside.
13   Cumulofuckus was preoccupied with cumulofuckus, and helofuckus.
14   And it came to pass that Injun met MakeReady, the short, stocky assistant maintenance officer who was not a pilot;
15   And Static, the radio and electronics lipstick lieutenant (a warrant officer who had red squares on his gold officer's bar to show warrant rank);
16   And CrossFire, the appropriately-named Catholic chaplain Navy man, who refused to use the out-in-the-open urinals because snipers on different occasions had shot at him while he was taking a leak.
17   Arguments spat forth as to whether CrossFire had quit voiding.
18   And when inquiries were made of CrossFire as to where he was pissing, he would temper a smile and make a tactful departure.
19   CrossFire was going to the Headquarters of the Holy Sea soon — thank God.
20   Vicar-major DingleBerry orchestrated happy hour.
21   And Vicar-major DingleBerry dedicated himself to every happy hour event so as to make every pilot want to live until the next happy hour;

22   For he had books mailed to him about how to be a master of ceremonies;

23   And he kept clerks working into the night each Thursday typing last-minute changes, and jokes from his files, and his joke book collection.

24   Vicar-major DingleBerry knew it was critical to the success of the war that the pilots' morale be kept high;

25   Besides, he didn't have to fly combat missions when he was busy preparing for happy hour.

26   And this also justified Vicar-major DingleBerry's subscriptions to sex books and other magazines,

27   Such was an essential source of information for happy hour planning purposes.

28   Vicar-major DingleBerry read each one with great dedication of purpose, sometimes late at night by flashlight under the blanket so that he wouldn't wake the Commander in the next room,

29   For Vicar-major DingleBerry had become multi-orgasmic in a war zone.

30   And there shown round about a special alcoholic happy hour punch served from the squadron "thunder mug."

31   All would ritually partake from the juice in the thunder mug commode bottom which had been erroneously shipped in the maintenance supplies as a necessary military item.

32   Upon first seeing the commode, Vicar-major DingleBerry had quickly recognized the throne of the god of shit;

33   And Vicar-major DingleBerry had the maintenance shop attach two long pole handles as mountings on the "thunder mug" commode bottom so that it could be carried stretcher-style around the room by two pilots.

34   The "thunder mug" had become the squadron mascot.

35   The numbers 777 were painted on one side, and the face of a lion was artfully painted on the other.

36   The back of the commode consisted of a sheet of magnesium metal shanghaied from the carcass of a deceased Dog helicopter from the helicopter graveyard.

37   And the metal sheet was shaped square like the square face of a commode tank and on it were written the names of all the dead pilots from the flight squadron.

38   Sometimes peeled bananas were floated in the Thunder Mug punch bowl for symbolic thought.

39   The liturgy of happy hour was one of the sacraments that Marine pilots worshipped.

40   It was an aviator's religious ceremony which one could get devoutly drunk at the Drinking Mass, and the mass drinking.

41   And the homily began with a prayer by CrossFire,

42   Then the calling of the roll,

43   Then the collecting of a kitty pot to keep the alcohol flowing through the collecting of fines.

44   Money was meaningless when death was close by, and the fines were sufficient to keep happy hours very happy.

45   Injun was introduced formally to other squadron pilots and was ceremoniously transferred the silver bullet.

46   The word of the parish children was that Injun was to carry this silver bullet on his person at all times regardless, of the circumstances;

47   And would be fined each time Injun was asked by any pilot to display his bullet and could not do so.

48   Injun knew the scripture for he would be relieved of the silver bullet only when a new pilot checked in to 777, thereby becoming the new guy with more time left in the war zone than anyone else in the squadron.

49   Upon motion duly made, seconded, and unanimously passed, TailWind was fined for farting in the mess line.

50   CrossFire was fined for not being seen at the piss tubes.

51   OverBoost contributed for breaking a helo tail-wheel locking-pin for which DingleBerry produced a red ribbon with the pin attached to be worn around Overboost's neck during the happy hour.

52   And the church aspects of the service culminated with every pilot holding his glass to a one-drink salute to their dead comrades who would live forever, for to die a Marine is to live forever.

53   Drunkenness prevailed.

54   Division artillery often flashed in the distance, and then shortly came the echo follow-up cannon roar signaling the weaving of war's tapestry to the non-chalance of the pilots in their dipsomaniac endeavors.

55   And it came to pass that choir director DingleBerry, with a tilted smile, announced that it was opera time.

56   Hymnals were distributed and the bar choir began,

57   For the first song was "The Whorehouse of Today."

58   And DingleBerry waived his short arms from the housing of

his tiger stripped camouflaged flight suit signaling for singing to begin:

> He took off so early one morning,
> The engine running a blast;
> At five hundred feet he lost power,
> Into the whore house he was cast.

>> Fuck him, fuck him, he died in a
>> Whore house today,
>> Fuck him, fuck him, he died in a
>> Whore house today.

> We buried him on top of two thirty,
> His head was facing the west,
> His coffin was made of a poncho,
> With the sign of the Korps on his chest.

>> Fuck him, fuck him, he died in a
>> Whore house today,
>> Fuck him, fuck him, he died in a
>> Whore house today.

> So take down your gold star dear mother,
> And replace it with one made of gray,
> Your son was a hard-chargin' co-pilot,
> But he died in a whorehouse today.

>> Fuck him, fuck him, he died in a
>> Whore house today,
>> Fuck him, fuck him, he died in a
>> Whore house today.

59   Someone yelled, "Telegram."
60   And another amplified voice responded, "A telegram?"
61   And with that, OverBoost stepped to the corner of the Club and knocked loudly on the wooden rear door; instantly the room silenced and OverBoost pretended to receive a telegram.
62   "Madam?" said OverBoost in a mocking fashion with a deep voice.

63   "Yes?" OverBoost responded to himself loudly to be heard in a makeshift female voice.

64   "I have a telegram for you — it's about your son."

65   "Yes?" Again came OverBoost's makeshift female voice, "Oh, O-Oh, I just love telegrams. Can you sing it?"

66   And with that, the pilots all broke into loud singing of the telegram:

> Your son is dead they say . . .
> He bought the farm today
> He lost his turns going into the
> Tru Lai L.S.A.
>
> He's thinly spread around
> All around the ground
> So what else is there to say?

(and another verse was sung).

67   SmegMa yelled out, "Pubic Hair!" Spontaneously, with DingleBerry in the lead (after a few boo's), the song broke forth:

> Pubic hair, you've got the cutest little pubic hair
> There are no others that can compare,
> Pubic Hair! Penis or Vagina,
> Nothing could be fine-a,
> Than pubic hair.
> I'm in heaven when I'm in your underwear,
> So there's no need to shove,
> I've got a mouthful of,
> Those tasty pubic hairs.

68   And Cumulofuckus went to his bunk to miss his wife and hate the Korps more;

69   For Cumulofuckus thought of his wife until his groin turned blue,

70   He also thought of 35,000 feet and 1,200 miles per hour. Both thoughts turned him on.

71   The Korps took both away — his wife and jets.

72   And Cumulofuckus knew helo pilots were second class

pilots — when you were about to flunk out of flight school, the Krotch sent you to fly helos.

73   "The grunts were right," he thought. "Eat the Apple, . . . and Fuck the Korps."

74   The happy hour festivities proceeded without Cumulofuckus.

75   And it came to pass that banter, then revelry, followed by pious inebriation was the order of the Church service.

76   Then Carrier quals began.

77   And the religious ritual of carrier quals consisted of shoving several tables end to end to resemble the landing deck of a bar room aircraft carrier.

78   And there came about six pilots carrying at their waist level some saturated soul around the room by the arms and legs, face down, like a plane would do approaching the carrier deck for landing.

79   As the qualifying pilot would approach the tail of the make-shift carrier, his church mates would bodily throw him toward the table deck like an airplane landing on an aircraft carrier.

80   The object of carrier quals was for the thrown pilot to catch the toes of his boots like a tail hook on the end of the table keeping him from sliding off the other end into the sea.

81   It was that carrier quals was true bar flying.

82   And DingleBerry would sometimes act as the Landing Signal Officer, yelling "too high," "too low", and "meatball," the signal which meant that the landing approach was in the green.

83   And when an airplane had to land with its landing gear up, or when it has to land while it was on fire, the runway was sprayed with a foamy fire-retardant chemical.

84   So DingleBerry would yell "on fire" signaling other pilots to foam the makeshift bar room carrier deck with the foam of shaken beer.

85   Amid laughter, the thrown pilot would zip across the foamy, slick beer to the floor at the other end of the table,

86   Followed by a chant of "He's in the drink, he's in the drink — is the S.O.B. goin' to sink?"

87   There was no formal termination of the church service happy hour.

88   The pain of war neutralized by alcohol with the singing and drunken orations would dribble away after the bar closed.

89   It was that Injun and DarkMoon drunkenly argued over

whether the red man or the black man had received worse treatment at the hands of the white man.

90   Then Injun told stories of the plight of the Osage, how his ancestors were massacred, how their land was stolen from them by the federal government and how, even after being moved on the Oklahoma reservation where oil was discovered, many of his tribe had been murdered or swindled out of their oil or land.

91   And DarkMoon said that slaves didn't have land to be run off of, blacks had to ride in the back of the bus but Indians didn't, the rich were still killing the poor blacks as evidenced by the large number of black Marines in the infantry battalions,

92   The blacks were carrying the largest share of the war because they were poor.

93   And DarkMoon spoke truth for white folks could send their kids off to college, get them married, or get them into the militia to avoid the draft.

94   TailWind redirected the conversation by asking the drunken Injun if he knew how to do an Osage war dance,

95   And Injun responded that he did but that he needed drums to do it.

96   Then TailWind said he had a drum and led a gaggle of pilots outside the Club.

97   Then TailWind turned a 55-gallon steel drum used as a garbage collector bottom-up, and began a drum beat with wooden tent stakes.

98   Then Injun let out a loud war hoop and rhythmically danced in a circle, gyrating his head down to the ground and back up while chanting in Osage.

99   And soon Injun fell to the ground—the week's heat, the hours of flying, and the alcohol exhausted both his body and soul.

100 TailWind looked at DarkMoon and said, "Alright, you airborne Step-n-Fetchit, it's your turn. Give us an African dance?"

101 And DarkMoon tapped a slow rhythm for TailWind on the drum to show him the desired tempo, then he drunkenly knelt on his knees and sang as he pretended to pick cotton:

I's jus a Mississippi cotton picker,
Straw boss says I's jus a nigger,
Got fo' hundred pounds in jus one day,
Kick me in the ass, das my pay.

    Mug-a mug-a mug-a, kis' my ass
    Mug-a mug-a mug-a, fuck you chuck

Owed sixteen hundred dollars to da Boss's sto,
Das why I join da Marine Korps,
Get three squares every day,
C O treat me right, what you say.

    Mug-a mug-a mug-a, kis' my ass
    Mug-a mug-a mug-a, fuck you chuck

102 DarkMoon fell to the ground in drunken laughter, fighting the hidden pain.
103 And he lay there next to the sleeping Injun with his comrades looking on;
104 And he croaked a few epithets, including "I'm hit, I'm hit, over" and "We're the meanest mothers in the valley."
105 DarkMoon looked up blankly to his brothers and said, "Why are they wasting the kid Marines?"
106 And the gaggle disbanded not wanting to think about DarkMoon's piercing question.
107 It came to be that Injun and DarkMoon were carried to their cots;
108 Whereupon, TailWind removed the stupored Indian's boots and painted the Indian's toenails red,
109 For Injun was now accepted into TailWind's inner circle, and TailWind grinned to himself, "Injun was lucky that the pilots hadn't played 'piss-out' " — a drinking game which results in urination on the first participant to pass out.
110 TailWind saw visions of the ash faces of the dead young Marines,
111 And TailWind cried, for he too was powerless to stop the killing.

CHAPTER 10

1   And it was that night Medical Evacuation (MedEvac) was a most dangerous of missions,

2   For darkness was itself an enemy.

3   And the blackness in an overcast reduced the visibility where unseen tree limbs, bushes, and hidden obstacles ate helicopter blades leaving the crashed crew naked in death's territory.

4   Split-second nightmares frequented helicopters on night rescue missions,

5   For the enemy set traps to snare the night rescue helos.

6   "No guts, no glory," became the better you than me words of the pilots poking at their aerial comrades who flew night MedEvac.

7   And Injun questioned StoneMan, "Why don't the majors fly night MedEvac?"

8   And StoneMan smiled for Injun suddenly realized Kiwi never flew at night.

9   And StoneMan said, "Temple just pencils it in on the flight sheet — 'parker pen' flight time we call it."

10   And it became known to Injun what other young pilots had learned, that the words "field grade moon" meant that some senior grade pilots would schedule themselves to fly at night only when the moon was full, or bright.

11   And the 'meat pilots' resented those senior pilots who avoided their fair share of the risks of death by using their rank as a privilege not to fly at night, and to jockey flight schedules.

12   The meat pilots at happy hour would sing in unison, "Let's say hello to the Vicar-major," and they would with great joy scream, "Hello!, Asshole!"

13   And the meat pilots would again scream in unison, "Let's say hello to the Asshole," and they would scream, "Hello Vicar-major."

14   It was that certain priest pilots earned a professional disrespect from the meat pilots.

15   And much hate was held in abeyance by the meat pilots until opportunities for retaliation could be placed against those of privilege.

16   But it was also that many Meat-majors flew among them, and shared the dangers.

17   Such was a pilot called Matty Wright.

CHAPTER 11

1   The siren screamed forth the whine of emergency MedEvac.
2   Injun and a new co-pilot raced for the two MedEvac helicopters.
3   And it happened that Injun saw the crew chief on the number two wingman chase helicopter waiving his arms wildly,
4   For in his excitement, the new co-pilot had mistakenly climbed aboard the wrong helicopter and was yelling for crew assistance to start what he was then discovering to be a helo without an engine.
5   Injun laughed, and the ground crew laughed.
6   The crew chief helped the embarrassed co-pilot get to the right helo.
7   And it was that daylight would soon turn to twilight, then darkness;
8   SnowWhite and StoneMan, with messages in hand, ran to the two waiting helicopters.
9   Injun, with SnowWhite strapping in, taxied the helo quickly toward the runway with the wingman, MedEvac Chase, close behind;
10   And then there came the gunship helos called Gun-1 and Gun-2.
11   For the two airborne ambulances needed brotherly firepower shot at the enemy while the MedEvac helo was naked on the ground in the open recovering the wounded.
12   Injun flew with precision, for he had quickly learned that time was of the essence—a brother Marine needed him;
13   And SnowWhite as the command pilot let Injun fly at the controls of their lead helo.
14   SnowWhite was different; he talked funny, but SnowWhite had righted a wrong when he got the Army gun pilots to fly cover for them up in the mountains.
15   Injun remembered TailWind saying that flying with SnowWhite was special.
16   And Injun had learned that SnowWhite gave StoneMan, OverBoost, RedLine, HalfRight, ShareCrop, BurnOut, DarkMoon, BolTer, and BirdMan their nicknames.
17   And the name SnowWhite was known round about to the

grunt Marines who learned that the pilot called SnowWhite would rescue the wounded even in the heat of battle.

18   **THE MULE SENT THE RABBIT TO DIE IN THE ALLEY**, came SnowWhite's words evoking a chill over Injun causing his already anxious body to feel a tightness form in his stomach.

19   "Death Alley," Injun thought to himself, "This is the entrance to the roadway to hell, to Baca Valley, and on to the Trail of Tears."

20   And it was that OverBoost had told Injun that Bishop-general Mu'Le' kept ordering child men Marines over and over back into the same landing zone at a hated place named by the victim Marines as Death Alley.

21   And many helicopters had been shot down in the Alley, and crew members had been killed, and wounded;

22   And many Marines would be killed around the same over-used landing zones in the floor of the enemy's valley.

23   Then they came unto the high hills on both sides of the narrow corridor which made helicopters landing in the bottom like shooting fish in Charlie's barrel.

24   **THUNDER WILL BE AT THE ALLEY**, SnowWhite told Injun on the intercom.

25   Injun felt some relief, but was sore afraid.

26   And it was that Thunder was the code name for the Marine jet squadron — two attack jets would join up in flight to provide the kind of close air support that only Marines can give.

27   And radio contact was made with the pinned-down reconnaissance patrol called "Rabbit."

28   And the heavy enemy bullets froze the nine-member Marine force to the earth, who had been sent as bait into the Valley of Weeping.

29   It was known that if the Marines were left overnight, they would be killed.

30   Rabbit's radioman prayed, and his prayers were answered.

31   **THUNDER, GIVE RAIN,** came SnowWhite's radio message instructing both the jets to attack just as helos were about to land.

32   And Injun knew two jets at once was an uncommon procedure, but he knew darkness was fast approaching and textbook procedures would take too much time;

33   The death demon was waiting for fresh flesh,

34   And Sir Charles had to be the momentary target sending the enemy into hiding long enough for the helicopters to quickly land and leave.

35   SnowWhite smiled at TwoDogs, and with an unrecognized accent said, THE SOLDIERS HAD BREASTPLATES OF MAGNESIUM; AND THE SOUND OF THEIR WINGS WAS AS THE SOUND OF CHARIOTS OF MANY HORSES RUNNING TO BATTLE, and SnowWhite took flight control as leader of the emergency mission, and sang to himself.

36   THUNDER TALLYHO AND GO! RUN RABBIT RUN, SNOWWHITE FLY PATH THAT LEADS TO LIFE, EVERYBODY OUT, came SnowWhite's radio words.

37   And the easy green flying targets headed to the front row of the enemy's shooting gallery.

38   Injun witnessed for the first time the magnificent flying aura of the Marine Korps;

39   "This is it," Injun squeezed thoughts above fear,

40   For there were nine men, two wounded, and the finest team in the world was now in action to rescue them.

41   "Charlie will get his balls shot off," Injun announced.

42   And SnowWhite tilted the helo downward in a hawk's spiral dive into the valley's barrel bottom rescue point.

43   Live combat zoomed into Injun's focus.

44   If art can have beauty, then the Mona Lisa of war was vividly portrayed on the sky's canvas,

45   For the two MedEvac helo's leapt from the sky to the earth while rockets fired from the two jets streaked past,

46   Instantly there were the wing tip to wing tip jets on each side of SnowFlight when the two close air support jets zoomed by with guns firing,

47   And instantly they released on tree top level pull-out fire bombs against the enemy hillside area.

48   Simultaneously, Gun-1 with perfect timing crossed on its tree level attack followed by Gun-2 protecting the two flying rescue mules.

49   Now it was and shall forever be that the close air support teamwork bought the less than one minute needed to load the Marines.

50   And both helicopters slowed their motion right over the ground capturing first the wounded and then gathering the living,

51   And the last man made a running leap into the open doorway of the escaping helicopter just as the jets made their second attack.

52   The helicopter crews fired their machine guns into the tree lines;

53   And the Gunships had continued tight flying orbits with guns and rockets blazing.

54   Marine close air support shown brightly round about,

55   For close air support separated the Marine Korps from the Sky Blue Church.

56   Brotherhood made a difference, thought Injun; the Marine jet pilot's allegiance to their ground comrades is alive and well.

57   And Injun smiled outside, and inside. "My father will be proud," he said unto himself.

58   SnowWhite nodded to Injun to take the flight controls and fly home.

59   And Thunder radioed back, "bar-b-que flight, goin home, out."

60   And the euphoric jet pilots flew up-side down and around the slow flying helicopter brothers.

61   And Injun, the crew, and the Marines yanked out of the jungle jaws of death gave praise.

62   And the two wounded were delivered to the waiting medics at the hospital.

63   It was that within thirty minutes of being wounded in the jungle, each child man Marine was being treated by a skilled surgeon.

64   Injun determined that if you had to be in a war, this War of all wars would be the one, and if you have to fight, the Marine Korps was the best.

65   Injun's first flight with this white haired guy called SnowWhite cemented Injun's confidence in SnowWhite's flying abilities—even if he talked funny;

66   For TailWind's extraction at the DMZ was magnificent, Injun thought, but SnowWhite's flying was the best.

67   And Injun was proud of his new pilot friend, SnowWhite;

68   It was important to Injun that SnowWhite be confident in him.

69   SnowWhite was blue steel, and steel blue.

70   Now when the helicopter taxied back in the darkness into the

MedEvac spot on return from its mission, Vicar-major Dingle-Berry stood at the wheel, waiting for SnowWhite to climb down;
71 "Hopper's dead," he said, knowing that SnowWhite had a common bond with Hopper and would want to know.
72 And when StoneMan joined up, the Vicar-major repeated, "Hopper's dead."
73 And SnowWhite stared squarely at the Vicar-major, who continued, "Egg Beater came apart, happened right above the ground, blades intermeshed and one blade spun through the cockpit;
74 Hopper took it through the neck,
75 And SnowWhite was saddened at the death of his cherished friend, and quietly said, **THE HERRODS OF WALL STREET CAN REJOICE. A MAN GREAT IN LIFE HAS PASSED FROM THE FLESH.**
76 And StoneMan bitterly spat,
77 And the others of SnowFlight came forth and said that they escorted the body of Hopper Honey unto the departing silver bird.
78 SnowWhite wept.
79 And it came to pass that DingleBerry said also that 777 was ordered to move away from war for forty days and forty nights to the Island of the Floating Dragon by carrier ship to get new helos.
80 SnowWhite, upon hearing such message, said, **IT IS TIME TO DEPART INTO A QUIET PLACE, AND REST A WHILE.**

CHAPTER 12

1 And it came to pass that 777 was sent by the High Priests and departed from the Nam Bo war to go to the Island of the Floating Dragon by Navy carrier ship privately.
2 And the Nam Bo children of the 777 orphanage would be without the food given by SnowFlight.
3 And SnowFlight, in the departure from Tru Lai to land on the ship, flew to the supply depot and lifted by helicopter cargo nets pallets of rations and delivered them unto the orphanage children.

4   And straightway SnowWhite constrained SnowFlight to get to the ship, and SnowWhite stayed behind.

5   And when blackness was come, the ship was in the midst of the sea, and in the hours of the morning SnowWhite was the last to leave the land.

6   And SnowWhite saw the carrier ship toiling in the sea; for the wind was contrary to the ship: and about the fourth watch of the night SnowWhite cometh unto the helo carrier out of the newly formed sea fog and haze.

7   And the bright landing light shown about from the Dog Driver helicopter.

8   But when they saw SnowWhite dangerously skimming the sea, they supposed it had been Saint Elmo's fire, and cried out:

9   For they all saw him and were troubled. And immediately SnowWhite radioed the ship, **SNOWWHITE WITH SOULS TO COME ABOARD**.

10   And the Navy radio priest on the carrier ship upon the sea made jest by requesting where SnowWhite wished to go and SnowWhite said, **LET US PASS OVER UNTO THE OTHER SIDE OF THE LAKE**.

11   And there was much laughter.

CHAPTER 13

1   And 777 came over unto the other side of the sea by ship unto the land of the Ryukyu and the Island of the Floating Dragon to get new helos.

2   And when SnowFlight came out of the ship to the new airfield, immediately on land there met them the merchant of motorcycle who had his dwelling among the passage to Futema.

3   And SnowWhite said, **LET THERE BE WHEELS AMONG WHEELS**.

4   And SnowFlight on land became called SnowPack, and SnowWhite, StoneMan, RedLine, OverBoost, Tailwind, Bird-Man, HalfRight, TwoDogs, ShareCrop, DarkMoon, BolTer, SmegMa, and BurnOut rode their motorcycles round about.

5   For they were free to meditate.

CHAPTER 14

1   For forty days and forty nights 777 was to absent itself from the horror of war on the Island of the Floating Dragon.

2   And SnowWhite led SnowPack to the quiet of the green mountains to where the raiments of war were silent echoes of the mind's immediate past.

3   There came an old leathered man with sheep wool hair who in silence watched the twelve from the volcanic rock wall at the end of the dirt floored primitive inn.

4   And the oriental stillness of the old man was broken by Bird-Man's gesture of friendship with the tender of a cool beer.

5   And it came to pass that the pilots discovered among their midst a Tokko Tai, a Nipponese suicide pilot who took off from land, not a ship.

6   And it came to pass that the old man would be waiting in the evenings for the arrival of SnowWhite and the twelve pilots who would meditate on the events of survival, and things that were, and things that would be.

7   And it was decided that the King of Cash was plundering the splendid little war amid the smiles of the Queen of Loot, for economic harvesting of war crops and vanity of royal power shown round about.

8   And it was decided that the Prince of Money obeyed his King and smiled upon the Herrods of Wall Street for in War there is money for the pockets and shekels for the mind.

9   And it was decided the church of the Marine Korps cast a devout religion more sanctified that any other church of the earth for when its clerical hierarchy whispered, unsolicited death emitted therefrom their mouths.

10   And the stoic old man, Lei' Merej, frightened the pilots with his simple words.

11   **YOU SPEAK BLASPHEMOUS THINGS OF YOUR RELIGION, MARINE KORPS, AND YOU HIDE THE WAYS OF ITS HIGH PRIESTS?** the Tokko Tai man queried.

12   **GOOD MEN CAN CHOOSE BLINDNESS,** said SnowWhite.

13   **IS THAT NOT THE HISTORY OF WARS?** the suicide pilot cleverly asked.

14   "But this war is different," inserted HalfRight, "We must stop the enemy movement before it creeps to our homeland."

15   The old suicide pilot responded, **SUCH IS NOT THE TRUTH; THE POOR PEOPLE OF NAM BO ARE SIMPLE FARMERS WHO TILL THE SOIL; SOME PRAY TO GOD FOR SURVIVAL. THE TRUTH IS THAT YOU CANNOT FACE THIS TRUTH . . . YOU ARE BEING ASKED TO RISK YOUR LIVES SO THAT YOUR PEOPLE CAN LATER LEARN THIS TRUTH, . . .**

16   The old man paused staring at the distant ocean, then said, **THE TRUTH IS THAT FORCES ARE BARGAINING FOR FLESH.**

17   And there was quietness among SnowPack for the old man's words carried a piercing softness.

18   **YOU MUST RISK DEATH RATHER THAN SURVIVE THROUGH CONFRONTATION WITH TRUTH, FOR TO TELL OF HARD-HEARTEDNESS WILL CAST YOU IN DIS-HONOR AND RELEASE YOU TO DEATH'S DISCIPLES . . .**

19   **. . . JUST AS THE COMMON PEOPLE FROM WHICH YOU COME ARE THE PRIZE OF YOUR FATHERLAND, THE COMMON PEOPLE OF NAM BO ARE ITS PRIZE. THE TRUTH IS THAT YOUR COUNTRY HAS CHOSEN TO FIGHT ON THE SIDE OF OPPRESSION AND CORRUP-TION AGAINST THE SIMPLE PEASANT, AND YOU ARE THE EVIL ENEMY IN THE EYES OF THE MANY POOR PEASANTS WHOSE LIVES YOUR LEADERS HAVE CHO-SEN TO WASTE WITH YOURS.**

20   And there was quiet among SnowFlight for the old soldier's words were penetrating.

21   "Hey, cut the deep shit," said SmegMa, "Let's talk about geisha girl pie or something more reverent," which gained a few chuckles.

22   And SnowPack revelled away from deep thought and dressed themselves in the vestments of alcoholic pleasure.

23   Then it became known that the old man of war had never landed on an aircraft carrier.

24   And it came to pass that a brown man named Lei' was wheeled around the room and pitched on a make-ship carrier deck from the tables.

25   Much laughter came forth in the hours of isolated comradery

and the flying stories from Lei' matched the tales of woe from SnowPack.

26   Then upon the suggestion of TwoDogs and the blessing of them all, the motorcycles were started and lined one beside the other in a row with rear wheels toward the volcanic rock front.

27   And it came to pass that each of the pilots climbed onto the flat roof, and one by one leapt from the roof to their waiting mechanical steed, and on nod of SnowWhite, SnowPack roared off into the night down the winding mountain highway.

28   "Where's BirdMan," yelled StoneMan with concern for his unseen brother pilot when SnowPack stopped on a curve near the bottom.

29   And SnowPack returned up the hill only to find BirdMan screaming from where he sat perched on his motorcycle hung in the top of a tree where he and his drunken motorcycle had, in flight, been caught after leaving the roadway into the air and into the top limbs of a tree on the steep hillside.

30   And there was much laughter and amusement after retrieving the scratched, but unhurt BirdMan.

31   And word spread about a Greek Marine pilot who had been captured by a tree.

CHAPTER 15

1   Now it came to pass that the lone Indian climbed to the peak of the hill;

2   He observed that the ocean could be seen from all directions from the dragon's hump looking at the chain of islands floating in the deep blue sea.

3   And the distant island humps cast the picture of a floating dragon.

4   After sitting motionless for hours in meditation, the big Indian spoke,

5   "Father, give me peace, for I have become the ways of the white man. As our fathers fought for their land with bows and arrows against the white man's guns and power, so do the poor common people of Nam Bo fight for survival against many enemies. I will do my duty, Father, but my soul sees the ways of the greedy white man."

CHAPTER 16

1   Holy Day, November 10, was celebrated by all Marines of the Korps church.

2   And DingleBerry abandoned whoredom with the dwarf slant eyes whose smallness made him feel large and he departed the Texas Bar from the brothel he called "the Ranch" to come forth to minister the eucharist of the Marine Korps Birthday.

3   On the Island of the Floating Dragon the papacy from the Holy Sea kept the best secret within the vows of the unholy church for thereon in a quiet setting over-looking the Lake of Indifference was a glorious Tabernacle of Alcohol.

4   And it was in this emporium that the American League, the National League, the beleaguered, the beguiled, and the devout assembled to honor their beloved Korps church.

5   And before formal assembly there was the consumption of much alcohol.

6   And when the mass was assembled, DingleBerry read forth a catechism mass while standing upon a stool behind a lectionary large cake in the window of the immaculate pilot's club.

7   And there were staccato toasts of champagne followed by a canteen cup with brandy, for it was a time of holy celebration.

8   And SmegMa came forth to the altar of cake with erect penis, which he stuck into the cake, smiling and saying, "Eat the Apple," and the room roared in a laughter response, "And Fuck the Korps."

9   And there were many hymns sang, but SmegMa yelled forth to sing DingleBerry a hymn, to which the pilots loudly sang, "Fuck him, f-u-c-k him-m-m-m-m."

10   Then it was that SmegMa yelled forth, "Anyone that can't tap dance is a muther fucker,"

11   Whereupon, the room of pilots all stood up in their combat flying boots, and commenced to tap dance on the table tops, on the bar, and everywhere.

12   And there were hours of celebration, for unto the Marine Korps Church was given only one day per year.

13   And it came to pass that SmegMa went unto the brothel and chose the whore he called "November Ten,"

14   Whereupon, November Ten on November tenth, while also engaged in the art of fellatio, hummed the Marine Korps hymn,

15 And SmegMa testified that it was a truly religious experience.

CHAPTER 17

1 And as there were days and there were nights to meditate;
2 And Injun increasingly searched his soul as to why to return to the Land of Nam Bo,
3 For it plagued Injun that war could be used to make rich men even richer,
4 That cleric priests could be paid with medals, and vanity promotions of the mind,
5 And that self-preservation of the mediocre King could prevail.
6 And that mothers would quietly give their sons for the Enterprise of War.
7 Injun concerned himself that other Indians swept into the white man's ways would be lured into the trap of placing honor before truth.
8 And he thought of the "around the fort" Indians who tried white men's ways,
9 And he thought of the Indian warrior who hopelessly challenged over-whelming odds while his wife and children were being slaughtered by the ruthless white men,
10 And he saw in the eyes of the Nam Bo peasants many dead indians.
11 "Why must we go back?" asked Injun of SnowWhite.
12 **BECAUSE YOU ARE BONDED TO YOUR BROTHERS,** answered SnowWhite.
13 And Injun saw also the secret of Marines, for a Marine cannot abandon his brothers, even in the face of wasted death.

CHAPTER 18

1 Now it came to pass that SnowPack sought wisdom from SnowWhite as to the why's of the Nam Bo war,
2 And there was much gnashing of teeth as to why they should die for such unworthy cause,
3 And there were thumping echoes of the mind screaming forth

mental vomit wreaking of great hate-seeking runaway survival yet knowing the truth;

4   And SnowWhite said unto SnowFlight, **YOU CARE MORE FOR YOUR KID BROTHERS THAN YOU DO FOR YOURSELVES.**

5   And the secret of the Marine Korps was revealed unto them, for there flashed visions of inches of past glory harnessed to miles of misery and death, and of brothers clinging to brothers with morsels of hope cast only in the dim light of survival by the bond of Marine to Marine.

6   And it was known unto them why uncommon valor is a common virtue.

CHAPTER 19

1   Tribedom, chiefdom, villagedom, fire and maneuver, Sun Tzu, Clausewitz, Geronimo, death without dishonor, each flashed haunting signals to the Injun of three names.

2   And there came visions of the blank stares of the dead faces of the child men of no name slipped into the 1369 green rubber bags of cancellation of the flesh,

3   Then Injun had visions of the wars that should have been, for the white men rode red stallions following the riking bitch many horned bride,

4   And the big Indian cried for the dead flesh that had been, that was, and that would be,

5   For there were fields of daisies spotted by acres of bittercup.

6   "I'm going crazy," the big Injun mumbled openly as he passed through the maze of innocent youth captured in old men's purse.

7   And it was that the man from a thousand tribes begat vomit of the soul and spasm of the mind seeing once again all that history had secreted on the young,

8   And on the poor.

9   But therein appeared an apparition of truth for the tan Indians were winning against the folklore of the white man,

10   And the spirit of a man on a white horse with a sword shown brightly, and Injun grinned.

11   "Am I going crazy," the big Injun asked of SmegMa, the near shrink, after explaining the visions and not wanting to go back to war.

12 "Why do you ask me," answered the sex driven mind as SmegMa arranged and rearranged the packages of condoms like a house of cards.

13 "Because you know things," responded the despondent Indian.

14 "There are only two things to this war," said SmegMa, as he lined the condom boxes in a row, "Flying n' fuckin," and he paused, "and fuckin n' flying."

CHAPTER 20

1 Now in the last days of Injun's peace on the Island of the Floating Dragon, Injun's prayer's were answered;

2 For Lei' Merej took Injun where there were many horses,

3 And Injun smiled for his soul felt free in the presence of the little man of leathered skin and penetrating smile.

4 Now it came to pass that Lei' Merej and his friends rode horses with Injun on the green hilltops overlooking in all directions the deep blue sea,

5 And the horses did glide in rhythm as if the wind were beneath their feet,

6 And the Indian wearing the small beaded cross was among many cowboys,

7 But the aura of these people who took him aside and befriended him in the island wilderness overwhelmed Injun.

8 And Injun awoke from a deep sleep in the shade of the war to come finding Lei' looking into his eyes,

9 "Who are you?," questioned Injun.

10 **I AM HE THAT LOOKS OVER THE SOULS OF MEN,** answered Lei'.

11 "But I do that . . . we helicopter pilots all do that, . . . You are a farmer," quivered the big Injun at the chill suddenly in his soul.

12 **YOU ARE RIGHT,** smiled Lei', **I AM A FARMER,** he paused, **OF TREASURES TOLD, . . . AND UNTOLD.**

13 And the evening rain came with the sea's mild wind drifting about as the shifting mind of the now unburdened Indian smiled knowing his place was with the tribe of child men Marines.

CHAPTER 21

1   Now it was that an Indian named TwoDogs knew the God of the Quapaw, the Cree, the Cherokee, the Chickasaw, the Cheyenne, the Crow, the Choctaw, the Calusa, the Colville, the Cowlitz, the Chinook, the Cayuse, the Caddo, the Creek, the Cayuga, and the Catawba, and gave blessings.

2   And the God of all the Indians could be seen by TwoDogs in the white cross with the red heart and the blue eyes.

3   Now it came to pass that out of the night 777 was called back from the Island to the banquet table of death at the war.

4   And so it was that the helo carrier ship carried many to the land of Nam Bo to make war.

5   The Dark Angel dealt greed, avarice, and false pride to the money hummers of war,

6   And men of powerful mind but invisible god whispered forth the wisdom of sacrifice under non-thinking excuses of hierarchical self-preservation,

7   And Satan danced for men were given unto pissing on God's laws, and issued forth legions.

8   But the Indian of content thought knew the white business men took food from the starving Indians,

9   And the white men's ways left room for God only after the meal of greed had been consumed.

10   And it came to be that 777 returned across the sea to the land of Nam Bo where the beast dispensed war.

11   There also came upon Nam Bo and Sam Bo the days of punishment for the men of the uncircumcised minds as leaders of the uncircumcised nations heard not the echoes of the past;

12   For the customs of the people were in vain: for the men of self-righteousness deck their minds with gold and silver but use nails not.

13   But they were altogether brutish and foolish: the stock is a doctrine of vanities.

14   They were the greedy dogs which can never have enough, and they were the shepherds that cannot understand: they all look to their own way, every one for his gain, from his quarter.

15   "What's attrition spelled backwards," screamed the King of Cash halfway around the earth to the Paragon of Piles.

16   And the man of narrow mind and long tooth knew not, for

the school book solution in the many years of sabbatical war study did not allow for backwards thought.

17 "When you are surrounded," the Paragon of Piles tweaked to the King, "You can attack in any direction."

18 And the King was amused not, for in the land of Sam Bo the victim peasants were seeing the lies of their King.

19 And there came wise men from across the ghettos of thought to counsel the desperate despot.

20 And the mental slot machines spun forth tails of statistics;

21 For falsehoods gain less disrespect when hinged to mathematical folklore.

22 And the Prince of Money staggered to the mental bar as the shock of reality of failure stained his perfect mind with visions of miles of yes men in yes outfits driven by yes clones.

23 And the demons who had suckled the flesh of thousands into evil thoughts and evil ways grinned for the money hummers of war could count much cash, and their souls could be counted upon.

CHAPTER 22

1 There came to be among the captives along the river Perfume the Duke of Darkness,

2 And the child men of captured spirit with unskilled mind did blindly obey, for it was their nature,

3 And the Duke of Darkness spoke of things great and small in a world confused by prophet over principle.

4 Then the dark spirits from the Emperor of Ego glistened forth battle heroics on the Pope, the Cardinal, the Bishop, and the other generals of lesser mind whispering deity doctrine, hiding the wrongs of economic war burdened on the backs of the child men Marines who could only choose honor over truth,

5 And Satan spewed forth a hideous laugh echoing battles flinging human entrails, arms, legs and souls, regardless of race, color, creed, age or sex.

6 Once again legions of the evil demons danced glory, medals, promotion, and elevated insignificance in the minds of those who understood not that the child men were mere children of the innocent flesh;

7 And once again ignorance begat death,

8   But the child men of blind mind with confused heart gave all,
9   And they did love each other, and they did let brotherly love prevail,
10   And it was that the child men Marines were asked to do for no reason at all.
11   And the child men increasingly knew such, and hurt with great pain;
12   The child men saw a father, whom they loved, giving them unto the priests of war to be burned in the Valley of Slaughter.
13   For their death was only a tithe to falsehood above truth;
14   And the meaning of their existence on this earth was reduced in the flickers of a mere muzzle flash.
15   There was a war, and there was a rumor of other wars, in a war,
16   And escape through survival became the only door.
17   And hate crystallized into the casual taking of life standing at Hate's Door.
18   The child men unleashed their hopelessness by killing all that flickered forth as an avenue of survival,
19   And they would take wagers as to how many bullets they could shoot into a peasant body before it hit the ground.
20   And the little people on all sides became the victims of demons homesteading the minds of the rich, and the powerful,
21   For when the forces of evil do battle, evil knows no uniform or army.
22   And the child men sang, "Napalm sticks to children, and the Dow doesn't give a shit."

CHAPTER 23

1   Injun stared from the shadows at the kid Marine and his shepherd dog.
2   And the attack dog with the attack trained kid provoked visions,
3   For the mind of the dog blindly knew not, unfettered to attack on simple command,
4   For the mind of the child man Marine blindly knew not, unfettered to attack on simple command,
5   And the dog would give its all, its life.
6   And the boy Marine would give his all, his life.

7 "War's Chow," Injun thought as his visions flickered at death and the stacked 1369 body bags.

8 And Injun hurt for he was powerless to stop the useless killing.

9 And Injun cried, for he saw love of the dog in the face of the boy;

10 And for he saw in the face of the dog his grandfather's two dogs, who gave all.

CHAPTER 24

1 Injun agonized over the killing fields and seeing the rows and rows of dead Nam Bo children in the long ditch graves used to instantly hide the harvesting of many lives by two bit bullets.

2 So it came to be that Injun drank much to hide the pain, and the hurt,

3 For in alcohol there lies escape's revolving door.

4 Injun confronted TailWind as he retaliated against one of the many flies that followed TailWind around.

5 And upon the table in front of TailWind crawled lots of flies, and Injun asked the drunken Pole, "Why don't you shoo away the flies?"

6 And the drunken Ski replied, "They aren't flies, . . . they're 'Walks'."

7 And Injun understood not the Ski's drunken stupor, and asked, "What do you mean they're Walks?"

8 "I pulled all their wings off," the grinning Ski said. "These here bugs are 'Walks.'" He pointed to the table top of wingless flies.

9 And in War, sometimes even the smallest of retributions gives temporary solace to a mind forced to live in a human hell.

CHAPTER 25

1 "War is good business, invest your son," commented Stone-Man to the medley of pilots who witnessed the rich Sam Bo laborers building war base runways for the profit of the King.

2 And the King's laborers' openly wreaked of money through exorbitant war contracting prices.

3   "I doubt that," responded BolTer, "those look like loyal hard-hat Mexicans in service of their King."

4   "Look like wet backs to me," said the Spanish OverBoost.

5   "Allah will grant you heaven if you die while serving him against the ungodly," DarkMoon countered with certain Islamic evidence and continued, "And the VC and NVA carry those tiny Budda's while driving the Sam Bo imperialists from their fatherland . . . [A]nd the Jews are the chosen people who killed Jesus in the chosen land . . . [A]nd we can't let those damn Yankees free our slaves — My god who'll do the field work?" DarkMoon poked at BolTer, his doubting friend.

6   And springing to disgust at the thought of the King of Cash using the war so the King could profit.

7   "Have the white men money whores always choked a war?" queried Injun.

8   "Why this is not a war, this is a live fire training exercise orchestrated by career priests and scored by the Prince of Money," DarkMoon espoused with anger, "And the careerists are too busy building their own personnel jackets and covering their own ticket-punching ass."

9   "You're a cynical bastard," BolTer stated to his black pilot friend. "And you doubt everything until you have counted it three times," DarkMoon replied.

10   Then Injun said, "How can you have a war without profits?"

11   And as SnowWhite listened to the frustration of why men who loved their country so much were being wasted in an unloving way, he said, **IT IS A TIME OF GREAT DARKNESS, BUT THE LIGHT SHALL AGAIN SHINE.**

The Word According to
SHARECROP

(Know Yourself and Seek
Self Improvement)

CHAPTER 1

1   ShareCrop was the only one that knew.
2   ShareCrop wouldn't tell—the Chief wouldn't want him to, for he learned when he and Injun had visited Injun's home and he had seen the remnants of the Osage.
3   Just as the carpetbaggers had robbed ShareCrop of his inheritance by taking several thousand acres of his great-grandfather's cotton land following the War of Northern Aggression, the greedy white men robbed the Osage first of their tribal land, and then of the money rightly theirs when the "worthless" rolling reservation land of northeastern Oklahoma proved to be rich in oil.
4   "Your Grandfather would be proud," were the humble words the weathered Indian father said to TwoDogs as he and a white boy called ShareCrop were leaving to make war.
5   "Our people will miss you." The quiet Cherokee mother cried slow tears that flickered as small moving, clear pearls of life trickled down her cheeks in the Oklahoma sunlight,
6   "My heart will ache for you till you return, you are a part of me, my soul is of your soul," she said.
7   "Take this with you and wear it until your return," then she removed from her neck a leather string necklace to which was attached a small beaded white cross with a big red bead center heart.
8   TwoDogs had made it for her when he was nine years old.

53

9   And the two young pilots departed for the land of Nam Bo.
10   "Why did they name you TwoDogs?" asked ShareCrop.
11   "When my Grandfather was a small boy," Injun began with a saddened expression, "his parents were very poor."
12   "The Five Civilized Tribes were at the mercy of continuous lies of the Eastern white men, and there was no food in the winter."
13   "Grandfather said he had two wonderful dogs, his best friends;"
14   "They swam in the river, hunted, and were his companions."
15   Injun began to cry. "Grandfather said in the bitter winter that the family was starving — and they had to eat the dogs."
16   Injun teared. "Grandfather said he named me TwoDogs because since that time he had not been able to love until I was born."

CHAPTER 2

1   It came to pass that ShareCrop quickly matured in the land of Nam Bo thrusting a child into mental numbness caused by instant stark terror from the horrors of war.
2   It was that the southern spirit of honor, duty, and father prevailed in ShareCrop's bean field mind.
3   And ShareCrop soon recognized that storybook pictures of war were displaced by the horrors of child men's body parts,
4   By children with severed or smoking flesh, stump limbs, and agony;
5   And by death with or without cause or purpose.
6   It was also that ShareCrop joined with other pilots seeking escape from the titanic whys of war.
7   And it came to pass that ShareCrop became bonded with a pilot called DarkMoon, whom he called Black Bart.
8   It was that DarkMoon smiled upon his new friend ShareCrop, and called him Delta Duke.
9   And it was that ShareCrop taught new meaning unto DarkMoon, for ShareCrop taught DarkMoon to say,
10   "Moin'n Massah;"
11   "Moin'n Mr. Pennyworth;"
12   "Mo'e T Suh;"

13 "Hole D Doe;"
14 "Moan back," and,
15 "Chitlins is good."
16 And DarkMoon taught unto ShareCrop new thoughts for ShareCrop was taught to say,
17 "Top of the morning, Sir Simoleon."
18 "Black books, black looks,"
19 "Pomme de Saint Jean,"
20 "Lebenesraum," and,
21 "The Harrowing of Hell," about which old Harry plundered, laid waste, and captured souls.
22 So it came to be that ShareCrop tried to teach DarkMoon about field hand blacks.
23 And it was that DarkMoon tried to take the country out of the boy.
24 Then it was that DarkMoon pricked his finger and exchanged blood with ShareCrop,
25 And ShareCrop gave his blood unto DarkMoon.
26 After that SmegMa called the inseparable two Vanilla-Fudge,
27 And it came to be that ShareCrop and DarkMoon gathered forth high-style humor in a low-style war.

CHAPTER 3

1 Soon, unto ShareCrop, he saw that death came easier for men who had no real name,
2 For unto many were given nicknames to salve away somehow the real name of the living man changed into 1369 flesh.
3 And time faded from memory the real name and residue gave forth SnowWhite, StoneMan, RedLine, OverBoost, DarkMoon, HalfRight, SmegMa, Birdman, BurnOut and BolTer.
4 Then there were others, but death tasted less bitter when the real name was no real person,
5 And comradery elevated great feeling at the special names given by special friends.

CHAPTER 4

1   Ada Sam was beautiful from the air—a vision of high mountains, waterfalls, and clouds that slipped silkily on and off the mystic mountain tops;
2   And there were clouds that drifted in the mild winds over the airfield changing bright day to wet white fog and then instantly back to bright day.
3   Ada Sam was deadly.
4   The high ground above the airfield with dense jungle cover gave the enemy easy shooting at the child men below.
5   Some said the Marines were encamped there as prey trying to lure the elusive enemy into a real fight in the war of attrition.
6   Others knew the Pope-general's staffers were deeply concerned that the Army not come into Tekoa Province—it was important that the soldiers of a foreign force, the Army, not get involved in Marine operations.
7   It was worth the lives of a few good Marines not to have to deal with the Army.
8   "Do what?" quipped SmegMa to the Lay-major assigned as an air priest in the Ada Sam command bunker.
9   "You want us to haul the Chaplain with the Salvation Army food to the Kidron Special Forces compound so he can make a goodwill pilgrimage in the Village of those loin cloth mountain people?"
10   "Affirmative," the soon to be confirmed for promotion Lay-leader-major replied, "it's part of the 'we are the people' program."
11   "Bullshit . . . Sir . . .," SmegMa surly retorted, "You and I both know those damn Nam Bo pilots will bomb the villages when there are no other targets of opportunity, just for the fun of killing them. They treat 'em less than animals."
12   SmegMa called his helicopter DoGooder-1, and the wingman was DoGooder-2 in honor of the Chaplain.
13   It was ten minutes from lift-off at Ada Sam to Kidron Special Forces Compound located on a hillside overlooking the road in from Bac Bo and the grass hut village.
14   And the natives were small, brown people—not black people.
15   Pigs, ducks, and other animals were kept underneath the

houses, and ShareCrop witnessed a woman suckling a baby pig beside the landing zone.

16   The young Chaplain armed with godly intent went among the natives in the "friendly" village ignorant of the short distance between the firing pin and the firing cap of a chambered shell in an enemy rifle which when properly aimed and ignited would send the Chaplain to instant eternity.

17   "Sick him on 5-P," grinned the Special Forces Sergeant giving instructions to the guards going with the Chaplain to the village.

18   And the gaggle of do-gooders maneuvered down the trail with the guard soldiers as quiet body guards.

19   After making gestures of friendship through the interpreter, the Chaplain commenced to pass out food, money, and his interpretation of God, in limited quantities, to the wonderful mountain people.

20   And it was that a large-breasted, missing-toothed woman smiled at the Chaplain with her beetle, stained black teeth;

21   And he gave her five piasters (5-P).

22   And she stepped back and opened her blouse so that the two cantaloupe breasts could be photographed by the boy preacher.

23   And the Chaplain turned red with embarrassment, and the soldiers laughed.

24   Baby food was passed out to the old people, and mothers with babies.

25   Then ShareCrop thought of Injun's story; the Osage Indian should have been mountain people, he thought, but then reflected how the white man treated the Indians may explain why the Nam Bo soldiers wasted the mountain villagers.

26   One man's death for another man's pleasure.

27   And it came to pass that the helos departed;

28   And a message came forth from Kidron:

Chaplain visit over-all successful. Food, clothing and money good. Do not send baby food. The enemy told villagers the picture on the can was what Marines put inside. Corn for corn, peas for peas. Marines grind up babies and put them in jars because of the baby's picture on the food jar. The villagers destroyed the baby food. Marines eat babies!

CHAPTER 5

1   ShareCrop was a man of big heart, and sudden gloom and doom thought.

2   ShareCrop cried, and his heart sobbed, and his soul fretted, for it could not possibly be done that all child men Marines be saved from the wrath of death of the flesh.

3   And ShareCrop ached at visions of wasted death of countless kids, and people, and beliefs.

4   And ShareCrop crouched at having decisions thrust upon him which implanted happen-chance death on his fellow man.

5   ShareCrop had great love,

6   And had great fear of not saving every brother in need.

7   ShareCrop saw the evil of the leaders of the tan-yellow men;

8   And he was seeing visions of evil of the leaders of the white man.

9   Then it came to pass that ShareCrop met face to face with a pilot called SnowWhite, a man of decisive character and sure thought.

10   ShareCrop was the first pilot unto whom SnowWhite asked, **COME, FLY WITH SNOWWHITE?**

11   ShareCrop came to know this white-haired pilot with blue eyes that sparkled comfort in the middle of a living hell.

12   It came also to be known to ShareCrop the wonderful flying talents of SnowWhite, for his touch of mastery gave the old dog helo the smooth performance of a yearling deer gliding confidently through the forest.

12   And it was that ShareCrop and SnowWhite came unto the mountains to a people known as SOG;

13   And on the faces of the hired men of many lands was a mission of murder for money,

14   For these men warred for the highest bidder.

15   There came from the midst of the men of SOG a man of yellow hair and pearly teeth, and he spoke to SnowWhite, "Why are you here?"

16   And SnowWhite rebuked him, and said also, **IT IS NOT YOURS TO QUESTION.**

CHAPTER 6

1   There came unto the fold of 777 Flight-Squadron in the Tekoa Wilderness an occasional rat, and many rodents.

2   And the crooks and crannies of the mind infested by rat and rodent experiences gave forth sympathy for mere animals seeking only survival.

3   Now it was that ShareCrop and BurnOut felt sympathy not; for in their youth the nightly scratching and roaming of rats left countless echoes of sleepless nights.

4   And it came to pass in the night that ShareCrop with the drunken gaggle of pilots were confronted with the destiny of one live rat caught in the mechanical live trap set under their hootch.

5   Some said leave the poor creature alone, for even rats are entitled to survival,

6   Some said the place for a disease carrying rat is in the trap,

7   Some said the only good rat is a dead rat.

8   Then there arose a need of sacrifice, for some said this rat doth protest when poked upon,

9   Whereupon, BurnOut called the rat "Mesha."

10   And the rat, Mesha was doused with fluid and set afire inside the trap to the drunken screams of "Burn Baby Burn" and "Start your engines."

11   Then out of the darkness came ShareCrop, tearing away at the killing frenzy over one simple rat quickly opening the trap and thereby releasing the burning and instantly running rat whose glowing hair was a moving fire-ball in the blackness underneath the wooden buildings,

12   And there were then screams of fire with stark terror drunken pilots chasing the burning animal through the darkness of the night for fear the hootch would be burned to the ground.

13   And it came to pass that the burning animal fell over dead provoking words of "He ran out of gas" and "Semper fi, mutherfucker," from among the pilots.

14   And there came forth a general order that pilots were not to burn the rats, but much confusion came therefrom as to whether priestly rats were excluded.

CHAPTER 7

1 There came a time of abundant death and much hate;
2 And the pilots ferrying the lots of the 1369 corpses knew not why the War,
3 Nor could their minds bear the horror of the waste of precious young men simply to train inexperienced career commanders and overaggressive promotion seekers.
4 Nor could their minds accept body count to justify an unjustifiable war.
5 Nor could their minds accept that the Fatherland they loved had abandoned them to the arrogant ways of the King of Cash, and of the Prince of Money;
6 For inwardly they knew they were temporarily entrapped under the thumb of the Dark Angel.
7 And it came to the mind of ShareCrop the answer to this fine little war.
8 "What's it called?" queried DarkMoon to ShareCrop's scaffold with a rope hanging down near the ground in front of a board wall ShareCrop built at the sandy ditch behind the "O" Club building.
9 "It's called piss'n up a rope, that's what this war is all about," grinned ShareCrop,
10 And with his penis withdrawn in a death squeeze,
11 And with an instant spurt, ShareCrop shot a urine-released stream aimed up the rope as high as his bodily force could reach.
12 Then ShareCrop marked his highest spot.
13 DarkMoon laughed, and tested the 'rope of faith,' as it became known.
14 And it came to pass that there were many pissin' contests at the wailing wall of the Nam Bo War,
15 And names were written on the wall as to the man who could piss the highest up the rope,
16 And the pissin' rope gained religious contestants from far and wide, for all knew the fine little war was no more than a pissin' contest for survival and eagerly cast a dissenting vote as high as he could in reverent disrespect.
17 And the sandy earth runneth over with the silent hate for a war of economic opiates, run by yes men for the fat people of the land.

CHAPTER 8

1   ShareCrop went into himself, for the image of war serenaded to the mind of his youth was not the war he saw as a child man.
2   But ShareCrop witnessed the pride of being a brother.
3   And ShareCrop saw miles of honor of child men unto child men;
4   With caring priests harnessed to that which they believed not.
5   But ShareCrop saw other leaders who dishonored the loyalty of the devout brother Marines.
6   And ShareCrop gathered much hate inside, for he screamed with silent horror when there were seven heads and six bodies of his dead brothers,
7   And ShareCrop lurched with great constant pain at stained visions of children with missing hope.
8   So it was that ShareCrop crawled deeply into the numbness of disbelief shock, and much alcohol.
9   And it was with great pride he gushed forth when he could save the flesh.
10   And he landed his helo in the heat of battle giving forth all he could give,
11   For he did love his brother Marines.

CHAPTER 9

1   Now the soldiers of Sam Bo gathered together their armies to battle, and were gathered together at Se'chu, and set the battle in array against the soldiers of Bac Bo.
2   And the soldiers of Bac Bo stood on the mountain on one side;
3   And the soldiers of Sam Bo stood on the mountain on the other side;
4   And there was a valley abyss between them with many peasants,
5   And the soldiers of Sam Bo were with much hate from the frequent vision of watching arms, legs, eyes, body parts, and flesh of their brethren removed, and taken by an invisible enemy who disappeared and reappeared with mystical madness.
6   Hate's hopelessness oozed from the hearts and minds of the

soldiers of Sam Bo, and the many peasants were easy targets about the places of battle.

7   And a hurting child man spoke forth and said, "You can kill some of the people all of the time; and you can kill all of the people some of the time; but you can't kill all of the people all of the time."

8   And the kid of horror movie lifestyle said, "If you ain't got no people, you ain't got no war."

9   And the horror of the Dark Angel unleashed many demons harvesting innocent flesh in the form of men, women, and children, regardless of age, creed, religion, or sex, for the weapons of war killed them all.

10   And the mother's sons who were little league players, scouts, choir members, and "apples of the eye," punched twenty-five cent bullet holes in priceless babies, and children, and parents, and grandparents, all in the disease of the mind that allows innocent youth to become duty-bound killers with old men's blessings.

11   And the demons of Satan's army gave secret passwords of: gook, slope, survival, get-even, hate, winning, and duty, to soldiers who knew not what they do.

12   Then there came upon the Valley SnowWhite, and from the helicopter he saw the killing fields, and witnessed the dogs of war returning to their vomit of war, for a killing frenzy was taking place.

13   And the air whistled with whispering prayers.

14   And SnowWhite with SnowFlight landed their helicopters among the peasant Nam Bo villagers who clung to the green machines of rescue, for death by assassin awaited those caught in the onslaught of the war machine eating upon the unleavened flesh being digested in death's reaper.

15   Threefold the number of passengers allowed were loaded aboard the departing helos which squeezed airborne only by the silent words of SnowWhite and the flying mules giving more than a green flying mule can give.

16   And the escaping Nam Bo peasants sang only to be heard as trickling tears amid the roar of the loud engine.

17   But the leaders of war hid from their eyes the killing of unarmed villagers by the soldiers of Sam Bo, Nam Bo, and Bac Bo;

18   And the leaders of war hid from their eyes the killing of children, for enemy flesh sometimes hid among the innocent and those condemned to the land, and those who could run fast not.

19   And troops numbly sang, "Napalm sticks to children, and the Dow doesn't give a shit."

CHAPTER 10

1   The heat of battle more and more placed the old Dog helicopter in the gun sights of the enemy.
2   And the Dog helos would come back with bullet holes, crippled, smoking, and sometimes bearing the wounded and dead bodies of a Dog's own pilot, co-pilot, or crew member.
3   The short space in time between life and death often was held in the hands of the wingmen gunship crews sent to guard the mothership Dog rescue helo during the few precious moments needed while on the ground in the enemies sights,
4   And among the gunships there were those pilots who knew not self-preservation, and gave all by the risk of their own life.
5   But there also came the careerists, the slender of mind, and the narrow of thought, and the few unproud flying Marines whose souls were not knit with the souls of their brethren on the ground.
6   ShareCrop believed not his ears for he heard the Curate-colonel commander of gunships order the gun pilots not to take any "hits," for the commander sought the statistics of non-war in a war,
7   And the commander priest of gun pilots blasphemed the Dog Drivers for unto his pilots he said, "There is no need to get down there with the MedEvac helo and get shot up, we can't loose helos."
8   And ShareCrop felt anger at the career priest who was more interested in promotion than in team work.
9   And ShareCrop knew MedEvac pilots, crews, and passengers would die as easy targets without the close protection of gunships;
10   And the gun pilots whose souls were knit with the souls of their fellow Marines listened not to the command cleric of career blindness who would exchange his brother's lives for sterile fatness in his personnel jacket.
11   And Pete and Re-Pete, the worlds greatest gun pilots, laughed at the silly non-leader who believed promotion came from not taking hits by flying high away from the heat of the battle,

12   And Pete and Re-Pete turned guns hot in the narrow confines of flying close to the rescue helo.

13   For Pete and Re-Pete saved lives while they risked their own, but such was the nature of caring.

14   And the Curate-colonel of gun pilots understood not the word brotherhood.

15   And the Dog drivers gave many alcohol blessings to Pete and RePete at the "O" Club Tabernacle.

16   And the Curate-colonel of gunships came unto the drinking temple, and the meat pilots in unison, loudly sang forth, "Hello AssHole."

CHAPTER 11

1   ShareCrop mentally yelled and sat up in the middle of the night seeing again and again in his dreams a clock with no hands,

2   And hearing voices mumbling unknown sounds.

3   "What does my dream mean?" ShareCrop asked Doc SmegMa as the Doc sat naked in the high noon sun with his pecker stuck inside the beer can without ends filled with Bones Baker's red dye paste prescribed to kill SmegMa's fungus,

4   His pecker checker,

5   And to temporarily halt the runaway penis hinged to an undisciplined mind.

6   "No time is the right time," instantly answered SmegMa without the least concern for the passers-by laughing at a pilot with his dick in a can filled with red fungus cream.

7   "But that's what I keep seeing in my sleep," ShareCrop responded seeking a deeper more meaningful answer.

8   "Well then," the red-dick man leaned over and whispered.

9   "It really means that the time is whatever you want it to be," and SmegMa smiled.

10   And it came to pass that ShareCrop accepted such wisdom and confidently faced the daily horrors of war knowing that all was OK for it would only be his time if he wanted it to be.

CHAPTER 12

1   Now it came to be that ShareCrop saw in the eyes of the peasant farmers the same missing sparkle he had seen of the faces of the tenant farmers of which he knew much;

2   And there came the Tetrarch of Tekoa, gathering graft, selling drugs, and dispensing fear on those who would give not, sell not, or conceive not.

3   And he did sodomize the children.

4   Then it was that ShareCrop saw Hopper Honey, crying in the Wilderness, poking at the high, and provoking at the blind;

5   And Hopper Honey screamed forth the sins of the High Church of the Marine Korps, for it sinned on its congregation while the Pope, Cardinal, Bishop, and other high clergy hid from their eyes the evil that prevailed.

6   But the High Church of the Marine Korps gave not the axe to be laid unto the root of the trees;

7   And every tree that which bringeth not forth good fruit was not hewn down and cast into the fire.

8   And many other things in his exhortation preached Hopper Honey unto the Marines.

9   And it came to pass that Hopper Honey was condemned to fly the Egg Beater helicopter, for it was known that such was to be shut up in a flying prison.

10   And it was that the Harrods of Wall Street reaped millions of shekels, for in the designing of quick money with dimness of twilight minds, the Egg Beater helicopter came apart in mid-air, a manufacturing defect acceptable to the money hummers of war.

11   And an Egg Beater came apart killing Hopper Honey, taking away his head as the broken Egg Beater slung its long steel blades through the cockpit killing its pilot.

12   And when it was known, there came members of SnowFlight who took up Hopper Honey's corpse and laid it in the silver bird.

13   When they were done, they came unto SnowWhite in the edge of night from flight, and when he had spoken, they were to go into a desert place, and rest a while;

14   For the Church ordered 777 with all its pilots, crews, and helos to go by carrier ship to the Island of the Floating Dragon.

15   There were many coming and going, and they had no leisure so much as to rest.

16   And it came to pass they departed unto a desert place by carrier ship privately, to go to the Island of the Floating Dragon.
17   That before leaving by sea, SnowWhite and SnowFlight took pallets of surplus food to the orphanage.
18   And SnowWhite in the night was the last to leave,
19   But in the toiling sea, SnowWhite came out of the midst above the sea, as the helo bright landing light shown round about glowing in the still fog.
20   And it was that they were afraid he would crash in the sea fog, but SnowWhite landed safely on the ship, much to their amazement.
21   Thus they departed to the Island of the Floating Dragon, away from Nam Bo, and war.

CHAPTER 13

1   While upon the high sea, ShareCrop came unto SnowWhite with guilt,
2   For it was in the distance that the heart cast waves upon the shores of guilt,
3   For the child men were without him.
4   For ShareCrop loved the child men Marines,
5   And feared for their flesh.
6   And ShareCrop felt his place was among his dying brothers, for he should not leave them.
7   It was that SnowWhite felt great compassion for ShareCrop, and said unto him,
8   **IT IS WRITTEN THAT YOU MUST DO ONLY THAT WHICH IN YOUR HEART YOU CAN DO.**
9   And it was that ShareCrop knew he would return back to war after forty days and forty nights.

CHAPTER 14

1   And it came to pass that the Triple Seven helos came out of the morning night from the carrier ship and landed on the Island of the Floating Dragon.
2   It was written that for forty days and forty nights they would

have a rest of non-war to repair and replace the flesh and machines of war, and meditate.

3   And there met them at the Gate of Futema on the Island of the Floating Dragon the merchant of motorcycle, and SnowWhite spoke, **LET THERE BE WHEELS AMONG WHEELS.**

4   And SnowWhite, StoneMan, RedLine, OverBoost, Share-Crop, TailWind, TwoDogs, SmegMa, BirdMan, BolTer, DarkMoon, HalfRight, and BurnOut bought motorcycles.

5   SnowFlight in the air became called SnowPack on land, and they rode motorcycles round about.

6   And ShareCrop rode a mechanical steed he called "Hog," for in farm animals he felt secure.

7   It came to pass that ShareCrop erased the visions of the mind flashing the atrocities of war for he became known unto a farmer called Lei',

8   And ShareCrop and Injun would ride Lei's wonderful horses on the mountain tops amid visions of the deep blue sea around the humps of the high hill-backs.

9   Then there came one day unto the hill village TailWind with much preoccupation and concern at how animals could expel such large quantities of gas,

10   And in the twilight of the evening, TailWind lit a mule fart sending forth a blue-red fiery mist burning the animal's tail and launching the frightened beast at top speed down the village street amid the laughter of SnowPack.

CHAPTER 15

1   It came to pass on the Island of the Floating Dragon that the son of the mother who barked cared not for the mental poison of the souls of the pilots of his parish command and Curate-colonel Temple ordered all pilots to stay overnight to the airfield contrary to his words and to punish whoever flew a helo under the big bridge at the end of the bay.

2   In the evening of frustration, there was a gathering in the ready room of the tormented souls who could only drink, and gnash their teeth to vent their great distaste for Temple.

3   And the Navy Chaplain major Brother Hebert Hebert Head came forth and consoled his fellow man;

4   For the wrong Reverend Richard Head believed the pilots were his lost sheep and part of his flock;

5   But they wept not at being grounded by the Temple man and consumed much strong drink.

6   So it came to be that Chaplain Head was sent forth and departed on the clergical mission to buy a divine native food called "flied lice" and "moo-goo gai-pan,"

7   For in tending to these souls confined to base, the Chaplain knew surely there would arise forth at least one convert.

8   And SmegMa summoned forth from his glossary of island sexual gnomes a plump psychiatric social worker indentured to governmental service whose single slit glory shown forth with great enthusiasm.

9   "I can fuck everyone of you to your knees," emitted words from the increasingly attractive receptacle of bodily fluids who knew not neither class nor style.

10   And the pilot with the short, red hair and the bulging chaw of tobacco spat in Temple's ready room coffee cup and saith, "Why lady, just park that pussy and let's make it smoke."

11   Now before such words could penetrate the air, the room came to darkness except for the flickering lights on the numerous radios and the bright flashes of the airfield rotating beacon sweeping through the windows.

12   And SmegMa echoed forth a voo-doo chant with the angry pilots joining in loud sounding rhythm. "A-h-h, O-o-om da'da, Ah-h-h, O-o-om da'da," to which the woman of conjugal bliss nakedly writhed to the male chants as she slithered to the quickly thrown rug and gyrated to the singing of the room of pilots.

13   Now it came to pass that Chaplain Hebert Hebert Head returned with arms loaded with much food, and heathen trinkets called fortune cookies,

14   For he knew these men of constant death were in need of good fortune.

15   Now when Chaplain Head shown round about, SmegMa ushered him through the encircled pilots in the dark ready room for food delivery,

16   And when the Chaplain saw the naked squirming body of the round-eyed fat woman, and heard the voo-doo chanting, he screamed a blood survival scream, like a braying donkey caught with his testicles in a spring trap,

17   And the Chaplain ran through the screen door ripping his way from the sin he knew not.

18   Chaplain Head ran round and round the building three times before making his way in the darkness across the runway at the airfield, not looking back to see if the ghosts of evil were in pursuit of his soul in the blackness;

19   And he hid in the laundry closet near his quarters knowing the demons knew where he lived.

20   "I saw Satan in the Ready Room," the Chaplain quivered while telling the curate Temple of his memory;

21   And not remembering that he had thrown fried rice and noodles over all the pilots in his get-away escape from evil.

22   "You did not see Satan in the Ready Room," the irritated Temple said, then grinned. "You saw SatanNita."

CHAPTER 16

1   There came unto SnowWhite the twelve of SnowFlight and sought his counsel for round about them on the Island of the Floating Dragon there could be seen the storage places of much money humming of War. When SnowWhite heard, he said,

2   IF ANY MAN HAVE AN EAR, LET HIM HEAR,

3   THERE WERE ONCE TWO MARINES, ONE WHO WAS BLIND, AND ONE WHO WAS DEAF, AND THEY SERVED THE HOUSE OF SAM BO WELL.

4   AND IT CAME TO PASS THAT THE TWO MARINES FOUND FAVOR IN THE EYES OF THE CLERGY, AND WERE CAST IN COMMON VALOR AMONG COMMON MEN OF THE COURT OF THE KING OF CASH.

5   AND THE BLIND MARINE HEARD THE COUNTING OF MONEY; AND THE DEAF MARINE SAW THE COUNTING OF GREAT CASH,

6   BUT THE BLIND MARINE SAW NOT WHO COUNTED THE MONEY, AND THE DEAF MARINE HEARD NOT THE DEMONS OF GREED COUNTING THE PROFITS OF A FINE WAR.

7   AND I SAY TO YOU, THOUGH A BLIND MARINE SEES NOT, HE CAN HEAR ALL;

8   AND THOUGH A DEAF MARINE HEARS NOT, HE CAN SEE ALL.

9   AND A MARINE WHO HEARS BUT CANNOT SEE, AND A MARINE WHO SEES BUT CANNOT HEAR, ARE THEIR BROTHERS' KEEPER.

CHAPTER 17

1   There was on the Island of the Floating Dragon special celebration, for the November 10 birthday of the Church, Marine Korps, came to be.

2   DingleBerry came forth from the den of fornication to plan the ceremony, and to perform the Korpsism eucharist.

3   And the man of short mind and short body summoned forth the building of a great cake; and SmegMa gave the cake the name November Ten.

4   And it came to pass at the "O" Club Tabernacle over-looking the sea that there was great singing and many him's, for the congregation of the Marine Korps forgets not the birthday of all Marines, living and remembered living,

5   For to die Marine is to live forever.

6   And the songs of the Nam Bo war were sung, along with the songs of men scheduled to die.

7   Then it came to pass that there was consumed brandy in a canteen cup,

8   And SmegMa came forth dick in hand and shoved his penis into November Ten, smiling and saying, "Anyone who can't tap dance is a muther fucker," and the pilot's laughed, and there was a mass of tap dancing, and a tap dancing Mass.

CHAPTER 18

1   "Black Bart, you are jus' an Ethiopian eunuch," the drunken ShareCrop poked at DarkMoon in surly banter because his black friend did not have the balls to bell the cat.

2   "Delta Duke, you are a HaySeed Hick, a man with a big heart and a down-trodden mind," effervescently giggled the onyx enigma.

3   And it came to pass on the Island of the Floating Dragon that one DarkMoon and one ShareCrop, in the accompaniment of other lesser souls, painted black shoe dye polish spots on the balls of the passed-out Vicar-major DingleBerry;

4   And when DingleBerry awoke in the thatched ranch house called "snake" in bed with the short woman in whom he could see eyes to eye, Vicar-major DingleBerry screamed aloud among the unpidgin minds at his sight of two testicles diseased by spotted black dots on his balls' skin,

5   And he ran therefrom straight unto the arms of the dispensary korpsman seeking the medicine man's salvation.

6   Doc Skurvy Skull, the island contract India Indian leprechaun, with palm money already given from DarkMoon, said with gold tooth smile to the petrified Vicar-major, "I uu. . .sally only see black balls on negroes and lepers," and quaintly whimsied, "and habu disease."

7   Then it came to pass that Vicar-major DingleBerry concerned himself inordinately at having contracted a mystical disease,

8   And then Dingle worried not, for he knew that he could not be grounded from flying and the habu disease did not affect his non-flying skills, which is where he visualized himself as best.

9   But DarkMoon and ShareCrop giggled greatly, for soap, water, and time would wash away the sins of the short Vicar-major who knew not why he had blackened balls.

10   And Vicar-major DingleBerry sat in the sun with the open ended beer can over his balls with red dye fungus medicine packed round about,

11   And DarkMoon passed by and laughed aloud, and said unto the Vicar-major who would cherish to be grounded in a combat zone, "Root rot."

12   And TailWind asked Vicar-major DingleBerry where he got the two spotted raisins.

13   And ShareCrop said, "Varicose scrotum?"

14   And Doc SmegMa said, "I wouldn't put that little of a meat in a refrigerator."

CHAPTER 19

1   Behold, 777 was called out of the night to return back unto the land of Nam Bo,

2   For unto 777 was given the message to return to the living hell in which flesh could perish.

3   And ShareCrop was sent forth to fetch materials and food from the fields of great war storage.

4   Thereupon, on the Island of the Floating Dragon, a vision came upon ShareCrop while in the presence of mountains of materials stretched across the vast plains of accumulation of war things that money can buy,

5   For ShareCrop witnessed the fine tune which sprang forth from the economic lyrics of the money humming of war.

6   And it was that defective shells were to be sent forth to be used by the sons of the people, for cost plus budgets shoot forth great cash.

7   And it was that the unbalanced artillery shells were to be sent forth to be used by the sons of the people, for war profits required neither accuracy nor tolerances,

8   And it was that child men Marines would die from the deadly enemy of weapon failure cast out by the defective minds who worshipped Mammon.

9   And ShareCrop saw massive food, and castles of frozen storage, and ShareCrop sought food blessings from the Keepers of the Horde for the common Marines,

10   But ShareCrop was given not, for it was told that Marines were to be lean, green, fighting machines.

11   And it came to pass that ShareCrop learned that it was shekels of the under-table that gave heart and sustenance to the men of non-war who held the survival of others in their hands.

12   Whereupon, ShareCrop sought counsel with SnowWhite, for his youthful mind wept greatly at seeing men abandon principles amid the loose money cast about, but DarkMoon wanted to sicca these men.

13   And SnowWhite counseled and said, **EVIL FLOURISHES WHEN THE PURSE OF UNGUARDED MONEY IS OPEN TO SELFISH MINDS.**

CHAPTER 20

1   Now it came to pass that 777 returned across the sea to Tru Lai.

2   It was that the feast of the unleavened flesh of the child men Marines drew nigh, which was called death.

3   And it came to pass that SnowFlight followed SnowWhite unto the big cathedral church yard at Tru Lai City and there were given unto SnowWhite eleven white doves,

4   And SnowWhite whispered unto the doves and set them free, and there came visions into the minds of SnowFlight.
5   And BirdMan cried for there was a white cross on the blue field,
6   And TwoDogs saw his dove glide over the blowing wheat plains,
7   And HalfRight saw his unknown mother from the window of his youth,
8   And TailWind saw the white of the boat school,
9   And StoneMan saw freedom from a fine little caged war,
10   And DarkMoon said, "free at last, free at last."
11   And RedLine saw a blowing trumpet, though he heard not,
12   And SmegMa envisioned one male and ten females,
13   And OverBoost saw smooth clouds,
14   And BolTer saw ancestral temples spread across time,
15   And ShareCrop understood, for from the fields of the mind he then harvested the crop of truth,
16   And BurnOut grew confused, for there were thirteen of SnowFlight.

CHAPTER 21

1   It was a time that many bodies were put to death of the flesh,
2   And it was the time of the liturgy of the Korps Church.
3   And on each beat of the big war drum, a 1369 body fell forth.
4   For it was unwritten in the articles of the Church that Marines will trade fresh lives for dead ones.
5   And the high clergy of the Church enraptured by a history not of their making followed scripture,
6   For in the Valley of Hinnom during the time of the Fox the bodies of three dead Marines were abandoned in the once again escape from the over used landing zone called Mu'Le's ass.
7   Then the child men indentured to a war not of their making and harnessed to honor before truth blindly obeyed the command to return into the living hell of the Valley of Slaughter from which the sole mission was the rescue of three dead bodies.
8   And SnowWhite cried.
9   And it came to pass that the shoals of man glistened forth from the banks of ignorance.

10   Then it was that there were five more child men dead, but the cause of the sacred Church went unblemished.
11   And five child men gave their lives to recover the dead bodies of three brethren.

CHAPTER 22

1   It was times of much death.
2   And the hidden enemy was much sought at the cost of many lives.
3   It is written in the book of war that those who seek pay greater than those who hide.
4   And the cannon fodder young knew not but rigid compliance with command,
5   And the keepers of the Church knew not but the rigid compliance with whispers of the King of Cash,
6   For the King sought not High Priests of independent principle who cherished the congregational flock more than career survival;
7   For the King of Cash knew that one elephant could squash many piss ants of life.
8   And death's banquet table was covered by the horn of plenty, for great money and vanities of the mind fill the soul coffers of hell.
9   And as the cash of life flows, men do ungodly things in the name of cash,
10   For cash has no conscious.

CHAPTER 23

1   Then it came to be that StoneMan, OverBoost, RedLine, Bird-Man, TwoDogs, DarkMoon, ShareCrop, SmegMa, BolTer, TailWind, HalfRight and BurnOut appeared at the rope of faith,
2   For their frustrations leapt forth pissin' up the rope of faith against the wailing wall of the war.
3   And there was dejection, weariness, hypersensitivity, tremors, anxiety, phobias, jumpiness, fatigue, and the fighting of a war because they were forced to,
4   And there was euphoria, glory, excitement, pride, caring, tal-

ent, dedication, loyalty, responsibility, courage, integrity, discipline, and much love of the brethren,
5   But there had been, was, and would be the detestable abomination of Why?. . .!
6   And DarkMoon sought to sicca the fat major who would not fly,
7   And TailWind farted silently in open disrespect,
8   And StoneMan pretended to drink from an imaginary grail,
9   And SmegMa sent a fake message that Vicar-major DingleBerry had been seen in bed with a chicken,
10   And OverBoost screamed out in the middle of the night, "incoming,"
11   And sleepless BirdMan laughed at OverBoost's bad dream, and screamed back "outgoing,"
12   And ShareCrop in the night burned Temple's outhouse,
13   And RedLine painted at night the number 769 on the general's airplane,
14   And BolTer nailed a water leak hole in the tin roof above Vicar-major DingleBerry's bed,
15   And HalfRight stuck a small pinhole leak in the rubber air mattress called "rubber lady" on Vicar-major DingleBerry's bed.
16   And TwoDogs shaved his head on the sides as silent protest.
17   And so it came to be that the combat helo pilots lived from day to day, knowing not which day carried the bullet with their number on it.

CHAPTER 24

1   For ShareCrop, SnowWhite, and the brotherhood of SnowFlight, there was much flying.
2   And great happiness when saving child men flesh,
3   And much pride in pilot's work,
4   For they had skills of artful masters.
5   And the good soldiers on each side summoned the guardian Angels of protection, and the spirits of survival;
6   But the demons homesteading the minds and souls of men puked forth messages of power, vanity, and greed, for it was a time for harvesting the blood of ignorant youth cast in the spell of honor, and not truth.
7   "We can't trade two or three of them for one of us," argued

BolTer to SnowWhite after seeing the field of blood with pits dug to bury the several hundred young enemy dead while the bodies of their wounded and dead Marine comrades were being continuously shuttled to the field hospital.

8   **THE WHORES OF WALL STREET COUNT CASH, NOT LIVES**, were the words of SnowWhite in response to the cause of attrition.

9   And roundabout men who loved their Fatherland refused to dishonor it;

10   But the High Priests accepted the tide of statistical human death and misery which emanated from the flicker of their lips and called the demon's blessing "body count."

11   And roundabout the High Priests feared the arrogant King,

12   But the High Priest clergy could not give loyalty back to the child men Marines by shedding their priesthood in the High Church to expose the King's ways;

13   And the child men Marines had no hope of survival, except to kill.

14   And the unleashed ego of the runaway error magnified itself over and over to the ever increasing ire of the people asked to donate their sons to Mammon's Priests and Money Parasites.

15   But the durable war goods index spoke forth jobs, fake light and the horn of riches.

16   So death was the essential by-product for the continued power of war good jobs.

17   And command titles, unearned medals, and fictional marriage to the High Church was needed for the careerists who would not speak out for self-preservation sake;

18   Wherefore, the young, innocent soldiers were left to give, and did give all, so that their Fatherland could through time learn the evils;

19   And the people could learn the ignorance of allowing selfish leaders to steer the ship of war through the seas of profits.

20   No greater price could be asked of the young men than to shed their life by a leadership that dishonored them,

21   And to convert their flesh to the cash pockets of money derelicts who quickly exchanged someone else receiving a burning bullet for the price of safety deposit box mind ego.

22   And ShareCrop decided, "It is the nature of the rich to market the poor in the stockyards of war."

The Word According to
DARKMOON

(Every Man Should Be
Kept Informed)

CHAPTER 1

1   DarkMoon hated bigotry, prejudice, ignorance, liars, and incompetence;

2   He concentrated on eliminating any appearance he was anything but a refined black gentleman;

3   DarkMoon knew class for his military attache' father had assignments throughout the world's different embassies where DarkMoon witnessed worldliness.

4   DarkMoon was skilled in the martial arts, the culinary arts, and could conjugate the universal navy term "fuck" as a verb, a noun, an adjective, an adverb, or other dangling modifier.

5   He took pride in being without the slightest hint of common black dialect.

6   But DarkMoon had a problem: he did not understand what it was to be black.

7   And he was crazed with hatred toward one human being who would abuse another human being,

8   For he marked a Frenchman with his constant companion curved boot knife after he caught the man sexually abusing a child the homosexual had lured into a Paris alley.

9   DarkMoon was a fine friend, and a deadly enemy.

CHAPTER 2

1   "If the Korps wanted you to have a woman," his words focused on the eyes of the pretty thing he had met at the terrace square on the pier section of the beach, "they'd issue you one."
2   "I've already got an instructor," she winked cleverly, casting rejection back into the sexual premonitions of the jar head flight student.
3   "Boatman?" he asked, getting a head nod yes, and with further questions was pleased he had cornered this sea duty Navy major's turf, and looking for a non-permanent relationship.
4   And it came to pass the two new friends went away privately,
5   And DarkMoon learned from Abbey about the stress of the Navy life, and even more so, the Navy's lay-priesthood.
6   It was that the Navy man did violence to this jewel of a woman because his ship boss played hard "brown shoe navy" with him.
7   Until then, this shore-bound woman, the idol of his world while he was off at sea, had corralled her ache for companionship.
8   She knew her distant fiancé would partake of other women, a tradition quietly alluded to, but unspoken.
9   Besides, DarkMoon thought, she was the first woman that he had ever brought to multiple smiles — he turned her on . . . again and again.
10   "Partaking of a swabbie instructor's woman was a mild retribution for the shit the Navy dumps on the Korps," he mentally rationalized.
11   "Older women are beautiful lovers;"
12   DarkMoon learned many things from her;
13   For she told secrets of how the Navy wives kept the pecking order of the ranks of their husbands in their social functions, and Abbey was a non-person civilian outsider.
14   And special tables were established for bridge games, for the Mrs. High Priest captains and the Mrs. Curate-commanders took false rank over the wives of the lesser junior women.
15   For it was that protocol was *grande dame* mission essential.
16   And it came to pass that Abbey opened up into DarkMoon.
17   "The club turned into a riot today," Abbey giggled as she and DarkMoon moved to the porch overlooking the surf slowly caressing the white beach.

18   "What happened?" DarkMoon grinned back with enthusiasm, eager to hear from this sparkling female.

19   "Mrs. Big Snoot and the other snoots, after having their quota of gin, proceeded to fake sincerity with a Japanese war bride brought back by an instructor pilot. They played all the social niceties with the quiet girl, poking cruelties in their resentment of anyone who would have the gall to bring one of those 'yellow-breasted rack thrashers' home." They both laughed.

20   "Anyway, this poor Japanese girl spoke pidgin. After being put through the social mill with a few sick innuendoes about her china pattern, and other shallow cat and mouse pokes, Curate-commander Junco's wife asked about their courtship," Abbey continued,

21   "My major 'rubs me vely much,' the Japanese bride responded to questions, but the old gal didn't quit, but asked, 'How do you know he loves you very much?' "

22   "The Japanese girl smiled then said, 'Him say him heart pump piss for me.' "

23   DarkMoon roared with laughter knowing the silent tolerance that the Navy wives bore about their husbands overseas tour which occasionally slipped into stories of their drunken stupor; about geisha's; and about hotsie baths—things left best unsaid.

24   "I guess that no one talked about 'made in Japan' after that," DarkMoon said and laughed with Abbey.

25   "Oh that's not the half of it—pour me a wine," she proceeded as she wiped the laughter tears from the corner of her eyes,

26   "After the echo of the girdle straps quit popping and the old snoots staff meeting had been dismissed, this dumb Georgia honey, cume' snob from Sophie Nookie, asked this poor girl if it would be imposin' if she could ask a personal question about Japanese women. The Japanese girl said okay.' "

27   "Is it true that Japanese girl's vaginas are sideways?" asked the Georgia darling, pointing her finger and moving it sideways.

28   "Oh Shit!" DarkMoon coughed simultaneously in a deep bellow that sent a sip of wine out in a spray while part went down his windpipe in guffaw. He fell to his hands and knees laughing and coughing with Abbey pounding on his back trying to help him get his breath back.

29   Tears rolled out their eyes in laughter.

30   "What did she say?" he deeply giggled.

31   "She handled it well," Abbey answered, grinning, "She just

said 'You no pay attention to th-at, is just old story told by sailors.' "

32   They both laughed.

33   This is one hell of a woman, thought DarkMoon, as they held each other, intermeshing little giggles between sips of wine listening to the rhythm of the surf.

34   An occasional drone of the aircraft engines on the night flying training missions could occasionally be heard overhead.

35   And it was the nature of training warriors that they be prepared to war.

CHAPTER 3

1   "Can you meet me at the beach house?" DarkMoon asked Abbey in an obviously strained voice on the telephone.

2   "Sure, when?" . . . "What's wrong?" she asked.

3   "Pooh's dead," he said, "mid-air collision."

4   "See ya in a few," said Abbey.

5   She was standing inside the screen door waiting as DarkMoon came up the beach house stairs.

6   "Just hold me — I hurt," he said, and they tenderly embraced and held each other while in silence tears flowed.

7   "It's not fair," he cried, "Pooh was the best, the cream of the cream . . ."

8   Abbey cried with him for she had developed strong feeling for her friend, and his buddy.

9   "I know it's part of Naval Air," he wept, "but why do we have to push so many flight hours so quick, why . . . why . . . why?"

10   And they moved to the rattan daybed on the porch where DarkMoon cried himself into a sleep with Abbey trembling inside with the realization of the powerful internal feeling she knew she would soon have to face.

11   And it came to pass that two non-committal persons laughed, and played, and loved amidst the thrill of high performance flying, and high performance romance uncommon among any they had known.

12   And it was that few words rendered a rising pulse and a quick dash — "ready," "6:00 o'clock," "my place" or the name of a pilot's hide-a-way.

13   It was a time of emotional blindness.

14 It was a time of unspent youth.
15 It was a time when life's cherished memories were forged.

CHAPTER 4

1 It came to pass that DarkMoon landed his airplane many times on the aircraft carrier,
2 And it came to pass that DarkMoon completed helicopter training.
3 DarkMoon was designated a Naval Aviator and received the cherished gold wings which the pilots called "Golden Leg Spreaders."
4 Tradition required the newly pinned pilots to proceed to the club where they placed their new wings in a glass and a concoction of different strong drink called an "overboost," was mixed therein.
5 And with proper toasts, the "overboost" drink was by honor to be consumed with only one tilt of the glass.
6 Giacomo, an already bubbly pilot from his pre-pinning celebration, turned his glass up only to find when he finished the swill, his wings were gone—he had swallowed his wings!
7 Giacomo was quickly driven to the Naval Hospital and X-rayed.
8 And the wings were found among the young pilot's intestine, shinning like a misplaced surgeon's scalpel;
9 The prettiest set of internal Naval Aviator wings ever eaten.
10 He was cross X-rayed, and it was determined that the safety pin catch was fastened—he could pass his wings!
11 And the pilots drew lots, for a gambling board was made as to the time of wing passage.
12 And it came to be under Naval Aviation history, the only man known to have swallowed his wings, also passed his wings.
13 Then word spread far and wide of a man called "OverBoost," and of his great feat.
14 And the X-ray was sent round about to display the unbelievable,
15 And DarkMoon wrote a poem about internal golden wings.

CHAPTER 5

1   And it came to pass that two souls faced their dedicated non-commitment to each other but feeling the addiction of one to another.

2   "How are we going to part?" she brokenly asked as the tears dripped down her face.

3   "Let it wait?" DarkMoon could not respond.

4   They held each other not letting go — even in the night as one would rise the other would follow.

5   "I'll not let you go," DarkMoon whispered.

6   "I'll not ever let you escape me," Abbey whispered back as the tears flowed with each sealing moment.

7   And it came to pass that a man named DarkMoon and a woman named Abbey consecrated themselves in constantness for thirty days while traveling across Sam Bo to the ocean where DarkMoon would leave for war.

8   Swimming, back-packing, trout fishing, gliding, and freedom fit their souls — with singing, and laughing, and giddiness throughout.

9   "Goodbye, my Sparkle," DarkMoon let go with parting tears at the airport by the bay where Abbey was boarding for home with DarkMoon going to war.

10   Sobbing, she handed him a small box . . ."Don't open it till you leave, and promise you'll come back to me," she tearfully smiled.

11   "So be it," he responded and handed her a white envelope. "Open it on the plane."

12   And they kissed passionately one last time, and she boarded as the last passenger.

13   As the plane taxied, Abbey opened the envelope:

14   TearLight
     by S. Bolevar Cana

     The mist of a diamond
     In the corner of your eye
     Carboned by a soul
     In happiness cry.

The texture of your star
In each night's twilight
Glistening from your heart
With radiant delight.

Tears mined from smiles
Will always be
The brightest sparkles
With you and me.

From a tear's sparkle
To a Sparkle's tear
Shine our soul's riches
Ever so clear.

I will always love you.

— SB

15   And it came to pass DarkMoon opened Abbey's gift as he
drove toward the Valley leading to the Marine air base.
16   And he withdrew the small folded paper first,

"I thought you'd need a scarf for those cold nights in
Nam Bo.
         I Love you,
            Cheeks

17   Then he lifted the pair of fine blue silk panties with the name
"Cheeks" embroidered in white thereon;
18   He laughed, and then he cried so hard he had to pull off into
the road side park where he breathed deeply, and cried aloud with
an agony he had never known before.

CHAPTER 6

1   "Human blood is all of the same color," DarkMoon spat at the
Anabaptist escapee from South Louisiana who came unto the tin
tent.

2   The unfazed Chaplain blindly continued, "Who are we to question the holy scriptures?"
3   "Is that so," DarkMoon smiled, "then if God wanted us to be Baptists, why did he send Jesus? . . . You water saints have vision problems on dry land . . . Jesus drank wine! . . . Jesus made wine! . . . Why do you Baptists first march to the tune of a guy who ate locusts and honey?"
4   Chaplain Hebert Hebert Head exited the futile conversation and departed the hallowed ground of the pilot's club – a vile place wreaking of alcohol and strained souls;
5   He had his last ridicule from this black man.
6   This Chaplain could handle being asked to partake of part of a quart of salvation;
7   He could absorb the stories of fleshy pleasures;
8   But no uppity nigger was going to blaspheme the very fundamentals of almighty God in his presence, besides, he knew sin when he saw it!

CHAPTER 7

1   "You're too white," DarkMoon emphasized standing tall next to his youthful new friend, "You're a white man with white hair and a name of White . . . and they call you 'Snow.' "
2   And DarkMoon followed SnowWhite as his flight leader.
3   And round about the meat pilots and the meat Marines called the bullet-dodging group of pilots "SnowFlight,"
4   For these special pilots came among them in the heat of battle.
5   And these gung-ho pilots answered the child men's radio prayers.

CHAPTER 8

1   The jet pilot ejected into the enemy sea off the land of Bac Bo.
2   Sea Air-Rescue could not find him and twilight had changed to blackness in the monsoon rain and fog.
3   The Cardinal and his Curates had deep concerns;

4 The Korps had lost an airframe to combat—what impact would that have after the war?

5 And there is a helicopter shortage—should we risk losing a helicopter?

6 Can the Korps let the Air Force Jolly Green Giant helicopter rescue a Marine pilot?

7 It was that SnowWhite and DarkMoon with StoneMan and BirdMan on their wing disregarded the radio message to their two helos to return to base, but proceeded north into the open and black sea hoping the downed pilot would be able to fire a pen flare or emit through his survival radio a traceable signal.

8 The enemy fishing boats would be looking too.

9 There was no choice but to turn on the bright search light underneath the helo's nose shining onto the water in search of a cold fellow soul.

10 But the light made the helo an easy target to the shore and boat gunners.

11 Fuel became critical and the crews checked their life jackets ready to join their unknown comrade in the sea.

12 Headquarters radio intermittently broadcast in the blind trying to get contact with SnowFlight to order them to abandon rescue efforts for just one pilot.

13 As coolness and confidence transitioned to fear and silent prayer, SnowWhite murmured gibberish unknown to DarkMoon.

14 Then a pen flare sped skyward on the horizon telling the enemy and SnowFlight the downed RainMaker jet pilot was casting his lot on helicopter rescue.

15 **KEEP ME AS THE APPLE OF YOUR EYE, HIDE ME UNDER THE SHADOW OF YOUR WINGS**, SnowWhite radioed to StoneMan.

16 Then SnowWhite turned off all the lights of the helicopter, leaving only the one light of a firey blue flame that shot outward into the night from the exhaust manifold of the roaring engine.

17 But StoneMan, like the mother quail in spring protecting her young at the surprise encounter of danger with her chicks, turned on his helo's bright lights and big white search beacon and circled low and away from the downed jet pilot, acting like a crippled bird summoning the enemy cat while SnowWhite invisibly flew to the source of the pen flare.

18 "Soul aboard! Go Nest," radioed DarkMoon to StoneMan.

19   The downed pilot had been rescued in spite of command concern for statistics of the High Church.
20   Radio silence was kept on the homeward trek until SnowFlight crossed into Nam Bo.
21   Birdman radioed of the downed pilot's rescue.
22   And there came cheers as echoes in the radio room, but the tabletop Bishop was angry — he had not approved the mission;
23   Who is this man that defies the authority — who is SnowWhite?
24   Who is this man who saves others without permission?

CHAPTER 9

1   Vicar-major DingleBerry stood at the refueling tanks as SnowFlight landed;
2   Then a chill ran up his deputy-command spine because immediately on landing the big radial engines coughed, then quit running from fuel starvation.
3   SnowWhite had run out of gas.
4   The wet, cold, and exalted fellow Marine pilot extracted from the sea hugged the crew and thanked BirdMan, DarkMoon, and then StoneMan.
5   SnowWhite removed his helmet and climbed down the side of the helicopter to greet the exuberant, but shivering soul — who halted his advance and stared in the face of the white haired pilot . . .;
6   "You are the One," he choked out.
7   **SNOW BE THE ONE**, came SnowWhite's words.
8   "The many flying skills of SnowFlight have become known to the pilots at Thunder, RainMaker and Eagle squadrons," the rescued jet pilot said.
9   **SNOW SON OF HEAVEN**, responded SnowWhite unheard by the others during the roar of landing nearby aircraft.
10   "You're a star out of the heavens," the trembling jet pilot replied, "You're an answer to prayers."
11   Vicar-major DingleBerry approached SnowWhite, coveting what was certain to be a career making event;
12   But he had to walk the straight and narrow, for the Bishop-colonel was livid with an underling making a right decision without his blessing.

13   SNOWWHITE NO WANT MEDALS, was the firm reply to the Vicar-major's proposals of awards.

14   "You don't understand," DingleBerry persisted, "the way you get promoted in this man's Marine Korps is by the size of your personnel file;"

15   "You've pissed off the Air Boss; he's after your head; let me get you a Navy Cross."

16   And the old fart twice unpromoted Vicar-major could not accept that a deserving act of valor was met with rejection.

17   SnowWhite mildly answered the Vicar-major, AT THE END OF THE GAME, THE KING AND THE PAWN GO INTO THE SAME BAG.

18   And SnowWhite grinned, then said, THE BEST MEDAL IS A LIVE MAN'S SMILE, and then SnowWhite stared with his steel blue eyes into the face of the unbelieving DingleBerry.

19   GOD'S SERVANTS HAVE NO NEED OF MEDALS; THEIR LIGHT SHINES.

20   And DingleBerry understood not, for unto the god Marine Korps he prayed,

21   And it was that the career pilots were victims of their religion,

22   And it was a time when the High Priests followed their arrogant King worshipping the priesthood trinkets of the mind.

23   But in the King they believed not.

24   And all the King's whorses,

25   And all the King's men,

26   Sought profits,

27   As a means to the end.

CHAPTER 10

1   Sometimes it was cruel, sometimes it was funny, but it was delightfully entertaining to follow the escapades of DarkMoon making jest of the unwanted, but homestead hootch-mate, Chaplain Brother (Navy-major) lieutenant commander Hebert Hebert Head.

2   "You see my mother stuttered," the skinny but tall Chaplain would try to explain with his Cajun drawl, "but the nurse just simply wrote down my name twice" — he would grin at the explanation of two identical first names.

3   "It's a good thing she didn't fart," responded TailWind.
4   "Or even worse," echoed DarkMoon, "what if she'd named you Richard?" Both TailWind and DarkMoon smirked to guffaw.
5   "Richard is a nice name," nodded the Chaplain, not even having the most remote idea that DarkMoon was referring to the nickname "Dick."
6   Thus, it became known round about among the pilots that a religious dickhead was among them, and they called him Richard in reverent disrespect.

CHAPTER 11

1   The airfield Chaplain's duties were different,
2   For there were no dying men in a battlefield needing last sacraments within the confines of the airfield compound.
3   And Sunday church services yielded few attendees for Sunday was a war day to the enemy, and to the Korps, and simply just one more invisible day among many days—it was a meaningless distinction.
4   So it was that the Chaplain was the keeper of the indigenous Nam Bo natives who were allowed to work menial jobs on the airfield:
5   The barbers; the cleaning servants; the old men who cleaned the privies by burning the fugal matter with gasoline and hauling off the live rats captured in the wire cage traps;
6   "Do you know if someone is boom-booming, ya know-fuck'n Missey Tuo," asked SmegMa to the Louisiana holier-than-thou while DarkMoon listened.
7   "Look Richard," SmegMa quickly said, while looking into the Chaplain's indignant face, "don't get your dander up, she's the prettiest house mouse on the base. She may not have big breasts, but I bet she could . . ."
8   The Chaplain interrupted, "Just quit. You're trying to spoof me won't work. Thou shalt not fornicate, lust, or commit adultery. Get thee such thoughts from me you donkey dick devil."
9   "Come on Richard, you mean to tell me you have never even beat ole one-eye?" asked DarkMoon.
10   "Who is one-eye?", the Chaplain queried, "One of the demons known only to you black folks, I suppose?"

11 "Your pecker," instructed DarkMoon, "the same one-eyed pecker I heard you pulling last night."

12 The now embarrassed Chaplain turned to leave the hootch and SmegMa verbally followed, "Better to sew thy seed in the belly of a whore than into the gutter . . . and you were starching a sock."

13 DarkMoon and SmegMa laughed watching the Chaplain scurry off to one of his many self-created duties designed to escape.

14 The Chaplain knew he had done something to irritate the Almighty for he had been banned to live among these sinners . . . besides, he had searched, and there is no such quote.

CHAPTER 12

1 The Chaplain reported to Temple for their weekly briefing.

2 "How is morale?" inquired the short, plump squadron commander to the chromosomal deplete Chaplain.

3 "It is fine, Sir," he replied, "But had no pilots at Chapel on Sunday."

4 "That's war," the ground-bound pilot commander continued, "I've heard a report that the maids are pissing in the bunkers — now you get that benny boy interpreter of yours and make sure those maids know they are fired if we catch them pissin' in the bunkers — understand?"

5 The Chaplain whispered; the Chaplain again leaned forward and whispered toward the cauliflower looking ear.

6 "Doing what!" bellowed Kiwi in the face of the Chaplain.

7 "Sex, sir, some of the men are having sex with the maids . . . I just thought you would want to know, Sir," the Chaplain meekly said.

8 "Chaplain, what the men do in their private lives is not your ecclesiastical business," bellowed the commander into the trembling Chaplain.

9 "If they can bomb 'em, strafe 'em, and kill 'em; they can fuck 'em!" the grinning Temple screamed.

10 "With all the diseases, I don't know why — but that is the business of that shanker mechanic doctor of ours — understand. You worry about their souls, and Doc can deal with their peckers!" the commander bellowed.

11   And the Chaplain shook his head in yes fashion and was dismissed, with parting words, "And if I was you Chaplain, I'd check with Bones Baker . . . there's a fungal disease you can get in the tropics if you put your dick in a cotton sock," the fat face laughed from the waist up.

CHAPTER 13

1   And it came to pass that Chaplain Hebert Hebert Head did not understand why he was being punished but accepted his fate.
2   He knew the Catholics prayed to idols; the Jews killed Jesus; the Church of England was born out of a King's adultery from which a split again occurred in the War of Northern Aggression.
3   He thought war should bring these men closer to their maker — was he a failure? Few sought his tutorage.
4   SnowWhite entered into the tin roofed and plywood constructed chapel occupied by the Chaplain.
5   And it was that quiet quickly came over both the room and the Chaplain.
6   SnowWhite faced the despondent Chaplain and said, **WHERE THERE IS A CHAPEL OF GOD, SO TOO WILL AN ALTAR OF SATAN BE NEARBY.**
7   "Words fitly spoken — like apples of gold in pictures of silver," The Chaplain responded, referring to scripture.
8   SnowWhite smiled with a smile that communicated comfort, and said, **AS THE COLD OF SNOW IN THE TIME OF HARVEST, SO IS A FAITHFUL MESSENGER TO THEM THAT SENT HIM.**
9   And it came to pass that the Chaplain and the congregation of one were able to communicate, though this man SnowWhite talked different.
10   And the Chaplain spoke of Hebrews,
11   And SnowWhite smiled.

CHAPTER 14

1   "You're a black man," flopped the fat tongue from the fat face of Poncho Pilot, "and you just keep yourself clean and take the medals awarded to you and you'll be on the inside track.

2   "Blood is red; Marines are all brothers; I cannot recommend you for a Silver Star, sir, for just flying around watching a battle — even if you think I deserve a medal," responded DarkMoon.

3   The stub cigar now wearing the red face stared in disbelief at a sure-fire Flying Cross being refused by this uppity black man.

4   Then DarkMoon said, "Medals are a career officers ticket for promotion, but only a reserve officer's pride in citizenship."

5   "Dismissed," was the command.

CHAPTER 15

1   And it came to pass that the firmament of the people questioned the King.

2   And the King sought counsel of the Divinity of Defense, for he was sore afraid.

3   And the Divinity of Defense sought counsel of those in the Puzzle Palace not trained in the art of war but those whose great academic skills were unmatched, but who knew war not.

4   There spoke forth the demons of *cum laude, summa cum laude* and *magna cum laude,*

5   And it was said that rich people don't need to fight wars . . . but don't tell the poor.

6   And more of the sons of the poor, the unpowerful, the disadvantaged, and those indoctrinated with honor before truth were cast into the Tekoa Wilderness.

7   And the innocent mothers recognized not that their sons were being given unto Molech.

8   And it came to pass that the many deaths and the many wounded were known as meat Marines, for they filled the quota, and nurtured the blindness, and worshipped the god of attrition with flesh.

9   "Two-thirds of your battalion is black," stated DarkMoon to the friendly command cleric armed with both a shot gun and a machine gun.

10   "We don't get to pick our men," he replied referring to the obvious youth in the distance, "we got a war to fight."

11   "Why are there so many of low rank?" DarkMoon queried.

12   "Why promote 'em, just cost Sam Bo more money."

13   And DarkMoon thought of his sicca as he listened to the Vicar-major dishonor the loss of life of the meat Marines.
14   But the black child men honorably gave their all, knowing their Fatherland abused them.

CHAPTER 16

1   **LAMBS   AMONG   WOLVES**, SnowWhite   said   to DarkMoon,
2   And DarkMoon wanted to disembowel with his curved knife the Vicar-major who was killing the children Marines through command indifference.
3   "I cannot sit idly by while they waste Marines just so they can train inexperienced revolving officers and give them combat command time in their promotion files," DarkMoon begged an answer.
4   And SnowWhite said, **WE KNOW THAT WE HAVE PASSED FROM DEATH UNTO LIFE, BECAUSE WE LOVE THE BRETHREN. A MAN THAT DOES NOT LOVE HIS BROTHER IS DEAD.**
5   **THERE ARE THOSE WHO WILL USE THEIR RANK FOR SURVIVAL, AND SEE THEIR BROTHER HAVE NEED, AND SHUT UP THEIR BOWELS OF COMPASSION FROM HIM.**
6   **LET US NOT BE FAITHFUL IN WORD, NEITHER IN TONGUE; BUT IN DEED AND IN TRUTH.**
7   **LOOK OUT FOR THE WELFARE OF THE CHILD MEN, FOR THEY HAVE BEEN ABANDONED BY THEIR KING TO FEND FOR THEMSELVES.**
8   And the soul of DarkMoon was knit with the soul of SnowWhite, and DarkMoon loved him as his own soul.
9   But DarkMoon was a fanatical believer in the brotherhood.

CHAPTER 17

1   It was called operation "Stryker" by the cleric staff of the Diocese.
2   Many helicopters were, in synchronization, to implant the pas-

senger flesh of the child men Marines to do battle with the enemy.

3   And the rhythm of land warfare was orchestrated to the tune of artillery, followed by bombing and concentrated weapons of death to pacify the landing zone in the midst of the river of the seven villages;

4   And much death did occur to the poor peasants indentured to the soil for their politics were only food for mere survival.

5   And it came to pass as DarkMoon looked from his window as the helo passed over the trees preparing to land to unload the Nam Bo soldiers to commence their warfare,

6   There appeared in the open field a lone farmer plowing his sparse rice field behind his life support tractor, a water buffalo.

7   And SnowWhite said on the radio intercom, **THIS MAN IS NOT ENEMY; HIS ENEMY IS STARVATION, OR A STRAY BULLET, AND HE HAS CHOSEN TO PLOW HIS FIELD IN ORDER TO SURVIVE FOR IF HE SHALL NOT PLOW, HE SHOULD SURELY DIE.**

8   And as the white smoke of battle drifted in hazy pockets across the field of Zo Phim, there appeared a running man in black clothes trying to cross the open rice fields along the top of the rows of checkerboard farm land.

9   And the jet pilot dove at high speed firing his mighty guns but missing the lone, little man as he ran for his naked survival.

10   And the gunship helicopter with guns blazing made two attack flights trying to kill the lonely running escapee, but the bullets only chewed the earth on both sides of the man's path.

11   And the gunship helo entered its death giving dive the third time seeking to kill the man, but he leapt under the water in the deep canal;

12   And the helo quickly altered its flight path and came to a quick stop whereby the helicopter hovered over the man submerged in the water;

13   And a lone crewman leaned out on the skid with a pistol and killed the unarmed escapee who had momentarily survived the mighty aerial fire power of the land of Sam Bo.

14   And the second gunship fired a single rocket at an attacking enemy soldier who came from a grass house;

15   On seeing the diving helo, the enemy man turned and ran inside the house's open door to be followed by the rocket and the immediate explosion.

15   And it was that the peasant farmers were the victims of all soldiers for they were indentured to the land to eat;
16   And could only humble themselves to whichever soldier possessed their land;
17   And could only hope their temporary captor would share with them the food that they grew.

CHAPTER 18

1   The King commanded the Deity generals, and the priests of the second order, and the keeper of the door, to bring forth more ravages of war;
2   And they burned the earth in the fields of Kidron;
3   And they carried the ashes of destruction whether they went;
4   And they cast the powder thereof upon the graves of the children of the people;
5   Behold, the machine of war did eat of the unleavened flesh among the brethren, all to be placed upon the altar of attrition, which did not become valid merely by the passage of time.
6   And SnowFlight came to believe that no man might make his son or his daughter to pass through the fire to Molech.
7   And there came forth from the battle of Ada Sam great hoards of rats who feasted on the bodies of the enemy dead;
8   And the Bishop-general sought counsel that his Marines should not die from the diseases and plagues carried by fleas on the nightly roving hoards of rodents hungry for the flesh of the sleeping living, or the dead.
9   And much hate arose from the meat Marines who waited for the High Priests and the King to remove them from the altars of waiting sacrifice.
10   It came to be also that the faith of the congregation of the people questioned the elevated blindness of those who knew not the feel of a burning bullet, the explosive removal of a leg, arm, or eye, and death in the name of the false god of attrition.
11   But the Paragon of Piles fretted not, for his was chapter and verse of things he understood not, for he was of mediocre mind and piss poor judgment – he was school trained to say "yes" to the King of Cash.
12   SnowFlight did have compassion, making a difference;

13   And others were saved with fear; pulling them out of the fire; hating even the garment spotted by the flesh.

14   There came also those who faked the worship of Korpsism; those who accepted death for image;

15   And destruction whispered through their self-preservation words;

16   And death by trial and error from those who reeked with ineptitude.

17   And Poncho Pilot again sought refuge high in the sky watching the ant like helicopters far below.

18   And Poncho Pilot again sought to be adorned with the medals of man offering badges of infamy to others for the reciprocal gestures of paper made heroics on his behalf.

19   And DarkMoon sought SnowWhite, for DarkMoon came into disfavor with the desk-trained man given command rank but who knew not the principles of leadership required thereof.

20   And SnowWhite answered, **THESE ARE MURMURERS, COMPLAINERS, WALKING AFTER THEIR OWN LUSTS: AND THEIR MOUTH SPEAKS OF GREAT SWELLING WORDS, HAVING MEN'S PERSONS IN ADMIRATION BECAUSE OF ADVANTAGE.**

21   And DarkMoon thought this white-haired man who talked with funny words now made sense.

22   These few unholy priests of command had been consecrated to power by the King summoning cashiered regular priests from desk jobs designed to insulate them from being able to have command of the congregational Marines.

23   And the children of the congregational people suffered, and died, in the unwashed hands of the discarded clerics elevated to priesthood by papal dictates in the name of "shortage," "need," and "command time."

24   And the High Priests of much devoutness cast their allegiance to the god, Marine Korps, for the survival of their god was essential to their religion.

25   "Which comes first, God, Country, or Marine Korps?" DarkMoon asked of the Priest-colonel sent to portray the image of leadership in a time of unknown victory.

26   "That's not yours to question," stammered the common Priest-colonel.

27   "But these Marines are being asked to go into the jungle and risk their lives so that the carcass of a worthless crashed helicopter

can be picked up to throw in the helo graveyard tomorrow," continued DarkMoon, not caring whether he made a career of the Marine Korps, or what was written in his personnel jacket.

28   "We can't let the enemy get the radios," was the Priest-colonel's self-created response.

29   "Not so," replied DarkMoon, "the reason is that the Holy Sea doesn't want to report it as a combat loss so the Krotch can have less statistical helicopter losses than the Army."

30   And DarkMoon hatefully continued, "Marines will die . . . not for their country, not for God, but because the Korps wants a wartime statistic."

31   "Marines are trained to die, for whatever cause they are told to die," sparked the hard-chargin', ring-knocking, desk Bishop-colonel irritated at the black pilot who would even think of questioning his command edict.

32   **GIVE TO THE KORPS WHAT IS THE KORPS'**, came words from the pilot with the white hair.

33   "Dismissed," jerked the now irate secular non-combatant Priest-colonel seeking peace from adverse thought.

34   **ZERO, ZERO, MIND FOG**, said SnowWhite to DarkMoon.

CHAPTER 19

1   DarkMoon, in the quiet, wrote himself a poem:

Oh Lord, take me in a pleasant way.
Don't let me become senile,
My mind withered away.
Or endure many miseries,
Traveling to judgment day.
Come in the night,
And quietly take my pay.
Oh Lord, forgive those
Who equate with thee,
That's the only way
They know to be.
But in the end,

All shall see
At one ment in eternity.

2   And DarkMoon felt his blue neck scarf, and he saw the smiling face, then he wrote a poem to Abbey,

I looked for you in the square
and found only pleasant memories there
your hair, your face, your smile
my heart pounded for a while.

I watched the tree shade flicker in the breeze
and remembered your thirsting quest to please
our temporary destiny cast on time's isle
my heart was melancholy for a while.

I felt your memory — a pearl it shall always be
and I shall keep it sealed in my heart's treasury
bound in spirit's thread of many a mile
my heart counted for a while.

I felt you far away
and agreed it was life's pay
tears of pleasure with no reconcile
my heart sundered for a while.

And if in the square you should look for me
our memory shall remain carved into the shade tree
chained in wood whispering our souls trial
may your heart pound for just a while.

CHAPTER 20

1   Triple Seven was ordered out of war for forty days from the Tekoa Wilderness to cross the sea to the Island of the Floating Dragon by carrier ship to get new helicopters.
2   And it came to pass that many pallets of food were to be destroyed by explosion and burying as the Navy unit changed its land based operation to sea.
3   Out of the mist came six helicopters led by SnowWhite, and

the helicopters dipped one by one over the storage yard hovering and attaching their cables to the cargo nets aerially hoisting the pallets of surplus food and departing.

4   And it came to pass that SnowFlight delivered the surplus food to the soccer yard of the orphanage as food for the children.

5   And the children knew also of SnowFlight.

6   And it came to pass that there was much gnashing of teeth by the High Priests of the Navy trained the perform much a do about nothing,

7   But SnowFlight had departed to the Island of the Floating Dragon.

8   And it was that Navy High Priests sought not that which they could find not.

CHAPTER 21

1   DarkMoon liked the idea, but he was deadly afraid of snakes.

2   Dr. Bones Baker, awakened from his noon day nightly nap, grinned and gave Injun the spool of thin, clear medical thread.

3   "You're sure he's dead," DarkMoon asked ShareCrop over and over while the head of the snake was tied to the invisible long line of thread strung from behind the commode bottom down the sandy pathway and across the grass into the store room.

4   Now it came to pass that DarkMoon, Injun and ShareCrop giggled, guffawed and cajoled with spurting tight lips watching the short MakeReady go into privy for his regular evening defecation.

5   And it came to pass that Injun pulled tight the invisible string dragging the snake from behind the pot out and between the feet of the thronesitting MakeReady,

6   There came a scream from the outhouse among the foliage as MakeReady leapt down the sidewalk with the chasing snake.

7   And the waist down naked maintenance man knew the snake would get him as he rounded the corner at dwarf speed disappearing into the long building.

8   Injun choked with laughter,

9   DarkMoon giggled while keeping his eye on the dead snake,

10   And ShareCrop gathered the carcass of the snake concocting other ventures that might give unto more laughter.

11   And it came to pass that the Military Police arrived but found

no snake as confessed to by the waist down naked man sputtering about not even being able to have nightly peace and quiet.

12   And SmegMa saw the naked MakeReady, and said, "I wouldn't put that much meat in a refrigerator."

13   And DarkMoon told unto MakeReady to be careful for a snake had bitten a man in that very same outhouse for which his leg had to be cut clean off at the knee.

14   And so it was that the MakeReady man forcibly changed his bowel schedule to midday and looked high and low before sitting upon the wooden privy throne with his special made little stirrup chair which held his feet off the floor while he relieved himself.

CHAPTER 22

1   "Spook," came the voice of ShareCrop with bad vision in the night to the unsleeping DarkMoon.

2   "Have we got us a tar baby?" he said.

3   "Negative," responded DarkMoon, "We're just in the briar patch of life."

CHAPTER 23

1   The sky was shallow sea blue,

2   And the winds were silken calm when DarkMoon took off piloting the helo.

3   It was a time of smooth flying above the airfield.

4   The instruments did sing forth balanced flight,

5   And to DarkMoon it was a wonderful calmness.

6   Then from the helmet bag ShareCrop pulled forth Rotor-Root, his pet black snake,

7   And it was that DarkMoon turned white, for unto snakes he was sore afraid — and cursed ShareCrop.

8   Then it was that DarkMoon sought retribution to the laughing ShareCrop,

9   And DarkMoon slashed forth with his sicca knife at the black snake with the helo dancing amid the cockpit squabbles;

10   And it came to pass that Rotor-Root slithered out the window into the open air above the airfield falling to earth.

11   Now it was that Chaplain Hebert Hebert Head sat quietly in

the tin roofed outhouse behind the chapel thinking of how he had made his fourth child,

12   When a thump banged forth from the metal ceiling.

13   Then as he looked, the black snake carcass fell forth to the ground, and he was sore afraid.

14   He went forth and fell upon his knees as he knew the snake message sent from the sky was cast to him for such thoughts.

15   And it was that Richard read his well-oiled good book seeking forth the messages of flying snakes.

16   And Chaplain Head was afraid to let anyone know, for he knew that he had been given a sign;

17   And he tried to ban sex from his mind.

18   And it came to pass in the drinking chapel that a round of drinks was had by all to the memory of Rotor-Root, the flying black snake.

CHAPTER 24

1   It was the time of the last day of the Celtic year;

2   It was also the last day of the Indian Harvest.

3   Injun dressed in a loin cloth and did stripe his body with much day-glow orange airplane paint with white stripings;

4   DarkMoon dressed in a loin rag with much white lines mixed with flickers of silver light reflective metal flakes;

5   ShareCrop rolled the white paint dipped motorcycle tire tread across the black back of DarkMoon to the hoots of the pilots preparing for Halloween on the Island of the Floating Dragon.

6   Then it came to pass that the Tabernacle of Alcohol gathered forth many costumed demons of the night unto the drinking chambers,

7   And there was loud music noise orchestrated by pidgin speaking duplicators of rock singing with an electronic folklore band.

8   And there were women whose eyes were round, and who spoke English between the antics of the war absent pilots;

9   And there were women whose eyes were slanted, and who spoke not English but knew the soldiers of war were at non-war play.

10   It came a time that SmegMa yelled into the horn of loud voice noise, "Any one who can't tap dance is a muther fucker."

11 Whereupon, the room full of decorated bodies leapt forth in a frenzy of tap dancing,

12 But it was that Chaplain Hebert Hebert Head was then peaking through the outside window glass into the dancing room of the chamber of alcohol and saw visions of many demons jumping up and down to the flickers of strobe lights and the wangling of mystical music,

13 And the Wrong Reverend screamed at such sight and ran in the night to the secret closet behind the water trough of the Chapel, for he knew these demons also knew where he lived.

CHAPTER 25

1 And it came to pass that DarkMoon returned from rest to instant war,

2 For 777 returned to Nam Bo after forty days.

3 And there were days of flight boredom with the stark terror moments when the familiar thunks of bullets hitting the helo were heard;

4 And there were panic driven nights when out of cautious sleep there came forth the enemy rockets exploding at the air field.

5 And DarkMoon witnessed death of the flesh first hand;

6 And the weeks of war became months of war with death's whistle lurking in the crevices of each flight.

7 And DarkMoon saw SnowWhite as a pilot of unbelievable talent;

8 And DarkMoon believed in SnowWhite,

9 And the miracle of SnowWhite's funny words.

CHAPTER 26

1 Three-D was a good man, a good father, a good Lay-major, and a three times divorced husband;

2 For unto the man of war his woman of all years divorced him each time he went off to far lands for his beloved other love, The Korps.

3 And upon return, the woman of set ways would re-marry the 3-D man of set mind.

4 "Dempsey Dilbert Doe," she would sermonize toward the

polite Seasoned-major, "I'm not going to be a war widow; You get yourself killed on your own time."

5   And 3-D would yield unto the make up of the other race, women.

6   And he would say, "Women don't think like people."

7   But D.D. Doe knew inside that when your number was up, your number was up.

8   So it came to be that 3-D accepted whatever would be.

9   And he quietly did his duty flying in the old Dog helos;

10   And unto him he knew he was safer flying with the meat pilots of war;

11   For he trembled with fear at inheriting a flight assignment with a jet pilot transitioned Lay-major co-pilot as his combat flying companion.

12   And it came to pass that his fear of fears shot nerve-endingly into reality,

13   For unto the flight schedule he was sent forth with the Texas-major who was labeled "co-pilot only."

14   SmegMa called the left-seat Texas man Co-Tex,

15   For SmegMa said of the desk flying conversion to war man that he was as close to a pussy as you could get.

16   Now it came to be that 3-D and Co-Tex did fly unto the mountain cliff-top landing zone to recover the child men patrol;

17   And the trailing enemy spied the easy shooting target of a slow flying helo-landing in textbook descent unartfully flown by Co-Tex;

18   Then it was that 3-D and Co-Tex were shot from the still air with instant crash and much thrashing about the rocky ground,

19   But Co-Tex screamed on the air waves for rescue; "Save my ass!"

20   And above the butcher shop of combat engagement, DarkMoon with ShareCrop took pictures of the crashing helo jerkedly kicking about the ground like a headless fluttering chicken;

21   And ShareCrop came back on the radio and said, "3-D, are you lettin' Co-Tex do the crashin'?"

22   And through the grace of God, no one was killed and few were injured.

23   And it came to pass that DarkMoon called in guncover;

24   And many shells of artillery;

25 Then quickly landed and flew out capturing the crashed pilots and crew.

26 And it was that the two lay-leader majors earned their pay; and they became known as "meat majors."

27 For they had become tenured in a job opportunity war.

The Word According to TAILWIND

(Set the Example)

CHAPTER 1

1   No name ever fit a human being more than "TailWind" adapted itself to T. Ski.

2   In his second year at the Naval Academy (Canoe U.), he was awarded a summer's sea duty aboard a nuclear submarine—a prime assignment which contradicted the respected Naval underwater catechism known as the "No farting in a submarine" rule.

3   "We have a man with terminal spastic colon," gasped the submarine radio operator to the Fleet Commander in fear that the crew would mutiny before Plebe Fartski could be ejected from the mid-sea submarine—ICBM, torpedo tubes, or however.

4   "If you fart one more time," echoed the Chief Petty Officer to the smirking plebe, "I'll shove this Boson's pipe up your ass so far that you'll blow lights out."

5   The sailor men cheered as the helicopter lifted the human fart generating machine from the submarine, thereby freeing the entire crew to smell the wonderful odors of machine oil, static discharge, and cigarette smoke.

6   The Naval Hospital poked, tested, x-rayed, re-tested, and diluted the barium supply for the whole hospital trying to establish a cure for "TailWind" Fartski—as he became known.

7   And it was that Senior Medical Corps Officers were denied

access to golf courses, racket clubs, and manufactured policy planning sessions to attempt to identify a cure for this biological enigma.

8   And special diets, exercise, and then no exercise, and retesting failed to curtail this magnificent mind entrapped in a four bowel farting machine body that randomly emitted in uncontrolled fashion noxious odors.

9   And it was written 'No Submarine Duty' conspicuously in his personnel file with a recommendation that TailWind be assigned duty whereby the constant blowing air might at least dilute his bodily signature.

10   "The Marine option, Sir," TailWind repeated to the Commandant of the Boat School.

11   And it was that the Commandant did not want to lose one of its top graduates to the Korps; however, on reviewing the personnel file, the Commandant observed that the Korps could have this farting quota.

CHAPTER 2

1   TailWind was a devout and school trained pious Marine, who lived a vision within a vision.

2   Like the others, he memorized the Marine's Hymn.

3   And he cherished the sermons of First to Fight, The Marines have Landed and the Situation is Well in Hand, Tell it to the Marines, Devil Dogs, Gung Ho!, and other foundations for Esprit de Corps, including Semper Fidelis — "Always Faithful."

4   Marines are special.

5   Marines fanatically, while in uniform, did not: put hands in pocket, chew gum, whistle, smoke on the street, embrace or hold hands with women, hold an umbrella — not even as an escort, or break step while walking with another person.

6   TailWind studied the early Marine prophets.

7   It was written that Pope Pious I had been an ancestral Marine, and the many other known popes had run the High Church with splendor and sacrifice.

8   It came to pass that the devout TailWind was summoned to the Land of Nam Bo to exercise his religion, Korpsism.

9   And the man of uncommon mind saw the school solution of war,

10   For it was that TailWind understood with chapter and verse the teaching of the art of war.

11   And round about in Nam Bo, TailWind witnessed the plague of unknown purpose,

12   And the High Priests of the Church of the Korps gave sermons written for other wars,

13   For in Nam Bo TailWind saw the mismarriage between duty and kingly indifference.

14   And TailWind witnessed the compass without a needle.

15   TailWind became violently pissed — not at his beloved Korps — but at its yes men High Priests who with all seeing and all knowing, saw not and knew not.

16   There was a shortage of pilots, helicopters, bombs, and there was the decaying equipment!

17   And there were plastic rifles, and plastic grenade launchers, and unround shells that met death for full employment standards.

18   And the ninety-day supply system of the Korps as only an Advanced Naval Base Assault force killed a few child men Marines.

19   "The Korps is not a second standing Army," mumbled TailWind to himself.

20   And worst of all, there were the defective minds of war,

21   For the D.C. Doxies reaped profits from the manufacturing madness.

22   And TailWind acquired a hate attitude and cried at each 1369 body bag placed on his helicopter — taking a part of his soul.

23   Death in war is, but wasted death was agonizing his mind.

24   Then it came to pass that child men Marines were ordered to die in order to build a "magic" wall between the land of Nam Bo and Bac Bo.

25   It was insane.

26   And the Prince of Money imposed on dedicated young Marines a defective weapon that they called Matty Matel's machine gun, for it jammed in battle.

27   And the unskilled and untrained indentured child men Marines with such new weapons were left knowing their imminent death met "low bid" commercial standards.

28   And the innocent child men Marines cried at giving loyalty to a Fatherland that gave not loyalty back.

29   TailWind heard their painful words; TailWind witnessed their honoring the unhonorable cause.

30   And it was that TailWind learned that Nam Bo was a rudderless ship abandoned to unprincipled war with the Pope-admirals and Pope-generals trying to sew sailcloth for a submarine in dry dock — it did not compute!

31   Likewise, it became known that among the clergy there were certain Vicar-majors and Curate-colonels who would manufacture excuses not to be sent on regular combat flying missions.

32   "Someone has to make sure these reports get in on time," they would say, or "You guys want good chow — don't you, then I'll see that it's done."

33   And the Academy-trained man of high heart and dedication witnessed firsthand line and staff corruption through career worship, and liked not what he saw.

34   And TailWind thought of all his teachings where the Korps was only to be skilled and trained to capture and temporarily hold an advanced naval base.

35   But TailWind saw the death sentence of making the Marines a land Army, and understood how old men of monocular thought perpetrated the madness.

36   And it was that the magnificent mind in a four bowel farting body preferred noxious bowel odor to the smell of the King.

CHAPTER 3

1   It was that patriotism, mom's apple pie, and god Bless Sam Bo were stained by body count, cover-up, field grade foul-up, and death by inter-service rivalry.

2   Because of all those men whom the Korps had shown glory, the new order could not be fulfilled.

3   "It is not ours to question," said the Pope-general, and echoed the Cardinal-generals, the Bishop-generals, and the curate officers and vicar staff helpers with line and staff elders who knew the King of Cash gave them a war without a mission, a compass without a needle.

4   "We shall do all we can to prove we are better than the Army, less they do battle at the end of this war to do away with our

beloved Korps," instructed the ecclesiastical hierarchy staff council who protected the unholy church.

5   And it was adopted that all would be done to generate proof that the beloved Korps could out sacrifice the Army.

6   And they worshipped the cookie cutter war plan.

7   It was whispered that all equipment and aircraft shall be rescued from enemy territory to show less equipment losses by the beloved Korps — even at the sacrifice of fresh lives, for the statistical scriptures shall bear testimony of the wonderful church.

8   It shall be that the beloved Korps shall do more with less — even if supplies are stockpiled.

9   It shall be that the enemy horde shall deal face to face with our beloved Korps, and it shall not waste artillery, bombs, and incendiaries, but shall frontally meet the bastards under the catechism of high diddle, diddle, run up the middle.

10   It was the blessed word.

11   And the can do attitude coupled with high church blindness killed many child men Marines.

12   And it became known that the shore-bound Marines were landlocked sea warriors.

13   And the Korps church leaders openly accepted the King of Cash, knowing the King was an elephant walking on the Marine pissants of life.

14   But the High Priests silenced their tongue against what they liked not, for priesthood mixed with the agony of arrogance.

CHAPTER 4

1   "The Devil made me do it," TailWind barked back to the demands of the Curate-major giving the operations briefing for the next day.

2   "If you fart one more time," the irate, teary-eyed major stated opposite the abandoned side of the briefing room where TailWind sat alone taking notes, "I'll put you on night MedEvac for a week."

3   "Don't throw me in the briar patch, Sir," TailWind responded, knowing that the night moon was full with clear skies meaning that this Lay-major helicopter pilot coveted being able not to fly at night, but if required, only to fly on a full moon clear night, and the Vicar-major would claim this night.

4   "I'm ordering you not to fart," he shouted sharply at TailWind.

5   "No intentional respect sir, but sometimes assholes get out of control," he paused amid the laughter, "but sometimes assholes listen to each other."

6   And there came much alcohol after the briefing, for these were times that make men's souls.

7   And there was much singing for vile songs in war vented the flying warriors' souls, and they loudly sang,

Ginsi fuckin' Cola
Hits the fuckin' spot
Twelve fuckin' ounces
That's a fuckin' lot
More fuckin' Ginsi
For your fuckin' money too
Ginsi fuckin' Cola
Is the only drink for you
Fuck, fuck, fuck, fuck

8   And they loudly sang in unison the pilots' fight song,

We're a bunch of bastards
Scum of the Earth
Born in a Whorehouse
Shit on, pissed on, kicked around
        the Universe
Of all the sons a bitches
We're the worst
We are the men of 7-7-7
Scum of the Universe

9   And it was in the middle of a man-generated hell that TailWind escaped in these precious moments with his other pilots who shared a common bond,

10   And they all anticipated instant death hidden among uneventful flight hours and forgotten days of moment-by-moment survival.

CHAPTER 5

1   And it came to pass that the drunken TailWind, on his hands and knees before God, breathed words and spewed vomit from his toes outward,
2   "In the name of the Father, the Son, and the Holy Ghost, I've changed my mind," prayed TailWind,
3   "I hereby enter my renunciation; I have a change of heart. I will do right. I hereby pledge to my fellow human being, my brother Marine, and sanctify myself and commit never to become a Vicar-major, a Curate-colonel, nor a Pope-general. May the D.C. Doxies who feed their egos and pocketbooks from the lives of these kids go to Hell!"
4   He cried amongst the visions of the 1369's in the green bags stacked on the helo pad as he lay across the barbed wire in the rain.
5   I will sacrifice my life for these kids," the tears continued, "but only for them! Not the Korps!"
6   As TailWind lifted his head he looked into the steel blue eyes of the pilot called SnowWhite.
7   **CAN I SHARE YOUR PAIN?** asked SnowWhite.
8   And SnowWhite carried TailWind from the rain to his cot.
9   And it came to pass SnowWhite and TailWind became common bond pilots, and common bond friends.
10   And it was that TailWind became part of a convoy of common pilots known as SnowFlight.
11   For it was that the meat pilots did flock among themselves.

CHAPTER 6

1   One Eye was a religious bigot.
2   One Eye was a hard-core snake handler preacher and had quietly escaped detection.
3   "Jesus spoke English," he said, "not Yiddish!" — as he glared rebuke toward BurnOut and TailWind, who were pre-occupied with the new girly magazine in SmegMa's mail.
4   "Ever eat any Pussy, Chaplain?" sparked BurnOut.
5   "Get thee away from me Satan!" he quivered, rapidly departing the hootch.

6   "Looks like a taco," said SmegMa toward the escaping Chaplain, "If it's not made to eat, why does it look like a taco?"

CHAPTER 7

1   DarkMoon and OverBoost traded the sailors on the ship for half a hoop of sharp cheese.
2   And RedLine brought back a case of canned refried beans, and fresh garlic bulbs from an unknown source.
3   Then a jar of jalapeno peppers appeared from a cult hiding place as the final gesture to complete the beginning of the Great Fart Fight.
4   With darkness, cold beer, and the ingestion of the vast portions of the acquired internal ammunition, preparations were laid for the incubation of intestinal gas build-up in the pilot's bland diet bowels.
5   A few misfired trumpets gained many laughs in anticipation of the scheduled great fart-off.
6   Contestants were given a five minute anticipatory warning for which to schedule their tribute.
7   Random honking was permitted; TailWind was the master, gasser of ceremonies.
8   With every loud fart there came a roar of laughter and an intellectual discussion of the quality, rhythm, and tone of such fart, after which a vote was taken.
9   Somewhere in the dark hours, the humor had lost its gloss and the alcohol had gained in strength—then it happened!
10   "Any you guys ever light a fart?" came an anonymous query from the beer drinking crowd.
11   And within moments, contestants vied in line sprattled at the end of the building atop a sandbag bunker and, at the proper moment, a lighted match was properly placed near the contestant's anal exit awaiting sphinxter release.
12   The blue-green, and sometimes reddish fire gained acclaim after acclaim.
13   TailWind bargained for firing position and a long narrow blue hue darter captured the envy of all amid cheers and laughter.
14   RedLine misfired, contracted, and suffered a rectal implosion; the hair of his ass was singed; cold beer was quickly poured

down the ass crevice of the teary-eyed pilot, and the laughter was immersed with drunken vulgarities.

15   Wounded, but not seriously, RedLine straddled in duck walk fashion in search of Dr. Bones, and ointment.

16   "You could have killed him!" — Curate-colonel Kiwi yelled.

"Killed Who?" TailWind standing at attention, replied.

"St. Jean," he glared.

"How . . . Sir?" TailWind responded.

"Lightin' Farts; You could have blown him back to the land of the big P.X. We're short of pilots — how the hell could I explain to Headquarters that we MedEvac'd a pilot from fart burnout . . . I can't make you not fart, but you'll light no more farts — that's an order — pass the word," he shouted and left.

17   And the crowd queried, "Does that mean we can't light a major?"

18   And there was much laughter.

CHAPTER 8

1   DingleBerry's happy hours blended to a history of many.

2   Happy hour became a way to ignore the unhappiness and bitterness of the horror outside.

3   Happy hour with alcohol was a means to dilute the days of boredom and to temporarily erase the moments of screaming sounds of human agony: to wash away the residual visions of the pieces of smoking or burned human flesh torn apart — the hidden truths of real war.

4   And happy hour allowed the exasperations of those who envisioned a Father gone amuck because the King had ignored those trained and skilled in the art of war to the preference of an academic fanatic who knew not that men would be required to die at the flick of *cum laude* lips, all in the name of experiment, postulate, trial and error, and his acceptable type I and type II error.

5   And the poor, the uneducated, the disadvantaged, those of slow mind and limp foot, were by design the fodder of the war.

6   And there was little sadness that a Bishop had been "fragged" by his own men, for the man could only say "yes" to the Divinity of Defense — a leadership trait not in keeping with the Thirteen Commandments of the Korps;

7   For a true High Priest would resign from the High Church

priesthood before being disloyal to his innocent child men brethren.

8   And loyalty allowed not for a High Priest to keep silent at war profiteering of his King.

9   And the name of the game at the club was "spike."

10   And the terms of the game were simple, toss your survival knife high in the air vertically where it would rotate and plan to catch it as it fell point downwards without cutting yourself.

11   And those who cut themselves were hooted by the other happy hour bleary-eyed pilots.

12   And the drunken Indian, blitzed at the death of BuckShot, his gunhelo pilot friend, misjudged and smiled cooly as TailWind withdrew the knife that stuck through Injun's hand, to the hoots of the watching happy hour crew.

13   Then Dr. Bones Baker poured good whiskey on TwoDogs' hand wound, and stitched the two holes with gynecological imprecision while the drunken pilots cheered at the Doc's antics as he performed barroom surgery.

14   And SmegMa was intrigued at how this man who played with pussies for a living could tighten up a bodily hole to specification, and asked many questions.

15   The nerve-dead Injun watched, and spoke of unknown tribal battles on the Oklahoma plains.

16   The bar cheered at the last stitch; at the hand held high.

17   And the pilots loudly sang Injun a "him,"

> Him-m-m . . .m
> Him-m-m . . .m
> Fuck Him . m. m. m

CHAPTER 9

1   The Prince of Money is coming.

2   And word spread round about that the Prince would make his divine presence known to the unwashed masses of common soldiers assigned to the unpopular common task of uncommon war.

3   And his economic glory shown round about, for the Prince of Money with his eminent power and his circumference of "yes clerics" knew the game of war not.

4   Any high priest rejecting the Prince of Money's ideas was removed from view.

5   And the Prince of Money accepted not the views of the men who knew war for he had graduated *cum laude* — cash.

6   "Economic power fuels this nation," the Prince of Money would say, "and we can out-money these impoverished hordes."

7   And thus war became a battle of numbers, "body count," "how many we lost to how many they lost," and to simply draw lines geographically across the terrain of the earth, for it was mean, medium and mode for the Prince to checkerboard the land and play economic chess with human life.

8   And the buzz words were more equipment, inventory orders, replacement gear, and war trinkets, for this pleased the money makers.

9   "We are winning," the High Priests were instructed to say if they were to keep their officialness;

10   And they would ask also for a larger army, for war time-motion study could be shortened with quicker numbers.

11   And the staff cleric would review the government contracts in light of the growth of the barons, the dukes, and the princes of profits.

12   "Nothing is too good for the Marines," the troops would recant knowing that 'nothing' is the support they would receive at the hands of the misguided strategy of the eggheads running the war who had never held a rifle much less been on the point of an assault.

13   "Tell the press there is no shortage of bombs," the directorate head told the Bishop who sought guidance from the office of the Prince of Money.

14   "But we're short of bombs," protested the Bishop behind closed doors,

15   And the Prince instructed the procurement lackeys to buy more lackey bombs, but the Marines would die in frontal assault philosophy.

16   "National security dictates that you are not to inform the press", mandated the PhD under-secretary to the High Priests who knew their men would die because of the stupid inefficiencies of the war-game mentality, but spoke out not.

17   And it came to pass that even the littlest of minds recognized that the war, and the shedding of human life, cannot be reduced to mere mathematical formula;

18   To the whims of egoists feeding to achieve mental satiation of power;
19   Or to a corrupt leadership scavenging on the economic morsels retrievably hidden among the mass procurement in government spending.
20   And the Prince of Money smiled and said, "the minerals hidden under the sea and in the mountains of Nam Bo will flow for years to come," and he became also known as the Prophet of Profits.
21   And it was that TailWind saw the misguided minds and counted the bodies, but he was powerless to stop the runaway beast.
22   TailWind sought release in alcohol.

CHAPTER 10

1   StoneMan, OverBoost, SmegMa, DarkMoon, TwoDogs and TailWind consumed great quantities of alcohol at the Elephant Bar before the race began.
2   It was a year's wages to the rickshaw drivers, but each of the six drivers agreed in pidgin to the rules of the race.
3   On the go signal, the first driver to get to Holy Sea dock side pier would win all the money.
4   The leathered men grinned at each other as the drunken passenger pilots lined them in gate fashion; the winner of this race would be wealthy.
5   "Go!" screamed the shore-bound sailor laughing at the trotter antics of the old men racing off in the evening sun.
6   And the hunger of the old men lead the racers down sidewalks, through fish markets, and alleyways toward victory.
7   And vehicle traffic ran amuck to the screaming pilots yelling giddy-up and other what-nots of horse motivation.
8   And it came to pass that TailWind's driver took to the hotel entrance racing across the lobby wreaking havoc and sprawling patrons on the way out the other lobby door.
9   And the High Priests of war in formal white uniform gathered at the hotel were dismayed at the antics of whoever disrupted their fine evening meal on the veranda of the old French Hotel.
10   And it came to pass that TailWind's driver, grasping for every bite of rancid air that lifted off the fecal matter of Stink River,

arrived clearly first, and fell to his knees smiling at his new found wealth.

11 And the pilots laughed at the clip-clop sing-song of their pier side collision.

12 And the Bishop-general was distraught and issued a "Letter of Reprimand" to T. Ski for disrupting the reception at the hotel.

13 And TailWind framed the Letter of Reprimand and told everyone that "A Letter of Reprimand is better than no mail at all."

CHAPTER 11

1 "Luke the Gook and Marvin the Arvin are victims of this war just like us," bellyached TailWind watching the dead and wounded little tan Nam Bo bodies taken from the helicopter.

2 **WHO IS THE ENEMY?** queried SnowWhite to the dismayed TailWind.

3 TailWind paused before responding, "The enemy of a soldier is whoever he is told is the enemy, but an enemy is also whoever or whatever brings on death, destruction, or takes away the body or soul of a human being."

4 SnowWhite smiled at TailWind's response, **WHAT IS EVIL?**

5 And it was that TailWind liked not his thoughts.

6 Then SnowWhite said, **CHILD MEN ARE BEING GIVEN UNTO MOLECH**.

7 And TailWind grew cold with vision chill, for he saw parents ignorant that they had delivered their children unto High Priests who would cast the children unto the brass to be burnt.

CHAPTER 12

1 "What are they all doing around the radio?" asked Dingle-Berry of the Operations Sergeant.

2 "They're listening to the Middle-East war reports," responded the Gunny.

3 "My people are whipping the shit out of the camel jockeys," quipped BurnOut.

4 "Jews 6, Sand-Niggers none," came his smiling quote.

5   And it came to pass that within a war there came great concern that real war was happening elsewhere.
6   And several pilots inquired if they could volunteer to go to the real war, one they could respect.

CHAPTER 13

1   There were many uneventful hours of flying that fulfilled the majesty of quotas and statistics in the Tekoa Wilderness.
2   And the hours of waiting were filled with chess, checkers, cards, and for those who would wait patiently for their turn at the game, m-o-n-o-p-o-l-y!
3   Into the blackness of the rain drenched nights the screams of money-humming, apartments, hotels, and arguments of loaded dice echoed through the tent area in the middle of a war.
4   Pilot teams were formed, and the day's flying suffered the addiction of the blood-thirsty battle of the Monopoly game.
5   It was during the heat of the afternoon in the middle of a major banking problem that the voice of the radio speaker screamed out, "Emergency, Mayday, Bug Killer on fire, inbound airfield."
6   The pilots ran to their helmet-bags, gathered their cameras and lined up along the dirt runway watching the smoke trailing spotter airplane trying to land.
7   And the pilot of the small plane radioed he could make it, and shut back the smoking, sputtering engine.
8   Hordes of cameras clicked at the landing approach, the perfect one-wheel touch down, for the other wheel was missing, and then the sudden rolling and tumbling with a cloud-ball of red runway dust, but no fire!
9   Then the cut and shaken pilot was pulled from the wreckage able to walk on his own, not knowing the massive number of pictures made of his crash.
10   And it became known that the pilot had stuck his grease gun machine gun out the window to shoot at a suspected V.C. only to shoot off his own tire.
11   And the ricochet bullets from the tire bounced back to hit the engine;
12   The Bug Killer pilot had shot himself down.
13   And much hoot went round about.

CHAPTER 14

1 "Flaming Hookers," smiled SmegMa to the challenged Navy pogue TailWind had retrieved from the boat on the sea.
2 "The trick is to light the brandy, tilt your head to the side, and drink the liquor without putting out the flame."
3 SmegMa instructed, then demonstrated drinking the alcohol but leaving a small amount of burning liquor with a blue flame in the bottom of the glass when he was through.
4 The Navy major, not to be shown up by a Marine helo pilot, lit his drink, tilted it successfully only to dribble burning liquor on one side of his moustache to the laughter of the crowd and a quick throw of water in his face saving him from serious burns, but leaving a scraggly, black, half moustache amidst the aroma of burning hair.
5 "Set your face on fire," grinned Dr. Bones Baker at the embarrassed sea-going line cleric as the Doc looked for facial wounds, and applied ointment.
6 "Leave 'em alone or those pilots will talk you into burning off the other half," Doc laughed and ordered a round of drinks.

CHAPTER 15

1 And it came to pass that again and again the arrogance of power with kingly difference shown round about.
2 The sea going force of the Korps as the least organized, least equipped unit for a sustained land warfare battle was placed next to the standing land army of the Bac Bo enemy.
3 And the Divinity of Defense allowed the unseasoned civilian analysts to control the decisions of battles and the strategies of war like unto a child's game.
4 It came to pass that the firmament of the people sickened at hollow success in the names of "body count," "captured," and "death of peasants who controlled not the powers of either side of the war."
5 And the Prince of Money dispensed the shekels of war for the harlots who suckled on the blood of power politics which ran amuck from the will of the people.
6 It came to pass that TailWind continued to suffer for the child

men, for the beautiful peasants who were victims of geography, for the mountain tribesmen caught between opposing forces on high ground, and for the fatherland caught by a King who understood only arrogance and private pocketbook fiscal heroics.

7   It was not clearly opposing forces slaughtering each other by unprincipled land warfare; it was "hide and seek" whereby the will of the common people crept to silent disbelief of betrayal by arrogance.

8   And TailWind sought counsel with SnowWhite at the new thing called limited warfare conjured by those who thought death by any other name was not death.

9   And SnowFlight was of much fret that the Prince of Money negotiated lives of the defenseless young captured through indoctrination in assembly line fashion without human feasibility study.

10   It was that the King knew he was King.

11   SnowWhite said to TailWind, **THE PRINCE OF MONEY IS A MAN WISE IN HIS OWN CONCEIT. THERE IS MORE HOPE OF A FOOL THAN OF HIM. THERE IS AN EVIL IN THIS WAR WHICH SNOWWHITE HAS SEEN, AND IT IS COMMON AMONG THESE MEN.**

12   And TailWind listened to such words but knew not what the words meant nor why this pilot with the white hair talked funny, but he was immaculate under fire.

13   And of the war, SnowWhite said, **POCKETBOOK MINDS HAVE POCKETBOOK HEARTS.**

CHAPTER 16

1   The cold rain and the night's blackness made the big white bobbing hospital ship with its red cross a mystical vision floating in the rolling sea.

2   SnowWhite and TailWind flew with a load of wounded on board their helo to be delivered via the ship's small lighted landing space just big enough for one helo at the rear-end platform of the ship.

3   Night MedEvac to a moving ship on a bouncy sea, thought TailWind, was the penultimate of helo flying.

4   And it happened that the big engine coughed, then sputtered and quit.

5   In the immediate silence, instant terror speared into TailWind's bones;

6   We will crash into the sea, he thought and yelled on the intercom to the crew to prepare to ditch; the helpless wounded would surely die.

7   SnowWhite calmly radioed the ship of the engine failure and flew the descending, engine-out helo in a glide better than TailWind had ever experienced.

8   Only perfect timing, and master flying skill could get the powerless helo to crash onto the small deck of the moving ship.

9   And SnowWhite smoothly trickled the airspeed, then the rate of descent, then the slight sideward unbalanced flight bleeding off speed to the proper point of closure to the ship.

10   TailWind was astonished for SnowWhite slipped aerially over the small moving helo pad and simultaneously hit vertically hard on the deck;

11   And the ship's crew quickly jumped to the wheels chaining the helo down to the bouncing deck in the rolling sea.

12   "It's a miracle," screamed the smiling TailWind into the microphone as all electrical power went blank.

13   And it came to pass that Kiwi insisted that SnowWhite be given a medal for extraordinary flight in saving the wounded from sure death from the possible crash into the sea by landing at night onto the moving ship.

14   And SnowWhite refused the awards and said, **SNOWWHITE NOT DESIROUS OF VAIN GLORY, PROVOKING ONE ANOTHER, ENVYING ONE ANOTHER. FOR MEN TO SEARCH THEIR OWN GLORY IS NOT GLORY.**

15   And Kiwi understood not why uncommon valor was a common virtue.

16   And SnowWhite said, **THE BEST RIBBON IS A LIVE MAN'S SMILE.**

CHAPTER 17

1   It came to pass that 777 with all pilots were ordered to depart by ship privately to the Island of the Floating Dragon across to the other side of the sea.

2   And SnowWhite lead the flight of six to a field where pallets of crated food were to be destroyed.

3   And SnowFlight captured the out-dated food by cargo nets under the helicopters and flew it to the soccer field of the orphanage as they departed the airfield for the ship to cross the sea.

4   And the children waved and the women of peace smiled as the boy with white hair and a face that sparkled flew by in departing flight for there was now food for the children.

5   And the Navy was distraught that it had not been allowed to burn the surplus and aged food.

6   And there was gnashing of teeth among the High Priests of war, for SnowWhite was not authorized to give government property away, even if it was to be destroyed.

7   And the starving children knew not how one man could feed so many.

CHAPTER 18

1   For forty days and forty nights 777 was to absent itself from the reignments of the War on the Island of the Floating Dragon.

2   And SnowWhite lead SnowFlight to rest in the quiet of the volcanic mountains to where the sounds of war were silent mental echoes of the immediate past.

3   And there came an old leathered man who watched from afar as the days passed by.

4   The oriental silence of the old man was broken and he asked of SnowFlight, **WHICH IS MORE IMPORTANT, TRUTH OR HONOR?**

5   It was decided that the King sought reward for that which he knew not, that the Divinity of Defense was more deadly than the enemy, and that the Korps was a devout religion more onerous than the churches of the earth for how many religions had brought to death the numbers of its congregation,

6   The strange old man, Lei' Merej, frightened the pilots with his simple words.

7   **YOU SPEAK BLASPHEMOUS THINGS OF YOUR CHURCH, BUT YOU DO NOT TELL OTHERS OF THE WAYS OF THE KING?** the piercing old man queried.

8   "But its High Priests are sworn to secrecy," TailWind did argue, "and besides, the Deacons of the People of the Congregational Church have cast a holy pledge, a vow not easily undone."

9   IS THAT NOT THE HISTORY OF THIS WAR? the suicide pilot of ancient time cleverly asked.

10   IS IT NOT A PRIEST'S DUTY TO SPEAK TRUTH IF THE KING MAKES PROFIT FROM THE PEOPLE'S TREASURY, OR FROM THEIR SON'S FLESH?

11   "But this is different," inserted HalfRight, "We must stop the evil system before it creeps to our homeland."

12   THE TRUTH IS THAT YOU FEAR THE TRUTH, the old man stared as if to pause and force them to listen, he lowered his voice and continued;

13   THE TRUTH IS THAT FORCES ARE BARGAINING FOR YOUR SOULS.

14   And Lei looked upon them, YOUR KING HAS COMMITTED YOU NOT TO THE SIDE OF FREEDOM, JUSTICE, HONESTY, AND KINDNESS . . . FOR THE PEASANT PEOPLE. YOU FIGHT ON THE SIDE OF GREED, CORRUPTION, CRUELTY, AND INJUSTICE.

15   And there was quiet among SnowFlight for the old soldier used piercing words and it was known of the Nam Bo atrocities.

16   And SmegMa made much joke to avoid the pain of the old man's words.

17   "We die because we are young and stupid," said StoneMan.

18   "It's the black dwarfs," inserted DarkMoon. "Those are the worst gnomes known to man," he joked.

CHAPTER 19

1   Now it came to pass on the Island of the Floating Dragon that SmegMa found favor with the fat girl with the fat face,

2   And the tiny pencil line moustache.

3   And in the nightly echoes of passion there came forth multiple conjugal moans signaling for all to hear the wonders of weight over beauty.

4   TailWind sought to counsel SmegMa.

5   And unto SmegMa DingleBerry presented a Lover's Medal,

6   For he donated beyond the call of duty.

7   And DingleBerry questioned SmegMa with intrigue as to the harmonic performance which kept many pilots awake at the silent ready in the middle of the night.

8   Then it was that SmegMa answered,

9   "There are only two kinds of pussy, big ole good ones, and good ole big ones."

CHAPTER 20

1   There was in 777 a Lay-major called Doe.

2   And Poncho Pilot blessed Lay-major Doe as the keeper of fuel, for it was that helos needed clean, healthy fuel.

3   And it was that Lay-major Doe followed the written safety law that there was to be no smoking within twenty-four hours nor drinking within fifty feet of any aircraft before a pilot could fly.

4   Behold, Lay-major Doe sought escape and insulation by special privilege, for he believed he was a Priest helper in the folklore of the career church,

5   And Lay-major Doe would mandate among the pilots that he be allowed not to have early flights.

6   And Lay-major Doe be not disturbed during the hour of fuel nourishment.

7   Then it came to be that TailWind secretly caused to be delivered unto Dempsey Dilbert Doe contaminated gasoline in a fuel sample jar.

8   And the Lay-major of fuel saw his life pass before his eyes, for helos have their engines fail with bad fuel; and Lay-majors who fail become lay leaders in the real ground war, a job called forward air controller.

9   Whereupon, the Lay-major ordered the fuel trucks to dump thousands of gallons of bad gas into the trench ditch that led to the sea.

10   And there came a great fire, for unto the mile of ditch, the poor farmers burned waste.

11   And it was seen around the island the mile long fire stick.

12   And TailWind named the Lay-major, "D. Dil Doe."

CHAPTER 21

1 Then it came to be on the Island of the Floating Dragon that SnowWhite taught unto TailWind, DarkMoon, HalfRight, SmegMa, TwoDogs, BirdMan, ShareCrop, BolTer, OverBoost, StoneMan, RedLine and BurnOut aerial salvation, and secrets.

2 And SnowFlight realized more the heart swelling pride of savings lives, not taking them,

3 And SnowFlight understood not of a man called Joseph who lived in Arimethia,

4 Nor the funny words and singing of SnowWhite.

5 And SnowWhite smiled a comfort issuing grin as SnowFlight sought wisdom concerning the uncommon flying talents which came over them;

6 And SnowWhite said, **A GREAT GIFT CAN BE WRAPPED IN SACKCLOTH OR IN FINE WHITE LINEN, BUT THE OUTSIDE OF A PACKAGE DOES NOT A GREAT GIFT MAKE.**

7 And SnowWhite told them funny words and taught them to sing in battle, and great comfort came upon them,

8 And the twelve could not remember the funny words nor hum the all familiar rhythm, but the twelve felt its presence.

9 And Tailwind, DarkMoon, HalfRight, SmegMa, TwoDogs, BirdMan, ShareCrop, BolTer, OverBoost, StoneMan, RedLine and BurnOut worried not for themselves, and knew not why.

CHAPTER 22

1 Then it came to be that TailWind went alone into the high hills to weed his mind of things he had seen, things he had done, and to question things that he should do.

2 And TailWind thought of man, space and matter, but the here and now reappeared in his troubled thoughts more than the everafter and nevermore.

3 And TailWind cried, for his pain was great.

4 And TailWind thought of the hopelessness of his ancestors and the Polish people, imprisoned behind invisible walls by men whose power emanated from fear and terror.

5 And TailWind thought of his inability to right this wrong.

6   And TailWind saw the eyes of the wonderful child men Marines who gave all, but understood not,

7   And TailWind wept, wept, and wept; and there came unto him a vision within a vision,

8   For the Great Temptor was sending messages of how to invoke selfishness,

9   And round about TailWind saw that the money machines of war cranked voraciously harvesting the crops of profit,

10   For money paved the way for those who knew not the words of the Lord.

11   And the umbrella of truth folded in the reign of glory chaining the blind child men to the living hell of war.

12   And evil begat evil under the dances of the mind sewn by the Dark Angel saying to all that death and destruction of the innocent was justified and acceptable,

13   For it was widely known that the donation of the poor people's sons interfered not in the King's business.

14   But men of poor pocket and disadvantaged stature were awakening to rich men's lies;

15   For righteousness of mind and heart requires no money, nor greed,

16   And TailWind sought counsel with SnowWhite, who said,
WAR LOSES IMPORTANCE WHEN RICH MEN DO THE DYING.

CHAPTER 23

1   And it was the rule on the Island of the Floating Dragon that TailWind always be at the end of the line, for those in front suffered not the sharp smell.

2   So it was when they stood in chow lines,

3   So it was when they rode motorcycles,

4   And so it was when and where the human fart generating machine could be segregated from the others.

5   And it came to pass that TailWind became a usable emissary securing places for the pilots;

6   For when TailWind gassed, rooms were vacated.

7   Thus, it came to be that TailWind was the procurer of territory for the acclimatized others of SnowFlight,

8   For with TailWind's slightest grin, crowds would flee from the

pungent odor surrounding his presence leaving ample room in the busy Inns for TailWind and his friends immune of his constant smell.

9   "You are worth a million bucks," emphasized the accountant Hapstein, "We can rent you out to businesses who pay you to go into their competitors enterprise."

10   Then TailWind started to smile, but BurnOut held TailWind's mouth, for if TailWind laughed, it could bring tears to one's eyes.

11   And it came to pass that the Polish pilot with the spastic colon trumpeted salutes in the Club of the Men of Sky Blue,

12   Who of a sense of humor had none.

13   And the gaggle of Marine pilots sought only food from the Inn of the Air Force;

14   But the Air Force Base Bishop, with tears rolling to his cheeks, explained TailWind's non-presence was required from the palatial building high on the mountain over-looking the deep blue sea.

15   And BurnOut slipped away through the empty kitchen,

16   And BurnOut departed from the back of the building, escaping with food meant for the table of the men of non-combat,

17   And BurnOut also took therefrom three fancy uniforms worn by the High Priests of the Sky Blue Church meant for the laundry.

CHAPTER 24

1   And among the dirty laundry from the Sky Blue High Priest's temple, TailWind, BurnOut, and SmegMa found the vestments of coat and tails with the squirrelly braid.

2   Then it came to pass on the Island of the Floating Dragon that TailWind, BurnOut, and SmegMa dressed in the dress uniform of three Sky Blue High Priest generals;

3   And these pilots in drunken priest uniforms were seen among the brothels and bars, and riding motorcycles round about.

4   It was also that in the Temple Club Tokyo, SmegMa in the Air Force Bishop-general's tuxedo, screamed out, "Anyone who can't tap dance is a muther fucker,"

5   Whereupon, it was witnessed that three drunken Sky Blue

High Priest generals danced a jig on the tops of tables and sang songs unknown to the foreign minds.
6   Now it was that word went forth from far and wide seeking who among the High Church of the Air Force congregated with the common masses,
7   And who among the High Priests would ride a lowly vehicle called a motorcycle,
8   And who among the High Priests behaved like a combat knowing soul.
9   Behold! It became known that agents of a foreign force, the Korps, had once again subjected the men of non-war to combat theology,
10   And a second sign was placed at the entrance to the Sky Blue Temple, beneath the same other sign, No Marines Allowed!
11   And the Sky Blue High Priests of non-war staffed the dilemma, for men of non-war were being driven crazy by men of war whose life expectancies delivered a care-not religion.

CHAPTER 25

1   Now it came to be that twelve helicopters were ordered forth to travel unto the Sky Blue Air Base on missions of secrecy,
2   And an unknown voice came forth on the Air Base tower frequency, "Bullshit."
3   Whereupon, the Low Priest of the Tower, a Curate, radioed forth, "Who said "BullShit?" seeking to punish him who cast such sin on the air waves.
4   And helicopter number one said, "Number One, negative bullshit, sir."
5   And helicopter number two said, "Number Two, negative bullshit, sir."
6   And helicopter number three said, "Number Three, negative bullshit, sir."
7   And helicopter number four said, "Number Four, negative bullshit, sir."
8   And helicopter number five said, "Number Five, negative bullshit, sir."
9   And helicopter number six said, "Number Six, negative bullshit, sir."

10   And helicopter number seven said, "Number Seven, negative bullshit, sir."
11   And helicopter number eight said, "Number Eight, negative bullshit, sir."
12   And helicopter number nine said, "Number Nine, negative bullshit, sir."
13   And helicopter number ten said, "Number Ten, negative bullshit, sir."
14   And helicopter number eleven said, "Number Eleven, negative bullshit, sir."
15   And helicopter number twelve said, "Number Twelve, negative bullshit, sir."
16   And the Tower Curate-colonel of Sky Blue was livid, but could talk not,
17   And the High Priest of non-war summoned forth the Curate-colonel Tower man, and screamed forth, "What's this bullshit on the radio."
18   And the Tower Curate-colonel wept, for men of war care less for the silly rules of the men of non-war.
19   Then there was much gnashing of teeth, for the High Priests of the Air Force knew they could ban Marines from their drinking temple, but men of war were entitled to the facilities of war, even if these men of the Air Force warred not.
20   And it came to pass that 777 was called out of the night to return to the land of Nam Bo, and the Sky Blue men gave thanks, for peace is hell when the Marines are present.

CHAPTER 26

1   Now it was that 777 left the Island of the Floating Dragon with great war preparation;
2   And it was also that men who were preparing to die adorned themselves with the what nots of war,
3   For BirdMan expropriated from the twenty-seven hole battleground of the soldiers of non-war the cart of green golf bearing the hidden markings of the High Priest of the Air Force Base beneath the fresh olive paint.
4   And DingleBerry had special tall man rubber boots to give him new heights,
5   And TailWind brought rubber farting bags that when hidden

under chair seats emitted forth a noise making him invisible from others in the blackness of night.

6   Now it came to pass on the high seas that TailWind had frightening dreams,

7   For the tone of his bodily horn was changing.

8   And TailWind sought counsel with Dr. Bones Baker because of his sore trumpet.

9   "Hemorrhoid," said the medicine man wearing the shark teeth necklace amid the ceremonial shirt, "You just have normal pilot's disease."

10   But it was that TailWind protested, "But Doc, there is nothing better than a crisp, narrow, artfully sliced fart."

11   "If it gets bad, you can always cut it out," said the voodoo clinician, "Besides," he grinned, "the Navy needs hemorrhoidal tissue."

12   TailWind looked questioningly in the face of the Doc and Doc responded, "Its replacement tissue, you see you have to do a frontal lobotomy before you can be promoted to major, the hemorrhoid tissue replaces what we remove . . . just to make sure we get a real asshole!"

13   And it was upon the high seas the humor transported men's minds into the numbness of war things to be.

CHAPTER 27

1   TailWind witnessed the sea frothing shores in the stormy grayness as the ship approached the Nam Bo killing fields;

2   And the eyes of the pilots watched the serenade of the Navy boats dancing in the rolling waters transporting the men of war back into the killing sport of survival.

3   It was that Triple Seven returned to Tru Lai airfield amid the clamor of unscheduled battle;

4   For it was the enemy crept about under the cover of the low clouds and the uniforms of the ordinary peasant people.

5   And the helicopters flew frenziedly at tree tops knowing the next palm row would bear machine gun fire into the suckling metal skin of the helo or into the vulnerable flesh on board.

6   Then it was in the thin slice of hours that the safety aboard the ship of sea was transposed instantly into the chamber of war.

7   And it was that the smell of the air, the taste of the mouth, and the inner soul knew that death was lurking about,

8   Seeking the flesh of the unwise, the vulnerable, and those who sought a morsel of the ring of glory riding the merry go round in the mind that zaps boys into hardened men.

9   And there came many hours and many days of wonderful flying for TailWind,

10   For no greater reward can be given to man than to witness the saved child men's faces who are rescued from death's door;

11   But no greater sorrow awaits youth than to see child men blindness converted to limp flesh and stacks of green 1369 vinyl body bags testifying openly the gift of all from the dead man inside,

12   And to witness the penetrating agony of smoking live flesh gone awry among the liquidness of the body.

13   For TailWind, there was great relief in revolving benders, but mental pain mixed with euphoric love of the brethren issued forth disbelief in warfare folklore.

CHAPTER 28

1   And the days became confused with weeks of time and space unto TailWind,

2   Then also there was the short, cold hard wait when flying in and from of the jungle hang-outs where death quietly sat perched ready to spring forth swipes of life surviving challenge to those who tread at the door.

3   TailWind witnessed the pride of the risk of life to save others,

4   And TailWind fell to the depths of despondency at witnessing that men who are trained to war, make war.

5   For it was written into the minds of the High Priests of war that non-war was achieved with many battles.

6   Soldiers are trained to war, not to peace.

7   It came to pass that there were High Priests who saw the wrongness of fighting on the side of corruption, whoredom, injustice, indentured servitude and mammon's glories;

8   And it was that there were lay leaders, and curate commanders who gave all unto the church, and unto the child men Marines,

9   For unto the church of the Marine Korps, they knew no other.

10   But the King of Cash spake forth the greatness of unknown purpose;
11   And the Prince of Money issued forth great economic decisions as a tithe unto mammon's treasury.
12   "Victory is sweet," said the Prince of Money, but unto all the Kings men the 1369 child men Marines were dead and the dead speak not.
13   Behold also, it was that the *cum laude* cash minds explained not the meaning of victory.
14   And it came to pass that the dedicated TailWind sought to expose to those who followed him the thoughts of the teachings of war which were given unto him with wonderful pride, and also with disbelief of the evil that men do,

"Behold, hear me all those youth who can learn from the written word, I, T.Ski, of engineering mind and deaf vision, say unto you that no greater love can be given than to willingly give your life for another. But hear me, in war the decision of the gift may not be yours. The High Priests of War are forbidden to unfaithfully follow their King. It is written in war that the errors of the King, or of the King's Priests, are death warrants to the King's men. It is written also that unto those that make war against us, youth carries the burden of the Father. There is also no greater love than the son to the Father that loves you, but to this War the Father has disgraced the flesh of the son. We die in the shadow of the arrogance of a man who believes himself King."

15   Then it came to pass that TailWind mellowed, for each day was a day of war business,
16   And TailWind tested ShareCrop's rope of faith and enjoyed much the piss'n contests,
17   And TailWind came forth from hours of flying in a hard day at war and tap danced when SmegMa screamed out, "Anyone who can't tap dance is a muther fucker, "
18   And TailWind enjoyed farting in the middle of pilot briefings, for he believed it was only fair.
19   After expansive time compressed into paper thin memories,

the happy hours were staccato flashes of the songs sang by child men pilots to escape the agony of heartache thoughts,
20   But there were miles and miles of laughter;
21   And there were great celebrations when a child man of 777 could go to a faded place called home.
22   Soon, TailWind knew his time would be up but he hurt at the thought of abandoning the child men from his aerial protection.

CHAPTER 29

1   Zip! Zip! Zip! came forth the familiar terror of enemy bullets hitting the helo with pings shattering the windshield as TailWind instantly twisted the engine throttle to maximum power departing with the wounded;
2   And he gained speed flying at ground level behind the rows of trees trying to hide behind natures foliage protection.
3   Then TailWind pulled the controls trading airspeed for quick altitude out and away from the enemy.
4   Combat helo flying is truly an art, he thought, while enjoying the euphoria of giving his penultimate talent in saving others.
5   And it came to pass that TailWind landed and quickly was assigned a separate helo for he was off and in the air again seeking out those who were calling forth for MedEvac rescue.
6   Then it was that TailWind sped forth back into the thick of an ongoing battle for there were more wounded in need;
7   Zip! Zip! Zip! came again the enemy's bullets punching holes in the landing helo's thin skin;
8   And Topsy Turvy screamed on the radio that they were taking hits;
9   And the Crew Chief yelled forth that the wounded were on board.
10   TailWind added power to the Dog flying machine peeling off to the tree line seeking to escape as the easy target;
11   And it was that the smoking helo crept skyward out of range;
12   Then TailWind and Topsy Turvy nursed the crippled machine back to the airfield with only the grace of God keeping them safely airborne.
13   And TailWind checked out another waiting helo, for on the radio he heard the calls for rescue of other Marines.

14   Now it came to be that TailWind and Topsy Turvy climbed skyward watching the beast of war trample across the terrain below;

15   And it was that TailWind shot from the sky downward gaining all the speed he could muster while flying right above the ground behind the trees injecting the helo into the rescue zone;

16   And it was that TailWind shut the throttle from the engine while quickly placing the old helo in a side flair trading speed and ground altitude for quick stop with proper power for an instant landing;

17   Now it was that the wounded sped forth into the passenger bay and TailWind departed;

18   Zip! Zip! Zip! with dings came the familiar enemy bullet sounds,

19   And Topsy Turvy screamed forth that "We're taking hits!"

20   But TailWind flew the wounded but surviving helo and passengers back to the airfield;

21   And DingleBerry grounded TailWind, for he had put three helos into the helicopter hospital;

22   But it was that the battle had quietened.

23   And it was that TailWind and Topsy Turvy went into the "O" Club to consume much drink.

24   Upon questioning by ShareCrop, TailWind said, "I've had a hard day at the office."

25   And it came to pass that ShareCrop told unto TailWind that the High Priests of war had volunteered SnowWhite to fly into So dau lau Valley to rescue two unworthies.

The Word According to SMEGMA

(Know Your Job)

CHAPTER 1

1   SmegMa was a patriot of the first order; he volunteered for Nam Bo.
2   SmegMa worshipped the Korps; the holy day of November 10, the Korps' birthday, was his adopted religious day.
3   He believed the world was base; men were fundamentally animals; and in an environment of survival it was dog eat dog.
4   SmegMa knew he was a male stud;
5   For he went from flower to flower, flowers to flowers, and only ceased after his female challenger would beg for mercy.
6   It was DarkMoon's idea — but it destroyed SmegMa.
7   It came to be that DarkMoon and SmegMa were in Hong Kong;
8   It became known as "The Great Hong Kong Fuck Off,"
9   For the pilots sent away from war for R & R (rape and rampage) bet the braggart SmegMa that the Chinese prostitute, Kitty Chow, could out-fuck him.
10   The rules of engagement simply required SmegMa to perform his broadcast sexual talents while the pilots played cards awaiting the fucking race results in the adjoining room.
11   And the humping, bumping, grinding and pleasure pidgin ensued.
12   Unknown to SmegMa, as timeouts from sexual combat

occurred, Kitty Chow would step into the double doored bathroom to be secretly replaced by her twin sister, Katy,

13   And then Katy would later secretly rotate back in Kitty's place.

14   SmegMa rallied his last time in the late darkness of early morning—his alter-ego had gone soft.

15   With screams of depression at having been done in by this Kitty Chow sex combatant, SmegMa yelled for mercy as he buried his embarrassed face in a pillow hiding his shame from sexual inebriation, and pecker stupor.

16   The pilots hooted the sexually defunct corpse.

17   SmegMa heard unleashed ridicule at his not being able to handle this little half-Portuguese, half-Chinese woman;

18   He had been out matched. "I love her," he said to himself, "I must have her again."

19   SmegMa the stud knew he had been just plain out-fucked.

20   On return to Nam Bo from Hong Kong, an ever increasing strange new pain randomly throbbed in SmegMa's groin;

21   He was scared—the diseases he had heard about: pus pecker, black balls, incurable venereal diseases, the creeping crud. . . o-o-o-oh!

22   DarkMoon wrote a poem entitled, "SmegMa".

Oh dear me,
It hurts to pee!
Stuck my pecker
In a fungus tree.
When its over
And I am well,
I'll get it again
As sure as hell.

23   SmegMa, "The Great Depressed," as he became known, knew he was about to die—and as a consequence of screwing the most effective woman he had ever known.

24   Bones Baker, a gynecologist drafted to be a Navy Flight Surgeon because the Navy had little use for him as a pussy poker, appeared.

25   "You ever had clap before this trip," he asked in the capacity

of a co-conspirator with DarkMoon achieving further ego dismantlement of this male nymphomaniac.

26 "Sure I have," SmegMa quietly, but quickly and proudly responded.

27 "Relax Smeggie," grinned the deranged squadron flight surgeon, "You don't have a disease," at which point SmegMa's pecker smiled, "but you have the worst case of dry-rub dick-rot I've ever seen. You must have tried to drill a hole in a sandy beach; ya know, a post will rot if you leave it in the ground," and Doc laughed at his joke.

28 SmegMa's depression ricocheted to the ecstasy of his beloved Kitty Chow — she had not infected him — O-O-Oh, to have her again.

29 "Zip it up," Doc instructed, but the Doc diagnosed to deaf ears.

30 And it was that the Doc prescribed covering the pecker for hours with a red paste salve ointment applied by removing the top and bottom lids to a can, placing the can over the pecker, and filling the can with a medicinal red dye placebo paste, burying the pastry penis inside.

31 And SmegMa would sit in the noon-day sun naked, with his pecker in a beer can full of red paste.

32 Doc hoped any woman upon seeing Smegma's solid red penis would run away.

CHAPTER 2

1 The Water-Saint had been cast among heathens, atheists, agnostics, coon asses, niggers, adulterers, spics, deviates, wops, whoremongers, and alcohol consumers in Arcadia, Louisiana, and now, at Tru Lai, the other side of the earth, the same sinners were present — but more devout.

2 "Thou Shalt Not Kill," quoted Chaplain Head to the passing group of pilots.

3 **IT IS THE NATURE OF MAN TO SILENCE THE TEN COMMANDMENTS IN TIME OF WAR**, responded SnowWhite.

4 "Kill or be killed," stated StoneMan, "as in the law of Moses, offer terms of peace to the enemy, and if refused, slay every male and take women, children, cattle, and the spoils as booty."

5   "Burn 'em and scalp 'em," smiled TwoDogs.
6   "Fuck'em all," grinned SmegMa.

CHAPTER 3

1   And it again came to pass that the Divinity of Defense avoided the high military priests, the Deity-generals, and those trained and skilled in the scripture and verse of war.
2   "It's simple," said one of the Puzzle Palace Humpty Dumpty think tankers casting the blank stare of a non-combatant who pretends to know the wisdom of a foxhole without ever having felt the grip of being point man in an assault,
3   "We'll build a wall between the land of Nam Bo and Bac Bo."
4   And to the fathers and sons of Wall Street whose lives would not be shed for such a magnificent idea — the clearing of land and building of an electronic wall across the face of the earth between Nam Bo and Bac Bo — was thought to be a scholarly idea.
5   But to the child men Marines, the engineers, and those in harm's way, it was both idiotic and deadly — they would die fulfilling the electronic fairy tale.
6   And the kids given unto the beast's feed lot smote the form letter:

(Insert Parents' Names and Address)

Sam Bo regrets to inform you that your son was killed in action building a wall between the Nam Bo and the Bac Bo. This essential task will help sanctify and protect the families and people of Nam Bo from their brother, sister, and family member enemies who live north of their border in Bac Bo. He served with the highest traditions of his Fatherland. You will be proud to know we killed * of their sons in exchange for him.

Maj. Jus One Moore, Adjutant

* Insert Body Count
(Standard Govt. Form A-1369)

7   And it came to pass that SmegMa the devout became SmegMa the skeptical, for he questioned the idiocy of wasting lives of fine young men for gurus who knew not that they knew war not.

8   And he had learned that death was the cost of doing war business.

9   And he saw High Priests whose veins were hard,

10   And he saw High Priests whose pecker was soft,

11   And he saw High Priests who could hide their own Easter eggs.

CHAPTER 4

1   The ground fog and drizzling rain with a coldness drifted in from the sea up the Chebar River and across the Aceldama terrain leaving low clouds and oozing about in the blackness;

2   And Charlie stalked about;

3   It was stark fear for the helicopter crews trying to locate wounded while having to fly at the easy shooting low altitude only split seconds away from crashing into the ground.

4   Flying in the night rain with fog was a death warrant.

5   It was a time when SnowWhite had volunteered for the night MedEvac standby.

6   A midnight call came forth summoning the helo for wounded.

7   Aceldama OutPost was under attack; the enemy would concentrate on shooting down the MedEvac helicopter to show the Marines that there was no hope for the wounded.

8   And the enemy had the landing zone zeroed-in with their mortars and were probing the lines for weaknesses.

9   The pockets of fog hid the attackers until they were into the barbed wire.

10   The wounded would die without rescue,

11   Prayers were repeated in the helplessness.

12   It was that the protection of the artillery had to cease fire when the helicopters were approaching the outpost for risk of shooting down the helo by friendly fire;

13   But when the artillery would cease, the enemy gained advantage.

14   Bac Bo wanted the Sam Bo people to learn that the principal outpost had been overrun and all killed.

15   SnowWhite instructed his wingman to stay behind on the ground, and SnowWhite with SmegMa as co-pilot flew the helo into the blackness for the short flight to Aceldama.

16   And it was that SmegMa mentally prayed as chilling fear permeated his body and perspiration trickled from around his helmet mixed in the cold rain that flickered in the air blowing in the open side-window.

17   SmegMa knew that the wingman Chase helo with StoneMan and BirdMan was turning ready to take off, to save them if they crashed, but not airborne so as to risk a midair collision in the foggy blackness.

18   And it came to be known that Aceldama was surrounded by the enemy, and there was fog covering the field of blood.

19   And SmegMa requested Aceldama to set off flares in the fog to give the helicopter a burning light for guidance as to the location of Aceldama in the pitch blackness.

20   "Oh Shit!" instantly expelled SmegMa on the intercom as three different flares, all visible within hundreds of yards of each other were set off and beamed bright lights in the drifting fog.

21   SmegMa radioed, "This is MedEvac, be advised Sir Charles is trying to get us to land in the wrong place."

22   And it came to pass that SnowWhite had the big Spooky cargo plane high above airdrop flares where the giant flares would fall and burn brightly on the ground in the enemy held valley behind Aceldama.

23   And SnowWhite flew the MedEvac helo above the bright ground lights in the fog like a snowy cluster of stars.

24   And it was that the brilliant earth bound light allowed SnowWhite to fly above the ground and not crash in the fog as long as he kept vision of the bright flares burning underneath the nose and ahead of the helo.

25   And the surrounded Marines threw illumination grenades making a long straight line on the landing zone with a landing center of the cross touch down point in the blackness.

26   And SnowWhite muttered some unintelligible words on the radio and performed the unheard of feat of landing a helicopter through the thick ground fog to the lights landing in the center of the cross.

27   The plan worked, and the wounded were rescued.

28   SmegMa was in awe; What magnificent flying talent of SnowWhite!

29   At daylight, SnowWhite and SmegMa again flew into Aceldama with HalfRight and BolTer on wing to evacuate the walking wounded and re-supply ammunition, food, and deliver the mail.

30   Whereupon, the fog had lifted after sunrise and a hundred or so enemy bodies were hanging from the barbed wire with an occasional enemy soldier lying dead well inside the perimeter.

31   It was that the enemy had failed, but there were smiles on certain dead faces.

32   "Wanna buy a pair of ears?" smiled and said the homely child man sitting on a case of rations to SmegMa and HalfRight, Twenty-five dollars unless of course you want 'em to match, one left and one right off the same gook. Get you a matched set right there," he said, pointing to a make shift table where it first appeared four soldiers were playing cards — then SmegMa and HalfRight deciphered the vision.

33   For it was the child men squad had propped up four enemy soldiers in the field chairs and had them playing poker . . .

34   "All losing hands, aren't they?" grinned the Corporal as he lit a cigarette and stuck it between the lips of one of the dead Nam Bo soldiers.

35   "Nah, don't need any," smiled SmegMa looking into the ten mile stare the front line child men got under the stress of combat, "but let me know if you get any surplus pussy," he grinned.

36   "Shucks, I can't do that, only Whore-Ma Ma San we caught we had to turn loose in three days" — he winked, "that gal fucked three guys to death, we just couldn't afford to lose any more guys to jus' plain fuckin'."

37   "I wonder if she is related to Kitty Chow?" BolTer poked at SmegMa.

38   And HalfRight turned pale, for there hanging around the neck of the young, dead enemy soldier was a necklace chain bearing a small silver cross.

39   And HalfRight shot with chill, for he saw the face of a thousand orphans of all races reared in Catholic belief only to be told to kill each other by men of darkness.

40   "What is religion?" HalfRight questioned himself.

41   "Is the Korps church a greater church than the Catholic church?" he thought.

42   HalfRight searched his perplexed soul and reeked with thought chill.

43   And it came to pass that in witnessing war SmegMa and HalfRight discovered they saw their own ignorance.

44   And SmegMa said, "Shit flows down hill."

CHAPTER 5

1   "Priority Mission," the operations officer said as he woke up sweaty SmegMa, and the fly-covered TailWind.
2   It was that mid-day heat made it impossible to sleep, but SmegMa and TailWind had flown in the dark morning hours to rescue a snake-bitten Marine.
3   "Whaz we got?" requested TailWind from SmegMa after he connected his helmet microphone.
4   "The new Bishop-general wants a priority cargo pick-up down at Holy Sea. We're to fly wing on SnowWhite."
5   "Well at least it's not a take 'n wait," said SmegMa as they taxied toward take off, "Maybe we'll get time to go to the Elephant bar," SmegMa grinned.
6   "Yeah," keyed TailWind, "some mama san will give your pecker san clap-e-osis," and there was laughter.
7   And it came to pass that a radio call came forth for SnowFlight to land and pick up two runaway Marines for transport to Holy Sea cantonment area.
8   **PEACE BE WITH YOU**, comforted SnowWhite to the two young Marines.
9   "We couldn't take it," cried out the youngest child.
10   "We're from graves registration," the other one spilled out. SnowFlight then understood.
11   And it came to pass that the young Marines explained the horrors of the constant embalming and the rows of dead brethren sometimes blasphemed by experience gathering surgeons, bro's of a man-made hell, "We just want to get our turn to get even," one of the two quietly spoke.
12   And after time they spoke from the heart of the escape by constant alcohol and the drugs sold by the corrupt Nam Bo police; but alcohol and drugs only temporarily eased the pain of their wounds to the body and soul delivered by the man made hell.
13   And the two graves registration Marines told the story of the dead body of a Bishop who had ordered his pilot down into the heat of battle killing all on board.
14   From the refrigerated slab the "death mason's" body was ceremoniously placed on a quad-four hole latrine top.
15   And the grave's grunt Marines did the shuffle with the stiff

carcass of the dead High Priest on the four holer tray to the middle of the room where they melted the wax bottom of a single candle onto the dead Bishop's forehead followed by encrusting the lit candle onto the middle of his frontal lobe.

16 And the kid Marines sang him happy birthday—a living grunt Marine's silent retribution for the Bishop's unnecessary taking of brotherly life.

17 And the pasty grave's Marines giggled and told SmegMa and TailWind he had the balls of a Bishop; then winked with both eyes.

18 And it was that there was nothing new under the sun.

CHAPTER 6

1 And it came to pass that squadron 777 with all its forty-three pilots fasted from war for it was ordered for all pilots, crews and men to take the worn helos and to leave the zone of the land of Nam Bo to get new helos on the volcanic rock called the Island of the Floating Dragon.

2 For forty days and forty nights, the escape from death by political hubris and academic warrioring sept from their daily thoughts.

3 Motorcycles and pack movement further united and bonded the gaggle of thirteen: SnowWhite, StoneMan, OverBoost, Red-Line, BirdMan, SmegMa, HalfRight, TailWind, TwoDogs, DarkMoon, ShareCrop, BurnOut, and BolTer.

4 The invasion of the temporary war escapees reeked havoc on the natives:

5 For Marine pilots were banned from the Sky Blue Officer's Club because unknown persons were accused of riding motorcycles while naked through the air-conditioned dining castle on the night of the non-war non-work day while the violins played.

6 And Navy wives were forewarned of the vast quantity of unspent chromosomes seeking inter-service transfer;

7 And SnowFlight sought escape.

8 But SnowFlight avoided the cities and the marketplaces to meditate at an isolated hillside quiet place squeezed between two volcanic rocks with a dirt floor and an obsolete ice block beer cooler.

9 And in the evolution of events, the face of the warrior god, Marine, shown round about to passersby.

10 An old man of frequent appearance and constant stare became known unto SnowFlight.

11 "To die Marine is to live forever," said DarkMoon into the sun-baked face of the old Japanese silver-gray haired hill farmer who stoically listened.

12 "Honor, Glory, and Country," spouted HalfRight.

13 "Right or wrong, Sam Bo is Mine," defended OverBoost.

14 "No Guts, No Glory," chimed in RedLine.

15 "Death before dishonor," spoke TwoDogs.

16 SnowWhite moved close in anticipation of hearing the seldom spoken words from the keeper of universal peace.

17 "What do you know about war Old Man?" queried BolTer.

18 Eerie quietness pervaded the brotherhood as the man with the sunset of life face responded, **MY PLANE WAS DESTROYED ON THE GROUND. LEI' FOUGHT ON THIS ISLAND, BUT IN THE END, THERE WAS THE TRUTH, THE EMPEROR AND HIS MINISTERS COULD NOT UNDO THEIR WAYS. INNOCENT FLESH JUMPED FROM SUICIDE CLIFF.**

19 "Then you dishonored your country, your people," verbally stabbed BirdMan.

20 **WHO ARE YOU TO SPEAK OF TRUTH AND HONOR** quickly but quietly came the old man's accented words. **EACH OF YOU HAVE PLACED HONOR BEFORE TRUTH. THE TRUTH IS YOUR KING AND HIS MINISTERS HAVE MADE A MISTAKE AND DECEIVED YOU AND YOUR PEOPLE AS THE EMPEROR DID MINE.**

21 The old man paused, then continued, **THE TRUTH IS SOL-DIERS ARE NOT ALLOWED TO THINK THE TRUTH, ONLY TO BE THE INSTRUMENTS TO INFLICT DEATH ON OTHER SOLDIERS WHO ARE NOT ALLOWED TO THINK THE TRUTH. THE TRUTH IS YOU WILL NOT SPEAK THE TRUTH FOR TO DO SO WOULD RISK DISHONOR.**

22 There was an oriental stare maintained from the old man's face followed with a fatherly sternness in his eyes for he had frightened the Marines with words, not bullets.

23 "But you were a behind the lines pilot who had no plane--how can you speak of the Nam Bo war," speared BolTer at the small leathery figure who had scared him.

24   DO YOU KILL THE CHILDREN SO THE WORLD WILL BE A SAFE PLACE FOR CHILDREN TO LIVE? came the accented reply with quickness, and a confidence that instant retaliation was not on the faces of these twelve and the one that sparkles.

25   And it came to pass that the messenger was accepted kindly into SnowFlight — his spirit of truth frightened yet comforted the uncontrollable dozen; but to the mismatched gaggle of the twelve wild geese pilots, there was an obvious electricity between SnowWhite and the old man of unending sight.

26   And SnowPack adopted Lei', as he became known, for the group felt in need of bondage of a wise man from the past.

CHAPTER 7

1   "Oriental women have pussies that are sideways," SmegMa explained to two unsuspecting FNG's (fuckin' new guys) watching the helo crews decorate the big room of the spacious top floor of the disrepaired hotel,

2   As preparations were underway for the Yellow Breasted Rack Thrasher Pig-Out Ball.

3   A grand piano was positioned; the flowers were being placed on the fresh linen table cloths;

4   The microphones were being tested, and Flight Sergeant Max "The Snake" was being tutored by Vicar-major DingleBerry in the rehearsal of the program to determine by popular vote the ugliest woman presented to the glorious Ball.

5   Monies from the Nam Bo cola fund made the extraordinary pig party possible.

6   Uncommon whores of uncommon talents were employed to titillate the common soldier.

7   The troops combed the island seeking out the ugliest of them all in order to win the big money prize — half to the escort and half to the female winning the title of "Miss Pig."

8   And it came to pass the Ball began and the Master of Ceremonies commenced the entertainment.

9   A comedian who had been rejected told vile jokes while much alcohol flowed freely;

10   And then the "Pig-Out" award challenge commenced.

11   It was that each contestant was paraded by escort to center stage.

12   One Corporal escort had the local tailor make him a tuxedo of first quality out of camouflage cloth—complete with a jungle green bow tie and matching dark green silk cumber bun. The crowd roared with applause at his appearance.

13   And he announced he was now ready to formally sip tea with Sir Charles.

14   Laughter proliferated with the introduction and the parade of the unbeauties.

15   Each non-English speaking ugly had been carefully coached to respond in Pidgin English to deplorable questions: "Would you rather fuck a Green Beret or a Donkey?" "Do hippies make you constipated?" and, "How many calories are there in seminal fluid?"

16   Decadent humor was a temporary substitute designed only to momentarily forget the pains of the visions of pieces of bodies of the immediate past and of the ills to come.

17   And there were flashes and flickers of the faces of comrades killed, or wounded;

18   And there was much need to vacuum out with alcohol and deep laughter the mental snakes.

19   And the ugliest of the ugly was chosen;

20   And her four-foot frame with sparse orange hair paraded down the rampway with roses and a queen's crown in winning fashion;

21   And the grand piano played, and the Corporal sang bawdy words to the tune of an institutional song.

22   And the unprintable words from the face of the beast flowed forth.

23   But it was an out.

CHAPTER 8

1   Seven sex profits smiled upon SmegMa, and SmegMa smiled much money upon them—it was a dream, seven women for seven days and at least seven times in one day—good ole triple seven.

2   Paradise found, he thought as he peered at the deep blue sea from the porch of the isolated native grass house hidden in a small cove and rented to island honeymooners.

3   And only nakedness shown round about and much fucking did occur.

4   And it came to pass on the Island of the Floating Dragon that SmegMa violated the laws of Georgia, Pennsylvania, Missouri, Mississippi, and Louisiana, among others, with seven women singularly, and sometimes simultaneously, resulting in sunburn on untanned skin.

5   On the seventh day SmegMa requested mercy, for he was deplete in body and soul, and his pecker was sunburned, chafed and marathon exercised.

6   And it came to pass that Bones Baker laughed. "Red on the head like the head of a dog's dick," he laughed again seeing the sunburn penis, "keep this ointment, . . . and your pecker on ice." Doc laughed again.

7   And SmegMa fasted from sex.

CHAPTER 9

1   The short, native housekeeping girl entered SmegMa's presence with intent to tidy the room — mixed pidgin was exchanged by SmegMa trying to communicate solicitation, and she responded "no" to sexual advances but allowed the advances to progress.

2   And it came to pass that the sexually starved Marine overcame the resistance barrier and copulated with the foreign maid.

3   And it was as the rhythm began, SmegMa's excitement heightened at the non-English moaning, groaning, and bucking of his small partner — a woman like this he had never satisfied this way before.

4   His thrusts became harder, deeper, and faster only exceeded by her tempo . . . the explosion came with a bucking orgasm of two excited bodies intertwined, a magnificent woman he thought with each spasmic jolt.

5   SmegMa withdrew to look down in surprise at the continual bucking, now rhythmically gyrating female whose eyes were rolled back and whose body continued to flow with rhythmic shakes — "Mayday," he yelled, "I've killed her"; he ran naked into the hallway yelling for help.

6   Other maids came running — one shouting Pidgin.

7   One maid ran in with an ammonia capsule and spoon.

8   And they revived the naked girl in SmegMa's bed with the then

towel-wearing pilot staring on watching the process of placing the spoon in her mouth and shaking her to reality with ammonia at her nose.

9 "Doctor say she no fuck — KiKo epileptic," yelled the head house mouse, "she wait and wait, soon she have to fuck, but she go crazy."

10 SmegMa's ego faded; he had not driven a woman wild, he had been out-performed by epilepsy.

CHAPTER 10

1 "You can't hypnotize me," dictated the tall, confident sky blue jet pilot who wandered in the bar among the Dog Drivers.

2 "Doc SmegMa can hypnotize you in less than ten minutes," explained DarkMoon about the abilities of the near psychologist turned Marine pilot.

3 And it came to pass in the bar of the fancy Navy officer's club elegantly constructed from hidden funds that a wager ensued in the amount of one keg of beer.

4 The bet was simple: The young stud jet pilot would lie on the floor in the middle of the room, have a cold cloth placed over his closed eyes, and would be hypnotized within ten minutes, and would be told under trance that he could not sit up. If he could sit up, he would win; if he could not sit up (no person could hold him down), then he would buy the Marine pilots a keg of beer. Money was held by the bartender.

5 And it came to pass that OverBoost pulled the cord from the music box, and the numerous onlookers circled the pilot lying in the middle of the floor,

6 Then it was that Doc SmegMa began to hypnotize by dipping and squeezing the water from a common bar rag and placing it over the eyes of the then-confident sky blue pilot.

7 "You are very relaxed," commenced SmegMa instructing the non-responsive mind of the procedure to follow.

8 Doc SmegMa rambled with quiet phrases, "Your toes are going to sleep, your ankles are beginning to mush, your whole body seeks a deep, deep sleep."

9 "You are now asleep," he announced in the presence of the bar congregation, "When I count to three, you will open your eyes but you will not be able to sit up," he instructed the prone pilot.

10   DarkMoon, standing quietly nearby, unzipped his flight suit bearing his naked dark moon butt, then squatted, cheeks-spread with his hands so as to place his rectum only inches above the nose of the floor bound pilot.

11   Then slowly, Doc SmegMa removed the bar rag cover from the closed eyes of the confident pilot and stated, "Three, Two, One, now you can open your eyes but you won't be able to sit up."

12   And the room broke into laughter as the open-eyed, now-dismayed pilot screamed, "You dirty bastards! There ain't no way I'm gonna sit up," as he stared eyeball to the black cheeks and anus of DarkMoon.

13   A new keg of beer was tapped, but the crowd waited for the next victim of "Doc SmegMa's beer making machine."

14   And it came to pass that the Navy Bishop Commander became irate for he inquired round about to the tale of a black man exposing himself in the Club.

15   But he could not ban Marine pilots from their beer chapel for they were of the congregation.

CHAPTER 11

1   SmegMa led SnowPack through the streets and gates of alcoholic idolatry to view hard-core survival of a captured race.

2   And it came to pass that SmegMa led the ten, without Injun or SnowWhite, into the valley called sin alley and a place called the Texas Bar with a reeking urinal labeled "The Ranch."

3   And there known to SmegMa, but not SnowPack, was a beautiful transvestite of the thin and lanky persuasion who performed on stage with the visual display of the best case study of how to present a female appearing body from hormonal injections rendering this transsexual man to be indistinguishable from a seductive, blonde femme fatale, except for the coal black crew-cut revealed only after removal of the dancer's blonde wig.

4   But the big Indian attended not, and knew not of the transvestite.

5   And the next night it came to pass that the big Indian came to the bar with the other pilots, and he fell in love at the singing and dancing of Minnie-Hand-Jobs, the sarcastic name SmegMa gave this beautiful dancer.

6   "I'll buy her for you," smiled the plotting SmegMa to the drunken Indian as the imperial blonde commenced her (his) elegant bump and grind gyrations on the stage in front of the reservation-seeking red man.

7   And SmegMa gave the smiling perfume man who owned the bar the fee for the Indian to have the pleasures of such magnificent creature;

8   And Injun believed SmegMa had bought the girl for his Indian friend.

9   And the big Indian smiled and yelled an Osage war-hoop as he jumped to the stage joining in the dancing performance of Minnie-Hand-Jobs with Injun dancing in tribal fashion around with the twitching blonde body avoiding the big Indian in a joint performance.

10   And it came to pass that there was much laughter for many were pleased watching the dancing antics of the screaming Indian and his teary eyed friends who were cheering the drunk Osage warrior in his temporary ecstasy.

11   And it came to pass that the music ceased, and the dynamic blonde bowed to the Indian and his audience while removing the wig at the bottom of the bow revealing for the first time to the cheshire cat smiling Indian the coal-black crew cut of his now discovered to be male dancing partner.

12   And the angry big Indian screamed obscenities at SmegMa, jumped from the stage, and ran out of the den of iniquity to return to the safety of isolated Marinedom.

13   And much hoot went round about bantering an Indian and a squaw called Minnie-Hand-Jobs.

CHAPTER 12

1   And it came to pass that SmegMa taught the non-English speaking massage queen to hum the Marine Korps hymn while performing fellatio.

2   And she became known round about as "November 10."

3   And SmegMa bragged about staying power to the third stanza, last verse.

4   And others bragged about holding off until "the Land, Air and Sea."

CHAPTER 13

1   And one among 777 had not been enriched by the covenant of circumcision, and was laid bare at the pier side hospital ship.
2   Now it came to pass that SmegMa, in sympathy for the sexually afflicted, delivered to the freshly circumcised pilot thought provoking magazines of an exciting sexual nature.
3   "You dumb bastard," screamed the irate Bones Baker physician of men to the smirking SmegMa, "If he had got a hard-on, he would have bled to death, you could have killed him."
4   And the smirking SmegMa departed.

CHAPTER 14

1   The drunken Indian grinned, then chortled followed by a burst of outright prankish laughter.
2   The Osage engineer removed the light bulbs and disconnected the light switches in the small military quarters.
3   And SmegMa's room was filled from wall to wall and floor to ceiling with inflated condoms to where the door had to be carefully closed so as not to burst the guardian balloons of sexual use.
4   And it came to pass that the big Indian, the teary-eyed wop, and the giggling DarkMoon were filled with joy and great expectations.
5   And SnowPack held its happy hour and gave great cause for SmegMa to become drunk, all to the pleasure of the waiting eleven.
6   And when the time was ripe, and SmegMa had been lavishly adorned with many lovers medals with numerous sex clusters, the magnificent eleven carried the knee drunk SmegMa to his rubber filled room shoving him into instant warfare.
7   Da, da, da! Boom! Pop, pop! Bang, bang! exploded the condoms to a drunken mind instantly swept back into live fire combat.
8   SmegMa hallucinated and screamed, "Incoming," amidst the bangs and pops not hearing the convulsing laughter of SnowPack with the big Indian doubled up on the floor spurting out an Osage horselaugh in choking peals of laughter.
9   And the maids came in the morning to find underneath several

hundred air-filled condoms the passed-out body of the drunken chopper pilot strewn among many broken rubbers.

CHAPTER 15

1   The Korps called 777 out of the night back into the darkness from its forty day stay to come unto the congregation of war.
2   And the Korps came to bring sacrifice of its flocks in the names of honor and duty sanctified by the unholy and unwashed in the fat of the land.
3   It came to pass that the deity generals allowed to be hid from the eyes of the congregational people the sins through ignorance and profit the academic clerics and the other gnomes resulting in the sacrifice of the child men Marines.
4   The elders of the congregational people began to question the King and his ministers,
5   And elements of the masses of the congregation were sermonized by the washed word.
6   But the deity High Priests allowed the innocent of the congregation flock to be sacrificed at altars.
7   And the people became sickened.

CHAPTER 16

1   And the words of Jonah, Amos, Hosea, Obadiah, Joel, Isaiah, Micah, Nahum, Habakkuk, Zephaniah, Jeremiah, Ezekiel, Daniel, Haggai, Zechariah, Malachi went unobserved by the King, his divinities, his chief priests, and the numerous vicars seeking self-preservation and presumption.
2   And SnowWhite said unto SnowFlight: **THIS WAR HAS A FALSE TONGUE.**

CHAPTER 17

1   And SnowFlight returned to Nam Bo from the Island of the Floating Dragon to be immersed in the horrors of self-created human hell on earth.
2   For forty days and forty nights Triple Seven had fasted from

the table of war and the mandates of the vicar clergy who knew not the true motives of the King and the money gnomes, but blindly enslaved the child men Marines to the demon of attrition.
3   And it came to pass that the countenance of SnowFlight was cast against the demons of darkness.

CHAPTER 18

1   "Did you ever eat any pussy?" inquired SmegMa in retaliation for the blindness of the already retreating Chaplain DickHead.
2   "Woe unto you . . . you champion of harlots," whined the snake-handling escapee who had been caught lusting through SmegMa's library.
3   "Bet you never even ever fucked a chicken," pursued SmegMa at the caught holier-than-thou who was lusting half-way around the world from his six children and smiling wife who worshipped the absence of the erection of this man of the uncertain cloth.
4   "A whip for the horse, a bridle for the ass, and a rod for the fool's back," yelled the disappearing religious regulation of a preacher.

CHAPTER 19

1   And it came to pass that the zealous SmegMa blasphemed the god, Marine Korps, and asketh of SnowWhite all those things godly and ungodly of a mind distraught at the deceit of his false god, his King, and those entrusted but who wasted the lives of the defenseless young meat Marines.
2   SnowWhite answered and said unto him,
3   WHAT SNOWWHITE HAS DONE TO YOU?
4   SNOWWHITE HAS GIVEN YOU AN EXAMPLE,
5   GREATER LOVE HATH NO MAN THAN THIS, THAT A MAN LAY DOWN HIS LIFE FOR HIS FRIENDS.
6   IT IS A TIME OF BLINDNESS.
7   IT IS A TIME OF FOOLHARDY ENCAMPED AMONG SELF-PRESERVATION CLERICS.
8   SANCTIFY THE TRUTH;
9   TELL OTHERS SO THAT YOUNG MEN SHALL NOT BE

SACRIFICED; SO THAT CHILD MEN SHALL NOT BE CAST TO DUST BY CASH.
10   THE GOOD PEOPLE ARE THE PRIZE.
11   THE KING USES HIS POWER TO HIDE HIS WAYS.
12   FOLLOW YOUR HEART AND WITNESS TRUTH.
13   IN THESE PRINCIPLES HIGH PRIESTS HAVE FAILED, FOR THEY ARE TRAINED TO THINK THE WAY OF WARFARE AND NO OTHER;
14   FOR THE HIGH PRIESTS ARE NOT ALLOWED BY THE LAW TO TELL THE TRUTH AND KEEP THEIR PRIESTSHIP;
15   FOR THEY MUST GIVE UP THEIR VESTMENTS TO EXPOSE THE TRUTH.
16   WE ARE IN THE MIDST OF UNWISE THINKERS AND WARFARE WHOREDOM RENDERING THE CHILD MEN VICTIMS OF A RUNAWAY POCKETBOOK HARNESSED TO PIECES OF SILVER.
17   And SmegMa became sore afraid, for he saw the young Marines who smote their leaders, and he now understood.
18   And the rumors were round about that another Death Mason had met the fate he dispensed so coldly.

CHAPTER 20

1   And unknown names of the days disappeared into unknown weeks and unknown months without hope, and much blindness was prevalent.
2   And it came to pass that SmegMa climbed down the side of the running helicopter leaving the new young pilot at the controls so that SmegMa could pee in the reported safe jungle landing zone.
3   Shortly after unzipping the heavy gauge zipper of SmegMa's flight suit and upon his commencing relief, enemy snipers opened fire towards the helicopter. SmegMa screamed as he zipped his fly as he ran back and climbed up and unto the pilot's seat.
4   "He's hit, SmegMa's hit," yelled the scared, young inexperienced pilot on the radio as he added power flying the helo out of the zone with the screaming SmegMa hanging half-in and half-out of the flying helicopter.
5   "Emergency, Emergency," continued the frightened new co-

pilot, having to fly so as not to throw SmegMa from his hanging position halfway in the pilot's cabin door.

6   And it came to pass that the screaming SmegMa crawled inside the flying helo yelling with great pain about his wound.

7   And the scared co-pilot landed the helo at the hospital pad where the medics littered SmegMa with much foreskin zipped into the flight suit zipper, but without any bullet wound.

8   And in the course of events Vicar-major DingleBerry presented SmegMa at the next happy hour with the first "purple pecker" award, a glistening phallic medal on a purple ribbon.

9   And much hoot went round about concerning a pilot with a frilly dilly.

CHAPTER 21

1   And SmegMa dreamed he ought to give the more earnest heed to the things which he had heard, lest at any time he should let them slip.

2   For if the word spoken by the victim Marines was steadfast, and if every transgression and disobedience received a just recompense of reward,

3   How shall the culprits who nourish their egos on the souls of others escape?

4   How shall the Herrods of Wall Street receive justice for capturing pieces of silver in exchange for the 1369 young flesh at the price of war profiteering?

5   And it came to pass that SmegMa awoke from the nightmare of watching the Egg Beater helicopter come apart in midair slinging pieces of metal blades and fellow Marines out into the open sky three thousand feet above the earth to fall to their death.

6   And SmegMa awoke SnowWhite seeking an answer of who to smote those for such gross injustice.

7   And ShowWhite said, **GOD UNITES, SATAN DIVIDES.**

8   And SmegMa wondered what the fuck SnowWhite had said.

9   And the pilots were powerless to stop a helo design defect,

10   But the Egg Beater pilots kept flying, for not to fly would render unbearable thoughts to the child men Marines abandoned to die in the wilderness.

11   Marines do not abandon Marines.

12   And their deaths were reduced to simple cold statistics.

13   And the mothers knew not their sons were being given to Molech.

CHAPTER 22

1   And SmegMa temporarily resided at Tru Lai City for he was ordered to chauffeur the High Priests from the Holy Sea, and SmegMa sent a message to SnowFlight.
2   Greetings: SmegMa, Servant of the Korps and of the SnowFlight, to the twelve which are scattered, from the Holy Sea Headquarters, I send yea hoos.
3   My brethren, count it all joy that ye not fall into the temptation of the self-preservation society;
4   Knowing this, that the trying of your faith in your fellow Marine worketh patience.
5   But let patience have her perfect work, that you may be perfect and entire, wanting nothing.
6   A double-minded man is unstable in all his ways.
7   Let the Marine brother of low degree shame in that he is known:
8   But the career ticket-puncher, in that he is made low: because he shall pass away.
9   And be it known to you that the High Priests of the tabernacle of the Holy Sea drinketh SmegMa waste water, for SmegMa pisseth in their water barrel.

CHAPTER 23

1   SmegMa got them in the mail—stick on plastic bullet holes that faked a picture of a clean bullet hole when stuck on glass.
2   SmegMa carefully placed a real-looking plastic bullet hole on the clear visor lens of his flying helmet.
3   Then the visor lens was hidden from view except when he pulled the lens down from the top visor cover over his face.
4   And it came to pass that SmegMa was flying with Topsy-Turvy as his co-pilot, and Vicar-major Topsy-Turvy, a freshly converted jet pilot into helos, resented the whole world, for it was a disease to have to fly helos.

5   And it was a real combat flight; and he detested having to fly co-pilot and with the likes of SmegMa.

6   But it was just another flight to SmegMa, and he took pleasure in tormenting the career priest blinded by obedience in the face of overwhelming logic to the contrary.

7   And it came to pass that a jet pilot missed his target with the friendly bomb;

8   And the defective bomb landed into the Marine unit killing and wounding many child men Marines.

9   "MedEvac going in," confirmed SmegMa on the radio diving in a spiral from the sky down to the green below while ignoring the co-pilot and instructing the mere passenger, Topsy-Turvy, to monitor the radios.

10   And in the heat of death by mistake and defect, the enemy attacked part of the Marine unit capturing the benefit of their already having been bombed by their own jet plane.

11   And the wounded were loaded aboard in spite of the occasional bullets whizzing by, and SmegMa artfully flew the helo packed with wounded to the field hospital quickly returning for the second load.

12   But the enemy had since silenced, and there were left only sight-seeing investigative clerics who tormented Marines at work.

13   And as they prepared to depart, the perimeter Marines fired their machine guns at an enemy area and SmegMa pulled his clear visor down with the fake bullet hole and slumped in his seat, faking death, while Topsy-Turvy was looking the other way.

14   And it came to be that Topsy-Turvy turned and saw the slumped SmegMa with a bullet hole in his face and screamed on the radio, "He's hit, he's hit, the pilot's hit."

15   And Topsy-Turvy tried to immediately take off but SmegMa had cleverly kept his knee over the controls and held the throttle closed.

16   And Topsy-Turvy panicked, knowing he would die as a low-life helo pilot.

17   And SmegMa laughed over the intercom at the major screaming over the wrong radio for a medic, for he was the MedEvac helo and had a medic on board.

18   And the major screamed seeing the dead body of SmegMa come to life before his eyes, and then became furious at having been the brunt of the joke.

19   And the Vicar-major complained to Poncho Pilot about the

antics of SmegMa, and Poncho Pilot grinned at seeing the field grade careerist having gotten years of pay without risk only to learn as a helo pilot he would earn it in just a few minutes.

CHAPTER 24

1   SmegMa's hunger for a woman, any woman, left his mind in the war zone without sense of reality.

2   And it came to pass that the only available place for the sexual encounter with the Nam Bo kitchen worker was standing-up in the privy, a place in the noon day sun of great stench, and of a wretched aroma of driving force.

3   And it came to pass that the mighty SmegMa succumbed to meeting the willing woman in the privy to dampen addiction in control of his body, for his mind knew not.

4   And DarkMoon opened the door of the privy only to find the crazed and copulating SmegMa entranced in the opium of a Nam Bo woman;

5   But in the land of Nam Bo the whores of the mind had cast many snakes into the heads of the innocent children of war among the stink of greed, arrogance, and vanity.

6   And DarkMoon laughed and said, "I knew a stiff dick had no conscience, but now I know it doesn't have a nose either."

CHAPTER 25

1   "I had a dream," said the voice emitted from the thin face with black eyelids surrounding pearly white eyeballs emitting the ten-mile stare in a two feet conversation.

2   "And what was your dream," understandingly asked Doc SmegMa.

3   "I dreamed that all the shitters were eight feet long with a four-holer lid, and after I wiped my ass and looked down, inside was a dead body of a High Priest who betrayed us. And around the hill side there were numerous four-holers with the bodies of those others who had betrayed us. And there was a long line of men waiting for hours just to take a dump on the King of Cash, and the Prince of Money;" and the kid Marine that had become seasoned in useless death asked, "What does it mean?"

4   "How long you been in country?" asked SmegMa.
5   And it became known that the kid Marine knew not any vision of time, and knew not anything but taking orders, for he had become numb of soul and absent of mind.
6   And Doc SmegMa screamed at the Vicar-major who laughed at learning that the glorious church of the Marine Korps had not sent the kid Marine home at the end of his tour of duty for the child man Marine asked not, and those who ask not, get not.
7   And it came to pass that the drafted young man's cup had runneth over for he had endured the catechisms of the holy church, and his body would survive because Doc SmegMa interfered with the Vicar-major indentured with career job opportunity by invoking threat of papal notification, and exposure if the blind mind gave not.
8   But in the land of Nam Bo the emaciated body of the rescued kid Marine also transported home a mind ravaged by animal survival and weakened by disbelief in the King of Cash, and the Fatherland, but who also knew that the wasting of human life without just cause was acceptable, for such was a belief in the land of Sam Bo.

CHAPTER 26

1   And it came to pass that the High Priests, the careerists, the ticket punchers, and the blind-divine were perplexed at this SnowWhite;
2   For SnowWhite had done no wrong and desired no medals, no promotions, no honorable mentions, no letters of commendation, no career advancement, no personnel jacket stuffing, and no special recognition.
3   And it was that the High Church protected the image of the Korps at the expense of a few good Marines.
4   And it was that exhaustive late nights were spent to window dress the statistics and to camouflage the truth.
5   And self-preservation of the Korps church was their altar.
6   And ghosts haunted them of the Army's efforts to close the church of the Marine Korps.
7   But the demons puked forth thoughts for the blind divine.
8   "So dau lau Valley," grinned the Curate-colonel, "He's good, he's the best — let's send him into So dau lau Valley."

9   Such was a silent judgment of sending a designated Marine pilot in a sure-death rescue raid into a known enemy camp high in the mountains.

10   And the High Church sent forth orders for SnowWhite.

11   But Poncho Pilot responded to the high priest's request that SnowWhite be scheduled to fly to the So dau lau Valley by saying, "SnowWhite has done no wrong."

12   Poncho Pilot accepted destiny, and ordered SnowWhite to fly the mission.

The Word According to HALFRIGHT

(Make Sound and Timely Decisions)

CHAPTER 1

1   The non-denominational baby was placed in the traditional basket and left at the convent door.

2   The Nuns named him "Matthew," a gift from God.

3   And it came to pass that no one would adopt the tan and hairy Matty Wright, so that he aged in the Catholic orphanage until he was allowed from parochial school to join the Korps church.

4   "The Korps takes care of its own," bellowed the Senior Drill Instructor loudly in the training barracks.

5   "For you few maggots that can pass the test," he continued, "the Korps will send you to learn how to work on our beloved Korps' aircraft, the finest killing machines in the world."

6   Private Matt Wright passed the test, completed the aircraft engines course, and finished two years of college.

7   Staff Sergeant Wright applied and was accepted for the cadet flight training program, and in eighteen months, he completed flight school receiving his wings of gold.

8   Pilot Wright's first assignment was to fly F4-U Corsair fighter aircraft, the ones left over from a police action called Korea.

9   Classmates that could not hack it were assigned to fly helicopters, the home of second rate pilots.

10   Matthew L. Wright worshipped the Korps — he bought a new convertible and had it painted olive green.

11   Matthew L. Wright excelled and paid homage and tribute to the Korps, and was duly promoted.

161

12   To criticize his Korps was blasphemy.
13   The Korps daily guided Matty Wright, and he lived for the Korps.
14   Matthew L. Wright was a lean, mean, green, older fighting machine.
15   "There is no way my beloved Korps would do that to me," were the mental screams passing through his brain as he read the orders to report for six weeks transition training to learn how to fly helicopters on route to 7th Wing in the land of Nam Bo.
16   And thus it came to pass that the high church inflicted helo disease on one of its cherished children.

CHAPTER 2

1   It was in Sam Bo that its leaders who gained their power from the people separated the philosophies of the leaders from the firmament of the people.
2   And the gods of the East, and the gods of the West watched with the patience of Sun Tzu as the Political Almighty and the Divinities of Defense flatulently made the shedding of life commercially efficient and politically inexpedient.
3   In those days came Hopper Honey, teaching in Tekoa Province in the Nam Bo wilderness,
4   And saying disrespectful things about the Korps, for many of its field grade priests were skilled in scripture and verse but without knowledge — for actual aerial combat was the pilot's penultimate university of war.
5   And knowledge of Hopper Honey spread about, and many career field grade priests were solicitous to be baptized by his holy touch and his permeating ease in flying a helicopter.
6   "If you'll pay attention, Sir," he would sermonize, "your fat ass will get to go back to a vinyl seat instead of a vinyl body bag."
7   But when he saw the many career blind come to his aerial baptism, he said unto them,
8   "O generation of desk pilots and jet jocks ruthlessly shanghaied into combat helo flying because of the critical shortage, didn't you know you bargained for the wrath to come?"
9   "Repent!" Hopper Honey would say, . . . and grin.
10   "You can't hide behind senior rank and the Uniform Code of

Military Justice to keep your varicose ass from getting shot at — be one of us."

11 Hopper Honey would piss them off, but they would learn helicopter combat flying scripture, and verse.

12 And it came to pass that Hopper Honey was looked upon with disgust and disdain by those who suffered his words,

13 But to his fellow Marines in the trenches and jungles, he taught the sources of aerial salvation in time of need.

14 It was that Hopper Honey and those who followed his teachings were called "Honey do's,"

15 And Hopper taught pilots to fast from the book sermons of the High Church of the Korps,

16 For such teachings were from Korps preachers who knew not aerial combat, and the flying instructions were only desk scripture.

17 And Hopper Honey also blasphemed the keepers of the High Church, for the keys to the church of the Marine Korps were disbursed unchecked unto the hands of the academic demons who treated loss of flesh as a trial and error business judgment.

18 Then it happened, near the river Perfume in the land of Nam Bo, that SnowWhite came to fly with Hopper Honey.

19 But Hopper Honey refused, saying that it was SnowWhite who was the teacher.

20 And SnowWhite answering said to Hopper Honey, **START YOUR ENGINE: IT BECOMES US TO FULFILL THAT WHICH IS WRITTEN.**

21 And the heavens were opened,

22 And Hopper Honey baptized SnowWhite into aerial flying.

23 And it was also that there was an uncommon bond between Hopper Honey and SnowWhite.

24 And it came to pass that Hopper Honey was confined to preach flying in the parish of the High Priest called Castle at the fortress of Machaerus,

25 And it was that Hopper Honey was cast into the prison of having to fly the defective Egg Beater helicopter, for the big twin rotor helo came apart in the air killing flesh and spewing out body and metal into the air to race in death's fall to the earth.

CHAPTER 3

1   StoneMan looked out into overcast blackness of night and thought of the seemingly never ending monsoon rain.

2   No one would believe the coldness of tropical Nam Bo, but the cold moisture captured every crevice.

3   "Why me Lord", he whispered openly not to be heard but to let a little exasperation escape, "Why the children Marines? . . . ?"

4   "Have the poor been the meat soldier victims of past wars?" he nodded to himself.

5   "Please Lord, give me the ornament of a meek and quiet spirit," he salved his soul.

6   Now as he walked by, SnowWhite saw StoneMan and Bird-Man fearfully anticipating having to cast their night MedEvac helo into the black sky to rescue from the jaws of death some flesh at death's risk.

7   And SnowWhite grinned, and said unto them, **FEAR NOT FOR YOU ARE THE BEST. COME SUP WITH ME.**

8   And as they followed in the chilling monsoon rain and darkness on the way to the club, they came upon OverBoost, Lay-major Wright, and Redline looking out into the dripping rain, and SnowWhite called unto them to gaggle-up, and they did follow.

9   And StoneMan, BirdMan, OverBoost, Lay-major Wright and Redline were astonished at what SnowWhite said and his doctrine, for he spoke as one who was in authority, but he also spoke blasphemy;

10   Not against his beliefs, but against the High Priests who were sanctifying the Divinity of Defense, in the name of self-preservation of the Korps, and statistical whoredom;

11   And against score keeping in the deadly game of inter-service rivalry at the expense of child men flesh.

12   SnowWhite spoke harshly at a separate race, the career priest.

13   And SnowWhite said about the war in the land of Nam Bo: **PROFITS FUEL WAR.**

CHAPTER 4

1 And it came to pass that SnowWhite answered field deities with truth's in which they liked not;

2 But as SnowWhite passed by Lay-major Wright sitting in flight operations, he said unto him, **COME FLY WITH SNOWWHITE.**

3 And lay-major Wright arose and joined SnowWhite.

4 And SnowWhite called him "HalfRight," for it was known round about that no major was all right.

5 And it came to pass that SnowWhite and the gaggle of the special twelve pilots came to be known as SnowFlight,

6 And they ate and drank with the grunt Marine friends and other lesser beings in the eyes of the career minded indoctrinated.

7 And the shanghaied child men saw SnowFlight as a hope;

8 And SnowFlight became them, and they loved the aerial emissaries who shared their victimness of an unholy war, for SnowFlight landed among them in the heat of battle when others would not.

9 And the child men made SnowWhite an honorary Corporal and pinned chevrons on his flight suit in an emotional ceremony making him one of them.

10 And when the priest careerists became aware, they were of jealous heart.

11 And when SnowWhite heard such questions, he said, **LOOK OUT FOR THE WELFARE OF YOUR MEN.**

CHAPTER 5

1 It was the nature of things that places of sacrifice, or the times of sacrifice to the god, The Korps, were given names;

2 And one such name was Operation Molech, for the Prince of Money opined that the enemy must be driven from his homeland in a narrow strip of earth from which he had lived from the age of all time.

3 And it was that the poor peasant people who lived there fought only the war for survival for their meager existence came from the gifts of the earth;

4   But the demons of death grinned for such places became "free fire zones," "targets of cause," and "suspected enemy activity;"
5   And HalfRight screamed inside with agony but made noise not as he witnessed the maimed and wounded innocent children of the peasant villagers brought to the helicopter from the big, white Catholic Church rising majestically, yet strangely, as the only building where the jungle and the rice farmlands met by the river Chebar.
6   And as he watched a spirit took him up in vision for he could see the horrors of dismembered bodies not;
7   And the vision came to him that the battles were of the forces of evil unleashed from man's wickedness for the enemy was evil itself and evil lurked about from those who profited in this fine little war.
8   And in the vision the words came to him, "And the prince that is among them shall bear upon his shoulder in the twilight, and shall go forth: they shall dig through the wall to carry out thereby: he shall cover his face, that he see not the ground with his eyes."
9   And HalfRight added power lifting the big green helo skyward and the MedEvac chase helo rose majestically alongside with the many wounded souls inside to be taken to the Nam Bo hospital.
10   And there at the church steps was the small human praying frame of the Nam Bo priest of the Catholic Church wrought in prayer seeking God's protection from the awesome firepower, the bombs, and the destruction inflicted by the evil Sam Bo war power fulfilling inhumane policy on a white church in the jungles of the mind.
11   And there were visions of the awesome $800.00 shells, the $4,000.00 bombs, and the thousands of twenty-five cent bullets which had been expended with ruthless economic efficiency;
12   For the soldiers of war sought survival;
13   And the child men eliminated doubt with firepower killing all who may be the imaginary enemy, regardless of age, sex, or religion.
14   And there were visions that the soldiers captive to a war not of their liking sought retribution.
15   And HalfRight was ill that the protectorate High Priests sworn by catechisms to covet the child men congregation rebelled not from the open war profiteering of the King of Cash, and the Prince of Money's whoregregation.
16   And the High Priests left the devout Marines innocent vic-

tims to dictates of political lay leaders unable to formulate what justified such a sacrifice.

17　And HalfRight sought solace with SnowWhite who saith, CHILD MEN ARE BEING MANAGED TO DEATH.

18　And HalfRight was afraid, for who is this man SnowWhite that had read his vision?

19　And HalfRight suffered great pain at seeing his Fatherland as the instrument of inflicting death and great pain on the Catholic children of Nam Bo.

20　"Who is the enemy?" HalfRight kept asking himself this tormenting question over and over.

21　And "we are the enemy" kept flickering through HalfRight's mind as the recurring vision came forth of the Catholic priest praying to God to protect the people from this Sam Bo enemy.

22　It was that HalfRight suffered great pain, for how could such wonderful people issue forth death and horror on the innocent, tiny, tan people.

23　But he was perplexed also, for the war ate child men brothers.

CHAPTER 6

1　It came to pass that the happen-chance welfare of the expendable child men was acceptable to the King.

2　And the shortages of bombs, pilots, and support strained, stressed, and at times killed a few good Marines.

3　And defective weapons, and defective helicopters, killed a few more good Marines.

4　And it became obvious that the High Priests liked not the ways of the King; But Vicar, Curate, Bishop, and Cardinal priests want to be a Pope, be he the biggest or smallest Pope.

5　And SnowWhite openly blasphemed the conscience for he would poke, WAR IS GOOD BUSINESS, INVEST YOUR SON.

6　And the high clergy priests would excuse themselves from loyalty for they witnessed the money humming of war and hid the King's war profits from their eyes.

7　And SnowWhite said, CAREER PRIESTS HAVE A SELF-PRESERVATION SOCIETY.

8　And SnowWhite repeated his words to the High Priest colonel sent to inquire about the blasphemy of this man, SnowWhite.

9   And SnowWhite answered his questions, saying, **CHILD MEN ARE DYING BECAUSE THE KORPS IS NOT A LAND ARMY.**
10   The livid High Priest colonel waned in the presence of this magnificent young pilot whose record and ability were matchless,
11   But who quaked forth publicly the fundamental flaws and open raw nerves which would cause the Marine Korps to diminish in the ever watchful eyes of the enemy, the Army.
12   **LOOK AFTER THE WELFARE OF YOUR BROTHERS,** said SnowWhite to the red-faced career priest.
13   **SPEAK THE TRUTH.**
14   **HIDE NOT BY SILENCE . . .**
15   **. . . HIDE NOT WAR FOR PROFIT, OR PROFIT BY WAR.**
16   And it came to pass that it was recognized that SnowWhite spoke the truth,
17   But Korps' clergy could not find one among them who would blaspheme the Political Almighty, for to do so against the King of Cash was career death,
18   And not one Pope, Cardinal, or Bishop general would forsake his career to tell the truth, for loyalty came up the chain of command, not down.
19   And who were they to question King's policy, even in the face of the wasting of their comrades.
20   And SnowWhite chose twelve, that they should be part of SnowFlight, and that they might save lives of the child men, which also required them to expose the loss of their own lives.
21   And SnowWhite, StoneMan, BirdMan, OverBoost, RedLine, BurnOut, HalfRight, TailWind, TwoDogs, DarkMoon, ShareCrop, SmegMa and BolTer became one in the name SnowFlight, and word of SnowFlight spread round about.
22   SnowWhite ordained the twelve and gave them secrets.
23   The twelve of SnowFlight had a confidence over all around them, and their goodness protected them.
24   And SnowWhite bid them to go forth and ignore the selfish High Priests of military dynasty enamored by a history not of their making,
25   But only theirs to revere for they had become apotheosized by man, not God.
26   And when SnowWhite's friends heard of his doings, many thought he was crazy.

27 "He is nuts," said MakeReady the trusted assistant maintenance officer, "They'll shit-can SnowWhite if he don't keep his
mouth shut."
28 But among the High Priests there were those who knew their
beloved church was being stepped upon by an elephant King who
regarded them as pissants.

CHAPTER 7

1 "The primary mission of the Marine Korps shall be to provide
fleet marine forces of combined arms, together with supporting
air components, for service with the fleet in the seizure, or defense
of advanced naval bases and for the conduct of such land operations as may be essential to the prosecution of a naval campaign,"
read aloud TailWind from the written law.
2 And SmegMa, HalfRight, and RedLine listened to TailWind
in the flight operations ready room while waiting on BolTer to
fetch the Navy major flown in from the sea flotilla to be the
contacting coordinator for Naval gunfire support.
3 "Well they sure fooled me," retorted SmegMa to TailWind's
reading of the lawful mission of the Marine Korps,
4 "Here the Krotch is settin' on beautiful Tru Lai Bay. We
must'a seized us a land locked Naval Base. Maybe the Navy will
pull to pier side here tonight and we can get some steak eats, a hot
shower, and sleep in one of those non-combat air-con'dition'eed
steel infested rooms," TailWind smiled.
5 The group laughed at the combat sarcasm.
6 BolTer, and a conspicuously starched, plump Navy major
entered flight operations—the mission, to deliver by helicopter
hoist to the destroyer escort ship on the sea one overweight navy
Low-priest.
7 The flight out over the sea was not only uneventful, but just
plain boring.
8 But the sea was choppy with large rolling waves—a common
malady to seamen; a death omen to any person vulnerable to sea
sickness.
9 And it was that radio contact was made with the destroyer
escort, and SmegMa aimed the helo at the ship for landing by helo
hoist to the small, square platform located on the fan tail rear of
the ship, right above the propeller.

10   And it was that the rough seas oscillated the bow and the rear of the mighty ship in and out of the water to such heights that the big propeller came visibly out of the salt water churning the sea with white froth, like a huge spinning eggbeater that drifted back and forth into the blue-white meringue.

11   "Hook 'em up," communicated SmegMa to the crew chief, signaling the crewman to place the horse collar survival hoist underneath the arms of the Navy Sea-Priest so that he could be dangled in the open air out of the helicopter on a steel thread with the pilot controlling the speed of the release of the cable by pushing the electrical raise or descent button on his flight control stick.

12   And SmegMa flew the helicopter so as to make a hovering interception with a moving ship in rolling seas—perfect timing and great ability were needed for the few seconds required to operate the helicopter at the final high flying performance and critical engine and airframe tolerance levels.

13   And the flying approach, changing to a high engine power hover, was magnificent;

14   Then SmegMa ordered the crew chief—"OK, put 'm out"—the Navy Priest was dangled aerially on the cable hoist arm outside the flying helicopter.

15   And SmegMa smiled at HalfRight and then slowly extracted the helo's cable lowering the Navy Priest—not to the bouncing platform—but in the open air beside the ship where the large turning propeller leapt up out of the sea water beside the screaming Navy major who held on for dear life.

16   And SmegMa laughed and said, "Navy omelette," then raised him up and over where the flying helo and the moving ship on rough seas joined so that the Navy Sea-Priest could escape from the cable connection and release himself to the ship's deck.

17   And the helo crew laughed;

18   And the shaken Navy Sea-Priest grinned knowing once again those damn Marines were simply performing combat foreplay, but he gave them the single digit finger signal.

CHAPTER 8

1 "I'm invisible", bellowed out HalfRight to SnowFlight at happy hour.

2 "Want'a see me run through that wall," the drunken HalfRight would ask a stranger in the makeshift bar.

3 And it came to pass that the pain of seeing the maimed children and the wasted souls stacked in body bags ate upon the mind of the previously pious HalfRight, and he found solace in the alcohol.

4 Soon, the attendees would solicit the "invisible man," as HalfRight became known, to run through the wall.

5 And HalfRight would run against the wall with all his strength temporarily dazing himself as he would bang and splat back on the floor.

6 After the numbness wore away, HalfRight would grin a drunken smile and say, "See, I made it through the wall."

7 And SnowFlight would take care of the angry HalfRight who would fret deeply at the ignorance of war and his foolish youthful worship at such an atrocious idol,

8 For his heart would ache at the faces of the young men caught in the trap of a youthful indoctrination for which they were inept to understand.

9 And his heart bled for the numerous common people whose minute political power left them defenseless when their sons were beckoned to the devil's slaughter pen and as an offering unto Molech.

10 And HalfRight thought of the screams from the stretchers below sometimes crying "MaMa,"

11 And HalfRight saw the partial bodies explosively mangled, and the fresh maimed children randomly harvested by the angel of death,

12 And HalfRight would say, "I'm invisible, wanta' see me run through that wall?"

CHAPTER 9

1   It came to be that the King of Cash, the Prince of Money, and the Lords of Wall Street shown round about for unbridled economic power was the firmament of the dark angel trickling the blood of the land from the shekels of greed and the vanities of the mind.

2   And as power shown round about in the money humming of war, so were the Priest generals paid by titles or status imposed on those who honored the beliefs of the Prince of Money.

3   But from the gnat of nothingness came forth the cry of the spirit of the body of the people questioning the sanctity of power assumed and not power conveyed.

4   And there was much gnashing of teeth for the homilies of the Political Almighty sold not,

5   And the Priests of war became unwashed from the rivers of deceit.

6   "Eat the Apple, . . . Fuck the Korps," stated HalfRight to his own surprise as he stared into the rainey blackness as the cold drops dripped from the bill of his hat to his face.

7   "The slimy muther fuckers won't stand tall to the thieving son-of-a-bitches," he bitterly continued.

8   And it came to pass that SnowFlight crossed the sea to the other side to rest and meditate on the Island of the Floating Dragon, for the machines and men of war were worn and in need of replenishment.

9   "I'm invisible," said HalfRight to the brother submariners whose blood flowed through their minds below the ocean like the men who challenged the aerial sea above.

10   And it came to pass that HalfRight in drunken stupor ran through the rice-paper wall of the Nipponese bar out and into the street amid the uninterpretable screams of the irate bar owner and to the tune of the laughing sailors.

11   "I did it," shrieked the surprised, drunken helo pilot as he and the giggling BolTer staggered off escaping into the many alleys in the darkness with the sailors to the submarine base.

12   And the sailors of the undersea cherished the emissaries of the air in whom the previous days eventful flight had been filled with scenes of scantily clad women along the ocean beaches,

13   And unusual flight attitudes as the pilots flew the submarin-

ers around the Island of the Floating Dragon among the shiny beaches and jagged rocks piercing volcanically up out of the deep blue ocean.

14   And HalfRight and BolTer commingled the submariners' flight with an occasional shutting down of the helo's engine to autorotational flight,

15   And there were quick dives between cliffs seeking amusement of their newly found drinking buddy passengers.

16   And it came to pass the men of the sea awakened the comatose HalfRight and the hyper BolTer to tender a ride aboard their diesel powered undersea boat for a day's "shake down" cruise from maintenance repairs.

17   And it came to pass that the submarine started its big engines and to the sounds of the Navy the hatches were closed with HalfRight and BolTer as the most special of passengers to the happy submarine crew.

18   Then the smell of galley food and the sounds of the undersea commands filled the minds of HalfRight and BolTer as time passed on the travail under the open sea.

19   And the horns blew, the whistles tooted, and the orders to dive deeper were given; and the day's tests of the maintenance repairs began.

20   Then it was that a small pipe broke in the command cabin spraying sea water to the petrified faces of the helo pilots and the accepting submarine crew.

21   And HalfRight and BolTer were locked in the captain's small room; for the "General Quarters" safety command was given sealing all the crew in the submarine's air tight compartments.

22   And HalfRight and BolTer listened on the intercom as the crew battled the minor undersea leak, but they were sore afraid.

23   And it came to pass that a second pipe broke in the captain's quarters with water spraying and slowly filling the small room to the knees of HalfRight and BolTer,

24   The pilots were assured by the captain on the intercom to be cool, that a destroyer ship was on the surface above with a doppler in case undersea rescue were needed.

25   The sound of scraping metal filled the tiny cabin with the two helo pilots who were reduced to raw fear — BolTer mumbled out loudly, "SnowWhite where are you", and HalfRight broadcast on the intercom, "Get us out of here."

26   And the submarine commander ordered HalfRight and

BolTer to standby for evacuation as the water was pumped from out of the small room.

27   And the hatch door spun, and the sailor in the life vest screamed "Run to the forward Hatch" sending HalfRight and BolTer at high speed to the ceiling deck hatch.

28   And it came to pass that the frightened HalfRight and BolTer climbed out of the open hatch to a beautiful day at pierside, for the submarine had never left its berth.

29   And there was much laughter at the two helo pilots wet to their knees who had learned that the men of the undersea were their brothers.

CHAPTER 10

1   There was a spirit about the land of the Island of the Floating Dragon that echoed in its silent visions of wars past, for among its historical castles and kingdoms had dwelt the human challenges of many wars gone by.

2   And SnowWhite lead SnowPack to the volcanic mountains to meditate on what was, what has been, and what would be.

3   And there came among them a weathered man of bright mind called Lei, who questioned the souls of nations gone mad in the pursuit of bloodshed.

4   And it was strange meeting the little man who had been a suicide pilot in his youth, for he spoke of wisdom as to the nature of man.

5   MAN CAN CHOOSE, commented Lei to the young pilots in search of answers to great frustrations.

6   WHERE THERE IS NO VISION, THE PEOPLE PERISH, added SnowWhite as SnowPack questioned why the King of Cash and the Prince of Money were in control of such a noble race.

7   MEN CAN BUILD CASTLES IN THEIR MINDS, said Lei.

8   WHO CAN BRING A CLEAN THING OUT OF AN UNCLEAN, answered SnowWhite.

9   And much levity transpired from the deep thought of men whose very being was cast in, out of, and to go back into the heat of battle.

10   Then Lei caught a large common fly in an empty glass which he carefully filled with ice water while speaking of the death of just one fly.

11   And the submerged fly's movements in the ice water ceased only after a short time, for the fly moved not.

12   And much discussion ensued as to the nature of one dead fly in a meaningless world.

13   And the fly floated stiffly and motionless under the water's surface just underneath the ice of the glass.

14   WHO AMONG YOU BELIEVES THE FLY IS DEAD? queried the words from the mellow mountain farmer called Lei, to which all the young pilots agreed that the fly was dead.

15   WHO AMONG YOU BELIEVES THE FLY IS ALIVE? again questioned the stone faced farmer, and there were none but SnowWhite, who said, REMOVE THE FLY FROM THE WATERY GRAVE TO THE TABLE OF TRUTH.

16   And the fly was carefully removed to the table with the twelve apostles of flight watching on.

17   "The bastard's dead," said SmegMa as he viewed the upside down, stiff insect carefully laid upon the table.

18   YOU MUST HAVE FAITH, came forth the words of SnowWhite.

19   "What's one dead fly," queried DarkMoon.

20   And it came to pass that Lei performed burial services for the fly by covering the fly with the common table salt, and spoke of locusts with the face of people and the mane of a lion as insects.

21   And HalfRight grew apprehensive, for he sensed an aura about this man called Lei.

22   And as the SnowWhite and the Twelve looked on, a trickle of movement shook beneath the mound surface of the small white salt grave,

23   There followed further movement and the now living, moving black fly crawled forth from the salt mound whiteness,

24   Then momentarily fluttered its wings and then flew from the table to the astonishment of the Twelve, and laughter of the captive audience.

25   Then Lei smiled at the young faces for in wars of other times the Imperial Marines had used the submerged fly to lure sailors into wagers where the winning Marines would get rewards from the ships crew.

26   AS THE FLY DOES SURVIVE, YOU TOO SHALL SEE THE KING OF CASH SMOTHER THE PEOPLE IN THE SALT OF BLINDNESS, said SnowWhite, BUT IN YEARS TO COME, THE TRUTH SHALL CRAWL FORTH.

CHAPTER 11

1   Much suffering endured the congregation of the church of the Korps, for the congregation suffered from High Priest hubris.

2   And the High priests were victims of their King.

3   And on the Island of the Floating Dragon, the patriarchs of other services had caused to be built, overlooking the sea, a pilot's castle of great magnitude whose halls housed great riches extracted from the taxpayers unknown to the keepers of the purse.

4   And this military pilot's club of the Sky-Blue knew not common things for the Mrs's of the High Priests of non-war commanded the protocols and grandiose seances sought to summons vanity in the name of the ill-conceived status.

5   And it came to pass that in the evening on the glory day of non-war there was much pomp and ceremony at the tabernacle above the sea.

6   For there were numerous formally dressed small islanders who spoke pidgin not,

7   And whose demeanor fictionized grande dames of unrefined blood lines from places like the Okeechobee Swamp, the Bronx, Rio Bravo, and Toad Suck, Arkansas.

8   For it was important that the men of non-war in high priestly places suffer not the heat, the hardship, the horniness, and the miseries of the lesser Marine souls waging economic battles for the King of Cash orchestrated by the Prince of Money.

9   And it was critical that the women understand not the death warrants issued by their High Priest husbands who would efficiently exchange the sons of other women for small ribbons.

10   When the violins sang and the flambe glistened forth, there came DarkMoon, Injun, TailWind, HalfRight and BolTer, naked upon their motorcycles riding through the dining room in search of beer.

11   And much gnashing of teeth echoed forth for the women of unrefined rank gushed forth faintness as the visions of the night disappeared out the door into the blackness of the twenty-seven hole golf course.

12   And the Sky-Blue colonel stood in line behind the Sky-Blue Bishop-general while the blue-suit Cardinal-general screamed into the telephone at the Corporal at the Marine base about a Nigger, a

Chink, a Wop, a Greaser, and a mojo looking Indian, who had to be Marines, attacking the serenity of non-combatants engaged in a day of rest from six days of air-conditioned sacrifice.

13   And the Corporal at the Marine base informed the screaming voice that he had heard that a special operations group was to practice infiltrating the nuclear storage area on the Air/Base to steal a nuclear bomb, and that this might be the diversion tactic.

14   Instantly, the telephone dropped as the Corporal heard the running feet of the panicked colonels and generals, for the chop-block of Sky-Blue careers came forth to those who lost mock wars, or misplaced one nuclear weapon.

15   And it came to pass that the god, Marine Korps, understood not the pleas of the Sky-Blue military men of non-war who clothed themselves in unsanctified pettiness wanting to snatch away Marine pilots needed in combat in order to appease inter-spousal vanities,

16   For to punish pilots took time and removed them from a greater punishment, helicopter warfare.

17   And SnowFlight laughed at the stories of the expressions on the faces of the old women, and goosey waiters, as the wild ones rode naked through the multi-million dollar building simply in search of cold beer.

18   And the High Priest at the throne of Air Force ordered a sign, "No Marines Allowed" posted at the entrance of the palatial club overlooking the sea.

CHAPTER 12

1   A call came forth in the night for the soldiers of the sea on the Island of the Floating Dragon to return to the splendid little war.

2   And the Bishop-general of the 7th Amphibious Marines frothed with much glee for with blind devotion to duty he was prepared to cast human lots for pieces of insignificant geography all in the name of a temporary tactical victory and compliance with the wishes of his King.

3   For the King of Cash, the Prince of Money, and the academicians who knew not war imposed no limitations on the Bishop-general, except to worship the homily of attrition,

4   And to disburse many shekels to the purses of the inner whatnots,

5   And to cast shekels of the mind to those who honored the beast.

6   But the mutually defenseless child men Marines who were indoctrinated to love their father understood not that mere survival was created by castles of the mind.

7   And the Cardinal-general of the western church, rather than resign, allowed his loyal men to shed their lives in policies and dictates he believed not;

8   For it was the nature of High Priests not to question the King of Cash or the Prince of Money, even in the face of academic idiocy.

9   And it came to pass that the demons of evil smiled, for death and destruction prevailed providing the harvesting of human flesh crops from the killing fields of many useless battles.

10   And it was also that demons smiled, for child men were trained to obey the beast and piss on the Word of God.

11   The individual child men Marines saith, "Eat the Apple, . . . and Fuck the Korps."

12   And it was that 777 returned to war.

CHAPTER 13

1   The Ada Sam Marine base sparkled as an ideal unspoiled tourist attraction — but it was the Dang Ling Headquarters for combat operations.

2   And helicopters were essential to resupply the several outposts strategically positioned on the mountain peaks surrounding the isolated airfield.

3   And the little nodules of child men Marines at these outposts were irritants to the enemy;

4   Like all irritants, the outposts were often attacked — sometimes with the unconventional means of casting poisonous snakes over the barbed wire in the middle of the night;

5   Sleep was impossible for garbage discarded by the hilltop inhabitants attracted jungle pests — rats and other night moving creatures, the noise from which nocturnally kept the young Marines at the adrenaline ready.

6   The rule of warfare was that the aerial nakedness of helicopters became even more acute in darkness.

7   And the camouflage of night lost its advantage when having to

land in the blackness where the simple striking of tree limbs or other objects by the delicately balanced tail rotor blades would cause the helicopter to crash.

8   The enemy knew serious wounds inflicted on just one hilltop resident would summon the rescue helicopter setting the stage to test both sides art of violence.

9   The night belonged to the enemy, Sir Charles, and sometimes the other enemy, unskilled Priests.

10   The field phone rang during the dark hours of morning, "Front Desk," answered TwoDogs startling the new staff captain calling from the command bunker,

11   "Come to the bunker pronto; outpost says they hear tanks; need an emergency recon look-see."

12   "A-Mergency", yelled the big Indian's deep voice intending to stir the helicopter crews toiling on cots interspaced in the mud floor bunker and to reflect anticipated disgust at risking human lives to see what the outpost could already hear.

13   The cold chill of the morning mountain dew and of having to fly into the unknown darkness permeated the room with thoughts of dying as crews laced their boots and stumbled in the darkness to the tasks of preparing to launch helos out into the blackness with death lurking about.

14   And it came to pass that SnowWhite, TwoDogs, HalfRight, and StoneMan entered the sanctity of the Ada Sam command temple to witness the laying on of commands.

15   And the Marine liturgy ensued with each curate staff minister standing tall one by one before the High Priest before a school solution wall size map with various plastic sheets called overlays which depicted various combat scenarios or contingent situations.

16   And it was that the High Priest knew not what he was told not, or knew not.

17   And it came to pass that the infrared pictures displayed enemy tanks approaching the Special Forces compound at the Kidron OutPost.

18   And the secret creepy people overlay showed enemy tanks approaching the Kidron OutPost.

19   And the OutPost reported motor noises in the valley that sounded like tanks.

20   And the Special Forces commander radioed the Kidron Com-

pound was under attack, and that tanks were coming up the winding mountain road.

21   And the herringbone clad implanted branch Bishop-commander indoctrinated under Ego Mania I spoke with the absence of long term conviction: "Verify those tanks."

22   And it came to pass that despite all the millions of shekels spent to monitor the enemy with sophisticated intelligence capability, the command cleric dictated the exposure of loss of Marine lives to visually confirm the already verified tanks.

23   **BEWARE OF PRIESTS WHICH WEAR THE VEST-MENTS OF A SALTY MARINE,** responded SnowWhite to the blasphemy of the helo crews at the disbelief that their lives were being risked to cast a night look-see by helo at what the Army Special Forces unit had confirmed on the radio,

24   **PREPARE TO CODE BLUE,** came the strange words of SnowWhite to the crews.

25   SnowWhite's helo lifted off into the Ada Sam blackness with his three trusted wingmen remaining on the ground at the ready monitoring the radios, and listening, and waiting SnowWhite's fate.

26   **HOLY SMOKE, HOLY SMOKE, THIS IS GLORY BEE,** catcalled SnowWhite on the radio easing the tenseness and earning a grin from those monitoring the radio transmissions.

27   **GLORY BEE, DIS HEAH IS H-O-L-Y S-M-O-K-E, WHAT YOU DOIN' OUT SHOPPIN' DIS EARLY AH MORNING, SNOWWHITE,** came back the Georgia Team Commander's drawl to his friend, SnowWhite.

28   **GOT AN ARM CHAIR CLERIC UP HERE THINKS YOU BOYS BEEN COUNTIN' TANKS TO GO TO SLEEP,** SnowWhite at the southern accent,

29   **WANTS US TO LOOK-SEE SO YOU GUYS DON'T CLAIM TOO MANY MEDALS.**

30   **WHY YA'LL COME TO THE PICNIC, HEAH, WE GOIN TO HAVE FRIED TURRET, AND BAKED TREAD WITH BAC BO SOUFFLE,** said the Kidron Commander.

31   **STRIKE A MATCH IN TEN, LET SNOW SEE WHAT YOU'RE HAVIN',** came SnowWhite back on the radio.

32   And TwoDogs, HalfRight and StoneMan listened and laughed at the radio banter during the short trip of SnowWhite to the Kidron OutPost.

33   **WHY GLORY BEE, YOU GUYS DONE CALLED UP A**

DOZEN OR SO IRON CHICKENS, came SnowWhite's radio call.

34   YOUR PICNIC'S GET'IN LOTS OF IRON RAIN, AN' YOU GETTIN' MORE GUESTS THAN YA INVITED.

35   SAY SNOWWHITE, HOLY SMOKE NEEDS TO TURN UP THE CHARCOAL AND LEAVE, REQUEST GREEN CHARIOT OUT OF HERE, CAN YOU CODE BLUE? came the request.

36   SAY SOULS ON BOARD, responded SnowWhite.

37   NINE PLUS NONE PLUS THREE WOUNDED.

38   SNOWWHITE CODE BLUE IN PLUS 15, responded SnowWhite to his ground bound army friend, and acknowledging the secret prearranged pick-up point in fifteen minutes.

39   SNOWFLIGHT, SNOWFLIGHT, RENDEZVOUS CODE BLUE, EMERGENCY EXTRACTION, PLUS 15, came SnowWhite's words to HalfRight, TwoDogs, and StoneMan on the radio, "SnowFlight to SnowLeader, copy," echoed the response back acknowledging the plan.

40   Explosive charges with timers were activated and the Georgia captain disappeared to the perimeter and returned.

41   Kidron OutPost defenders with the wounded made their escape,

42   And it was as if angels were about ministering unto those who deserved not the frenzy of the demons.

43   And the Lord of Hosts heard the children's radio prayer cries in the wilderness.

44   Occasionally, the escaping souls would look back at the distant outpost under siege with fires, gasoline, and random explosions timed to trigger when several of the enemy tanks entered into the compound.

45   And it was that the explosions hurled tanks and assault troops into the air lighting the morning sky with billowing fire and smoke.

46   And the pick-up of the soldiers by SnowFlight commenced as flickers of fiery orange sunrise began creeping between cracks in the overcast clouds.

47   It was also that the low clouds compressed the helos into tight treetop flying just underneath the clouds and around the jungle hillsides to the pick-up point on a jutting rock peak sticking sideways out of the mountain.

48   Then each of the three helo's in front of SnowWhite per-

formed the penultimate of helicopter artistry by flying to the hillside peak without landing,

49   But by entering a gradual engine power reduction,

50   And then quick surgical power addition in order to momentarily hover the helo with only one wheel placed on the rock point cliff edge as each of the escaping passengers were rapidly loaded.

51   **HONEY BEE, SNOWWHITE ON FINAL,** radioed SnowWhite to the ground commander who waited to be the last person to leave the zone.

52   "You're taking some fire, SnowWhite," came the radio message.

53   **IT'S ONLY FAIR,** came SnowWhite's response, his helo at high speed twisted into a side flair for rapid deceleration,

54   And an instant hover capturing each of the four running soldiers with the fourth leaping airborne into the open door of the departing helo grabbing the life line tether of the door crewman to hold on.

55   The intercom mike keyed, **MANY TANKS, SNOWWHITE,** came the ground bound commander's familiar voice,

56   And he handed up to SnowWhite a polaroid picture of two tanks tracking across the Kidron OutPost perimeter wire.

57   **ALL IN A MORNING'S WORK, LEIRU,** responded SnowWhite as the helicopter crewmen stared at the young, black sturdy Special Forces captain with white hair and eyes that gleamed in the sunrise from a mystic looking man who somehow knew SnowWhite.

58   **WE'LL HAVE TO PUNCH OUT ABOVE THE CLOUDS,** SnowWhite commented on the intercom to his friend, **ADA SAM IS IN THE SOUP.**

59   TailWind radioed the Ada Sam command post and reported the visual citing of the enemy tanks,

60   And the rescue of the Army Special Forces Team from the Kidron Compound.

61   "Be advised the commander requests that SnowFlight land; you weren't authorized to rescue the Army people, wants report on tanks," came the command radio response.

62   **NEGATIVE, ADA SAM ZERO ZERO IN FOG, CANNOT LAND, WOUNDED SOULS ON BOARD, DESTINATION EAGLE,** answered SnowWhite.

63   "You hear me boy," came the voice of the school solution

High Priest who personally took control of the radio, "I order you to land."

64   "You get them Army boys on the ground, they can take care-a their own."

65   TailWind keyed the mike and sucked air through his teeth making a sound like static on the radio causing the ground bound clergyman to scream in his microphone radio transmission,

66   "I'm ordering you to land, damn-it! I'll have everyone of you throttle jockey's ass if you don't land now."

67   SnowWhite smiled, TailWind smiled, each of the other pilots in the flying formation hand signaled out the helo windows with a visual thumbs up to each other and smiled;

68   For it was a glorious morning, the sun was rising above the overcast below and hot coffee was minutes away to comfort the altitude chill.

69   The demon of darkness had once again been cheated from victory—the career priest schooled in sacrifice understood not saving lives by not wasting them.

70   And Injun thought, brothers are brothers, who is this High Priest cleric who knows not the common redness of our blood.

71   And HalfRight questioned his church, the Marine Korps, for soldiers of the Army were not the enemy.

72   And across the earth, the Pope-general bowed before the King and signed death warrants for child men for the King bought the Pope's soul by embarassment if Ada Sam were lost.

CHAPTER 14

1   And it came to pass that the Priests of High Command secretly wailed behind closed doors.

2   News release by the Army of a Marine High Priest who needed a photograph of tanks in order to see tanks in warfare,

3   Or actual visual sighting by Marines instead of sound military intelligence pleased the clergy not.

4   And the safe rescue of an Army outpost by Marine helicopters tempered the inter-service rivalry wound,

5   But the cleric not preventing such feat was promoted to Holy Sea Headquarters as the Assistant Admin Officer in charge of Nam Bo fish market analysis.

6   The words of the Political Almighty, the Divinity of Defense, and the Elders continued to spill forth blessing the fine little war,
7   And the choir of fifty sang loudly by casting millions of shekels for the immediate now and for the near evermore.
8   And the money machine did eat of the unleavened flesh,
9   And the money gnomes went forth harvesting the money crops from the fields of war.
10   The Pope, Cardinals, Bishops, and Monsignors considered themselves masters at the art of violence,
11   But were greatly frustrated at the mounting heretics and understood not,
12   For they were callous to granting death to sharecrop the fields of profits,
13   Including child men Marines who increasingly knew loyalty came not from above.
14   And their flesh fed the slot machines of capitalism.
15   The Political Almighty looked down upon the dissenters as impudent children and stiffhearted, for they are of a rebellious house.
16   And the King of Cash said, "The world is full of elephants and pissants, and I'm an elephant."
17   And young Marines died in the name of unsound and untimely indecisions.

CHAPTER 15

1   "I find in him no fault at all," said HalfRight to BurnOut concerning the whitehaired SnowWhite.
2   "Why do you wish to pilfer from his flying marvels," HalfRight continued further, "SnowWhite has done no wrong."
3   "He hasn't done it by the book," blasted the suddenly changed BurnOut, "He does not fly by the book."
4   "And did the generals not hold their tongue when they knew the Prince of Money personally took military command to sop his own ego?" said HalfRight.
5   "And did not our brethren Marines die so that the Prince of Money could cast commercial lots among the money-hummers?" forcefully responded HalfRight.
6   And it came to pass that SnowFlight accepted not BurnOut, for he became not of them.

7   And a High Priest of war summoned BurnOut to a place of great power, but of little knowledge;

8   And a High Priest gave unto BurnOut an assignment of easy office, for the High Priests sought knowledge of SnowWhite.

9   BurnOut sought statistical sanctity, and his new candy-assed assignment fulfilled him not.

CHAPTER 16

1   In the land of Nam Bo Marines also died because of the inter-service inexpediency.

2   And it came to pass that the Cardinal-general cloaked with the sanctity of WWII, the Banana Wars, and Frozen Chosen, only knew the homily of high diddle diddle — run up the middle,

3   But was captured by political ineptness and inter-service pedagogy.

4   "Fuck the Army", he would say, "they only get wounds in their ass running away",

5   And he would mechanically zip a grin across the wide corn crop face signifying to all in his presence to laugh at his humor.

6   And it became known to the high clergy in their general conference that one among their parish was blaspheming the King.

7   "Who is this SnowWhite?" foamed the Pope's on-site cleric wearing forehead lines of rhythmic new thought and Korps' self-preservation.

8   "SnowWhite, is SnowWhite," answered CrossFire, the transient Catholic Chaplain solicited to summons through prayer almighty God to assist this communion of war saints in their endeavors to separate the souls of the enemy from the bodies of enemy, regardless of race, religion, sex, creed, or age.

9   "We don't know," quickly inserted the Cleric colonel trying to shift the big Cardinal-general's stare at the perceived to be thoughtless joke of the Catholic Chaplain.

10   "You Navy folks will never understand what it is like to be a Marine," barked the Cardinal-general at the sole vestige of the Navy's presence in the form of a meek Catholic Chaplain,

11   And the Cardinal-general gave the edict, "Kill 'em all, let God sort 'em out;" and laughter came from his surroundings.

12   "Now what do you mean you don't know," demanded the Cardinal-general to the fresh ironed uniform housing the behind

the lines staff Curate-colonel in constant search of fulfilling the ever-changing formula for promotion.

13   All the personnel records were blown up in the mortar attack on the helicopter base, Sir," was the prompt response.

14   "Get Hapstein in here," came the order of the Cardinal-general, which brought forth BurnOut.

15   And the high clergymen in the presence of the communion of generals and other high Marine theologists queried the career destined Curate-major well versed in the semantics of truth avoidance.

16   "Did SnowWhite say, **KNOW YOUR MEN AND LOOK AFTER THEIR WELFARE?** to which major Hapstein answered, "Yes sir."

17   "Did a follower say 'This war is the incompetent leading the unwilling to do the unnecessary for the ungrateful?' " to which Curate-major Hapstein answered, "Yes, sir."

18   "Did SnowWhite disobey unwritten policy not to help the Army at Ada Sam by rescuing the Army Special Forces Team at Kidron OutPost?" to which Curate-major Hapstein answered, "Yes sir."

19   "Did SnowWhite disregard orders and proceed into Bac Bo waters to rescue a downed pilot?" to which major Hapstein answered, "Yes sir."

20   "Did SnowWhite give away food?" to which Curate-major Hapstein answered, "Yes, sir."

21   "Did SnowWhite say, **EGG BEATERS MAKE EGG OMLETTES**, to which Curate-major Hapstein answered, "Yes, sir."

22   "Did SnowWhite say, **DEFECTIVE GUNS COME FROM DEFECTIVE MINDS**, to which Curate-major Hapstein answered, "Yes sir."

23   "Did SnowWhite say, **THE MARINE KORPS IS NOT A LAND ARMY**, to which Curate-major Hapstein answered, "Yes sir."

24   And it came to pass that the Cardinal-general recognized not the church of the Marine Korps.

25   And the Cardinal-general was sore afraid, for those learned in the law explained that "truth" was a defense.

26   And the innocent young Marines knew not High Priests who would expose loss of their garments in order to give back loyalty.

27 And the Cardinal-general knew others gave "yes" verdicts knowing the Prince of Money sought out yes men,

28 And there were High Church Priests who stood up not for their men.

CHAPTER 17

1 It was a time of great bias and prejudice for the Holy Sea headquarters did much battle within and without its counsels of war and protocols of political ineptitude.

2 And many High Priests feared the dismantling of their church.

3 The Divinity of Defense traveled great distance to assure himself that the soldiers of war were following the plans of the academic deities who knew not war.

4 And it came to pass that the Congregation of the People wept at the blood of its sons donated to verify the inaccuracy of those who knew all, but also knew nothing.

5 And the words of the yes-men shown round about, for they honored not the principles of leadership.

6 Then there came to be much gnashing of teeth and career survival for the Divinity of Defense was sent to Nam Bo by an unhappy Political Almighty who cared not for excuses.

7 And the Congregational People were seeing the horrors of allowing only yes-underlings in yes-made offices guiding yes-minded regular career priest surrogates to inflict self-serving yes-theories on the innocent and defenseless souls of youths unable to fend for or understand for themselves in a war rigged so as not to raise the ire of the firmament of the People.

8 And the Prince of Money smiled at the imaginary vision of the endless oil fields thought to be beneath the Nam Bo sea,

9 For such great wealth more than paid for the fine little war,

10 And he was thus also called the Prophet of Profits.

11 And it came to pass that the words of "body count" were manured by the academicians of war to appease mothers; for the death of one son in exchange for three was a mathematical victory,

12 And it had to be winning where mothers of three dead enemy were to have exchanged their sons in the eyes of the mother of only one dead Sam Bo child. Hallelujah!

13   And many shekels of war were loosely strewn about.
14   And the greed demon living in the house of the Political Almighty smiled, for great things happen to those who help themselves, particularly when the merchants of murder go on a shopping spree.
15   And the mothers of child men were learning that the High Priests gave their sons unto Molech.
16   And SnowFlight sought counsel of SnowWhite, for they were bitter.
17   And SnowWhite said unto them, **DO NOT WORRY ABOUT BLIND MEN; AND DON'T BECOME ONE OF THEM, FOR THERE SHALL BE NO REWARD TO THEIR CLOSING OF THEIR EYES.**
18   **THE CANDLE OF THE WICKED SHALL BE PUT OUT. THE WICKED BUY THEIR ETERNITY.**
19   And SnowFlight understood not, and pressed SnowWhite for an answer as to "why" such horror and misery was prevalent.
20   And SnowWhite answered, saying, **GREED, VANITY, AND SELFISHNESS HAVE BEEN HARNESSED TO THESE WAGONS OF WAR.**

CHAPTER 18

1   HalfRight dedicated himself to the new order, for he liked not what he saw.
2   And SnowWhite said, **IN WAR, FATHERS BURY THEIR SONS.**
3   HalfRight had no father to bury him, and he was of great concern.
4   **ALL MEN ARE EQUAL IN THE PRESENCE OF DEATH**, responded SnowWhite to HalfRight's fears.
5   "We are being deceived about this war," stated HalfRight to SnowWhite.
6   **IT IS THE NATURE OF THE RICH TO DECEIVE THE POOR**, said SnowWhite, and continued,
7   **THIS WAR IS DESIGNED BY THE RICH TO BE WORN BY THE POOR.**
8   "But what is happening to the Korps?" inquired HalfRight to the white-haired pilot with comfortable answers.
9   **CASH RULES**, answered SnowWhite.

10   "But why so much unnecessary dying?" focused the man dedicated to his Korps church.
11   **CASH HAS NO CONSCIENCE**, said SnowWhite.
12   And HalfRight understood not, for he spoke the catechisms of the god, The Korps, without question,
13   But he also witnessed a disgust for leaders who cherished not the principles of leadership.
14   And HalfRight cried inside for the useless wasting of his brother Marines.

CHAPTER 19

1   When Poncho Pilot heard of the gnashing of teeth of the High Priests, he inquired of which forth their pain came.
2   We must not let our beloved church, Marine Korps, suffer at the tongue of the Army,
3   For they love us not, came Pilot's thoughts and visions in the middle of the night to the noise of DingleBerry practicing his nightly deep breathing exercise.
4   And as soon as it was day, the Elders, and the Chief Priests, and the Scribes came together, and summoned SnowWhite into their council, saying,
5   "Did you say, **THE KORPS IS NOT A LAND ARMY?**"
6   And SnowWhite said, **SNOWWHITE SAID IT.**
7   "Did you say, **CASH HAS NO CONSCIENCE?**"
8   And SnowWhite said, **SNOWWHITE SAID IT.**
9   Then said Poncho Pilot to the chief priests and to the assembly of career blindness, "I find this man to be one of the best pilots we have."
10   And they were the more fierce saying; "He stirreth up the troops, teaching throughout the Korps, from the Headquarters of the Holy Sea to the Tekoa Wilderness."
11   When Poncho Pilot had heard, he asked whether it was not better that Headquarters of the Holy Sea handle this matter.
12   And as he knew that SnowWhite belonged unto Headquarters jurisdiction,
13   He sent him unto the Cardinal-general of the Holy Sea, who was at Sapporis at that time.
14   And when the Cardinal-general of the Holy Sea saw

SnowWhite, he was exceedingly glad: for he was desirous to see him of the monsoon season,

15   Because he had heard many things of him;

16   And he hoped to know of some miracle of flight done by him.

17   Then he questioned with him in many words; but he answered him nothing.

18   And the chief priests and scribes of war stood and vehemently accused him.

19   And the Cardinal-general of the Holy Sea with his men of war set him at nought, and mocked him, and gave him in a tattered poncho and sent him in the monsoon rain back to Poncho Pilot.

20   And Poncho Pilot, when he had called together the Chief Priests and the Curates who wore the mind of career blindness,

21   He said unto them, "You have brought this man unto me, as one that perverteth his brethren Marines,"

22   And behold, I, having examined him before you, have found no fault in his flying nor his abiding by the principles of leadership, nor touching those things whereof you accuse him."

23   And the Curate-colonel of the Seventh Ground became livid.

24   And the career-minded staffers cried out all at once saying,

25   "Away with this man, let him that blasphemies the Marine Korps in the name of his brethren fly the rescue mission into So dau lau,"

26   For they knew there was much anti-aircraft and enemy in the Valley of the Skull where sure death was lurking about.

27   And Poncho Pilot ordered the flight schedule be posted with SnowWhite to fly the helicopter into the high mountain valley to rescue the two thieves who had taken secrets, and in their escape were evading capture but seeking rescue.

The Word According to BIRDMAN

(Set Goals You Can Reach)

CHAPTER 1

1 Protokletos Andreaus had escaped the sponge diving and fishing fleet for he suffered from the scourge of incurable sea sickness.

2 From his home in Bethsaida near St. Petersburg, he had migrated to Virginia to live with his Gunnery Sergeant uncle while attending college.

3 Soon he was indoctrinated into the salt life in Marine Town where he was subjected to the trappings of the glorious Korps Church and received many evangelical sermons that spontaneously flowed from the pious local flock who congregated in the local beer chapels.

4 And it came to pass that after college, Andreaus completed Naval Flight School where he was awarded wings of gold;

5 He was proud of his religion, the Korps, and devoutly practiced the tenets of the Korps Church.

6 And it was also that Andreaus quietly performed;

7 For he was first to fly; first in line to ride as a co-pilot on a test flight; and he flew more hours than any brother pilot.

8 And it came to pass that this child man who loved flying was sent to Nam Bo to practice his two great loves: the Korps, and flying.

191

CHAPTER 2

1   In the land of Nam Bo, Andreaus became a flying disciple of Hopper Honey, a man who knew the scripture and verse of many things, including flying.

2   And Hopper taught him secrets omitted by the flying standards book written by the desk-bound pilots who knew war not,

3   For there were combat flying maneuvers which tricked the enemy,

4   For the enemy would shoot where the image of the helo appeared to be flying thereby missing the vulnerable mechanical flying mule when in deceptive flight attitude.

5   And one trick was a high speed rapid descent in an awkward corkscrew, tilted sideways downward flight path,

6   And there were artful ways to make the helo jump out of the sky to the earth by more than just cutting engine power.

7   It became known unto Andreaus that pilots who wrote the books of war spoke with twisted tongues.

8   And it was that Hopper Honey taught the anxious Andreaus the aerial art of saving lives while protecting crews;

9   For Andreaus learned of things unknown to the common pilot.

10   And it was that Hopper Honey pointed out to the hungry Andreaus a white haired pilot with the name of White who was also called Snow.

11   **WHAT DO YOU WANT?** asked the white haired pilot looking into the determined Greek's eyes approaching him in the shade of the helo repair shack.

12   "To fly with SnowWhite," said Andreaus looking at the snow white hair that flickered brightly in the sun,

13   And he felt a sudden surge in the presence of his soul's very reason for being.

14   **FLY WITH SNOWWHITE, COME SEE!** . . . **COME SAW!**, said SnowWhite, and it was that Andreaus and SnowWhite took to the heavens in flight.

15   **SNOWWHITE LOVE SKY**, were the words from the best check pilot Andreaus had experienced.

16   Then it was that Andreaus felt in the sky the magnetic chill of the man with surgical blue eyes who became instantly known,

17   For from his hands came the smoothest touch of flying ever witnessed by this man who loved flying.

18   SNOW HOME, came the words as they climbed high above the clouds and danced among the cotton fluffiness in the cool Nam Bo air high above the steaming earth housing a brutal war.

19   Andreaus became euphoric, for SnowWhite was like no other instructor he had known;

20   He drifted into being with a common bond flier,

21   And engine power settings with synchronized rotor turns spun the big blades perfectly to tolerances and to the calm rhythm of SnowWhite's touch.

22   SnowWhite out flies all other pilots, decided Andreaus.

23   And Andreaus probed SnowWhite in the midst of the flying ballet, and expressed disbelief at some of the Vicar-majors not liking to fly.

24   A GOOD PILOT IS WORTH A THOUSAND MAJORS, grinned SnowWhite to the vocal frustrations of Andreaus about a priest pilot who confused rank above duty.

25   And Andreaus expressed disbelief that the Bishop-general would send the helos over and over into the same landing zones controlled by the enemy.

26   HIGH PRIESTS ARE TRAINED TO MAKE WAR, NOT TO MAKE PEACE, commented SnowWhite.

27   Andreaus liked what he heard from the man who had eyes that made you smile, and Andreaus said that the only answer was to drop nuclear bombs on the enemy.

28   NUCLEAR PEACE FOLLOWS NUCLEAR WAR, advised SnowWhite.

29   Then Andreaus questioned the granting of medals by the High Church to its career priests while the child men who fought the battles were given glory badges not.

30   MAN'S GLORY IMAGE OF WAR IS NOT TO BE CONFUSED WITH THE GLORY OF MAN, responded SnowWhite, THE BEST MEDAL IS A LIVE MAN'S SMILE.

31   And it came to pass that SnowWhite and the Greek addicted to flight soared until evening establishing an uncommon bond between pilots who can do more than just fly.

32   And SnowWhite called Andreaus "BirdMan," for no other pilot loved to fly more than BirdMan.

CHAPTER 3

1   BirdMan brought his hootch-mate, Rusty Stoner, to meet his new friend and magnificent pilot, SnowWhite.
2   **A BIRDMAN AND A STONEMAN**, commented SnowWhite to the two.
3   And StoneMan laughed at the new name, but he also liked the new found fellow pilot with white hair and penetrating blue eyes. Even if Andreaus is right, who is he to . . . ?
4   **STONEMAN HAS BEEN FLUTTERING DOVE, COME FLY WING WITH SNOWWHITE**, requested SnowWhite of Stoner.
5   This flight leader of men is crazy, thought Rusty to himself,
6   Calls me StoneMan,
7   Stoner's mind spun the gamut; he was safe; he now flew wing on squadron commander Temple — the Kiwi — the safest flying place in the Nam Bo war.
8   One glance was all it took from SnowWhite's eyes.
9   "War's hell," said StoneMan, and he agreed to fly wing on SnowWhite.
10   And the bevy grew — and the child men Marines called it SnowFlight, for word spread roundabout of brothers in the sky.
11   And the young Marines captured by honor at the expense of truth sought and got bodily salvation through the emissaries of the air,
12   For the pilots of SnowFlight landed among them in the heat of battle.
13   And there was hope in the eyes of the child men who knew they had been abandoned unto Molech,
14   But SnowFlight would abandon them not.

CHAPTER 4

1   And it was that BirdMan was known unto DarkMoon as a pilot who felt the presence of God in the sky,
2   And DarkMoon wrote a poem for BirdMan,

I stole the earth one day,
And silently hid pain away,

. . . From the Devil's view.
For the time was due,
High above the inhumane dew.

The winds whispered through my soul,
Secrets few know — of ages' toll,
. . . and I feel mere.
Only pilots share the space up here,
And see what earthlings cannot hear.

God opens up on high,
At each prayerful try,
. . . that God could be.
What pilot's souls see,
High in the aerial sea.

Let me drift in the peaceful blue,
As light as the clouds would do,
. . . in God's hue.
With the heavenly kroo,
. . . The faithful crew.

3   BirdMan felt great compassion;
4   And BirdMan saw young men thrust into a world in which
they were blind to deal.
5   BirdMan suffered for he was powerless to stop the useless
killing machine;
6   So he spoke to God while flying on high, hoping in the clean
air God would hear his cry.
7   And he prayed, and he prayed, and he prayed.
8   And BirdMan saw a white cross on a blue flag over and over in
his mind, but he carried the pain,
9   The burden of knowing the truth while ignorance paraded
false gods about.

CHAPTER 5

1   WAR IS TO YOUTH WHAT A FLAME IS TO A MOTH, said SnowWhite as SnowFlight listened to the words of the combat-eager child men Marines unloading from the arriving aircraft.

2   "We have to stop the heathen enemy here on their ground," patriotically said the Greek devotee to SnowWhite.

3   And SnowWhite answered, IT IS MORE IMPORTANT TO KNOW WHAT YOU ARE FIGHTING FOR THAN WHAT YOU ARE FIGHTING AGAINST.

4   "Then why are you here?" asked BolTer cautiously soliciting answers from the most unusual person he had ever encountered, "Are you here just to survive?"

5   And SnowWhite answered, saying, IT IS THE MISSION OF SNOWWHITE TO BE HERE,

6   IT IS ALSO KNOWN TO YOU WHAT YOU CAN SEE, FOR SNOWWHITE WORSHIPS NOT THOSE WHO DANCE SELF-RIGHTEOUSNESS TO MEN, BUT WHO ARE HYPO-CRITES, AND THOSE WHO SUCKLE FROM THE UNFORTUNATE.

7   IT HAS BEEN SAID THAT A MAN'S FOES CAN BE THOSE OF HIS OWN HOUSEHOLD.

8   SNOWWHITE WILL ENDURE, BUT THE HOUSEHOLD OF THE HIGH CHURCH SUFFERS.

9   AND THE CHILD MEN WILL DIE TO PROTECT THE CHURCH, FOR THE HIGH PRIESTS FEAR THE ALTAR OF IMAGE.

10   Then SnowWhite smiled, and said, REMEMBER, LOOK AFTER THE WELFARE OF THE CHILD MEN . . .

11   . . . SNOWWHITE HERE TO ANSWER CHILD MEN PRAYERS.

12   And there was quiet, for the helo pilots knew they were the rescue hope of the kids,

13   They were the last hope to many radio prayers.

CHAPTER 6

1   TopsyTurvy, the cleric major, mumbled, moaned, and accepted the flight as co-pilot with BirdMan;

2   TopsyTurvy loved flying jets, climbing high above the clouds sailing along at high speed listening to the echoes of the mind;

3   And TopsyTurvy let it be known unto BirdMan his great distaste at flying low and slow.

4   And it came to pass that BirdMan flew the helicopter higher and higher above the Nam Bo jungles and mountains;

5   Soon TopsyTurvy twitched, fumbled, and mumbled about being high above the clouds and the earth below, in just a mere helo;

6   Then BirdMan smiled and flew higher and higher over the mountains toward the jungle outpost;

7   And TopsyTurvy complained because it was cold with the open helo windows at such great height;

8   TopsyTurvy bitched because the old Dog helo shuttered and sputtered in the winds at such great height;

9   And TopsyTurvy was scared.

10   Zing Zing! Zing! Shot the new noise through the helicopter as the tail rotor gears slipped, then failed.

11   And TopsyTurvy screamed on the radio yelling "Emergency, Emergency," that the Dog helo was about to crash; he displayed a Lay-major panic, and a panicked Lay-major.

12   BirdMan laughed at TopsyTurvy for BirdMan had easily drifted into autorotational flight and there was no need to fear;

13   And BirdMan radioed to TailWind as wingman that a straightjacket was needed for TopsyTurvy;

14   And the dog helo did glide, and it did glide, and it did glide, for unto great heights it had flown and it took great time to get back through the hole in the parted clouds to the green earth below;

15   Then it was that BirdMan saw the green rice spot by the mountain village and landed the helo without engine power and with great talent,

16   And TopsyTurvy leapt to the ground kissing mother earth and swearing that he had escaped death by helo;

17   But BirdMan laughed; a tail rotor failure high in the sky was no danger at all.

18   TopsyTurvy sought to give BirdMan a medal for saving his life, and the crew, and the helo,
19   But BirdMan simply said "I'll take two at-a-boys and a beer."

CHAPTER 7

1   "The colonel says," sheepishly said Vicar-major DingleBerry to BirdMan, "you go fly out of the zone ole number 7 that got shot up and crash landed at Aceldama."
2   And it came to pass that BirdMan came unto Aceldama and examined greatly the bullet ridden and mortar hole torn helo that had been mechanically patched and partially repaired.
3   And with much heart and due reverence, BirdMan started and hovered the vibrating flying machine that whistled and slung forth great weird sounds from missing rotor blade pockets and holes in its sides.
4   And birds flew for their lives while animals scampered from the horrible in-flight sound coming from the piecemeal carcass of a shot-up helo;
5   The child men Marines laughed, watching the helicopter that did not want to fly as it danced in big hovering circles from side to side and yo yo'ed up and down trying to crash back to the earth;
6   And BirdMan test danced with the unwilling helo in its bucking and snorting refusal to be flown.
7   Then BirdMan nursed the wounded craft skyward wobbling with aerial disfunction as he herded it airward in a one flight challenge toward the airfield repair facility.
8   Passers-by, the pilots, the crews, and many people came out of their tents, their grass houses, and tin buildings to see what made such awkward noise in the sky.
9   There it was, the machine of man that should not fly, screaming forth with wind blowing through the metal holes in its sides whizzing strange shrill toned whistles interspersed among the awkward chop chop of blades with missing pockets.
10   And behold, for BirdMan was in his finest hour dangling above the earth connected to a fifteen hundred horse power flute.
11   Upon hearing the shrill sky noises, Injun radioed BirdMan to push left rudder to get C sharp;

12   And StoneMan radioed and asked BirdMan where he got the perfectly good helicopter,

13   And DarkMoon answered, "With coupons at the King of Cash's country store."

14   And ShareCrop said by radio, "BirdMan, you done landed on a land mine?"

15   Whereupon, as BirdMan smiled trying to fight the partial controls while wobbling away, the big engine coughed, then quit;

16   It became raw talent to BirdMan in the controlled crash decent but in his ears he heard SmegMa on the tower radio, "Bird-Man, why did you turn the engine off?"

17   And it was that BirdMan again heard SmegMa as the helo landed on the house, sinking through the grass roof, "Watcha doin' BirdMan? Are ya' a crashin?"

18   And it came to pass that BirdMan performed the perfect autorotational crash through the grass roofed house on the edge of the airfield with the spinning steel blades trimming flatness to the roof top.

19   And it came to pass that the Cardinal-general was pleased, for unto the graveyard was salvaged one helo carcass that would not be reported as a total loss,

20   And the Church of the Marine Korps would shine in the face of the Cathedrals of the Army over one less helo loss in the war of inter-service statistics.

21   And SnowFlight laughed, and laughed, at the story of Bird-Man crashing an already crashed helicopter.

CHAPTER 8

1   BirdMan, the maintenance check pilot, climbed alone as the sole pilot into the crewless helo to flight check the repaired helicopter;

2   BirdMan liked flying alone.

3   Then BirdMan performed all those mechanical test things pilots do to check the performance of a new engine;

4   And BirdMan flew high in the sky becoming a small dot above the Tru Lai Airfield.

5   BirdMan stopped the forward speed of the helicopter and froze the controls where the helo would just hover in one spot over a mile above the earth.

6   Then BirdMan turned-off the radios, and sat above the Tru Lai earth staring into the distant billowing clouds forming over the purple mountains.

7   "What did I get myself into," he whispered to himself.

8   "Death and wounds were to be clean."

9   "Everyone was to get some glory, some excitement."

10   "Sure, . . . death happens."

11   "I lied to myself; they suckered us kids."

12   And BirdMan sat high above the earth hovering and thinking.

13   And it was that flying alone allowed the mind to slowly cleanse itself from the recently discovered horror camouflaged from youthful inability to evaluate risk of death at old man's tarot.

14   BirdMan smiled as he scanned each critical reading from the many gauges showing the wonderful performance of the new engine.

15   "Lies, damn lies, and statistics," he remembered the words and saw the abomination of "body count."

16   BirdMan saw the arriving fishing boats of his youth which killed the innocent dolphins trapped in the nets;

17   And he saw in his mind lemmings with rifles jumping into the sea of stupidity.

18   "Am I going crazy?" came the self-examination thought.

19   Then the cool air shifted BirdMan's thoughts; and with the smooth flicker of the wrist, BirdMan pushed the nose over commencing the descending glide back to the Tru Lai world below.

20   **BIRDMAN BESIDE HIMSELF?** questioned SnowWhite as BirdMan walked in from the flight line.

21   "This war sucks," BirdMan responded, then wondered how SnowWhite knew.

22   **BIRDMAN IN HIGH HOVER LONG TIME**, said SnowWhite, grinning to BirdMan.

CHAPTER 9

1   BirdMan needed happy hour, for unto happy hour came stories of mental escape.

2   And unto happy hour came great laughter along with the stories of getting child men back from risk of the loss of flesh.

3   But DarkMoon, Injun, ShareCrop, StoneMan and SmegMa consoled BirdMan, for unto him ate the doldrums of war reality.
4   Vicar-major DingleBerry and the happy hour pilots sang the words to a new song,

Your son came home in a rubber bag,
   doo-dah, doo-dah,
Your son came home in a rubber bag,
   ooh, de doo-dah day.

Went in little and it came out big,
   doo-dah, doo-dah,
Went in little and it came out big,
   ooh, de doo-dah day.

5   And it was that happy hour lost its flavor;
6   For it was learned that SlingShot, the trusted gun pilot, had been hurt with wounds received in his close flying protecting the MedEvac helo.
7   And it was there was no hope to stop the war for the King of Cash knew not that he knew not.
8   BirdMan became much drunk.
9   Then in the pain of drunkenness, BirdMan hobbled out into the monsoon rain to be captured as he fell in the darkness by the round fence row of barbed wire.
10   And BirdMan cried, and cried, and cried, not from the pain from the cuts of the wire, but from the mental barbs cutting away at a tormented soul forced to accept the living hell of watching child men die for unworthy reasons, and at the wounds of SlingShot.
11   "War is human hell," he mumbled, watching the flashes of visions in his mind of the 1369 rubber body bags and the child men ripped apart with weapons of war, and smelling the charred flesh.
11   In the darkness a dry hand came forth in the rain, lifting BirdMan from the wire barbs of mental pain for SnowWhite untangled the pilot who more than loved to fly, and shouldered him to his bunk.
12   "I hurt," said BirdMan unto SnowWhite.

13   THE   SOUL   WITHIN   BIRDMAN   MOURNS,   said SnowWhite,
14   BUT MARY, SWEET MARY, SHARES YOUR PAIN.

CHAPTER 10

1   There came the time that all of squadron 777 was ordered out of Nam Bo across the sea to the Island of the Floating Dragon by helo carrier to get new helicopters and replenish for forty days and forty nights.
2   And the pilots of SnowFlight swooped down over the pallets of surplus food to be thrown away by the men of Navy and captured the food in nets as cargo carried underneath the helicopters.
3   And the food was delivered to the orphanage for the children of Nam Bo.
4   And as they departed the land, DarkMoon radioed to Bird-Man to fly in close in tight formation for DarkMoon wanted to take his picture.
5   BirdMan moved in close formation flying in one rotor blade distance to DarkMoon's helo.
6   But it was that DarkMoon only meant to moon BirdMan, for there three thousand feet above the earth was the dark moon butt of DarkMoon pointed out the pilot's window at BirdMan,
7   And DarkMoon said on the radio to BirdMan, "Smile, I just winked at you;
8   "Did you see the shutter click?"

CHAPTER 11

1   777 came to the Island of the Floating Dragon, with much confusion circling about.
2   And in time many nameless and faceless new pilots checked in to the 777 Squadron to prepare to go to the war.
3   BirdMan filled out the paperwork and checked-in a new pilot he called Isa A. Hoel into the squadron;
4   OverBoost checked out a survival radio and flight equipment in the name Isa A. Hoel;

5   RedLine assigned Isa A. Hoel into the small living quarters for pilots;

6   TailWind signed Isa A. Hoel into the medical clinic;

7   DarkMoon joined the pilot's club mess with the name Isa A. Hoel;

8   HalfRight wrote the name Isa A. Hoel in the roster at the chapel;

9   StoneMan scheduled a new pilot named Isa A. Hoel to fly on the flight schedule, but would cancel him from the flight manifest right before each flight.

10   TwoDogs listed Isa A. Hoel for receiving mail;

11   ShareCrop announced at the morning flight briefing that Isa A. Hoel had been sent for sea survival school at the big Navy Base.

12   BolTer ordered two flight suit name tags, metal dog tags, and calling cards under the name Isa A. Hoel.

13   BurnOut got Isa A. Hoel a computer code number that revealed Isa A. Hoel to have political connections.

14   SmegMa smiled, and passed out calling cards which said Isa A. Hoel on one side and Kraven Moorehead on the other.

15   And it came to pass that everyone knew Isa A. Hoel;

16   And no one knew Isa A. Hoel

17   And it was that no one could quite remember what Isa A. Hoel looked like.

18   Then it came to be that Curate-colonel Kiwi Temple sought to meet the new pilot named Isa A. Hoel, but he was nowhere to be found.

19   And the Ritual Reverend Chaplain Brother Navy-major Hebert Hebert Richard ("Dick") Head sought to meet the new pilot, Isa A. Hoel.

20   And the angry non-in-control Vicar-major DingleBerry screamed forth at the drunken happy hour did anyone know Isa A. Hoel?

21   And amidst the laughter, dozens of pilots screamed forth "yes"!

22   And they laughed and yelled, "Usa Ass Hoel."

23   And DarkMoon, with cheeks spread, yelled forth, "Here's Isa's brother."

24   And great laughter prevailed.

CHAPTER 12

1   It was on the Island of the Floating Dragon that a new pilot flew the helo with BirdMan above the airfield to train the new guy for war.

2   "What's that noise?" came BirdMan's words with a smile to the suddenly turned pale new pilot upon hearing the deafening silence of no engine.

3   "Umph-h-h," moaned BirdMan at the speechless with stark terror co-pilot. "Seems you lost an engine, you fly it, now don't kill us."

4   The terrorized co-pilot did fly the powerless helo to the earth and safely land on the runway.

5   And the "kid", as BirdMan called him, smiled with great confidence, for he had landed a helo without an engine, just like happens in battle when the engine gets shot out with a bullet.

6   And Vicar-major DingleBerry screamed at BirdMan that it was not within the desk book to shut off the engine in flight just to train co-pilots.

7   And Vicar-major DingleBerry told BirdMan not to tell him if he was going to shut the engine off ever again just to train a pilot.

8   And it came to pass that BirdMan would smile when flying above the airfield with the new pilots as he would shut the fuel off, stopping the engine, and would say, "In a pretend war with pretend leaders, just pretend I didn't shut off the engine."

9   Then BirdMan would teach flying confidence to the new pilot by performing a perfect engine-out autorotation to the runway.

10   "You're crazy," giggled HalfRight to BirdMan, "if they think you are good, they'll send you out on the sandwich missions."

11   "I'll ask that you be my co-pilot," responded BirdMan, "matter a' fact, I'll ask that you just fly with me all the time."

12   And the two pilots laughed, and HalfRight said, "You're crazy."

CHAPTER 13

1   BirdMan led the new fledgling co-pilots to meet SnowWhite; but it was that BurnOut accepted such not.
2   And there were many questions from the young pilots who knew war not and sought answers not wanting to hear truth.
3   And the young pilots wanted to hear how they could survive.
4   And the young pilots asked whys of the war of Sam Bo with Bac Bo,
5   And the young pilots asked why child men Marines should die for a no win war,
6   And the young pilots were void of wisdom or war.
7   "Give us the secret," asked one new child man Marine pilot, "How have you survived?"
8   **BY ELECTION,** came the words of SnowWhite.
9   And the clean skin faces sought what election?
10   And SnowWhite asked, **WHAT ARE YOU FIGHTING FOR?**
11   And hearing no Answer, SnowWhite asked, **WHAT ARE YOU FIGHTING AGAINST?**
12   And hearing no Answer, SnowWhite said, . . . **ARE THERE TIMES OF UNJUST WAR?**
13   . . . , **ARE THERE TIMES OF JUST PEACE?**
14   . . . , **ARE THERE TIMES OF JUST WAR?**
15   . . . , **ARE THERE TIMES OF UNJUST PEACE?**
16   **LISTEN TO YOUR HEART. WHAT DOES YOUR HEART TELL YOU?**
17   **IS THIS A WAR TO ALLOW MEN TO BE FREE?**
18   **IN THE MELON THERE IS HEART, AND YOU MUST LEARN TO FLY AS TENDER THE HEART OF THE MELON, FOR IN THE HEART THERE IS GREATNESS.**
19   **KNOW YOUR HEART, AND YOU SHOULD FLY THE WAY OF THE TENDER HEART.**
20   And it came to pass that the child men pilots knew not what SnowWhite had said, for he talked in riddles; for he talked funny.
21   But it was also that round about the child men pilots cherished the time when flight could be with SnowWhite,
22   For SnowWhite could do flying things no other pilot could do.

CHAPTER 14

1   BirdMan flew, and he flew, for BirdMan accumulated more flying hours than any other of his fellow pilots.

2   And it was that the serenity of flight washed away spooks of the mind and the mental sounds of unsolvable human misery.

3   And it was that BirdMan found atonement above the earth looking down on the evil things that men do.

4   And it came to pass in the middle of the night that BirdMan heard the whir, . . . whir, . . . whir of a strange, loud noise.

5   And BirdMan went to see.

6   And there was SmegMa with a very small car tethered to a long chain;

7   And the driverless car tied to the chain was throttled to drive round and round in a circle.

8   And the car did go round and round by itself.

9   And SmegMa went forth with the leather bullwhip cracking the whip and beating the circling, tiny car.

10   "The noise of a whip, and the noise of the rattling wheels, and the prancing horses, and the jumping chariots," said SmegMa as he beat the passing car.

11   "And there is a multitude of slain, and a great number of carcasses; and there is no end of their corpses; they stumble upon their corpses . . ." came SmegMa's drunken words in stupor as he fell to the ground, exhausted in mind and soul.

12   And it was that BirdMan went forth and rescued the pained SmegMa.

13   And so it was that the sights of dead young men and young men in agony of the flesh burst forth in the mind even when one is away from war.

CHAPTER 15

1   After a time, Curate-colonel Artimes N. Temple did promote BirdMan to flight leader, and advanced him, and set his seat above the seat of his common meat pilots,

2   For it was known unto all that BirdMan liked to fly.

3   And it was also known unto Temple that blindness made unto volunteers in times of great battle.

4   Now it came to pass that BirdMan would fly wing, and second place, with his brother pilot, StoneMan.

5   And there came a day that BirdMan and StoneMan danced among the clouds and mellowly flew high above the mountains on the Island of the Floating Dragon;

6   Then as birds in the sky, BirdMan dove downward with Stone-Man in chase;

7   And BirdMan flew between the narrow mountains and under the high bridge with StoneMan close behind.

8   Then it was that the two children of flight returned to the airfield amid much laughter and comradery for the aerial antics;

9   But there came much gnashing of teeth, for unto Temple was told secretly that his pilots were flying under bridges.

10   And the Temple man knew that pilots were more important than principles;

11   And it came to pass that the pilots were confined by Temple to remain one night at the airfield as a punishment not to fly under bridges.

12   But such was a punishment not,

13   For there are times when pilots should not go to town.

CHAPTER 16

1   The children of the mountain village on the end of the Island of the Floating Dragon liked the little porch house;

2   And their small tan faces glowed with uncommon sparkles with the BirdMan who shared with them and brought them the small house dangling under the helicopter.

3   And the children freely gave of their inner spirit to the Bird-Man's friends who sat among them in the shade of the afternoon.

4   But the Sky Blue Bishop-general at the air base understood not, for the gazebo in the middle of the twenty-seven hole golf course had disappeared in the night,

5   And there was much gnashing of teeth with hierarchial occultation, for to men of non-war the loss of a gazebo is a clergical event.

6   It was that great search was given surrounding the mystery of the missing gazebo; it was also that explanation was undiscovered.

7   "It had to be the Marines," mumbled the Sky Blue com-

mander, "but they are all far away in the mountains to the north, and no Marine trucks came on our base; and there weren't any on the base."

8   So it came to be that the thick file investigating the missing gazebo found its way unto the unidentified flying object cabinet, where it was rightly so.

CHAPTER 17

1   It was written in the Church of the Marine Korps law that while on the Island of the Floating Dragon, 777 shall get helos not worn by the rigors of war;

2   It was also written that new pilots were to train to go to war;

3   And it came to pass that 777 was called out in the night to quickly return the pilots to the land of Nam Bo;

4   Then it was that there was silence, for unto them was known that death awaited many in the battles to come;

5   And there was tightening of heart with parking of soul upon seeing death gathering about.

6   But out of the midst of gloom and doom, BirdMan brought much laughter, for BirdMan, in the night of departure, captured and carried underneath the helo the sky blue cart used by the Sky Blue Bishop-general in his war on golfs.

7   And it was in the night that the cart was quickly turned dark green and packed deeply into the carrier ship to go to the land of Nam Bo.

8   And it is an unwritten rule of war that the haves sometimes unknowingly give unto the have nots;

9   So it was that Sky Blue Bishop-general fretted greatly and there was gnashing of teeth for unto him secretly had been cast a Marine Korps' woe.

CHAPTER 18

1   It came to pass after 777 returned back unto the land of Nam Bo that BirdMan came unto the airfield of the zoomie, the jet pilot.

2   And there came BoxGutters, a short-stack jet pilot with low

manifold pressure who befriended BirdMan, and BirdMan befriended him;

3   And it came to pass that BirdMan strapped on behind Box-Gutters the mighty jet airplane to climb into God's sky.

4   Then BoxGutters cork-screwed the mighty jet from take off to high in the sky seeking to frighten and stress the mere helo pilot;

5   And BoxGutters dove and flew up-side down through the valleys and over the ocean finally allowing BirdMan to fly;

6   And BirdMan dove and flew up side down through the valleys and over the ocean, finally allowing BoxGutters to fly again;

7   And it came to pass that BoxGutters climbed into the helo to fly with BirdMan;

8   And BirdMan took off backwards, then jerked back to the earth in a panicked smoothness signaling death by helicopter to the whitened BoxGutters;

9   And then BirdMan climbed vertically spinning the helo around and around vertically in candy cane striped fashion over one spot confusing the jet pilot who knew all about flying;

10   And then in the middle of stable non-confusion BirdMan's climb ceased, for BirdMan turned off the engine, beginning a death leap in BoxGutters eyes to the earth where BirdMan landed without power among the Nam Bo villagers;

11   And it came to pass that BoxGutters worshiped not helicopters and sought safety at 25,000 feet and 1,000 miles per hour, for unto great speed and high altitude came survival;

12   And BoxGutters feared the unknown of a flying machine that fled backwards, upwards, and jumped straight at the earth when its engine failed.

13   And the pilots of SnowFlight laughed, laughed, and laughed, for unto 'jet jocks' there was a heaven, and helo's were their hell.

CHAPTER 19

1   Then there came the times of much suffering, for child men pilots died in the middle of the steamy jungles and on the flat rice field plains in the name of repeat victories for the same hilltop;

2   And it was that good child men were being asked to die for causes unknown;

3   And it was also that war without cause or purpose pumps up the economy and vomits the mind.

4   So it came to pass that BirdMan sought refuge higher and higher in the sky, for above the earth there is escape from witnessing the evils that men do.

5   But BirdMan could not stay skyward forever, and he landed and sought counsel from SnowWhite.

6   And SnowWhite unto SnowFlight said, **THE HOUR GLASS WHEN FILLED WITH SAND GIVES ONLY AN HOUR, BUT THE HOUR GLASS WHEN FILLED WITH WATER FLOWS QUICKLY.**

7   **AND THE HOUR GLASS WITHOUT SAND OR WATER FLOWS NOT.**

8   **THE GRAINS OF LIFE ARE NOW FORCED THROUGH THE NECK OF THIS WAR, AND IT SHALL COME TO YOU THE WISDOM OF TIME.**

9   **BUT THERE WILL BE MEN WHO WORSHIP THE SEEDS AND PLANT WARS,**

10   **AND THERE WILL BE MEN WHO MISDIRECT GLORIOUS CAUSE,**

11   **BUT IT IS THAT EVIL CORRUPTS THIS WAR AND DISPLACES THE FLESH.**

12   **WE FIGHT NOT AGAINST FLESH AND BLOOD, BUT AGAINST PRINCIPALITIES, AGAINST POWERS, AGAINST THE RULERS OF THE DARKNESS OF THIS WORLD, AGAINST SPIRITUAL WICKEDNESS IN HIGH PLACES.**

13   **KEEP THE FAITH,**

14   **YOU CAN ANSWER PRAYERS OF DYING CHILD MEN,**

15   **FOR THE SONS ARE GIVEN UNTO MOLECH.**

CHAPTER 20

1   "What's that noise?" came BirdMan's words with a smile to the suddenly-turned-pale BurnOut.

2   "Umph-h-h," smiled BirdMan at the speechless co-pilot, "Seems we really lost the engine."

3   And it was that the powerless helo with real engine failure did

glide to the earth and land artfully on the side of a bomb crater with BirdMan's flying touch.
4   Then it was that TwoDogs rescued BirdMan, BurnOut, and the flight crew in the middle of the jungle nowhere;
5   And BirdMan departed last, and burned the abandoned helo.
6   And it was that BirdMan smiled, for the Cardinal-general would have by edict sent forth child men Marines to die in the rescue of the carcass of the old, worn-out helo,
7   For it was known that the Church of the Marine Korps sought worship of war numbers against the enemy Army.
8   But it was known also that the burned carcass of a dead helo saves the kids risk of death;
9   So it was that the child men Marines were sent not to chase the mystical numbers of Korps self-preservation.
10   And it was also that BirdMan, StoneMan, RedLine, Over-Boost, TwoDogs, HalfRight, ShareCrop, TailWind, DarkMoon, SmegMa, and BolTer smiled,
11   For saving lives sometimes meant killing helo's.
12   And BurnOut said unto SnowWhite that BirdMan had destroyed government property.
13   And when he had spoken, SnowWhite said, **BETTER IS A LITTLE WITH RIGHTEOUSNESS THAN GREAT REVENUES WITHOUT RIGHT.**

CHAPTER 21

1   And BirdMan sang to himself as he walked,

He'. . .lo Bird,
High above yon tree,

Wo..on you please,
Come down and rescue me.

He'. . .lo Bird so high
Way up in the sky
Please come down and rescue me.

2   "HeloBird," came forth the word from SmegMa sitting naked on top the bunker with his pecker stuck in an open-ended beer can filled with red fungus paste.

3   Then SmegMa confronted BirdMan whether DingleBerry had grounded him for burning the Dog helo,

4   And BirdMan grinned, for to ground him meant that Dingle-Berry and Temple might have to fly BirdMan's missions,

5   For there was a shortage of pilots,

6   And there was greatness of rescue need.

7   But DingleBerry and Temple gave great frustration, for the secret of burning a Dog helo had to be kept from the clerics at the High Church,

8   For the clerics at the High Church expressed great dismay that the carcass of a dead helo was left lying deep in the enemies' jungle terrain.

9   Then DingleBerry and Temple sought not to ground BirdMan, for to ground BirdMan would signal inquiry from the High Church.

10   Both DingleBerry and Temple gave forth great gnashing of teeth at priestly indecision.

11   Then it came to be that DingleBerry ordered BirdMan not to crash when he flew,

12   And if BirdMan didn't crash, then BirdMan couldn't burn another helo, and if BirdMan crashed, he would have disobeyed orders.

13   SmegMa listened to such story from BirdMan, then laughed.

14   Then SmegMa told BirdMan of putting his pecker in the beer can, "Its fashionable."

15   And BirdMan confused said, "What's fashionable?"

16   Then it came to be known unto BirdMan that the new pilots and other passersby had been convinced by SmegMa of the wonders of placing one's penis in an open ended beer can with red fungus paste.

17   And there sitting in the sun behind the bunker were other naked new pilots partaking of the wisdom of SmegMa by putting their pecker in a can of red paste to get good luck.

18   Then BirdMan laughed, for blindness begats blindness, and those who seek ignorance will find ignorance.

CHAPTER 22

1   Now BirdMan, captain of the host of flight, was a great pilot with honorable soul, because by him SnowWhite had given unto him the power of deliverance unto the child men Marines: he was a mighty pilot in valor, but he was nuts also.

2   And it came to pass that the Bac Bo enemy built unto themselves a fortress on the edge of the wilderness.

3   And the enemy forthright did display its great flag on a tall pole for all to see.

4   And it came to pass that out of the cloud-covered sky leapt through the small hole of light between the clouds a lone helo directly above the enemy camp;

5   And the soldiers of Bac Bo ran unto the many hiding and protective places awaiting the bombs of battle and the guns of war;

6   But there came none for the helo hovered next to the flag pole and a child man Flight Sergeant Marine cut forth the flag of Bac Bo;

7   And the helo rose unto the clouds leaving only the rudiments of noise without gunfire as BirdMan with his crew escaped with the captured Bac Bo flag.

8   "You're nuts," giggled SmegMa at seeing the enemy flag stolen away from the flag pole at the risk of death in the palms of the Bac Bo lands.

9   "They'll be ready next time," said HalfRight examining the flag badge.

10   "What will you take for it," asked BurnOut thinking of the profit that could be made on resale and remarketing, "its single stitched and hand sewn!"

11   "Sands of Iwo Jima," came BolTer with a twisted grin, "Yoa done got tha flag before we capture the city."

12   And Vicar-major Berry glorified the capture of the enemy flag and sought its ownership for him, or for the mighty Temple as the desk pilot of men; but such was not meant to be;

13   And it was proper for unto the Flight Sergeant did BirdMan deliver the flag, for Sergeants are the pack mules of war.

CHAPTER 23

1   There was a time of much battle, and of much death.

2   And it came to pass in the land of Nam Bo that BirdMan was sent forth to rescue from the dark demons wandering about the battle field the flesh of the child men Marines.

3   And it was also that in the heat of battle that there were things small in the minds of non-warrior men who knew not the pain of death from those who practice god;

4   Then it came to be that the air cover for MedEvac helo's ceased for unto the coffers came abstinence of helo gun support by selfishness, and command fake heart;

5   "I'll go," said BirdMan, knowing that the child men lay in agony against the mindset of arrogance.

6   And it came to pass that BirdMan was cast into the furnace of machine gun fire to rescue the child men who blindly dove into the kiln splashing forth their blood in old men's challenges.

7   And as BirdMan sat in the open while the wounded were gathered into the helo perched to fly away, BirdMan was shot squarely in the heart.

8   And HalfRight screamed on the radio as the helo sped away with the bullet hole windshield face;

9   And BirdMan said, "I've got it," taking the controls away from the panicked HalfRight, "didn't hurt a bit."

10   Then it was that HalfRight saw that the miracles of man and the bullet-proof flight jacket of life had stopped the bullet, and BirdMan flew away.

11   And pilots came from far and wide to see the bullet proof vest that stopped the bullet that sought the heart of BirdMan.

12   And the drunken with happiness BirdMan tap danced the night away.

13   And SnowWhite saw into the night the drunken BirdMan, and said, **WHOSE GLORIOUS BEAUTY IS A FADING FLOWER, WHICH ARE ON THE HEAD OF THE FAT VALLEYS OF THEM THAT ARE OVERCOME WITH WINE!**

CHAPTER 24

1   And it came to pass that BirdMan dreamed over and over the vision of dying on an up-side down X with his head to the bottom.
2   "Protokletos," came SmegMa's words for the first time calling BirdMan by his real name, "it means you are in second place."
3   "But its the white of SnowWhite cast against the blue-sky," protested the still un-sober BirdMan into the eyes of the amazing 'Doc SmegMa.'
4   And SmegMa listened.
5   "But the cross shall never vanish out of the sky," BirdMan cried, "And the cross shall never vanish out of the sky," he said again, and BirdMan slept.
6   And it was and it came to pass that BirdMan served over and over as the target while the flesh of the child men Marines were jerked out of the ravages of ignorance wrapped in blindness.
7   And BirdMan became swollen with the pain of knowing.
8   But the heart of pleasure when capturing from death the flesh of the child men Marines knew no equal,
9   For unto few men are given this moment's flash of pureness.
10   And BirdMan saw fields of wasted flesh and was thankful to be allowed to partake in removing children from immense pain.
11   And it came to pass that BirdMan saw SnowWhite, and knew.

CHAPTER 25

1   For BirdMan, for SnowWhite, and for the brotherhood of SnowFlight, there was much death all around.
2   And those facing death prayed the Angels of protection and the spirits of survival;
3   But the demons homesteading the minds and souls of the leaders puked forth messages of power, vanity, and greed, for it was a time for harvesting the blood of ignorant youth cast in the spell of honor and not truth.
4   "We should trade one of the King's court for four of the enemy," came forth BirdMan's disgust for the King of Cash justifying war with body count.

5   And there were pits dug to bury the enemy dead who desired not death at any statistical number,

6   And old men, the women, the children, and an occasional animal were given the undignity of being one dead enemy in the folklore of body count.

7   But also there were the dead Marine comrades, and the wounded were being carried to the hospital.

8   **THE WHORES OF BABYLON COUNT CASH, NOT LIVES**, were the words of SnowWhite in response to BirdMan's penetrating questions of the whys of war.

9   And round-about men who loved the Fatherland refused to dishonor it but the King of Cash issued orders for the tide of human death and misery which emanated from the flicker of his lips;

10   And round-about, men who were loyal to their beloved Korps and refused to dishonor it were asked to die by the High Priests who believed not in the King of Cash, the Prince of Money, or the Paragon of Piles,

11   But priests of the High Church would give loyalty not back to the child men Marines by exposing the King's deeds, using truth as a sword of child men survival.

12   And this the unleashed ego of the runaway error magnified itself over and over to the ever increasing ire of the people asked to donate their sons for the Harrods of Wall Street,

13   For the continued power of the misguided vanities of the kingly mind,

14   And for the careerist priests who would not speak out for self-preservation sake;

15   The young, innocent soldiers were left to give all, and did give all, so that their Father could, through time, learn the evils and ignorance of allowing selfish leaders to steer the ship of the people through the seas of profits.

16   No greater price could be asked of a young man than to shed his life for an up-tick in the market,

17   And to convert his flesh to the cash pockets of rich derelicts who cared not at the pain of poor others, and others poor.

The Gospel According to STONEMAN

(Set the Example)

CHAPTER 1

1   Once upon a time, there was a mixed breed white man who sought and obtained atonement within the confines of the church, Marine Korps.

2   It was that Rusty Stoner had **INTEGRITY**, for the stakes of combat were too high to gamble on a dishonest man,

3   It was that Rusty Stoner had **KNOWLEDGE**, for he knew his helo and the techniques that could be used to make it perform,

4   It was that Rusty Stoner had **COURAGE**, both physical and moral; for he knew what was right and stood up for it; for he served God, country and the Korps—and in that order,

5   It was that Rusty Stoner was **DECISIVE**, for he would say what he meant and mean what he said, and wouldn't pass the buck,

6   It was that Rusty Stoner was **DEPENDABLE**, for he got the job done regardless of the obstacles,

7   It was that Rusty Stoner had **INITIATIVE**, for he thought ahead and stayed mentally alert and physically awake.

8   It was that Rusty Stoner had **TACT**, for he said the right thing at the right time in an effective, courteous way,

9   It was that Rusty Stoner dispensed **JUSTICE**, for he was fair, impartial and equal in his thinking and doing,

10   It was that Rusty Stoner was **ENTHUSIASTIC**, for he was at his best teaching the right way,

11   It was that Rusty Stoner had **BEARING**, for every where he

walked eyes knew there was a confident pilot within the well-kept flight suit, and he spoke plainly and simply,

12   It was that Rusty Stoner had **ENDURANCE**, for he kept himself fit, physically and mentally, and he could endure,

13   It was that Rusty Stoner was **UNSELFISH**, for he got and gave the best to those around him,

14   It was that Rusty Stoner was **LOYAL**, for unto his fellow Marines he gave all he could give,

15   And it was that Rusty Stoner was learning **JUDGMENT**, for **JUDGMENT** came with experience in learning how to understand; and as he was acquiring **JUDGMENT** in the land of Nam Bo, and the living sermons of the combat church came unto him.

16   And in the maze of youth, StoneMan was learning to separate in the fog of innocence the burning phosphorus of making choices.

17   Rusty Stoner was a lifer,

18   For he was an acknowledged career man, a "regular" of the Korps Church.

19   Someday Rusty Stoner would be a Lay-leader, or a Vicar, or a High Priest,

20   So Rusty Stoner did not have an "R" tattooed in his personnel file signaling for all to see that he was an outsider temporarily quartered as a member of the church like a visitor, or a distant cousin,

21   For unto the unholy inner circles of the Korps church, these outsider Marines were called "reserves."

22   And while unction was given that the reserve Marines were members unto the unholy church,

23   It was known far and wide that the church had two classes of members,

24   And one class of privilege.

25   Rusty Stoner's vows of regularity set him apart from the common reserve pilots of the Korps Church.

26   It was that Rusty Stoner extended his tour of duty to remain in Nam Bo in order to please himself, and to please his church.

27   He was devout.

CHAPTER 2

1   Rusty Stoner explained to his brother pilot, Andreaus, "You have to learn to live with the reality that most of the careerists have never seen combat, you have to be patient with them."

2   Andreaus protested, shaking his head negatively, "Somebody will have to die -somebody will pay the price so the Korps can train some desk pogue every few months giving commands in combat. I don't want to die cause Temple wants medals in his personnel jacket; he's fight'n for career survival; look'n for promotion. It's our asses that will be hung out so's he can get medals to dress up his file. You know he takes the milk-run missions; You know he has you fly'n wing on him so you can rescue him if he fouls up on a cake walk flight."

3   And it was that Andreaus was pissed at the individuals who defiled their brothers.

4   "That begs the question," Rusty Stoner sharply answered, "Can you let one Marine down cause we didn't do our best?"

5   Andreaus knew the answer, but Andreaus knew Stoner was right, but it just wasn't fair in an unfair war for anyone to shirk tough missions off to the child men.

6   "I perform," said Stoner.

7   And it was that St. Jean giggled and pretended to ice skate symbolically meaning 'skate mission' for Stoner's flights with Temple.

8   And it was that Giacomo laughed and mockingly pretended to eat a piece of cake.

9   And PennyWorth said, "Yeah, don't throw me in the briar patch."

10   But it was that the congregational pilots knew the church was sometimes possessed by deadly clerics,

11   And it was also known that flying high commanders stayed away from the battle, a blessing!

12   Alone that night, Stoner reflected on Andreaus' disgust;

13   He thought about the stupidity of a war without objective;

14   He thought about the blank eyes of the innocent child men Marines who loaded their dead and wounded brothers into his rescue helicopter;

15   He saw the faces of the dead pilots;

16   He heard the echoes of command and staff preoccupied with medals and window dressed statistics,
17   Stoner fought such thoughts.
18   Then Stoner smiled at those times he had pulled Marines out of the claws of death, the times he had saved lives—he grinned to himself, but he also cried.
19   Stoner hurt, he hurt for the killing;
20   He hurt for the insanity;
21   He hurt for the children;
22   He hurt because he was powerless to stop the hurt.
23   He ached with the pain of the vision of the attrocities of the mind seen as miles of countless victims.
24   "War is the horror of horrors," he whispered silently to himself as he faded toward a forced sleep, "but there has to be hope."
25   And Stoner thought a selfish thought, one that bothered him, "As long as I fly wing on Temple, I'll make it."
26   But Rusty Stoner liked not being assigned to the casper milktoast flights, and liked not himself for letting his extended tour flying skills be wasted covering the Temple man.
27   And a sweet dream came to Stoner, one that swept away the fog of the inhumane dew, for Stoner flew silently and wonderfully with others who confidently swept down in the heat of battles yanking the child men Marines away from the altar of innocence.
28   And in the sweet dream, the light did shine.
29   And in the sweet dream, it was an honor to be a Marine.

CHAPTER 3

1   And it came to pass that Andreaus sought out Rusty Stoner to tell him of a new pilot that had appeared while he was out to the ship on the sea.
2   And Andreaus took Rusty to meet SnowWhite, for he sang praises of the flying abilities of SnowWhite.
3   Then it was that SnowWhite smiled at the anxious Greek and the tall man in close stride, who was guided to SnowWhite.
4   A BIRDMAN . . . AND A STONEMAN, said SnowWhite.
5   And Rusty Stoner was taken aback by the immediate gloss of such words,
6   But SnowWhite said further, WHY BE DOVE, COME FLY WITH SNOWWHITE.

7   "This flight leader of men is crazy," Rusty Stoner thought to himself.
8   "Calls me a 'StoneMan'."
9   "I'm safe, I fly wing on Temple, safest place in the Nam Bo war, why should I fly with him?
10   One glance was all it took from the penetrating blue eyes of SnowWhite, "Wars hell, SnowWhite, but I'll fly wing on you."
11   And the bevy of pilots grew with StoneMan, OverBoost, RedLine, BirdMan, TwoDogs, DarkMoon, ShareCrop, BolTer, SmegMa, TailWind, HalfRight and BurnOut,
12   And they flew, and they flew, and they flew.
13   Round about the child men Marines called the gaggle of gung ho pilots, "SnowFlight,"
14   For word spread of the aerial brethren, and a white haired pilot.
15   And word spread of the SnowFlight pilots who flew about in the darkness, in the rain, in the clouds, and in the minds of wounded child men shouting prayers of survival.

CHAPTER 4

1   StoneMan learned to fly with a new perfection with SnowWhite,
2   For SnowWhite did fly at the high performance stresses and limitations of the helo bird,
3   And SnowWhite flew tactics unthought of by the pilots unskilled in the art of helicopter combat flight.
4   StoneMan the great pilot became StoneMan the flying aerial artist,
5   For with whispers of hand strokes on the flight controls the old dog became a wonderful portrait of performance.
6   StoneMan loved the innovations and flying tricks taught by SnowWhite to protect the vulnerable helo during the precious moments required to land and safely leave during the heat of battle.
7   And many secrets were given unto StoneMan by SnowWhite;
8   For he learned how to use the side flair while quickly pointing the nose of the big green flying mule skyward immediately before touching down to the earth, deceiving the enemies' mind as to where the helo was flying, and landing,

9   And he learned to escape to the right because the helo uses less engine power when in takes off to the right,

10   And he learned to fly decoy while SnowWhite flew at high speed at tree top level instantly appearing with an immediate in-flight quick stop right above the landing zone; then squirting back out the other side with wounded on board.

11   SnowWhite taught StoneMan special songs, or tunes, the words he understood not,

12   But it was that a special peace came over him when in the heat of battle for StoneMan grinned forth and chuckled while humming SnowWhite's tune.

13   These flying talents saved the child men Marines, and saved the helo to fly again,

14   But such were not the 'school solution' textbook thoughts written in the articles of religion of the High Church.

15   StoneMan was the flying companion of SnowWhite.

16   It was that SnowWhite taught these aerial delights to all of SnowFlight.

17   And it came to pass that SnowFlight knew fear,

18   But they also knew that they had the strength and tutorage of SnowWhite, which gave unto them great confidence.

CHAPTER 5

1   It was that StoneMan became spiritually high,

2   And it was that StoneMan cared not for the trinkets of man nor for the career vices occupying the corners of the minds of the ticket punchers,

3   And those who without the job opportunity war would be homeless.

4   "I want you to put Doltish in for a medal," Vicar-major Din-gleBerry stated to StoneMan with an attempt to wear an authoritative look on his beer can-opener face.

5   "He nearly got us killed today," StoneMan squelched, "He flew the flight by the book into the wrong landing zone, and downwind. That's not distinguished flying — just because he took a few hits in his helicopter — you ought to convene a flight evaluation board."

6   "Look Stoner," Vicar-major DingleBerry quipped, "Temple says he wants Doltish to get a DFC."

7 "You tell him," StoneMan straight-eyed the penguin looking Vicar-major, "that if he will fly co-pilot with Vicar-major Doltish and lead the next night flight when it is raining with no moon on emergency MedEvac, then I'm confident that a medal will be in order."

8 And it was that StoneMan walked away knowing that a deserving Purple Heart was not the type medal that either the ground-bound Poncho Pilot squadron commander nor the paper pushing Doltish wanted.

9 And it came to pass that StoneMan believed himself not,

10 For he cared not for the ribbons of these false men,

11 But he was of the rock of the soul.

CHAPTER 6

1 Far away in the land of Sam Bo, the King of Cash gnashed his teeth greatly for his darkness shown to the common people of the land,

2 And the trumpeters of the door announced to the regalness of the demons possessing the decisions of the pocketbook minds.

3 And the King summoned forth his trusted ill advisors who knew in warfare that death was necessary to harvest the quarts of hubris needed to wet the thirst of the dollar demons.

4 Behold: it was that the King spake forth of infamy, glory, and history, for in the King's mind there were many visions that his wisdom would long endure him above the Kings of the past,

5 And he spake of elephants and pissants, saying he would walk upon the pissants that agreed not with his power.

6 And the fat man with the fat face in the King's court spoke of war need,

7 Then it was also that the Queen of Loot smiled, for it was that the beads and bangles brought forth brothel businesses from the marketplace of war need.

8 "Gold, silver, jewels and pearls, fine linen, purple, silk and scarlet, all kinds of scented wood, cinnamon, spice, incense, myrrh, oil, rubber, tungsten, and the cheap labor," were the behind the door code words as to why the money gnomes believed in the geography of Nam Bo diseased by analness of the selfish mind.

9 And the demons danced visions of wealth, power, fame, and

greatness, but the ill advisors spoke of failure for the people were learning that their children were being sacrificed unto Molech.

10 Then it was that the demon horseman cast a trusted message of pride into the minds of gluttonous men, and one demon spoke forth, "The sons of the rich, our friends, and those who could cast shadows on the life of the King are not needed for the war."

11   And it came to pass that the Father sinned greatly on the Sam Bo sons, for the uneducated, the poor, the meek, the disadvantaged, and those with slow mind and limp foot were summoned forth in the name of honor, glory and duty.

12   And the clock of standards was reset so that press gangs of the mind could summons forth field hands to harvest shekels from the money plants and row crop the fields of war.

13   And the Sam Bo mothers blindly gave their sons unto the High Priests in charge of the altar of unnecessary war.

14   And the kindle glowed while hubris danced,

15   For there was fresh flesh in the Valley of Slaughter.

16   And the hierarchy of hell owned the King.

CHAPTER 7

1   There came to the land of Nam Bo a child man Marine of great heart and much love who of slow mind and slight limp was cherished by his fellow Marines.

2   The god, Marine Korps, gave him clothes, money to spend, and much food; a sustenance uncommon to his past,

3   For war was his only job opportunity.

4   And he was called PorkChop, for he savored the unlimited quantities of food and partook greatly of nourishment of the body.

5   And PorkChop knew no wrong, but gave his all for all was only what he was trainable to give.

6   And PorkChop was defenseless against mere intelligence of a common man;

7   And he understood not how to defend himself in the land of Nam Bo.

8   And amid the many deaths at Aceldama OutPost building the wall between the land of Nam Bo and Bac Bo, a sniper's single bullet took the life of the mascot, PorkChop, in the presence of StoneMan.

9   "Don't die on me you PorkChop," StoneMan screamed into the limp face of the kid Marine canon fodder snatched from life into 98 cents worth of chemicals by a two-bit bullet.
10   And StoneMan wept greatly at the limp mass in his arms,
11   And StoneMan hurt that flesh and blood of a beautiful human being was wasted;
12   And that he was powerless to stop the insanity.
13   StoneMan screamed inside till the echoes of disbelief rebounded only with the flow of mere tears at the evil that men do when Satan teaches them to piss on God's laws.
14   "Fuck you, whoever you are," he moaned loudly while holding one dead Marine who would help the King of Cash's body count statistic.
15   An unimaginable hate wreaked forth through StoneMan at the ignorance of war,
16   But the throttle of death ruthlessly twisted onward in the land of Nam Bo.
17   And SnowWhite approached StoneMan, and cried with him;
18   With mere death there is great pain, but with useless death for selfish gain the numbness of the mind adds shock to the soul.
19   And SnowWhite said, **LORD, YOUR SERVANTS EAGERLY AWAIT YOUR HOUR.**
20   In the depths of pain, StoneMan felt the shoulder of SnowWhite, and heard the soothing echoes from his words.

CHAPTER 8

1   And it came to pass that SnowWhite, DarkMoon, OverBoost and RedLine returned to Tru Lai from Aceldama Out Post,
2   But it was that StoneMan and BirdMan flew forth on to AdaSam.
3   And as they flew, StoneMan stared forth at the green earth below from the high above sky,
4   And in his mind he saw forces of evil crossing the earth telling men to kill,
5   And he visioned spiritual beings whispering to the High Priest generals that it was okay to take and re-take the same hills;
6   And he saw in his mind's eye the Father of Evil Arts crafting

short change to those who needed to believe their sons were worthy of three for one death of the flesh ratio.

7   And StoneMan saw a selfish King masquerading among fields of money punctuated by poppy flowers of ego.

8   And StoneMan wondered if there were demons on all sides of war dancing messages that it was alright for man to release the soul of men from the flesh of men,

9   And whether men puppeted through these forces were able to defeat the spirit within?

10   And were there angels of the Lord protecting the merciful, the righteous, and the meek?

11   It was therefore great frustration to StoneMan, for he knew not the answers and hurt for the tan people, the children, and the child men who were spirited to believe that they were mighty warriors.

12   And StoneMan saw the price of needless child men's death because the King's played war chess,

13   And he saw great and powerful men crawfish from the word of God.

14   But StoneMan saw also the vision in the clouds of a man on a white horse with his sword glistening forth at the ready.

15   And StoneMan drifted into shallow sleep in the cool of the high altitude and with exhaustion.

CHAPTER 9

1   BirdMan flew onward to AdaSam as StoneMan slept.

2   And it came to pass as StoneMan awoke high above the earth he looked down at the green quietness far below and was given unto another vision.

3   It was that StoneMan again saw spirits playing in the jungles of the mind telling men that it was acceptable for men to release the soul from the flesh.

4   And it was that the forces of evil knew no uniform but that of evil,

5   And it was that the King's evil swapped lives for power and money.

6   Behold! Stoneman grew chill at thought, for while evil was all around, were there the guardian angels of God about also?

7   Then it was that StoneMan rebelled in his mind, for he knew not any answers,

8   But he knew that war displaces right;

9   And he knew that war turns child men into disciplined assassins,

10   And the smell of self-preservation wreaked an odor on the high command.

11   And the smell of war profiteering reeked an odor about the King of Cash.

12   Satan dances when men pisseth on God's laws.

13   But StoneMan saw in vision also snow flakes of hope twirling in disc-like slow circles like little ice helos,

14   And StoneMan witnessed the solidness of good men abandoned to row crop the money fields of death for the rich.

15   But StoneMan also shook his head admitting to himself that the price of freedom is wrapped in poor man's choice.

16   Then, StoneMan smiled, for he remembered the words of the tune of SnowWhite.

17   And StoneMan confessed unto himself that the war indeed was the incompetent leading the unwilling to do the unnecessary for the ungrateful.

18   Instantly! Vision shot into StoneMan,

19   For he saw the face of SnowWhite;

20   And he knew that SnowWhite was answering the prayers of the wounded, and saving flesh;

21   And he knew SnowWhite was of the Holy Heart.

CHAPTER 10

1   The AdaSam High Priest gave the priority flying mission to StoneMan, for he knew of snakes and things.

2   Great chortle came forth at the thought of the Marine jungle team capturing a twenty-two foot snake in the pool of water beneath the water falls that sprang outward from the mountain overlooking AdaSam;

3   And the spiraling winds twisted the green mule helo while StoneMan fought with all his coordination to rise through the narrow gorge walls to land the helo on the big, jagged rock at the lower water falls edge,

4   And it came to pass that the mighty snake captured in the jungle was brought to display at AdaSam,

5   And released into an underground bunker as a cage,

6   And there came great common concern that the snake not starve for in war there is displacement of thought,

7   And a plain village duck was purchased to feed the uncommon tenet snake releasing the High Priest from concern that cruelty to snakes was not a command shortcoming.

8   And when night had passed and it was daylight again, many gathered to look for the tiny not duck in the stomach of the snake as devoured pray,

9   But all were dismayed, for perched in the middle of the great snake's forehead was the tiny duck, which had pecked-out both eyes of the now blind, twenty-two foot disabled snake;

10   And again there was great concern for there was no rehabilitation program for snakes available in the mental villages.

11   And BirdMan sought out the Sergeant of Supply, for he asked if sun glasses,

12   And a white cane could be ordered for a blind snake.

13   And there were visions of a Bac Bo duck pecking out the Sam Bo eyes.

CHAPTER 11

1   The Egg Beater helicopter came apart in the air,

2   But as it was in flight right above the ground.

3   And its innards spewed outward and downward.

4   For it was written into the law of nature that objects in the sky without wings or rotors swiftly leap to the earth.

5   But it was also written that the mighty Herrods of war profiteering could harvest money crops from defective money plants . . . and defective helicopters.

6   So it was thus that a pilot of pilots, Hopper Honey, felt not the swift rotor blade severing his head from his body.

7   For what is the loss of one flesh to achieve rich men's nourishment?

8   And what is the loss of one flesh to please a King's or Queen's mind?

9   And it came to pass that StoneMan, RedLine, OverBoost and

others of SnowFlight escorted the body of Hopper Honey from the synagogue of graves to the silver bird,
10   And it was that the shining Hopper Honey was of the flesh no more,
11   And he had died imprisoned in the olive green flying tomb at the hands of them whom he gave sermon.
12   And it was that StoneMan witnessed the defective shells;
13   And the defective guns;
14   And the defective ammunition;
15   And the trow-away weapons of low bid profits;
16   And he was distraught.
17   For it was that StoneMan witnessed the man made mistakes of war, the killing through error, and death by profit.
18   It was also that the child men saw the evil, the corruption, the man made hell that the tan man Prince inflicted on the poor peasant people.
19   And StoneMan said, "We must put a stop to this madness."
20   StoneMan sought the wisdom of SnowWhite, for the anointed one questioned why the High Priests of the Church were not protecting the child men congregation.
21   SnowWhite answered saying, SNOWWHITE HEAR STONEMAN THROWING STONES?
22   And StoneMan laughed.

CHAPTER 12

1   There then came a time when the men and machines of war of 777 were ordered out of the land of Nam Bo to the Island of the Floating Dragon to get new helicopters and to get fresh flesh of replacement pilots for war.
2   And it was that HalfRight did fret greatly, for the Nam Bo children at the orphanage hungered.
3   And SnowWhite grinned, then said, CAST YOUR NETS INTO THE SEAS OF NAVY SUPPLY.
4   And it was that the departing helos dipped into the Navy storage gathering underneath in cargo nets much food destined for destruction by the mandates of war business.
5   StoneMan wept with pleasure, for the small tan children along the big soccer field waived and the women of the Catholic cloth

smiled for unto them the helos brought forth their prayers for food.

6   And HalfRight saw the nakedness of his youth captured into abandonment, yet fulfilled.

7   And the helos shuttled men and war gear from shore to carrier ship;

8   And it came to pass that in the night all were aboard the ship on the churning sea to leave the confines of war for forty days and forty nights,

9   But SnowWhite and StoneMan stayed behind.

10   And it was that the big carrier ship was cast into total darkness, for unto war blackness the big ship hid from enemy boats on the high seas.

11   The pilots of SnowFlight were scared for SnowWhite, for the low clouds skimming above the sea would hide the ship from view.

12   But out of the blackness over the ocean came the sharp blue glare of the hue of SnowWhite's engine exhaust,

13   And SnowWhite made joke on the radio of the big Navy boat being a floating parking garage – he requested space number 1;

14   Then it was that SnowWhite landed on the carrier ship deck in the blackness to the many tiny lights sewn to the suit-front of the Navy landing deck man,

15   Who looked like a quiet cross with open arm's in the darkness of night.

16   So it was that the pilots and men of 777 departed across the sea unto the Island of the Floating Dragon by carrier ship, privately.

CHAPTER 13

1   The meandering trail of green islands rising out of the deep blue sea with a big long humpy body shown forth as a big sea dragon to the eyes of the helo pilot's arriving from high in the sky;

2   And it came to pass that the pilots of SnowFlight bought motorcycles from the island man merchant homesteading the gate to Futema.

3   The pilots laughed, and giggled, and made great humor for unto their minds was not war, but play;

4   And they rode round about with gaiety and new found happiness.

5   BurnOut rode an old motorcycle off the end of the pier amid great laughter from the pilots and constant disbelief stare of the small island people.

6   ShareCrop rode the big engine motorcycle machine great distance on the back wheel.

7   Injun blew forth the motorcycle horn of great noise scaring BirdMan into a water ditch;

8   And it came to pass on the Island of the Floating Dragon that the skies gave forth great thick rains blowing across from the sea to the land and back to the sea;

9   And many of the SnowFlight pilots raced on their motorcycles to beat the winds with distant rains seen coming in from the sea;

10   So it was that ShareCrop rode hard and fast at seeing the oncoming wall of rain water blowing down the highway;

11   And it happened that just as ShareCrop topped the big hill going into the airfield that the heavy rains came slicking the road and spilling the speeding motorcycle and ShareCrop onto separate sliding parts;

12   Now it was that the motorcycle slid through the open military gate whereby the guard properly saluted the passengerless vehicle;

13   And it was that ShareCrop slid shortly behind through the open military gate receiving promptly the second salute.

14   ShareCrop thus became the victim of much hoot in the heavy rain by the other wet pilots of SnowFlight who witnessed the one man slide show.

CHAPTER 14

1   Much comradery among the pilots of SnowFlight came forth in the times of rest on the Island of the Floating Dragon.

2   And it was that soldiers of war who escape the horrors of daily death found greatness in the smallest of things,

3   For on the Island every day was a holiday, and every meal was a banquet, and every night a Saturday night.

4   Such was the nature of child men forced to vision the end of life at the beginning of youth.

5   And StoneMan's thoughts were the thoughts of how to be a better pilot,
6   And how to give wisdom quickly to the new pilots who knew war not;
7   And how to be a better brother.
8   So it was that StoneMan flew days and many nights, sometimes with the ever present BirdMan, practicing the art of combat helo flying.
9   And so it was that StoneMan polished ever caressingly each fine tune performance needed to squeeze the Dog helo in and out of the ultimate adventure of survival.
10   And it was also that StoneMan went about at the places of the child men headed unto war to teach the art of helicopter salvation.
11   The many good works and the great heart of StoneMan could be seen by all,
12   And SnowWhite said unto StoneMan, **YOUR LIGHT SHINES BY HEART BEAMS.**
13   And it was that StoneMan was proud.

CHAPTER 15

1   And it came to pass on the Island of the Floating Dragon that SnowWhite took StoneMan, RedLine and OverBoost high unto the mountains;
2   And it was there that they came to know men who spoke words in riddles understood by SnowWhite,
3   For there came forth a leathery man with wool white hair named Lei' Merej, and another man called Leiru.
4   And it was that StoneMan, RedLine and OverBoost were overcome, for they witnessed the holiness of those messengers who answer prayers,
5   But they were stupefied, and there was fear at the aura of what they blindly had not seen.
6   Then SnowWhite charged them not to tell any man.
7   For unto men would be given them great disbelief,
8   And unto them had been given great weight.
9   And it came through time that 777 returned to war in the land of Nam Bo.

CHAPTER 16

1 "Who is this SnowWhite?" queried the High Priest to the staff helpers around the ecclesiastical headquarters.

2 The Chief Priest and Vicars gathered about witnesses against SnowWhite, and his sayings in efforts to put him away;

3 But SnowWhite's devoutness to the child men shown brightly against the careerists concerned with images, medals, citations;

4 And to ticket punchers whose object was time passage to get their personnel jacket emnued and embossed off the backs and blood of others.

5 We heard SnowWhite say, **MONEY WHORES PROFIT GREATLY FROM THIS WAR**, came words of witnesses.

6 But the Cardinal-general knew this wasn't blasphemy, for he too saw war profits being worshipped,

7 And he too knew of battles with the Divinity of Defense over the think-tank genius' lack of knowledge of the principles of combat and ignorance of the art of warfare,

8 For the war had become a matter of fiscal heroics;

9 And the people were to donate the lives of their sons for capital causes.

10 SnowWhite was summoned before the High Priest.

11 "Did you say **CHILDREN ARE BEING SACRIFICED?** the Bishop asked of SnowWhite.

12 **SNOWWHITE DID,**

13 "Did you say, **THE MARINE KORPS IS NOT A LAND ARMY?**"

14 **IT IS SO WRITTEN IN THE LAW,**

15 "Did you tell others of the numbers of war?"

16 **DO NOT THE HIGH PRIESTS HEAR VOICES OF DISBANDING THEIR CHURCH AND SEEK TO GIVE IT THE IMAGE OF NUMBERS?**

17 "And who are you to question?" sternly barked the irate Bishop.

18 **SNOW IS.**

19 "We'll court-martial your ass," screamed the Bishop.

20 **SNOWWHITE HAS NOTHING TO HIDE.**

21 And it came to pass that there was great gnashing of Chermarim High Priest teeth.

CHAPTER 17

1   And straightway in the morning the Bishop summoned the Chief Priests, the curate clerics, and the lame of independent thinking, and his unilingual advisors with their elders and scribes, and staffed the issue.

2   And it came to pass that the careerists, the ticket punchers, and the blind-divine were perplexed.

3   For SnowWhite had done no wrong, and desired no medals, no promotions, no honorable mentions, no letters of commendation, no career advancement, no personnel jacket stuffing, and no special recognition.

4   And it was that the tenured Chief Priests and the curate clerics had instilled policies and procedures with the Pope-general's blessings to protect the image of the Korps with the loss of a few good Marines.

5   And it was that exhaustive late night hours were spent adjusting body counts, and recovering the carcasses of downed aircraft to create a non-total combat loss statistic, and to portray the faltering ninety-day supply system as capable of supporting a sustained land operation while young Marines died to window-dress the statistics and camouflage the truth.

6   "The Army will bury us after this war if we don't deal with it now," commented the Cardinal-general to the "club of regulars" anointed with self-preservation of the Korps, and themselves.

7   Ghosts haunted them of the Marine Korps' history of the Army's assault on the very existence of the Korps church after the big war.

8   Then the spirits puked forth thoughts to the blind divine.

9   "So dau lau Valley," quipped the Curate colonel, "He's good, he's the best — send him on the rescue operation into So dau lau Valley to save the two Nam Bo thieves, Satset and Samsyd. With a little luck, we'll be able to give him a posthumous medal."

10   The reaction of the Chemarim Priests was one of having to accept the silent judgment of sending SnowWhite on a certain death rescue flight high in the mountains.

11   And it came to pass that the Chief Priest's suggestion became through High Church channels an edict for SnowWhite.

12   Poncho Pilot responded to the High Priest's request that

SnowWhite be scheduled to fly to the So dau lau Valley by saying, "SnowWhite has done no wrong."
13 But Poncho Pilot accepted destiny and scheduled SnowWhite for the sure death mission.

CHAPTER 18

1 It's suicide," StoneMan argued unto SnowWhite.
2 And among the covey of SnowFlight, all were afraid for the place of the skull meant anti-aircraft guns, entrenched enemy . . . and certain death, and they were greatly distressed.
3 Why would SnowWhite accept the mission?
4 And SnowWhite answered,
5 YOU HAVE NOT CHOSEN SNOWWHITE.
6 THERE ARE TIMES WHEN YOU HAVE TO ABANDON THE MULE, AND ACCEPT YOUR MISSION.
7 SELF-PRESERVATION KILLS. . . ,
8 INTER-SERVICE RIVALRY KILLS. . . ,
9 THE WHORES OF MONEY DINE ON CHILD MEN'S FLESH.
10 IT IS A TIME WHEN CASH RULES.
11 IT IS A TIME OF GREAT DARKNESS, BUT THE LIGHT SHALL AGAIN SHINE.
12 And SnowFlight witnessed a smile from the finest, for ShowWhite accepted the mission, and said, PIECE OF CAKE.

CHAPTER 19

1 So dau lau Valley lay high in the mountains where the thin air of the high altitude took away the wonderful helicopter flying performance taken for granted by pilots when sea level flying.
2 And the round eyes and rock teeth of the huge valley formed skull emitted a receptive grin to those who were asked to fly into the landing zone in the skull's flat nose with the steep rock cliffs jagging about along the overlooking valley walls.
3 "I understand you have volunteered for this mission," smiled the High Priest sent from the Holy Sea.
4 IF YOU SAY SO, smiled SnowWhite.
5 "There are two trapped in the valley," said the High Priest of

command as he personally briefed SnowWhite on the mission selected by Holy Sea Headquarters, "and the enemy are using them as bait, hoping that a rescue attempt will be made."

6 It came to be known that the two men sought for rescue were keepers of secrets, for they had absconded with knowledge of the Prince of Money and the King of Cash in their many endeavors to make profits from their splendid little war.

7 And it came to pass that SnowWhite told his crewmen to remain behind for the helo needed less weight,

8 And SnowWhite flew the helicopter alone without any co-pilot or crew onward past the gates for the mission of rescue in the grassy landing zone in the middle of the place of the skull.

9 The enemy grinned as the single small green flying mule above the floor of the valley drifted from between the clouds into plain view descending into the open trap.

10 And it came to pass that the easy victory of a willing target fooled the waiting demons, for SnowWhite intended not an aerial rescue,

11 But quickly corkscrew landed, and left in the open with the engine running and blades turning, a mechanical flying machine,

12 Giving the enemy the appearance of preparing for flight while SnowWhite escaped into the jungle in the twilight of the suddenly stormy monsoon blackness and heavy rain in custody of two disoriented souls in search of salvation.

13 The Captains of Blackness understood not, for the gloom of many bombs being dropped on them from a code name Arc Light shown round about, and the earth in the valley shook with man made earth quakes, and suddenly silence cried out for the mist of the unknown crept forth like a battle suddenly stopped.

14 The enemy searched not, for the carcass of the green flying machine lay filleted in the nose of the skull, a target of opportunity until the blackness of night shed its skirts over the earth.

15 SnowWhite was reported killed in action all in satisfaction of those who had demanded that this man who blasphemed the High Church not be allowed to spread his gospel.

16 And the King of Cash understood not that the firmament of the people was changing to unleash its wrath on him that had suckled and financially benefitted on the young;

17 And the Prince of Money understood not for he was of high intelligence and cared not for the lesser things such as the efficient loss of one human flesh, for such was the cost of war business.

18   Likewise, the Chief Priest mocked SnowWhite, with the staff scribes and line and staff elders, and said,

19   "He saved others; himself he cannot save."

20   SnowWhite was reported killed in action until the third day, when SnowWhite appeared from the mountainous jungles of the Tekoa Wilderness and walked unto the area of the Temple of the Holy Sea by the rice paddy plains, thereby fulfilling his mission.

21   And the two thieves with secrets of truth had been rescued, for they had gone separately.

22   And SnowFlight rejoiced and made attendance with SnowWhite;

23   And their eyes were opened, and they knew him;

24   And SnowWhite's tour of duty was over, and he with the eleven of them went forth to the place of the international airfield;

25   And it came to pass that SnowWhite was parted from SnowFlight, and was carried away by the silver bird up into the heaven.

26   But they were not able to resist the wisdom and the spirit by which SnowWhite spake.

27   And SnowFlight stirred up the brethren, and the elders, and the scribes;

28   And all that sat in the council, looking steadfastly on the vision of SnowWhite, saw his face as it had been the face of an angel.

29   Then the High Priests suborned men, which said, "We have heard SnowWhite speak blasphemous words against the King of Cash.

30   And the High Priests, scribes, elders, and career clergy of war continued the self-preservation bond and offered sacrifice of the child men Marines unto the idol, and rejoiced in the works of their own hands.

31   And the voice of SnowWhite came unto StoneMan in the night as he slept with vision, **THE LEATHERNECK AND UNCIRCUMCISED IN HEART AND MIND, WHO HAVE RECEIVED THE LAW BY THE MESSAGE OF LIGHT, AND HAVE NOT KEPT IT, SHALL ONE DAY HAVE TO ACCOUNT.**

The Gospel According to REDLINE

(Take Responsibility for Your Actions and the Actions of Your Marines)

CHAPTER 1

1   The burden of RedLine,

2   The book of the vision of RedLine, the Canuck.

3   And he turned in vision, and lifted up his eyes, and looked, and behold, there came four helos out from between two mountains; and the mountains were mountains of the high brass.

4   The first helo was red, the second helo was black, the third helo was white, and the fourth helo was a bay color.

5   Then he answered and said unto the angel that talked with him, "What are these, my lord?"

6   And the angel answered and said unto him, **THESE ARE THE FOUR SPIRITS OF THE HEAVENS, WHICH GO FORTH FROM STANDING BEFORE THE LORD OF ALL THE EARTH.**

7   And the angel spoke to him as a man of violent temper and intolerant heart.

8   And there was war in heaven,

9   Michael and his angels fought against the dragon,

10   And the dragon fought with his angels,

11   And prevailed not.

12   Neither was their place found any more in heaven.

13   And the child men Marine pilots were sent forth into the

Tekoa Wilderness all in the name of glorious, but unknown, reason.

CHAPTER 2

1   "RedLine" had stuck — a name tagged while in flight school on the hot headed young pilot;

2   His deep projecting voice rattled windows when he yelled and screamed — an event which was commonplace as the mounting number of disagreeing persons crossed his philosophy.

3   "I would rather have a sister in a whore house than a brother in the Navy," he would say in the House of Squid, provoking inter-service confrontation between the men of the sea and those who guard the streets of heaven.

4   It was also that RedLine called the ships of the sea, "boats" and "sea cabs," to the disgust and dismay of the brown shoe clerics who savored on tradition without progress.

5   Behind RedLine followed those in the Navy inner circle of small time line clerics who, but for a runaway war in Nam Bo, would have cast the talented flying student back to plain soldier Marinedom,

6   For unto the Navy was given the power to anoint child men Marines as Naval Aviators.

7   And the Navy appreciated not those who worshipped not the ways of the air above the sea.

8   And it came to pass that the skinned, battered, and mentally tattered RedLine went forth with his victorious wings of gold, having escaped from the confines of living among the Church of Sailors.

9   And as RedLine departed the hallowed ground of Naval Flying Folklore, he said unto the four stripers, "You dodged the draft, You joined the Navy."

10   So it was that the most devout of devout, the RedLine of redlines, parted from the flying church of the sea by the sea.

CHAPTER 3

1   It was written that RedLine go unto the family of the Korps and journey to the land of Nam Bo to make war.

2   "The height of optimism," quoted Vicar-major DingleBerry to the RedLine new guy, "is a Marine Helicopter pilot who believes he will die of lung cancer from smoking,"

3   Then DingleBerry grinned that he had so suavely captured someone else's joke and repeated it with field grade finesse'.

4   RedLine was told that the enemy were everywhere,

5   And the enemies look like the friendlies, so there are no friendlies.

6   And RedLine was told of his dead value, for a bounty was placed upon the head of all pilots.

7   RedLine believed himself a devout and pious Marine.

8   He worshipped the exclusive Church, Marine,

9   And with fiery heart and due reverence, he would follow the war sermons.

10   It was his duty to obey;

11   It was his duty not to question.

12   And RedLine accepted what he saw not;

13   For RedLine arrived at the gates of seeing war with the magnetic trappings rich men give as ornaments of the glory of war for the poor;

14   And RedLine witnessed the teachings of war,

15   For unto his family church had been given the rancid portion of the meat of war.

16   And unto the child men Marines there was issued death by indecision, death by retaking the same hill, and death by profit.

17   And it came to pass that RedLine understood and gave forth with a voice of thunder denunciation and condemnation.

18   For RedLine the devout became confused, then shattered, for he witnessed in his church obeyance of a uniroyal King.

CHAPTER 4

1   Among the young field Marines there was uncommon misery heaped with irresponsible waste of human life.
2   And the young became shocked to learn in war there is no meaningful escape from the old men's rules,
3   For honor prevails over truth when defenseless young minds are enraptured with serenades.
4   But the fine little war in Nam Bo cast ever increasing sour notes, for which the young soldiers sang,

> "Napalm sticks to children,
> And the Dow doesn't give a shit."

5   "We can't give him a medal," said the Bishop-commander to the disbelieving young leader at the death of one corpsman at Aceldama OutPost.
6   "But he deserves the Medal of Honor," responded the young officer trained in the principles of leadership. "He ran in front of the holes with a coat hanger unjamming Matty Matel's defective Machine Gun in the heat of battle; he gave his life saving us, Sir."
7   "We can't let the enemy know the guns don't work," sternly barked the Bishop priest who knew that in order to give the Medal of Honor the people would learn the defective truth.
8   And the young leader was distraught for his men gave all to their Fatherland but the leadership of Sam Bo gave not loyalty back.
9   And there was disgrace of the child men blood throughout the land of Nam Bo for it became known that the careerists cast a dark shadow for the citizen soldiers who desired not the full-timer's mentality.
10   But it was that yes men gave yes decisions in a yes man's marketplace.

CHAPTER 5

1   It came to pass that RedLine was sent on a routine 'take n wait' helo flight mission to pick up a Vicar passenger at Holy Sea headquarters and fly him to Tru Lai City.

2   A radio message came forth in flight for RedLine to make an emergency medical evacuation for a child man Marine with a head wound – a prayer to be answered.

3   And it came to pass that the wounded child man Marine was rescued and taken by RedLine unto the special hospital.

4   RedLine was proud, the flight crew was proud, and RedLine landed his helicopter at the Church of the Holy Sea to carry as their special passenger, a High Priest-colonel.

5   "Sir," the Sergeant Flight Crew Chief said to RedLine over the intercom as the High Priest prepared to board the turning helo, "He says to shut down."

6   And the Vicar was standing, with back arched, and round belly forward facing RedLine as he climbed down the side of the helicopter.

7   "Marine," he said in an old man's voice, "there's blood in my helicopter" – the High Priest pointed in the floor of the helo where the wounded Marine just delivered to the hospital had ridden, "I don't fly in dirty helicopters! Do You Understand!" he yelled.

8   "Prick," RedLine thought, as he nodded his head affirmatively seeing from the corner of his eye the Sergeant Door Gunner giving the Vicar the "bird" behind his back.

9   Then it came to pass that the helo departed,

10   And RedLine jerked the helo aerially about evasively in free spirit flight,

11   And RedLine angrily flew at twenty feet above the ground across the rice fields, between the palm trees, up the rivers, and with rolling and banking quick turns;

12   And RedLine sought to get shot at by an enemy called "one-shot Charlie," a farmer who despised the helicopters that chased his water buffalo and scattered his ducks.

13   And it came to pass that RedLine asked the crewman on the intercom radio, "Is the fat priest toting one of those ice water jugs?"

14   And it was that RedLine instructed the crewman to secretly pass the Vicar's ice water jug up between the co-pilot's feet.

15   For it was that the ice water privileges of non-war were given unto the High Priests who were to share not the ordinary misery of common field hand Marines.

16   And RedLine dribbled piss unto the Vicar-colonel's water jug, which was secretly returned.

17   And it came to pass that after the helicopter landed, the fat Vicar took a swill out of the jug, "a la RedLine piss."
18   The Flight Sergeant laughed, and laughed, and laughed.
19   And Redline understood not why the Church would ordain such a machine minister.

CHAPTER 6

1   Throughout the land of the great money malls common people of common pocketbook knew not of the uncommon deaths imposed by an uncommon king without common virtue.
2   And in War mothers want to know not that their sons died so that a War Priest could have privilege;
3   And in War mothers want to know not that their sons died so that the money gnomes of Wall Street could eat flambe' in a fine restaurant from the ill gotten profits of a defective weapon,
4   And in War mothers want to know not that their sons died so that a ticket punching priest could be promoted for successful deaths in unsuccessful battles for ill conceived principles,
5   Nor that they donated their sons for capital causes.
6   But in War mothers wail helplessly to the shock of an empty death notice paper quoting empty dreams about child man memories while the lords of the rich defile the mothers of the poor so that powerful Princes of Profit can achieve survival as unlabeled cowards and reap the fruits of the money fields.
7   But lo there will come a time when the whiners, the mealy-mouths, the patriotic grandstanders who suffer war not, and the cowards in heart and mind shall be cast into the pit,
8   And the sons of the rich shall suffer sucking chest wounds, missing arms and legs, and the living hell of economic wars on earth.
9   But the importance of merchant wars can erode away for it is the nature of the rich to war not when they profit not.
10   And it is the nature of the rich to devalue war for which the rich have to pay the market price.

CHAPTER 7

1   "They're just niggers, . . . wonderful, human, loving, kind, field hand, child men, niggers," cried the words of the drunken ShareCrop at the rubber bags filled with the black 1369 children who died only because it was said my father can whip your father.

2   And DarkMoon cried too, and said, "We're all niggers, we're red niggers, white niggers, and yellow niggers in the hands of the Prince of Money, for he is *cum laude* greed."

3   And RedLine cried, and cried, and cried, and thought of ways to get even with the King of Cash.

4   So it was that the field hands of war suffered greatly while enslaved to the trustee boss men.

5   It was that a black shake N' bake Cardinal-Priest of war recognized not the white-man lackey smeared upon his face,

6   Nor did he see the perils of subterfuge about his spirit.

7   Then it came to be that the lame, the helpless, and the slaves of confusion silently fought back against the surrogate demons of devoutness under labels of fragging, purple heart, million dollar wound, and survival.

8   And DarkMoon whispered round about into the ears and minds of the forgotten sons of unconscious mothers certain piercing things about the alter boys for the King of Cash.

9   It was also that the black child men Marines knew of the horror of their abuse, but stood tall; and proud; and died.

10   And it was too that the High Church and its High Priests hid from their eyes the evils of the King of Cash, and all the King's men.

11   For the Choir of Fifty were pocket change to the money things known unto their King.

12   But RedLine was, of the pilots of SnowFlight, the deep voice sending forth screaming questions of the whys of war.

13   **CASH RULES,** came the unwanted answer from SnowWhite.

CHAPTER 8

1   RedLine was given unto deep sleep with staggering vision, for in dream unto the Tekoa Wilderness on the road he was captured,

2   And the enemy soldiers of Bac Bo dipped his body unto burning oil, but his body jumped forth into the daylight.

3   Awakening, RedLine sought out SmegMa, and ask of him of such dream of surviving being dipped in hot oil.

4   Then the SmegMa pilot, named "Doc" by some, spoke forth, "You're horny, just plain horny. It happens to the best of us, go forth and seek the heated pussy, for unto you there has been told the wisdom of a hot piece of ass."

5   RedLine repulsed such thought and issued forth rebuke at SmegMa,

6   And RedLine further lectured the genius mind harnessed to a runaway penis of the great rewards of those who adhere to the system.

7   And RedLine looked into the face of the man who suspected not that he worshipped Priapus.

8   Then RedLine smiled, for RedLine grasped that SmegMa knew not that SmegMa knew not.

9   And SmegMa smiled, for one never knew when the big pilot with the deep voice would rattle his body.

10   And it came to be that the Frenchman called RedLine and the Italian called SmegMa shared burdens of the hows and whys of war.

11   It was that SmegMa called RedLine, "Froggie,"

12   And it was that RedLine called SmegMa, "Dip Stick."

13   And it came to pass that Froggie and Dip Stick met Peat and Repeat, the two gunship pilots who cared greatly for the bare naked MedEvac pilots sent into the heat of battle,

14   And they drank away the confusion.

CHAPTER 9

1 It was a most magnificent structure, the little temple of the big Temple,

2 For unto one man there was built a royal throne of defecation;

3 And upon this throne did Artemis N. Temple alone sit.

4 ShareCrop called the little house a one holier than thou, but SmegMa said it was a glorious shit house.

5 And unto the regular Temple man was built a special "shitter lid" upon which to place his royal ass.

6 And it was known unto Marinedom that there were those who were known as regulars,

7 And it was known also that there were those who were known as reserves.

8 And it was that there were many of the tribe of the Marine Korps who cast a careerist shadow upon the regular,

9 For it was written unto the secret books that those who came forth unto the church named "regular" of the congregation were set apart in a special place.

10 So according to scripture, those who chose not the congregation of the regular church were given forth unto indifference.

11 RedLine liked not what he saw, for unto the regular Temple man was given privilege,

12 And unto the regular Temple man was given the condiments of non-sacrifice;

13 It came to pass in the night when the enemy mortar shells landed upon the Tru Lai Base, RedLine did secretly set fire to and burn the outhouse of Temple.

14 And there was gnashing of Temple teeth, for the Temple man cherished the idol of one holer,

15 And it came to pass that the Temple man did pass gas and release bodily waste like common men in a common privy in an uncommon war.

16 And RedLine would laugh at seeing the fat man in the distance in the six-holer out house.

CHAPTER 10

1   It came to be that the King of Cash was sore afraid, for in his visions flashed the end of his power and the end of his season for he saw the last money harvest.

2   And the spirit of greed fretted inside the soul housed in the body of the man who had been delivered great wealth;

3   And the King paid the Devil his dues;

4   And vanity cast the horror visions of being a common man into the eyes of the man harnessed to uncommon edicts;

5   For the Elephant King would kill to protect his power lair;

6   And the demon of power struck jaggedly into the mind of the self-proclaimed Almighty the horror of suffering by the angels who would lay his shallowness in the bright light;

7   Whereupon the King of Cash called forth the Pope-Marine and made him swear in writing that the little tan men in the land of Nam Bo would not have victory;

8   And the Pope-Marine dispatched the death warrants of child men Marines, for it would be a great sin to not please the wishes of the King of Cash;

9   And the spirit spoke to the Pope, stay here where you are comfortable.

10   And the Cardinal of closed heart heard not the hue and cries of the choked principles of leadership.

11   The child men were given unto Molech so that the King of Cash would wear not the rags of his mistake;

12   Nor the mediocrity of the eyes.

13   So it was that the dark angel counted souls for abstinence of God was the seed of a great harvest;

14   And the Captains of Blackness went about their work turning good men into vicious killers at the urging of the demons whispering survival.

15   And the King of Cash sought survival as he pisseth upon the rivers of blood flowing from child men hearts.

CHAPTER 11

1 The MedEvac siren blew.

2 BurnOut, as the standby co-pilot, raced in the overcast night air to the standby helicopter accelerating his efforts starting the engine,

3 The big round aircraft motor cranked and ignited with the purring roar pleasingly familiar to the Dog Driver pilots;

4 For the 1,525 horse power engine hummed with a mechanical grace.

5 In his haste, BurnOut erred – the engine exploded, WHOOM! – followed by high speed zings shooting loudly into the night signaling all to hear BurnOut's mistake.

6 BurnOut's haste destroyed the engine and grounded the helo;

7 Then BurnOut was attacked by the screams muffled through a cheap pipe wearing a fat face belonging to Artemis N. Temple.

8 "You matsaball maggot," he screamed regarding the mistake as unforgivable pilot error. "You get your ass out of there. I'm a good mind to handcuff you to that fart'n whirlwind."

9 BurnOut was saved by the familiar roar and commencement of blade rotation of the other standby helo with RedLine at the controls.

10 But the fat commander was still screaming obscenities from alongside the roadway as RedLine taxied the helo for take off into the blackness while BurnOut strapped himself into a night MedEvac rescue mission.

11 BurnOut escaped the presence of the ground bound Temple.

12 "Don't sweat it," comforted RedLine on the intercom, "We got more helos than we got pilots."

13 Then it came to pass that the darkness engulfed the pair of rising helo's on the emergency night mission like an overhead chasm of blackness seeking to suck the souls from inside the aerial corks cast into ebony nothingness; like a submarine crew in the mystic deep black sea awaiting the deadly unknown.

14 "Night Scooter, Night Scooter," transmitted RedLine, "this is DogDriver MedEvac inbound, over."

15 "MedEvac, this is Night Scooter, six wounded, zone cold," came the radio response, "Charlie on the run."

16 "Roger, pancake in ten," communicated RedLine signaling

the Marines that he would land in the zone in ten minutes, "standby for signal light."

17   The landing was hairy,

18   And the wounded were quickly placed on board the helo.

19   Then RedLine throttled to maximum take off power beginning the departure lift out of the dry abandoned hillside rice field — -Then All Hell Broke Loose!

20   Enemy bullets ripped through the thin metal helicopter hitting vital linkage parts initiating the commencement of a spinning crash.

21   "Chase this is lead, we've been hit, goin' in," coolly broadcast RedLine.

22   "Leave us room to get ya," came TailWind's radio reply.

23   Eternity was condensed into fifteen seconds as the aerial machine fell spastically back to earth in the open rice field with all the emergency crashing techniques RedLine could muster.

24   BurnOut turned useless in his minute of panic as the green mule fell sideways beating itself into metal pieces.

25   "Hell BurnOut," RedLine screamed on the radio as the helo beat itself apart, "you can't be a good pilot if you can't learn how to crash."

CHAPTER 12

1   Chaplain Sir Richard Head paused as he entered the hootch in the heat of the day in the Tekoa Wilderness reflecting on the need to look kindly on two of his roommate pilots — a nigger tagged DarkMoon and a hell-bound jew called BurnOut.

2   As a potential lost sheep, he must gain them into god's flock.

3   "You guys hear the joke that lebanese HacJack told in the mess hall," Sir Richard quietly choked out secretly hoping to avoid confrontation with these heathen pilots. DarkMoon and BurnOut anticipatorily grinned shaking their heads "no" while gearing up for the preacher, who was a joke.

4   "Seems a little boy from down Orleans Parish, Louisiana asked his PaPa, 'Is we niggers, or is we jews?'"

5   DarkMoon's spring loaded mind turned to full throttle as both he and BurnOut focused a mocking ear as if to lend support that they were really interested in the disgusting human excuse with a grocery sack mentality.

6   "Why would you say a thing like that son," the man asked the boy. "Well, the boy said, 'Farmer Jones has some watermelons for sale for a dollar and I didn't know whether to offer him a quarter or steal one'," with which the shining Chaplain laughed voraciously at his joke anticipating again that two of his unwashed hootchmates could be won into friendship.

7   Smiles with solicitations of approval sped to doom and rejection as DarkMoon and BurnOut consciously withheld laughter at the first stage of the ecclesiastical entrapment by this holy roller camouflaged in the image of a religious counselor.

8   "Well kiss my hymie ass, that's funny," quipped BurnOut looking at DarkMoon.

9   "Yeah," picked up the deep voice from the already resentful black man, "that's better than jack'n off in one of those starched socks you keep hid under your mattress," speared DarkMoon, letting the South Louisiana bible belt thumper know these pilots knew his late night chromosomal secrets.

10   Chaplain Head ran from the hootch wishing once again he had not tried to repatriate the already condemned.

11   DarkMoon smiled at the grinning BurnOut, then removed and taped the nude centerfold from the girly magazine, mons veneris forward, to the top front of the aged refrigerator in direct eyeball view of the Chaplain's bunk—"The Last Temptation and Self Coital Destruction of Sir Richard Head," he grinned with the responding laughter of BurnOut.

12   And it came to pass that the Chaplain touched not the filthy picture taped to the refrigerator door, for it portrayed a visual source of relief of interoccular tension through auto-eroticism.

13   And RedLine removed the picture form the door, for he felt compassion for the Chaplain cut of biased cloth.

CHAPTER 13

1   MakeReady cherished being a non-flying combat Marine Assistant Maintenance Officer who drew combat pay;

2   He was an integral part of the war effort; he was the best at repairing and maintaining the big engines and the numerous hydraulic systems on the helicopters.

3   Even though 777 was miles from any known enemy and was surrounded by the Division, MakeReady was convinced that he

would be killed so that he took every unnecessary precaution that would reduce the odds.

4   MakeReady would never walk the same path between the buildings inside the compound;

5   He would stay indoors as much during the day so as not to be able to be seen by a sniper that lurked in his mind but was nowhere near the maintenance shack.

6   MakeReady traded the Sea Bees fuel for some bunker sheet steel plates which he placed underneath his cot just in case the enemy threw a grenade underneath his hootch floor.

7   MakeReady was the most combat prepared, and most unlikely to see combat Marine of the war, and the pilots knew MakeReady was a target of opportunity.

8   And it came to pass that RedLine became saturated with MakeReady's continuous phobias,

9   For MakeReady kept a machine gun, and a pistol, and grenades hidden in his hootch.

10   Unknown to MakeReady, but known to the select group of pilots, a test attack alert was planned.

11   And it came to pass MakeReady prepared for bed in the traditional way;

12   He placed the unauthorized machine gun so as to hide it underneath the poncho beside his bed;

13   He confirmed his Colt forty-five pistol did not have a chambered shell and carefully felt the locking pins of the two grenades he had snitched.

14   MakeReady was prepared for instant war and carefully raised the double mosquito net sides which were mounted over his cot in box fashion carefully tucking both sets of the netting all around under the mattress so as to prevent the deceptive infiltration of even one malaria ridden mosquito into his presence.

15   A content sleep surrounded MakeReady; He didn't hear the pilots carefully remove the machine gun, the pistol, and the grenades.

16   The siren blew! – the beginning whining escalated into a loud crescendo signaling enemy were all around, at which time Make-Ready bolted upright in the darkness.

17   And BurnOut had thrown a brick size rock high in the air so that its trajectory would fall straight down on the tin roof above MakeReady's head, and BurnOut yelled . . . "incoming" . . . signifying enemy shells were on their way.

18 Wham! Boom! Banged the rock hitting the tin roof over MakeReady's head, shocking the already panicked multi-phobiaed MakeReady as he tore out of bed wearing two full sets of mosquito netting with mounting poles attached;

19 MakeReady screamed for he could not find his machine gun — he could not find his pistol — he ran outside to screams of "get in the bunker."

20 MakeReady tripped, fell and rolled into a ball of netting knowing the lightning flash of light that hit him carried a bullet only to quickly realize the laughing pilots that were now standing around him had just taken his picture.

21 And MakeReady once again earned combat pay as a strategic non-combatant.

CHAPTER 14

1 "Who is this SnowWhite?" queried the High Priest to the staff helpers around the ecclesiastical headquarters.

2 The Chief Priest and Vicars gathered about witnesses against SnowWhite, and his sayings in efforts to put him away;

3 But SnowWhite's devoutness to the child men shown brightly against the careerists concerned with images, medals, citations;

4 And to ticket punchers whose object was time passage to get their personnel jacket emnued and embossed off the backs and blood of others.

5 We heard SnowWhite say, **THE KING PROFITS GREATLY FROM THIS WAR**, came words of witnesses.

6 But the Cardinal-general knew this wasn't blasphemy, for he too saw war profits being worshipped,

7 And he too knew of battles with the Divinity of Defense over the think-tank genius' lack of knowledge of the principles of combat and ignorance of the art of warfare,

8 For the war had become a matter of fiscal heroics;

9 And the people were to donate the lives of their sons for capital causes.

10 SnowWhite was summoned before the High Priest.

11 "Did you say **CHILDREN ARE BEING SACRIFICED?** the Bishop asked of SnowWhite.

12 **SNOWWHITE DID.**

13   "Did you say, **THE MARINE KORPS IS NOT A LAND ARMY?**"
14   **IT IS SO WRITTEN IN THE LAW,** were SnowWhite's words.
15   "Did you tell others of the numbers of war?"
16   **DO NOT THE HIGH PRIESTS HEAR VOICES OF DISBANDING THEIR CHURCH AND SEEK TO GIVE IT THE IMAGE OF NUMBERS?**
17   "And who are you to question, sternly barked the irate Bishop.
18   **SNOW IS.**
19   "We'll court-martial your ass," screamed the Bishop.
20   **SNOWWHITE HAS NOTHING TO HIDE.**
21   And it came to pass that there was great gnashing of Chemarim High Priest teeth.

CHAPTER 15

1   And straightway in the morning the Bishop summoned the Chief Priests, the curate clerics, and the lame of independent thinking, and his unilingual advisors with their elders and scribes, and staffed the issue.
2   And it came to pass that the careerists, the ticket punchers, and the blind-divine were perplexed.
3   For SnowWhite had done no wrong, and desired no medals, no promotions, no honorable mentions, no letters of commendation, no career advancement, no personnel jacket stuffing, and no special recognition.
4   And it was that the tenured Chief Priests and the curate clerics had instilled policies and procedures with the Pope-general's blessings to protect the image of the Korps with the loss of a few good Marines.
5   And it was that exhaustive late night hours were spent adjusting body counts, and recovering the carcasses of downed aircraft to create a non-total combat loss statistic, and to portray the faltering ninety-day supply system as capable of supporting a sustained land operation while young Marines died to window-dress the statistics and camouflage the truth.
6   "The Army will bury us after this war if we don't deal with it

now," commented the Cardinal-general to the "club of regulars" anointed with self-preservation of the Korps, and themselves.
7 Ghosts haunted them of the Marine Korps' history of the Army's assault on the very existence of the Korps' church after the big war.
8 Then the spirits puked forth thoughts to the blind divine.
9 "So dau lau Valley," quipped the Curate colonel, "He's good, he's the best — send him on the rescue operation into So dau lau Valley to save the two Nam Bo thieves, Satset and Samsyd. With a little luck, we'll be able to give him a posthumous medal."
10 The reaction of the Chemarim Priests was one of having to accept the silent judgment of sending SnowWhite on a certain death rescue flight high in the mountains.
11 And it came to pass that the Chief Priest's suggestion became through High Church channels an edict for SnowWhite.
12 Poncho Pilot responded to the High Priest's request that SnowWhite be scheduled to fly to the So dau lau Valley by saying, "SnowWhite has done no wrong."
13 But Poncho Pilot accepted destiny and scheduled SnowWhite for the sure death mission.

CHAPTER 16

1 It's suicide," StoneMan argued unto SnowWhite.
2 And among the covey of SnowFlight, all were afraid for the place of the skull meant anti-aircraft guns, entrenched enemy . . . and certain death, and they were greatly distressed.
3 Why would SnowWhite accept the mission?
4 And SnowWhite answered,
5 YOU HAVE NOT CHOSEN SNOWWHITE.
6 THERE ARE TIMES WHEN YOU HAVE TO ABANDON THE MULE, AND ACCEPT YOUR MISSION.
7 SELF-PRESERVATION KILLS. . . ,
8 INTER-SERVICE RIVALRY KILLS. . . ,
9 THE WHORES OF MONEY DINE ON CHILD MEN'S FLESH.
10 IT IS A TIME WHEN CASH RULES.
11 IT IS A TIME OF GREAT DARKNESS, BUT THE LIGHT SHALL AGAIN SHINE.

12   And SnowFlight witnessed a smile from the finest, for ShowWhite accepted the mission, and said, **PIECE OF CAKE.**

CHAPTER 17

1   So dau lau Valley lay high in the mountains where the thin air of the altitude took away the wonderful helicopter flying performance taken for granted by pilots when sea level flying.

2   And the round eyes and rock teeth of the huge valley-formed skull emitted a receptive grin to those who were asked to fly into the landing zone in the skull's flat nose with the steep rock cliffs jagging about along the overlooking valley walls.

3   "I understand you have volunteered for this mission," smiled the High Priest sent from the Holy Sea.

4   **IF YOU SAY SO**, responded SnowWhite.

5   "There are two men trapped in the Valley," smiled the High Priest of command as he personally briefed SnowWhite on the mission selected by Holy Sea Headquarters, "and the enemy are using them as bait hoping that a rescue attempt will be made."

6   And it came to be known that the two men sought for rescue were keepers of secrets, for they had absconded with knowledge of the Prince of Money and the King of Cash in their many endeavors to make profits from their fine little war.

7   And it came to pass that SnowWhite told his crewmen to remain behind for the helo needed less weight,

8   And SnowWhite flew the helicopter alone without any co-pilot or crew onward past Bethphage for the mission of rescue in the grassy landing zone in the middle of the face of the skull.

9   And the enemy grinned as the single small green flying mule above the floor of the Valley drifted from between the clouds into plain view descending to the open trap.

10   And it came to pass that the easy victory of a willing target fooled the caissons of battle, for SnowWhite intended not an aerial rescue, but quickly corkscrew landed, and left in the open with the engine running and blades turning, a mechanical flying machine giving the enemy the appearance of preparing for flight while SnowWhite escaped into the jungle in the twilight of the suddenly stormy monsoon blackness and heavy rain in custody of two disoriented souls in search of aerial salvation.

11   And the Captains of Blackness understood not, for the

gloom of bombs being dropped on them from a code name Arc Light shown round about, and the earth in the Valley shook with manmade earthquakes, and suddenly silence cried out for the midst of the unknown crept forth like a battle suddenly stopped.

12   And the enemy searched not, for the carcass of the green flying machine lay filleted in the nose of the skull, a target of opportunity until the blackness of night shed its skirts over the earth.

13   And SnowWhite was reported missing in action all in satisfaction of those who had demanded that this man who blasphemed the god, Marine Korps, not be allowed to spread his gospel.

14   And the King of Cash understood not that the firmament of the people was changing to unleash its wrath on him that had politically suckled and financially benefitted on the young;

15   And the Prince of Money understood not for he was of high intelligence and cared not for the lesser things such as the efficient loss of one human flesh, for such was the cost of war business.

16   Likewise the Chief Priest mocked SnowWhite, with the staff scribes and line and staff elders, and said,

17   He saved others; himself he cannot save.

18   And SnowWhite was missing in action until the third day, when SnowWhite appeared from the mountainous jungles of the Tekoa Wilderness and walked in the accompaniment of two thieves unto the area of the Temple of the Holy Sea by the rice paddy plains, thereby fulfilling his mission.

19   And SnowFlight rejoiced and made attendance with SnowWhite.

20   And their eyes were opened, and they knew him;

21   And SnowWhite's tour of duty was over, and he with the eleven of them went forth to the place of the international airfield;

22   And it came to pass, SnowWhite was parted from them, and carried away by the silver bird up into the heaven.

23   And they were not able to resist the wisdom and the spirit by which SnowWhite spake.

24   And SnowFlight stirred up the brethren, and the elders, and the scribes;

25   And all that sat in the council, looking steadfastly on the vision of SnowWhite, saw his face as it had been the face of an angel.

26   Then they suborned men, which said, "We have heard SnowWhite speak blasphemous words against the King of Cash and the Prince of Money, and against our Church, the Marine Korps."

27   And the High Priests, scribes, elders and career clergy of war continued the self-preservation bond and offered sacrifice of the child men Korps unto the idol, and rejoiced in the works of their own hands.

28   And the voice of SnowWhite came unto RedLine in the night as he slept with vision, **LOOK TO THE LIGHT.**

The Gospel According to
OVERBOOST

(TeamWork)

CHAPTER 1

1 OverBoost did not want a funeral like all the others, so he wrote an invitation of his own.

You Are Cordially Invited
to
The Aerial Burial
of
OverBoost
(a/k/a T. J. Giacomo)

Time: To Be Announced

Place: Just Underneath the Sky

RSVP

P.S. No present or past Muther Fuck'n majors allowed (except Matty Wright: honorary damn good guy)

(see reverse side for instructions)

2 And on the back, OverBoost requested:

T.J.'s Recipe for Departure:

Zone to be marked with Red, White, and Blue smoke.

Fine Wine and Liquor to be copiously consumed.

Drink from Canteen Cups.

Do the flag bit with rifles and the silly horn.

A helo fly by would be nice (Keep it tight).

Take a lock of my hair and mix it with a lock of my children's hair in a little gondola bag. Tie the bag to a helium balloon. Anchor the balloon with numerous blue ribbon tethers. Cut one of the tie down strings at a time, one string to be cut by each attendee, and my children as the last persons will cut the remaining strings letting the balloon with me and the memory of my children free to roam the heavens.

P.S. Piss on a major for me.

3 RedLine grinned as he read the burial wishes of his constant flying companion and friend, and said, "Wetbacks don't die, . . . besides, I'll pour good wine on your grave after I've passed it through my kidneys." They both grinned.
4 "I hear you Froggie," OverBoost responded, "but I wouldn't expose that little of meat to a refrigerator."
5 And it was that RedLine and OverBoost shared laughter, sadness, flying, friendship, stark terror, tears, and war.

CHAPTER 2

1 "If god wanted us to fly, he'd ah given us rotors," OverBoost quoted the overused cliche' to MakeReady, the non-pilot junior maintenance officer who was being forced to fly in the co-pilot's seat with the Mexican maniac pilot on a post-maintenance test flight to check the engine repair work.

2   OverBoost obtained tower clearance and climbed high above Tru Lai Airfield while asking the short-shit assistant maintenance officer needless questions,

3   And casually invoking death by crash and burn in the conversation as the consequence if MakeReady had erred with the wrong engine adjustments performed by his young pimply-faced child men Marine helo mechanics.

4   The big engine suddenly coughed, sputtered, and quit.

5   "Tower, Maintenance-1 with dead engine coming in," OverBoost radioed as he coolly began autorotation procedures and keyed the intercom while eyeballing MakeReady, "I'll land over there by that drainage ditch, you won't feel the fire at first so quickly jump in the water in the ditch to put it out."

6   MakeReady was frozen with fear; non-combat flying was about to kill him.

7   OverBoost looked out the window away from MakeReady's view while he laughed in the wind knowing the helo could safely land with an engine failure but wanting to scare the ground-bound yes maintenance man into earning his behind the lines combat pay.

8   The fire truck moved out in view of the descending helicopter and OverBoost smoothly adjusted the flight path with gradual but steady flight control in the bottom of the landing thereby cushioning the landing like that of a powered landing.

9   As they touched down, OverBoost screamed into the intercom to MakeReady, "Get Out! Get out before we tumble over, I smell gas, run for the drainage ditch!"

10   In the excitement, MakeReady panicked, made his emergency exit and ran and jumped into the drainage ditch just as the fire trucks arrived.

11   And there, standing knee deep with ditch water dripping from his splash was the bald-headed deputy maintenance officer.

12   The crash crew laughed at seeing the squatty MakeReady run away from a perfectly good helo and jump into a drainage ditch.

13   And they took MakeReady's picture with the wet, green vines hanging from his head.

CHAPTER 3

1   Behold, for unto the land of Nam Bo came a big helicopter with a set of big blades on each end,

2   And the child men called it an "Egg Beater,"

3   And unto its making did it come apart and beat itself into pieces.

4   It was that anxious money begat hidden defects in the greed worship of this piece of flying equipment of war.

5   And it was also that the big Egg Beater helicopter would come apart in mid-air slinging rich pieces of faulty manufacturing profits among Marine flesh high above the earth.

6   "Like flying a coke machine," said the demoralized Egg Beater driver to OverBoost. "You just put in your quarter; when she comes apart, ya' meet death on the ground."

7   "Why don't you just give up your wings?" asked RedLine to the Egg Beater pilot.

8   "Can't say that I haven't thought of it," the Egg Beater driver responded, "But what would you Dog Drivers do if we quit?"

9   And it came to pass that one by one, numerous Egg Beater helos came apart high in sky casting pilots, crews, and passengers into a mass of metal and bodies for a death fall to the earth.

10   And the Prince of Money smiled on the Egg Beater for it academically performed to expense tolerance,

11   And the re-design would allow many shekels to come from a different line item of the budget of the King of Cash.

12   Death sells easier when others pay the price.

13   Thus it was that many child men died at the hands of mammon.

14   And unnecessary death was an economic necessity.

15   And the Pope, the Cardinals, the Bishops, and the Clergy hid from their eyes the scripture and verse of the Church.

16   For the Prince of Money was not a Marine,

17   And belonged not to the Korps Church.

CHAPTER 4

1   Behold, the horror of horrors, the terror of terrors, the fear of fears!

2   For unto RedLine and OverBoost came the true vision as they flew wing on the Egg Beater helo in the sky, for the Egg Beater helicopter came apart before their eyes in mid-air,

3   And there were pilot's death screams on the radio as the pieces of helo carcass surged earthward,

4   And there were bodies thrown outward into the open sky high above the earth,

5   And what was one minute a flying machine with twelve souls on board became in an instant flash mere metal and 1369 flesh fired in scatter shot chunks toward the earth.

6   And the disassembled helicopter met commercial standards, for in the money humming of war cash is cranked out though purchase and repurchase, repair, and crash.

7   And there was great pilot anger throughout the Tekoa Wilderness, for it was known that the Prince of Money's helicopter fulfilled economic profitcy.

8   And it was known throughout the Tekoa Wilderness that child men pilot Marines would continue to die through leadership defect,

9   And defective leadership.

10   But the High Church generals exposed not those who tampered with their child men Marine brethren,

11   And the High Church protected the self-preservation society with child men blood,

12   For in Korps' religious doctrine there were haves, and there were have-nots.

13   And there were no's, and there were know nots.

14   And it was that the child men Marines were expendable.

15   And the child men hurt, and felt betrayed.

16   And round about, it was said, "Eat the Apple . . . and Fuck the Korps."

CHAPTER 5

1   OverBoost lived in the shadow of RedLine.

2   Whenever they could, RedLine and OverBoost would fly together.

3   And the inseparable two became one in the teamwork of SnowFlight.

4   And RedLine and OverBoost with StoneMan provoked the pilots of SnowFlight.

5   Then it was that the two pilots of violent temper and voices of thunder came unto SnowWhite seeking counsel,

6   For it was that the High Priests of the Navy were to destroy pallets of food while hunger appeared in the faces and bodies of the innocent children of the orphanage,

7   And it was that the feudal Nam Bo landlords cared not for the peasants, nor the orphan children of peasants.

8   It was a time of cash carcasses, and the Premiers of Nam Bo were busy harvesting shekel fruit slung loosely about from the Sam Bo money trees,

9   For the Dragon ladies of the Nam Bo feudal lords went a whoring with the children peasants, and extorted greatly from poor peoples labors, and took greatly of the promises of the dark angel.

10   And the good people of Sam Bo were told not of the atrocities on the Nam Bo poor, the disadvantaged, and the meek.

11   And the good people of Sam Bo were told not of the High Potentate Nam Bo drug dealers.

12   It was that SnowWhite listened to RedLine and OverBoost, who became men of intolerant heart, for they sought retribution against the evil doers, and they sought with great passion a means to expose the truth of the fine little war.

13   And SnowWhite said, **THE TRUTH IS A SECRET THE KING HIDES FROM THE PEOPLE.**

14   When SnowWhite had spoken, the two angry pilots carried forth disgust for the wicked men were given not unto justice.

15   And the High Priests hid from their eyes the sodomized children, the murders, the corruption, and the ungodly acts of the King's Nam Bo friends.

CHAPTER 6

1   In the madness of the Tekoa Wilderness there was a teacher of teachers,

2   And he was known as Hopper Honey.

3   As a pilot of pilots, Hopper Honey preached the aerial gospel of how to survive in combat with the vulnerable helicopter machines of war.

4   And the Vicar-majors cared not for the truth, for even if they believed, they were ordained into the inner circle of the Church of the Korps.

5   And the High Priests cared not for the truth, for they were part of the ordained blind.

6   Now it came to be that Hopper Honey preached once too often, and was imprisoned into flying the Egg Beater helicopter,

7   For it is unwritten in Korps scripture that it is unforgivable to blaspheme the church of the Holy Sea, even if its High Priests pisseth upon the foundations of the Church.

8 And it came to pass that Hopper Honey was chained to strong beliefs that allowed no dispensation to those who ignored the evils that men do.

9   But through time, Hopper Honey stayed true to course and changed not his belief in his child men brethren but cast a guilty shadow on the High Priests in hiding.

10   Then it came to pass that there were money dances and mental ballets serenading those who suckled on war.

11 And there were machine guns that failed and faulty ammunition that condemned the child men Marines to death,

12   And there were unbalanced shells that missed the target and exploded into the foxhole homes of the child men Marines,

13   And there were defective bombs,

14   For in the Prince's war business, one must accept random weapons of money humming quality.

15   And friendly fire lurks among imperfect trial and error training.

16   And in the evening of the demons of the mind, the Herrods of Wall Street prevailed, for Hopper Honey died when the Egg Beater helicopter came apart right above the ground, casting like a sword the steel blade spar through the cockpit, decapitating the pilot of pilots.

17   And it came to pass that the pilots of SnowFlight delivered the body of Hopper Honey unto the silver bird which departed into the heaven.

CHAPTER 7

1   SnowWhite said on the radio to SnowFlight, **LET US KICK THE TIRE, AND LIGHT THE FIRE.**
2   And it came to pass that 777 departed to go unto the Island of the Floating Dragon,
3   And SnowWhite lead SnowFlight to the supply field and lifted by helicopter many nets of food and delivered the wastage of war to the open field at the house of orphans.
4   And the women of God smiled and waived to the man of white, for they knew him.
5   And the little children of unearned misery waived, for they too were the keeper of secrets.
6   Then it came to be that SnowFlight went unto the Navy carrier ship without SnowWhite, for SnowWhite stayed behind.
7   And there was blackness and heavy seas,
8   And in the middle of the night SnowWhite drifted into view, for SnowFlight saw bright landing light visions,
9   Then OverBoost worried greatly, but SnowWhite radioed the ship saying, **SNOWWHITE WITH SOULS TO COME ABOARD.**
10   And the Navy radio man sought direction as to where SnowWhite wished to go, and SnowWhite said, **LET US PASS OVER UNTO THE OTHER SIDE OF THE LAKE.**
11   Then there was laughter on the high seas.

CHAPTER 8

1   The great ship of metal carrying all twenty-four of the 777 worn helo birds of war crossed the sea to the Island of the Floating Dragon.
2   While upon the sea, OverBoost was given unto deep sleep, and dream.
3   And in the dream he became a matador at El Padron,

4   And there came forth the mighty bull of great strength,
5   And there was a great fight between the man and the bull,
6   But at the moment of truth, the matador and the bull instantly turn into bleached white stone.
7   And in the morn, OverBoost sought counsel of Doc SmegMa to understand the dream.
8   "It means you don't like women," SmegMa said to the puzzled OverBoost, and he continued,
9   "You see albino bulls are castrated in their youth so as not to reproduce — a ball-less bull — ."
10   But OverBoost knew himself to be macho, and he could do battle with such a bull.

CHAPTER 9

1   It was that StoneMan and SnowWhite with RedLine and OverBoost on wing would fly as a two helo team;
2   It was also that they rode motorcycles on the Island of the Floating Dragon.
3   And it came to pass that SnowWhite led OverBoost, RedLine and StoneMan unto the mountains to the house of the small tan man called Lei,
4   There SnowFlight knew Lei, and Lei knew SnowFlight.
5   But OverBoost, RedLine and StoneMan understood not how such men of differing worlds shared such uncommon knowledge.
6   And there was a great calmness in the presence of SnowWhite and Lei, for they spoke with a constant smoothness.
7   And SnowWhite and Lei spoke of many wars in history as if it were now.
8   SnowWhite and Lei spoke also of evil forces dwelling in the hearts and minds of mankind,
9   For scripture and verse went unheard but spoke of such.
10   And it was strange unto OverBoost, RedLine and StoneMan, for SnowWhite and Lei spoke of others known not, but such names and places were known not by them.
11   SnowWhite and Lei talked of the heavens, healing, those awaiting the end of time, those who violate the spirit, and the repentance of men.
12   And it was that StoneMan, RedLine and OverBoost were

dumb with tongue, for they listened intently learning that SnowWhite could speak in simple riddles, and other words.

13   And SnowWhite said unto them, **PUT ON THE WHOLE ARMOUR OF GOD.**

14   **WE FIGHT NOT AGAINST FLESH AND BLOOD, BUT AGAINST PRINCIPALITIES, AGAINST POWERS, AGAINST THE RULERS OF THE DARKNESS OF THIS WORLD, AGAINST SPIRITUAL WICKEDNESS IN HIGH PLACES.**

15   Then it became known unto the inner circle, that SnowWhite was not of them, nor they of him, but SnowWhite was ordained of talents known and unknown unto them.

CHAPTER 10

1   It came to be that OverBoost, RedLine and StoneMan smiled for they knew SnowWhite, and SnowWhite gave unto them.

2   And the inseparable OverBoost and Redline became amazed at what SnowWhite taught them.

3   And StoneMan flew number two on the wing of SnowWhite, for in StoneMan there was an open gift.

4   It came to be on the Island of the Floating Dragon that on the twentieth day that there were asked many questions, for it was written that they could rest and meditate only twenty days more.

5   And SmegMa, TwoDogs, TailWind, HalfRight, ShareCrop, BirdMan, BolTer, DarkMoon and BurnOut sought counsel for they believed not in the sacrifice of their lives in the name of numbers.

6   And it was said that their Fatherland loved them not, for how could the father abandon the children and clothe them with ineffective weapons of war,

7   And how could it be that the High Priests were abandoning the congregation of the child men Marines in exchange for mental pieces of ribbon silver?

8   SnowWhite gave them comfort, and said unto them to fret not, that they would go and fly,

9   For who could selfishly deny their brother in time of need.

10 And there was much guilt among them, for it was known unto them that their thoughts of selfish survival cast them into the lake

of indifference with those who gave not, and who suckled survival on the backs of others.

11 Then it came to be that SnowFlight understood the horror of runaway war for once the beast is let loose, only the tethers of time and the harvesting of much flesh corral the beast.

12 And runaway war incapacitates the minds of men into blowing the trumpets of fiction while eating of blackness.

13 And SnowWhite said unto them, **NO MORE CAN BE ASKED A MAN THAN TO LAY DOWN HIS LIFE FOR HIS FRIENDS.**

14 **CAN YOU STAND BY AND LET THE CHILD MEN CARRY THE BURDEN?**

CHAPTER 11

1 "You've gone mad," said OverBoost to the laughing SmegMa.

2 "They are just lice, everybody has them, why not have pet lice?" responded the man of perverted entertainment.

3 And it was that inside his homemade laboratory SmegMa grew, cultured and nurtured his crawling friends.

4 And it came to pass that the sky-blue generals scratched their heads and groins in dismay, for scratching helped solve non-combat problems,

5 And it came to pass that Poncho Pilot scratched, but he knew he was allergic to combat and thought nothing of it,

6 And it came to pass that Vicar-major DingleBerry knew something was wrong for he itched all over.

7 Then it came to be that Bones Baker, the "flying gyno," diagnosed crabs, and told the infested that they best stay away from the combat zone clubs on the Island of the Floating Dragon, for the other pilots weren't going to the same places.

8 And for reasons unknown to the rest of the world, SmegMa giggled, guffawed, and sometimes gave strange hallucinating laughs each time Poncho Pilot and Vicar-major Berry would scratch.

9 For it was that SmegMa secretly sprinkled holy lice round about.

10 And it was also that Vicar-major DingleBerry boiled with great flame at SmegMa naming DingleBerry's short, fat whore, "Itchy Pussy."

11   Behold, in war, small retributions may be small bedfellows.

CHAPTER 12

1   The violence of temper and thunder of voice echoed forth from OverBoost from seeing the maps of the secret planners of war who spoke forth of things called "strategy,"
2   And OverBoost liked not the wall maps from the minds of those who practiced death by graph.
3   For behold, the Nam Bo battles were not to make men free,
4   And the Nam Bo battles were not to give men God,
5   And the Nam Bo battles were not to save the poor,
6   And the Nam Bo battles were not to establish justice,
7   For unto the minds of the thinkers not there was thought not.
8   But there were fields of storage on the Island of the Floating Dragon from the manufacturing money plants of war.
9   And there were men who begat death to other men for the sake of proving they could out-death the tan men.
11   And there were men of straw house mentality who believed that blowing down the straw houses of peasant farmers was a great victory.
12   And OverBoost became angry, for unto the undisciplined minds came forth war plans designed by machines at child men's death.
13   And unto the unseeing minds, there was entrenched hubris.
14   Behold! Men trained to kill understand not how to kill not.
15   For such men thrive on an opportunity war.
16   And OverBoost came unto SnowWhite seeking permission to kill men who without purpose took the lives of child men, all in the name of career blindness.
17   And SnowWhite answered, saying, **THE FALLEN ARE LEGION. IF YOU TAKE ONE APPLE, WILL THE ORCHARD GO BARE?**
18   **AND HAVE YOU NOT JOINED FORCES WITH EVIL IF YOU CHOSE TO FIGHT EVIL WITH EVIL?**
19   **REMEMBER OF SUCH MEN THAT THE WORM SHALL FEED SWEETLY ON THEM; . . . ,**
20   **AND THEY SHALL NOT BE REMEMBERED.**

CHAPTER 13

1   And it was that there was a death in Sam Bo of the mother of a Flying Sergeant on the Island of the Floating Dragon,

2   And the High Church gave grace upon him and sent him forth back to the land of Sam Bo.

3   And it came to pass that the Flying Sergeant did grieve and did give of himself in the spirit of death;

4   Then there came return passage through the big Sam Bo place of airplanes to send the Sergeant of Men back to Nam Bo,

5   And upon his chest there were the ribbons of pride of his cloth of the Korps Church dress;

6   There appeared a squalling woman who spoke filthy of the Church of the Marine Korps,

7   And the squalling woman said unbearable thoughts staining the love of his fellow Marine,

8   And the squalling woman spat upon his ribbons of sacrifice,

9   Whereupon, the Sergeant of Marines decked the woman, sending teeth and blood into separate places.

10   And the Sergeant of Marines hurt, for his death would be the source of freedom to those who spat upon him.

11   And the Sergeant understood not of those who understood not that the land of Sam Bo cared not.

12   So it was that men given unto sacrifice were placed upon the altar of knowing that the King's people cared not for the war trophies of the King, but spat upon the duty-bound soldiers.

CHAPTER 14

1   It was written that 777 absent itself from war for only forty days and forty nights,

2   And 777 was called out of the night back on the fortieth day to return unto the land of Nam Bo for the uncertain war had become a certainty.

3   And it was that the inseparable RedLine and OverBoost did fly many hours into the night returning the child men back by helo to the mighty ships of the sea.

4   And they laughed at BirdMan's capturing of the golf cart of the High Priest of the Air Force for Marine combat use.

5   And as the sun rose, great shadows begat images of black and gray across the faces of the high cliffs whispering eerie departure thoughts to the helo crews crisscrossing from sea to land,
6   And land back to sea.
7   "Death awaits us," said OverBoost unto RedLine.
8   "Death awaits us all," he responded, "it is just when."
9   And then RedLine said, "Haven't you heard, 'To die Marine is to live forever.' "
10   And it was that the men of 777 bulged with thought of imminent warfare,
11   And it was that the great ships of the sea moved away from the Island of the Floating Dragon toward the sea of the land of Nam Bo to cast the human livestock cargo flesh into the furnace of war.

CHAPTER 15

1   There came a High Priest who blessed with almighty words the invocation of war upon the tan men of Nam Bo.
2   **THE TRIBE OF THE KORPS IS OF ONE BLOOD**, said SnowWhite to Injun and OverBoost in answer to Injun's disgust at the High Priest's sermon of war.
3   And it was that the High Priests of war sought to inflict the wrath of the poor against the poor in the name of victory,
4   And it was that the Prince of Money envisioned the Church of the Marine Korps as an oxen plowing the fields of war,
5   It was that the High Priests of war gave allegiance at the altar of death by cost of goods sold,
6   For the highways of the art of violence were marched blindly by a King's ego.
7   And it was that the High Priests chose the garments of priesthood for unto them would be cast sackcloth and commonality if they exposed the doings of the King.
8   And OverBoost protested unto SnowWhite of how the brothers of the High Church would abandon the brothers of the Low Church,
9   For the High Priest gave forth death in the name of glory.
10   And SnowWhite answered, **THEY KNOW NOT WHAT THEY DO.**

11   And it was that the passenger Marine warriors on the ships of the sea were cast back in war onto the land.

CHAPTER 16

1   It was that SnowWhite, StoneMan, RedLine and OverBoost were sent unto battle,

2   And it was to be that the four helo's were to implant the soldiers in the high mountains among the enemy encampments.

3   It was that Legion did grin, for the spirits and their police did watch the men of the flesh quickly drift into the jungle nothingness from the flying machines;

4   For it was written that one must find the enemy to kill the enemy,

5   And to kill the enemy, one must find the enemy.

6   The soldiers of Bac Bo did seek and find the war painted figures of the tiny Sam Bo tribe;

7   And the flesh did rip and tear with the man-made implements of war.

8   Then there came the radio call of the men for help unto the High Priests,

9   But unto the tiny group of men the High Priests acknowledged not,

10   For the High Priests sought not the saving of the small group of men of war in the enemy land,

11   And they should stay and fight to death.

12   And SnowWhite, StoneMan, RedLine, and OverBoost did hear their unrewarded cries,

13   SnowWhite, StoneMan, RedLine, and OverBoost, though they heard, they heard not the High Priests who sought not the survival of a few good men.

14   And it came to pass that the four of SnowFlight captured the escaping child men team of brethren from the awaiting demons,

15   And the presence of SnowWhite in the heat of battle did issue forth the stopping of war time,

16   And the answer of radio prayers.

CHAPTER 17

1   And it was that OverBoost, RedLine and StoneMan smiled,
2   For it was also that the confidence of SnowWhite was their confidence.
3   And they would merely think at the controls of the green mule helicopter and the whispers of their hands and feet would give aerial flying performance that would even surprise them, for they knew not from whenceforth their talent came.
4   And there were days of constant flying whereby they would glide in and out of the midst of battle without incident making the impossible seem commonly accomplishable.
5   But it was that sadness filled their hearts, for among them were other helos that were shot from the sky,
6   That were riddled in the landing zones,
7   And that were the green hearses of unfair death in an unfair dream.
8   And RedLine screamed, and OverBoost screamed, for with great pain it was known unto them the death of one Navy korpsman, the saver of lives in the heat of battle,
9   For unto his comrades the korpsmen ran in the heat of battle from jammed gun unto jammed gun with a simple coat hangar of life, openly exposing the Navy man;
10   For the battlefield medicine man ran in the front of the weapons so he could ram the wire rod down the barrel of the jammed weapons of low-bid capitalism,
11   And he died.
12   And the High Priest said that such death could not be recognized with a medal,
13   For to give such medal would tell the enemy of the defective weapons given to the child men Marines.
14   And the child men Marines who died with the defective weapons in their hands received medals not, for the cost of the King's capitalism was camouflaged profits, and high sheriff greed.
15   And efficiency on written charts, graphs, and paper lies are meaningless to the child men who learn the truth that they have become trinkets on the watch chains of Wall Street's whores.
16   Then the inseparable OverBoost and RedLine appeared with StoneMan in tow to seek wisdom from SnowWhite.
17   And SnowWhite spake unto them, **THOSE WHO DWELL**

ON EARTH SHALL BE TORMENTED. AND HIGH PRIESTS
WITHOUT HEART WILL SAY IT HAS ALWAYS BEEN THIS
WAY. SUCH IS NOT THE LAW: FOR THE LIGHT SHINES
BRIGHTLY FOR THOSE WHO CHOOSE THE LIGHT.

CHAPTER 18

1   "Who is this SnowWhite?" queried the High Priest to the staff
helpers around the ecclesiastical headquarters.
2   The Chief Priest and Vicars gathered about witnesses against
SnowWhite and his sayings in efforts to put him away;
3   But SnowWhite's devoutness to the child men shown brightly
against the careerists concerned with images, medals, citations;
4   And to ticket punchers whose object was time passage to get
their personnel jacket emnued and embossed off the backs and
blood of others.
5   We heard SnowWhite say, **THE KING PROFITS GREATLY
FROM THIS WAR**, came words of witnesses.
6   But the Cardinal-general knew this wasn't blasphemy, for he
too saw war profits being worshipped,
7   And he too knew of battles with the Divinity of Defense over
the think-tank genius' lack of knowledge of the principles of combat and ignorance of the art of warfare,
8   For the war had become a matter of fiscal heroics;
9   And the people were to donate the lives of their sons for
capital causes.
10   SnowWhite was summoned before the High Priest.
11   "Did you say **CHILDREN ARE BEING SACRIFICED?** the
Bishop asked of SnowWhite.
12   **SNOWWHITE DID,**
13   "Did you say, "**THE MARINE KORPS IS NOT A LAND
ARMY?**"
14   **IT IS SO WRITTEN IN THE LAW,** were SnowWhite's
words.
15   "Did you tell others of the numbers of war?"
16   **DO NOT THE HIGH PRIESTS HEAR VOICES OF DIS-
BANDING THEIR CHURCH AND SEEK TO GIVE IT THE
IMAGE OF NUMBERS?**
17   "And who are you to question?" sternly barked the irate
Bishop.

18   SNOW IS.
19   "We'll court-martial your ass," screamed the Bishop.
20   SNOWWHITE HAS NOTHING TO HIDE.
21   And it came to pass that there was great snashing of Chermarim High Priest teeth.

CHAPTER 19

1   And straightway in the morning the Bishop summoned the Chief Priests, the curate clerics, and the lame of independent thinking, and his unilingual advisors with their elders and scribes, and staffed the issue.

2   And it came to pass that the careerists, the ticket punchers, and the blind-divine were perplexed.

3   For SnowWhite had done no wrong, and desired no medals, no promotions, no honorable mentions, no letters of commendation, no career advancement, no personnel jacket stuffing, and no special recognition.

4   And it was that the tenured Chief Priests and the curate clerics had instilled policies and procedures with the Pope-general's blessings to protect the image of the Korps with the loss of a few good Marines.

5   And it was that exhaustive late night hours were spent adjusting body counts, and recovering the carcasses of downed aircraft to create a non-total combat loss statistic, and to portray the faltering ninety-day supply system as capable of supporting a sustained land operation while young Marines died to window-dress the statistics and camouflage the truth.

6   "The Army will bury us after this war if we don't deal with it now," commented the Cardinal-general to the "club of regulars" anointed with self-preservation of the Korps, and themselves.

7   Ghosts haunted them of the Marine Korps' history of the Army's assault on the very existence of the Korps church after the big war.

8   Then the spirits puked forth thoughts to the blind divine.

9   "So dau lau Valley," quipped the Curate colonel, "He's good, he's the best — send him on the rescue operation into So dau lau Valley to save the two Nam Bo thieves, Satset and Samsyd. With a little luck, we'll be able to give him a posthumous medal."

10   The reaction of the Chemarim Priests was one of having to

accept the silent judgment of sending SnowWhite on a certain death rescue flight high in the mountains.

11 And it came to pass that the Chief Priest's suggestion became through High Church channels an edict for SnowWhite.

12 Poncho Pilot responded to the High Priest's request that SnowWhite be scheduled to fly to the So dau lau Valley by saying, "SnowWhite has done no wrong."

13 But Poncho Pilot accepted destiny and scheduled SnowWhite for the sure death mission.

CHAPTER 20

1 "It's suicide," StoneMan argued unto SnowWhite.

2 And among the covey of SnowFlight, all were afraid for the place of the skull meant anti-aircraft guns, entrenched enemy . . . and certain death, and they were greatly distressed.

3 Why would SnowWhite accept the mission?

4 And SnowWhite answered,

5 YOU HAVE NOT CHOSEN SNOWWHITE.

6 THERE ARE TIMES WHEN YOU HAVE TO ABANDON THE MULE, AND ACCEPT YOUR MISSION.

7 SELF-PRESERVATION KILLS. . . ,

8 INTERSERVICE RIVALRY KILLS. . . ,

9 THE WHORES OF MONEY DINE ON CHILD MEN'S FLESH.

10 IT IS A TIME WHEN CASH RULES.

11 IT IS A TIME OF GREAT DARKNESS, BUT THE LIGHT SHALL AGAIN SHINE.

12 And SnowFlight witnessed a smile from the finest, for ShowWhite accepted the mission, and said, PIECE OF CAKE.

CHAPTER 21

1 And it came to pass that those of SnowFlight witnessed the war as sacrifice unto the fire god, Molech,

2 For the tribe of the Korps had Priests of many ranks,

3 And the Chemarim High Priests accepted forth with open arms the child men donated with blindness,

4   For it was the people understood not the death of the flesh of their sons for capital causes,
5   And it was that the defenseless child men were given unto the hands of the High Priests,
6   And the High Priests placed the flesh of the children in the burning fires of the altar of sacrifice,
7   And the child men gave up the ghost.
8   So it was, and so it is, that mothers will give forth their sons when blessed with magic hollow words,
9   And sons dance forth to piper tunes written in Priestly lure,
10   For smoke and mirrors words salve the mind,
11   And hide secrets of capital wars.

CHAPTER 22

1   So dau lau Valley lay high in the mountains where the thin air of the altitude took away the wonderful helicopter flying performance taken for granted by pilots when sea level flying.
2   And the round eyes and rock teeth of the huge valley formed skull emitted a receptive grin to those who were asked to fly into the landing zone in the skull's flat nose with the steep rock cliffs jagging about along the overlooking valley walls.
3   "I understand you have volunteered for this mission," smiled the Temple Police Priest sent from the Holy Sea.
4   THOU SAYEST, responded SnowWhite.
5   "There are two men trapped in the valley," smiled the Temple Policeman as he personally briefed SnowWhite on the mission selected by Holy Sea Headquarters, "and the enemy are using them as bait hoping that a rescue attempt will be made."
6   And it came to be known that the two men sought for rescue were keepers of secrets, for they had absconded with knowledge of the Prince of Money and the King of Cash in their many endeavors to make profits from their fine little war.
7   And it came to pass that SnowWhite told his crewmen to remain behind for the helo needed less weight,
8   And SnowWhite flew the helicopter alone without any co-pilot or crew onward past Bethphage for the mission of rescue in the grassy landing zone in the middle of the face of the skull.
9   And the enemy grinned as the single small green flying mule

above the floor of the valley drifted from between the clouds into plain view descending to the open trap.

10   And it came to pass that the easy victory of a willing target fooled the caissons of battle, for SnowWhite intended not an aerial rescue, but quickly corkscrew landed and left in the open with the engine running and blades turning a mechanical flying machine giving the enemy the appearance of preparing for flight while SnowWhite escaped into the jungle in the twilight of the suddenly stormy monsoon blackness and heavy rain in custody of two disoriented souls in search of aerial salvation.

11   And the Captains of Blackness understood not, for the gloom of bombs being dropped on them from a code name Arc Light shown round about, and the earth in the Valley shook with man made earth quakes and suddenly silence cried out for the mist of the unknown crept forth like a battle suddenly stopped.

12   And the enemy searched not, for the carcass of the green flying machine lay filleted in the nose of the skull, a target of opportunity until the blackness of night shed its skirts over the earth.

13   And SnowWhite was reported missing in action all in satisfaction of those who had demanded that this man who blasphemed the god, Marine Korps, not be allowed to spread his gospel.

14   And the King of Cash understood not that the firmament of the people was changing to unleash its wrath on him that had politically suckled and financially benefitted on the young;

15   And the Prince of Money understood not for he was of high intelligence and cared not for the lesser things such as the efficient loss of one human flesh, for such was the cost of war business.

16   Likewise the Chief Priest mocked SnowWhite, with the staff scribes and line and staff elders, and said,

17   He saved others; himself he cannot save.

18   And SnowWhite was missing in action until the third day, when SnowWhite appeared from the mountainous jungles of the Tekoa Wilderness and walked in the accompaniment of two thieves unto the area of the Temple of the Holy Sea by the rice paddy plains, thereby fulfilling his mission.

19   And SnowFlight rejoiced and made attendance with SnowWhite.

20   And their eyes were opened, and they knew him;

21   And SnowWhite's tour of duty was over, and he with the

eleven of them went forth to the place of the international airfield;

22   And it came to pass, SnowWhite was parted from them, and carried away by the silver bird up into the heaven.

23   And they were not able to resist the wisdom and the spirit by which SnowWhite spake.

24   And SnowFlight stirred up the brethren, and the elders, and the scribes;

25   And all that sat in the council, looking steadfastly on the vision of SnowWhite, saw his face as it had been the face of an angel.

26   Then they suborned men, which said, "We have heard SnowWhite speak blasphemous words against the King of Cash and the Prince of Money, and against the church, Marine Korps."

27   And the high priests, scribes, elders and career clergy of war continued the self-preservation bond and offered sacrifice of the donated flesh unto the idol, and rejoiced in the works of their own hands.

28   And the voice of SnowWhite came in vision unto OverBoost in the night as he slept with thought of war, **THE LIGHT WILL SHINE AGAIN.**

The Malspel According to BURNOUT

(Respect the Rank, Not the Man)

CHAPTER 1

1   BurnOut had whizzed the midnight oil to become a certified public accountant;

2   And he balanced the ticket on each phase of Naval flight training.

3   He knew the mechanics; his double entry lifestyle balanced with each mental credit and moral debit.

4   His superior knowledge yielded him to be qualified as a pilot, and as a keeper of books.

5   BurnOut was quickly promoted to Lay-major by flying a desk.

6   There he made an equal number of takeoffs and controlled landings in the surplus dreg aircraft assigned for flight to desk pogues predestined not to be real pilots.

7   The Cardinal-general delighted in reading the personnel file of Ioudas C. Hapstein.

8   The map of Israel shown from his face;

9   His file disclosed a man pious in the Marine Korps;

10   A man devoted to the paperwork so detested by battle priests;

11   And, a man celibate to independent thought.

CHAPTER 2

1   And it came to pass that BurnOut knew each scripture and each verse of each desk generated book designed by thinkers of the sacred word;

2   And the teachings of the Covenant: The Guidebook for Marines.

3   BurnOut faithfully memorized its leadership principles thereby fulfilling the sacrament.

4   He could say his hail Marine Korps in his sleep.

5   It became known that the long hours and devotion to duty of Hapstein constituted extraordinary paper pushing which solidified in the presentation by the Cardinal-general himself of a medal to this line item major.

6   "You're sure the Egg Beater is defective?" inquired the Cardinal-general to his jewish information sleuth about the Korps' new helicopter.

7   "Yes Sir," he continued his secret oral report, "there is a flaw that causes them to come apart in the air. Holy Sea Headquarters says we have to keep this truth a secret. The old Dog helos will have to take up the slack. The Egg Beater will have to keep flying. The Prince of Money bought a death trap helicopter."

8   "We'll have crashes?" questioned the Cardinal-general, "What do the engineers say?"

9   "They're working night and day on it, they think they know the problems; a few crashes are just part of the risk, Sir."

10   "Find out who dropped the ball on this," the old flying High Priest sternly drilled at his information ferret, "I need to know the Pope-general's knowledge of this foul up."

11   The Cardinal-general mentally viewed the promotional chess board — it would be convenient for his career goal if the Holy One or the Divinity of Defense had to face the heat of irate mothers who lost sons not to war but because of procurement ineptitude, or money grubbing He-whores.

12   And it came to pass that the Pope-general's inspector detected the silent intrusions into the papal headquarters by an insignificant desk jockey as to how and who made purchasing decisions to obtain this defective helicopter,

13   And to its dialing for dollars flight history.

14   And immediately, orders of transfer were issued:

TO: Lay-major Ioudas C. Hapstein
FROM: The Pope

Report for immediate transition into helicopters to be completed not later than 21 days for further assignment to Seventh Air, Tekoa Wilderness, Nam Bo.

15   "I can't countermand the Pope," responded the Cardinal-general to the sheep white Lay-major. "You have served well, this is your chance, good luck."
16   Hapstein had cold fear;
17   He would have to become a common helicopter pilot;
18   A guinea pig with adverse statistical odds;
19   A test pilot in a faulty Egg Beater helicopter in actual combat.
20   He was distraught at his Church, the Korps.
21   "I hate helos," he screamed at the pilot's club bar sending a flurry of jet jocks running askance, not wanting to admit knowing a helo pilot, or a helo pilot to be.
22   "Just hold your hands above your head and yell 'unclean' " yelled the irate jew at being helo contaminated.
23   And it came to pass that a pious fighter pilot jew was ordained in the clergy of helicopter flying and sent forth to the Tekoa Wilderness on a mission from his beloved Church, the Korps.
24   And BurnOut preyed, and he was delivered into 777 to fly the Dog helicopters,
25   And he gave great thanks he was not given unto certain death in the helo designed from a common household Egg Beater.

Diary

of

Ioudas C. Hapstein

June 1
June 2
June 3
June 4

June 5
June 6
June 7
June 8
June 9
June 10
June 11
June 12
June 13
June 14
June 15
June 16
June 17
June 18
June 19
June 20
June 21
June 22
June 23
June 24
June 25
June 26
June 27
June 28
June 29
June 30

July 1   The trip across the ocean was long. The island is a strange land. There were people simply pissing and shitting along the street. There was a long ditch and I was told it was called a benjo ditch. It was their sewer system and the raw sewage simply washed with rainwater through the town to the ocean. The odor is sharp in places when there is no wind.

July 2   They shot me like a pin cushion. A Gunny told me to go to town and get drunk and laid — said it may be my last for a while so do a good job of it. I took his advice.

July 3   Woke up around noon with rain pounding the roof like I never heard before. Mouth tasted like dried anchovies. Somewhere in the fog I remember a place called the Texas Bar and laughing at the urinal with a sign above it "LBJ Ranch". No one spoke English and all the women were called something 'san.

July 4   The many battles on this Island cover the landscape with monuments, cemeteries, and war relics of the past. I feel like an athlete stretching my tendons and warming up to go into battle. New tightness in my gut.

July 6   I tried to find a Temple this morning. I feel like the wandering Jew. The pilot came up on the speakers and announced Nam ahead. The talking stopped. I wonder how many of the 135 Marines aboard will go home. Everyone glued their eyes out the window to where the ocean stopped and the land began. I can't see any jungles, but there are rice paddy fields from the ocean to the mountains. Then you could see bomb craters, and a bridge was blown up and lying in the river. Somehow it is silently frightening but I am anxious to get with it. Kill or be killed. How in the hell did I get myself into this?

July 7   It worked! I deliberately checked in late. All the Egg Beater slots were taken by the earlier new pilots. I got Dogs. 777 at Tru Lai. I am happy, scared, anxious, and apprehensive all at the same time. I see Tru Lai out the window from the Deuce — it's peaceful looking from up here in the sky. The ocean, the distant mountains and the landing field can all be seen at one time.

July 8   Got survival gear today; I fly tomorrow. I feel good. They have only lost one helo this year. Did I luck out. The Commander is a shanghaied desk pilot named Temple. He knows the system. I'm the new keeper of all the monies and funds for the base; I knew my accounting would someday pay off.

July 9   I flew with DarkMoon today. They call him DarkMoon because of his black butt that he moons. His father is an embassy officer. We flew cake walk missions all day; resupply, water, take n' wait, mail. I can't believe the jungle — grass is higher than the helo when we land. The country is beautiful. The Nam Bo people all look alike. You can't tell a friendly from an enemy. I reached for my pistol twice today only to find out that it was just a "friendly." I bet a lot of Marines unload and ask questions later.

July 10   I saw my first killed in action today (KIA). They called him a 1369, an unlucky cocksucker. First time I had heard that. It was perplexing. I knew guys died in war but somehow it was distant to know it and it grabbed me inside to see it firsthand. They never teach you the simpleness of here today, gone today.

July 11   I met a bunch of new pilots today. They came in from flying a week in the mountains at a place called Ada Sam. Bird-Man, SmegMa (in my hootch), an orphan called HalfRight, and a funny talking guy named Nowel White who they called Snow because of his white hair.

July 12   Night MedEvac. Last night was my first time in the barrel. We went out about three this morning to pick up a kid that had been bitten by a snake. Its the first time I realized that flying under the overcast made us an easy target. We turned off all the helo lights but the engine shoots out a long blue flame that can be seen for miles. I was scared shitless. We got shot at with tracers. The bullets started out like small red dots and looked like basketballs passing by the helo. I don't like this shit. We got the kid out; DarkMoon went nuts when the Crew Chief told him that the kid was on board and had the snake in a bag.

July 13   I flew with SnowWhite today. He is great. I have never flown with a pilot who can fly like he can. He autorotated to a zone today and stood the helo straight up on its tail right above the ground then instantly grabbed in all the power the engine had right in the bottom. I've never seen anything like it. It was a great day.

July 14   Happy hour. Everybody drank and sang. DingleBerry is funny. I don't know where he comes up with all the jokes. Temple just homesteads the bar chair and seldom speaks. Flew down the sea coast today to a fishing village with BirdMan. The artillery unit shot a shell out right across our nose. It scared me to death seeing the distant gun flash and the barrel size shell pass by us. I don't want to die — much less from a stupid mistake. BirdMan is a big Greek, and when we landed, he screamed and yelled at the Nam Bo advisor.

July 15   It rained heavy all day. We didn't fly—even the MedEvac. It would be nice if it would rain heavy every day—then there would be no war. It's funny watching pilots who don't have to fly. Some played cards; some acey deucey. An Egg Beater came apart with OverBoost watching last week; he just sat and stared in the rain all day today. I hurt for those guys. War's hell without having to fly a helo that comes apart in mid air. Its double dog hell with what they have done to us. Someone ought to go to jail.

July 16 Rain!
July 17 Rain!
July 18 Rain!
July 19 Rain! Went to Ada Sam.
July 20 Rain!

July 21   I spent a week at Ada Sam. It is a beautiful airfield but we sure are exposed. I saw elephants, tigers, parrots and all kinds of things. We flew to the little hilltop outposts all around the airfield and over into the valleys. They said the enemy were all around but I didn't see one soldier. There is a cliff at one end of the runway and just as you lift off and pass over the edge you are high above the valley floor with a white water river rushing downstream a thousand feet below. I liked it.

July 22   Shit sandwich. I flew with SnowWhite. He seems to like me. We had to go right down between two high hills and we were the perfect target. Somehow he got us in and out of there. I just knew we would be hit and crash at anytime. He told me to sing and gave me words I forgot. Boy did he not know I was silently yelling away inside from the time we came into gun range until we were out and high in the sky. We saved the kids.

July 23
July 24
July 25
July 26
July 27

July 28
July 29   I'm home.
July 30
July 31   Just another bullshit day.

Aug 1   Hours and hours of boredom interrupted by moments of stark terror.

Aug 2   The children of the villagers are wonderful kids. We went to the village and helped build a school today. It was wonderful. I met a little Nam Bo man called Peepers by the Marines. He had thick glasses, a tiny body and carried a grease gun. They paid him for every enemy he killed. The caretaker Gunny said they started out with eight dollars but had to reduce it because he was making so much money. I think this is the way to fight a war — just pay those who will benefit to kill those who are warring against them. Mammon's Mafia-ha!

Aug 3   I flew with HalfRight today. We followed a ground unit around as it burned villages and chased an invisible enemy up the river. HalfRight is ok. He gets with it. I found out he is Catholic and the Korps is his home. We both like SnowWhite but don't understand him. He is thick.

Aug 4   We are scared. They want us to fly high in the mountain to let lose some teams to chase after radio signals. They will be mince meat. They have dogs with the teams. There are stories of how guys have died rather than let their dog get killed. And there are stories of how the dogs get killed. I am confused.

Aug 5   Just another day.

Aug 6   I saw three Egg Beaters crashed in one zone today. The lead pilot briefed everyone how he was going to land into the wind before they took off. When they got to the attack zone, the enemy were not where he said they would be in the briefing but on the opposite side. He approached into the wind right across the top of the enemy — but just like he briefed he would do. Several Marines were killed and wounded from such stupidity. RedLine and I followed SnowWhite in and out of the same zone and did not get one round in our helo.

Aug 7   Rumors that we will be ordered by carrier to Okinawa to get new helos, equipment, resupply, and new pilots. I flew with BolTer today; his father is a Cardinal. Strange seeing a Chinese pilot in an oriental war.

Aug 8   Boy you wouldn't believe what happened to me. I flew wing on SnowWhite and we got in the middle of a sandwich right out in the open. We took several hits; no one hurt. DingleBerry wanted to get us a medal; I wanted it but SnowWhite said **THE BEST MEDAL IS A LIVE MAN'S SMILE.** I would feel guilty taking a medal when I saw the misery of the kids having to do the dirt fighting, and death by stupidity.

Aug 9
Aug 10
Aug 11
Aug 12   I got a letter from Pop today. First time in years.

Aug 13   Rumors keep coming about shipping out to the Islands for forty days.

Aug 14   Landed back at 77 Headquarters. I couldn't believe the food. Steaks, fish, assembly line food, /// Makes you hurt after seeing the misery of those in the field.

Aug 15   I flew night MedEvac last night. Rain and fog moved in from the ocean. I was scared but it went off without a hitch. RedLine was the lead bird. SnowWhite told him some words to sing while he flew. I don't understand but BirdMan said they flew around the fog and picked up someone that had stepped on a mine. This war business is a challenge.

Aug 16   Lots of take n' waits today. Some Navy High Priest wanted a ride out to the sea. TwoDogs gave him the ride of his life; we never got more than two feet off the trees. CrewChief said the braided swabbie stared out the door all the way to the ship.

Aug 17   There weren't enough helos today—Hoorah I thought! But they called over short of gun pilots. I flew co-pilot in a gunship. I thought I might get into the thick of it but it didn't happen. We flew cover for a patrol out in the rice fields.

Aug 18   Out of helos again today. More pilots than flying machines. It was hilarious. SmegMa sat naked in the sun with his dick poked inside a beer can with the top and bottom cut out. Doc made him fill it with a red paste to get rid of the fungus he caught. I wrote Pop a letter.

Aug 19   I am pissed. They made me ride in an Egg Beater today. We needed an extra pilot to pick up a repaired helo at the Aceldama Airfield. I was scared the whole trip. Those damn helos are death traps even without a war. They keep grounding them because of the crashes.

Aug 20   Rumors again that we will have to keep the old helos. We won't go to the islands. I need a rest.

Aug 21   A Crew Chief got shot in the ass today. It was the pilot's fault. He had to play hero and land the way the book writers wrote. RedLine and I zoomed in three times into the same zone without a hit. I'm beginning to understand why desk pilot thinkers are just as dangerous as the enemy.

Aug 22   Rape, Pillage, and Burn. We got the gooks on the run. Saw a jet shoot a rocket right in the front door of a house. That will teach them to fuck with us. We drank too much.

Aug 23   War's hell when you deal with Marines. If you fuck with the best, you'll die like the rest.

Aug 24   One of the High Priests came by today; a real asshole. SmegMa sang him a him at the club. He didn't know whether to get mad or not. He just simmered and outwardly smiled. A good Marine don't give a shit.

Aug 25   What a day. I flew in and out of battles all day and pulled 34 wounded out without one death and no one hurt. I got drunk. This war business stuff is exciting when you are good.

Aug 26   Chaplain Head is such a dink. How they get these preachers is a mystery. We don't have a Rabbi but there is one down at Holy Sea. Dick Head whimpers at night when he plays with himself.

Aug 27   BirdMan taught me how to do a zero airspeed autorotation. It is great to set there motionless and kick out the engine falling backward in a death spiral to the earth pulling back in the cushion at the bottom right above the ground. Damn, I love flying with these guys.

Aug 28   SnowWhite and I flew to the mountains today. I don't understand him but he has what it takes. Some Army guy came into the Ada Sam Camp that had woolly white hair. He seemed to know SnowWhite and they laughed aloud. I don't know if this black guy was laughing at me or they were making Jew jokes.

Aug 29   We landed at Aceldama OutPost this morning after a battle. I don't understand but some of the dead enemy had smiles on their faces. BolTer was stoic; wouldn't talk about what had happened. Chinese are different. SmegMa said the Nam Bo people hate the Chinese and we have to protect BolTer.

Aug 30   Siren went off in the middle of the night. Suicide squad made it in through the wire. They blew up a gasoline truck but were killed before they got to the helos. A drunk pilot outside the club sat openly in a beach chair watching a suicide gook running toward him in the moon light. The drunk killed the gook with pistol fire; he landed at his feet in front of the chair. It was crazy. The explosive didn't go off.

Aug 31   They made the Egg Beaters evacuate a village. One farmer wouldn't leave without his water buffalo. They got the beast in the helo. At 5000 feet the animal bolted, broke loose and jumped out the back. The farmer jumped after the water buffalo.

Sept 1   Another day another dollar. Went into Tru Lai City today. The people are very poor. There is little to fight over except land. A big Catholic Church was in the town. The Nam Bo general came where we were. He was a schlemiel. The attached Gunny said the Gook-general likes young boys, and winked.

Sept 2   Hours of flying and no excitement.

Sept 3   Flew out to the carrier ship. The hospital ship with its big red cross was bobbing in the water nearby. We brought some high mucks back to plan some battle.

Sept 4
Sept 5
Sept 6
Sept 7

Sept 8   Met the most unbelievable pilot today. Big guy with a bellow voice. Flies all the time; supposed to be the best instructor around. They call him Hopper Honey. Boy he tells it like it is. He wears mouse ears with a trainee to startle his flying.

Sept 9   Rumors of getting out of this war still are going on. They keep worrying what the Bac Bo army will be doing. I saw the charts today; the enemy is massing up North. It rained today while the wind blew dust at the same time.

Sept 10   Flew maintenance check flights all day. We have good mechs but someone is tampering with the supply. We can't get new engines.

Sept 11   SnowWhite landed on the carrier last night even after the engine quit. He is the best pilot I've ever known. I wish I was that good. He talked to me the other day about why men could not stop wars. I am confused, but he talks in riddles.

Sept 12   I am getting used to this thing called war. Its just like work at home except you get up and go to war and you go to bed late and tired, knowing you will get up and go to war tomorrow. Death is so commonplace it doesn't shock you any more.

Sept 13   Field grade moon scheduled tonight. Dingle was up at the operations ready room seeing if he could get on the night flying schedule. Strange how a pilot could dedicate himself to a career of not flying or flying the cake walk missions.

Sept 14   I saw a message come through that we are going to pull out for forty days and the ships will carry us up to the islands to get these worn out helos repaired and exchanged. I can't tell anyone because it might get canceled.

Sept 15   We sang, and we sang, and we sang.

Sept 16   A gun pilot was killed today. They couldn't stand to let a patrol in the Valley get wiped out. They flew right in the thick of it. One of the helos took a round right in the controls and flew right into the ground. Killed everyone. Shit!

Sept 17   Poncho Pilot tried to get to be a hero today. He asked several pilots to recommend him for a medal. We must be in the dregs for leaders. There are good commanders, Temple is just too old.

Sept 18   The Great Fart Fight. They all got drunk last night and had a farting contest. Somewhere in the middle of it they decided to start lighting farts. I laughed till I cried.

Sept 19   Nothing
Sept 20   Rain
Sept 21   Rain
Sept 22   Rain
Sept 23   Rain
Sept 24   Rain and Cold
Sept 25   Rain, Cold and more rain.
Sept 26   Rain and monopoly.
Sept 27   Rain
Sept 28   Rain
Sept 29   Rain, maintenance flight hover.
Sept 30   Rain
Oct 1   Rain,
Oct 2   Rain,

Oct 3   Hopper Honey was killed in an Egg Beater crash today. Spinning blade cut his head off. We followed his body till they put in on the Evac plane for home. We are going to the Island!

Oct 4

Oct 5   Hallelujah. We're out of this place. Took old C rations to the orphanage as we left. Thought SnowWhite would crash at sea. Fog and blackness; He looked cosmic flying right over the water with the big search light on in the distant fog.

Oct 6   Navy has it made — food, dryness, showers. I'd forgotten what it was to be this clean.

Oct 7   Except for showers and eating, I've slept for two days.

Oct 8   Beautiful! The islands look like a big floating dragon in the sea. After we unloaded, all of us bought motorcycles.

Oct 9   BirdMan caught a big fish off the pier. He put it in SmegMa's bed with its head on the pillow and a cigar in its mouth. SmegMa came in drunk and slept with it.

Oct 10   What a day. Flew over the nudist beach. Never saw so many naked women in my life. They don't have hair! and the men aren't jewish — ha.

Oct 11   The Air Force reported that someone flew a helo underneath the big bridge. Temple was pissed; ordered all pilots confined to the airfield. SmegMa got a round eye nurse naked in the ready room and when Chaplain Dick Head saw her, he went nuts — ran out into the raining black night across the runway.

Oct 12   We followed SnowWhite up to the mountains to a dirt floored place. It was pure peace. Met a common farmer with an uncommon brightness called Lei; First wool haired oriental I've seen.

Oct 13   Loose lips sink ships. Keep your mouth shut.

Oct 14   Trained in the mountains today. The machine gunners got to where they could hit the target as I flew by.

Oct 15
Oct 16
Oct 17

Oct 18   Spent three days up North. The island is beautiful. The sea is spectacular—until we saw the school of sharks. Can't help but think pilots in a helo going into the sea would be like sardines in a tin to the sharks.

Oct 19   I couldn't believe it. Injun blew up several hundred rubbers and put them in SmegMa's room. The got him drunk and shoved him in around midnight. It was funnnnnnnney.

Oct 20   Got word today that two pilots were killed at Ada Sam. I thought the war was over. We have several new pilots. Hard to know anyone's name.

Oct 21   Kinda childish. Several of them had special name tags made for their flight suit—Harry Balls, Dick M. Dumpem and they checked in an imaginary guy they called Isa A. Hoel. Drove 'em nuts. SmegMa had a name tag he wore around with the name Kraven Morehead on it.

Oct 22   I flew with Snow today on a confined landing zone training mission. He continues to amaze me how good a pilot he is.

Oct 23   Weather terrible. Typhoon coming. We all drank at the club.

Oct 24   Rain, rain, rain. Boring. Tired of philosophy, reading and thinking.

Oct 25   Typhoon came. Unbelievable. The wind hit 85 mph. We got high at the club but had to crawl in the wind back to the quarters. I tried to stand up but couldn't. It was funny, we laid there and laughed and laughed.

Oct 26   SnowWhite wants me to kinda watch out for the others. I don't understand; StoneMan, RedLine and OverBoost follow him around everywhere.

Oct 27   I flew a new kid today-TreeTop they call him. He was plain lost. I guess they have to pump 'em out for fodder.

Oct 28   I was at Air Force today on secret mission; They all carried machine guns and were handcuffed to boxes; BirdMan asked the spit clean major why all the fuss over shake a' puddin. He didn't laugh.

Oct 29   New helos; new pilots; new equipment. I'm gettin scared that someone will recognize us for gettin back in the shit.

Oct 30   Slept all day. I feel good. Apprehensive.

Oct 31   Halloween. The guys went nuts. Injun painted himself with orange war paint and wore a loin cloth. SmegMa is SmegMa; aargh. They danced and drank the night away.

Nov 1   I couldn't believe it. BirdMan flew over to the Air Force Base and externaled the gazebo from the golf course up to the mountains. I know nothing. Ha.

Nov 2   I flew sea air rescue off the end of the island. A sailor fell off a ship at sea last night and they don't know where. It was scary for we saw sharks.

Nov 3   Rumors of new fighting breaking out in Nam Bo.

Nov 4   I rode down to a place called suicide cliff today. I couldn't understand how so many people would just jump off with their children into the sea rocks way below. They said their leaders told them the Marines would torture them.

Nov 5   I assembled a new survival kit of my own today to carry back to the war.

Nov 6   I got a letter from Pop.

Nov 7   Hurry up and wait mission; flew some take n' wait jockey around the bases.

Nov 8   DarkMoon mooned the club last night. Some boatman got mad at the antics. Temple told him to leave DarkMoon alone.

Nov 9   We leave in five days, I fear the unknown.

Nov 10   Unbelievable. The Feast of Tunn Tavern. Everyone got drunk. They stuck their dicks in the birthday cake. I tap danced on the bar top. SmegMa had a brothel queen hum the Marine Hymn while getting a blow-job. What a celebration.

Nov 11   My tongue still feels thick. I had no business flying today but it was routine. We are going back but don't know when.

Nov 12   I witnessed SmegMa eating local food he brought for lunch in a round tin bucket. He was sitting in a circle with the native workers and jabbering. He thinks he is one of them.

Nov 13   I saw SnowWhite for the first time in a while today. He seemed drained. He's ok.

Nov 14   Rain blew in and out; stormed long enough to give us the day off.

Nov 15   We were ordered out during the night. Had to load the carrier starting in the dark. Madhouse for a while. They tell us that they expect a big battle and we need to full steam to the war. I don't want to die. BirdMan stole a golf cart and brought it to the ship under the helo.

Nov 16   Stormed at sea. Strange how ominous. The kids on the ship are preparing to fight. Someone painted a duck on the doc's door.

Nov 17   The radar has us close to Nam Bo out at sea. They don't know when or where we will assault but everyone is preparing for battle. I don't like it; the rain and low clouds will make helos shooting ducks having to fly around at treetops.

Nov 18   We did it. I am back at Tru Lai. It was crazy. Several times we came out of the clouds staring in the face of a helo headed right at us. Several helos took dings from one shot Charlies.

Nov 19   War is all around us. I flew into the Nam Bo hospital last night with a cargo of tiny tan men all shot up. I had forgotten the smell of wounded flesh.

Nov 20   I am a Marine. I am a Marine. I am a Marine.

Nov 21   We lost a helo yesterday. They just flew into a mountainside in the fog. I knew the desk major was an accident looking for a place to happen. He took some good people with him.

Nov 22   I can't remember eating. I miss good food. This will do.

Nov 23   There were rows of 1369's on the ramp today being flown to Graves Registration. A cold reminder.

Nov 24   A Nam Bo leader came by today. Offered to sell us a high medal for green money. I wanted to kill him. Are these shitheads what we are dying for?

Nov 25   Flew with StoneMan today. He's good. We extracted a team in the mountains by cable. Eternity passes in the time we had to set there in the open as a sure thing target.

Nov 26   Mail run; beer run. They chipped in and bought a pallet of beer from the Navy boys.

Nov 27   I flew in an eight helo flight to a village near the Tru Lai City. They said lots of villagers were killed. It doesn't make sense; why are we killing the people we're saving?

Nov 28   Another day.

Nov 29   Another day.

Nov 30   Another day.

Dec 1   Another day.

Dec 2   Another day. Two dry farts.
Dec 3
Dec 4
Dec 5
Dec 6
Dec 7
Dec 8
Dec 9
Dec 10
Dec 11
Dec 12
Dec 13
Dec 14
Dec 15
Dec 16
Dec 17
Dec 18
Dec 19
Dec 20
Dec 21
Dec 22
Dec 23
Dec 24

Dec 25   What's this cease fire for Christmas shit! Let's cease fire
for 364 days and flight only on Christmas.

Dec 26
Dec 27
Dec 28
Dec 29

Dec 30   So what.

Dec 31   I'm ready to go home.

Jan 1   I saw two Marine jets fly between the trees while I was sitting in the hot zone today. It felt great. The Air Force never gives close air support.

Jan 2   I caught the Chaplain reading SmegMa's sex books. He is such a wimp. I told DingleBerry.

Jan 3   Rain, rain, rain. TailWind and I pulled out a patrol right at dark; no action. They said they were being trailed.

Jan 4   Aceldama OutPost. Seems there is a nightly attack every night lately. BolTer keeps talking about how the dead enemy have a smile on their face. Masada?

Jan 5   Back to the OutPost today. They made the Marines dig up and recount the bodies. Didn't believe them. Strange watching a mass grave being dug by the tank dozers.

Jan 6   Took three holes in the helo. Had to fly with Doltish. He thinks he is good but he flies low and slow. He hinted at me putting him in for a medal because we took hits.

Jan 7   SmegMa sat around all day with his dick in a beer can filled with that red paste. Doc says its root rot.

Jan 8   I don't know what day or week it is. If I forget to write in this diary, I have to ask someone the date. We are just trudging through time and space without feeling.

Jan 9   The sight of dead children is pure horror—we killed them. We are all victims. Where is mercy?

Jan 10   A kid cried to me today because he was just a mere mechanic and wanted to fight in the war. Stupid. He wants to be made a machine gunner and fly door gunner. Strange how some of them fight to get out of the shit and some are lured into it.

Jan 11   SnowWhite talks funny but boy can he fly. We circled out over the ocean and skimmed through the fog to get to a patrol with a wounded Marine. Unbelievable how the fog lifted long enough for us to get the kid out and socked back in as we left.

Jan 12   A day of rest. Not enough helos repaired today.

Jan 13   Its cold, wet and the food is bland. Nice to be alive — they brought in some dead enemy with their weapons this morning. Caught them at the wire last night. We are a target.

Jan 14   Tru Lai was attacked last night with mortars. TopsyTurvey had to watch the explosions and took a tiny fragment hit right in the head. Dumb. One less promotable careerist — his record should read wounded while thinking like a dumb ass.

Jan 15   The Nam Bo police beat some of the workers to find out if they had helped in the mortar attack. They treat their own people as throwaways. Had a good day flying with TwoDogs.

Jan 16   Saved several Marines today. Feels good to get them out and to the hospital; horror at seeing the wounds. HalfRight and I flew wing on SnowWhite and StoneMan. Seven hours flight time.

Jan 17   Egg Beater commander got shot in the leg flying low and slow over a village. Mistakes over and over. Same old trial and error mistakes training a new inexperienced commander.

Jan 18   Special Operations Group over the other side of the mountain. There were many hired killers there getting ready to rape, pillage and burn. You could see murder for money in their faces.

Jan 19   Spent the night with the SOG group at the base camp. I was scared. They had captured girls and put them in wire cages. If any man wanted one, he just pointed. The girls were like caged animals. I was told to keep my mouth shut.

Jan 20   I am exhausted. slept all day. I keep seeing the eyes of the little girls in cages forced to screw all the killers. We are fighting on the side of evil animals.

Jan 21   SnowWhite shared my pain. I am angry that our leaders would side up with such creatures.

Jan 22   RedLine and OverBoost went down today. Took a hit in the engine oil cooler. No one hurt.

Jan 23   DingleBerry wants us to start putting in more people for medals. Says 777 is not recognizing all the good work. Bullshit.

Jan 24   SnowWhite and I landed at the orphanage today. It was inspiring to see SnowWhite with all the kids. If the earth were covered with just kids, there would be no wars.

Jan 25   SmegMa talked MakeReady into sitting in the sun with his pecker in a tin can filled with paste. SmegMa told him every-one would get the fungus and carry it home if they didn't cure it before they left.

Jan 26   Just another day of war. We need a warrior's union.

Jan 27   I lost an engine today; warning light worked. I shot the best autorotation I have ever flown. Landed on the side of a bomb crater. BirdMan rescued me, HalfRight and the crew.

Jan 28   Dingle gave me the day off.

Jan 29
Jan 30
Jan 31
Feb 1
Feb 2
Feb 3
Feb 4   I don't care any more. Fuck you diary.
Feb 5
Feb 6
Feb 7
Feb 8

Feb 9
Feb 10
Feb 11
Feb 12
Feb 13
Feb 14
Feb 15
Feb 16
Feb 17
Feb 18
Feb 19
Feb 20
Feb 21
Feb 22
Feb 23
Feb 24
Feb 25
Feb 26
Feb 27
Feb 28
Mar 1
Mar 2
Mar 3
Mar 4
Mar 5
Mar 6
Mar 7
Mar 8
Mar 9
Mar 10
Mar 11
Mar 12
Mar 13
Mar 14
Mar 15
Mar 16
Mar 17
Mar 18   I've got to get out of this place.
Mar 19
Mar 20
Mar 21

Mar 22
Mar 23
Mar 24
Mar 25
Mar 26
Mar 27
Mar 28
Mar 29
Mar 30
Mar 31

Apr 1   I got a Silver Star. I deserve it and it will get me pro-moted. I told them SnowWhite said the Korps is not a land army. Don't mess with the nose. No one knows what the nose knows.

Apr 2   All hell broke loose.

Apr 3   SnowWhite got what he deserved. If he is so good, he'll be able to fly to the Valley of the Skull and get out. He is good at miracles.

Apr 4   I got mine. You get yours. Its a dog eat dog world.

Apr 5   He who gets in line last, gets in line last.

Apr 6   I am better than he is. You don't have to fly if you count.

Apr 7   You good looking son of a bitch.

Apr 8   StoneMan lied over and over.

Apr 9   Asshole. Better thee than me.

Apr 10   No people, no problem.

Apr 11   SnowWhite took off by himself. Killed in action. What have I done? Fuck the Silver Star! They won't take it back. I threw it out the window somewhere over Aceldama. I hurt, I am in pain, it does not compute, I'm spinning inside, what now tan sow.

Apr 12   Dippety due, up yours too. You'll wonder where the yellow went, rubber bag, rubber bag, douche bag

Apr 13
Apr 14
Apr 15
Apr 16
Apr 17
Apr 18
Apr 19
Apr 20
Apr 21
Apr 22
Apr 23
Apr 24
Apr 25
Apr 26
Apr 27
Apr 28
Apr 29
Apr 30
May 1

Form 1369-B		Page 4

Investigation Report

Conclusion:

Iodus C. Hapstein died as a result of intentionally jumping from the passenger compartment of a flying helicopter above Aceldama Airfield. His death was suicide. The note in his diary simply read:

"Forgive this schmuck."

(Official Use Only)

The Revelation According to BOLTER

(The Faithful Messenger)

CHAPTER 1

1   In the land of the big shopping malls in the post-war baby boom, the Marine cleric of the High Church had twin sons.
2   And it came to pass through the years of careful coaching and constant occultation that the twin sons joined the church and became lay leaders: one with a congregational platoon, and the other a common helo pilot.
3   The platoon leader son sustained disabling wounds at a muddy high ground south of the river Chebar at the Aceldama OutPost because his newly issued machine gun had failed;
4   Both the helo pilot brother and the deity Cardinal-general father were perplexed.
5   The Cardinal-general wore dismay on his chinese ancestral face when he had audience with the Prince of Money at the chamber of the Divinity of Defense to engage in a subordinates combat at the idiocy of body exchanging warfare.
6   And it was unknown to the ego of he-whores the fallacy of body count,
7   And the Prince of Money knew he erred not.
8   It was the time when the academic men of non-war dominated his Holiness, the King of Cash, and the demons of darkness and greed homesteaded the inner circle of those blinded by the grandeur of power, money, and vanity.
9   And the Prince of Money was skilled in the inefficiencies of business, but also understood not that death cannot be sold as a

mean, median or mode ratio—even though the Prince of Money knew that war was good business;

10   And the showboat man of Kingsian mind and two-tone heart knew himself to be the greatest;

11   But the people would not continue to donate their sons for business causes, or for a Prince's piece of mind.

12   The Cardinal-general of Holy Sea West was distraught that those unskilled in the art of warfare were instituting policies fundamentally defective at the fighting level of the victim field Marine,

13   Who did therefore die.

14   "We can do nothing to stop him," responded the Pope-general to the Chinese Cardinal, "he is accountable only to his Holiness—who fears only the inquisition by the House of Ill Gotten Gains."

15   And it came to pass that the fears of the Cardinal-general were right, that the conceit of the King's lay-leaders fueled by the money-hummers of Wall Street first sought pocket book victory as they believed that their goliath war machine could promptly conquer little Bac Bo's commonplace army.

16   And it came to pass that the Prince of Money in the awning of the King of Cash interfered more and more into warfare, and would seek yes decisions for the yes market's sake.

17   Acts of frustration to an uncontrollable enemy skilled in patience and armed with an unlimited quantity of time was understood not by the money gnomes advising the Prince of Money and the King of Cash.

18   And the captains of darkness smiled for the evils of vanity, greed, and power shown round-about, and the flesh was sent to death,

19   And the rich sent the poor to war's market.

20   And good child men were harnessed to a runaway war chariot.

21   Vain deaths blossomed under the harvest moon for statistical death was sold under the trade name of body count,

22   And the sucking chest wounds, or missing arms, legs, or eyes were the cost basis for geography neither wanted, occupied, nor kept.

23   But it was that the King of Cash reaped War profits;

24   It was that a great economic society could be built on the blood of the lesser child men of the land;
25   It was that honor, duty, and Fatherland were the smoke and mirror songs used to serenade the minds of those who knew not that they knew not.
26   And the necessity of dying for an unknown cause, or for an unknown purpose, became unknown commonplace;
27   Survival became the password of the victim soldiers.
28   The King of Cash and the Prince of Money preyed upon the havenots, particularly the black poor, for they had power not and were the silent fodder upon which the money machine could feed.
29   There was summoned forth the afflicted, the not-so-bright, the crippled, and the poor, under glorious cause but camouflaged purpose, for these persons were least able to defend themselves against indoctrination;
30   And survival by wealth was not within their group,
31   100,000 were shipped unto Molech.
32   And the unskilled, the untrained, and the blindly versed sons of the unpowerful were used for a war tithe unto the mammon's altar of attrition.
33   And the black child men marched to the High Priest's altar with dignity.
34   And mothers blindly handed their sons to be sacrificed to Molech.

CHAPTER 2

1   BolTer knew that he might die, but never for disloyalty to the cause — but what cause?
2   And BolTer sought to be left alone.
3   "This is not a war," he thought, "this is a battle between the haves, and the have nots. This war is being waged for the principles of making money, . . . and to salvage the Prince's ego."
4   And the Marines were a stubbornly independent race of warriors whose very fiber prohibited disgrace of faith, and were of unquestioned loyalty to their brothers.
5   And voices said unto the minds of the Priest-generals,
6   "It is alright to take and retake the same hill,"

7   "And it is alright to hide from your eyes defective weapons and ill gotten gains,"

8   "And you can't do anything to stop it, so keep your Priesthood."

9   The voices sought blind dedication and harnessed obedience to ungodly causes.

10   "My Father," BolTer wrote, "We have been used, our blood has been taken to fill the coffers of those who deserve not, and we are the blind soldiers who have killed and taken away the lives of the peasant people, all for pieces of ribbon and enrapturement of the demons of greed, vanity, and power. Hear the words of my friend, SnowWhite, in whom I gave much doubt, **CHILD MEN DIE BECAUSE THOSE SWORN TO COVET AND PROTECT THEIR FLESH HIDE FROM THEIR EYES THAT WHICH THEY SEE.**

11   "Father, we must expose this great lie," wrote BolTer to the Cardinal-general of the West, the guardian of Holy Sea for half the earth. "We cannot trade our lives one for one, two for one, or three for one,

12   And we fight for such an evil and corrupt Nam Bo government."

13   "And my friend SnowWhite also said, **KNOW FIRST WHAT YOU ARE FIGHTING FOR, THEN WHAT YOU ARE FIGHTING AGAINST.**

14   "Father," BolTer wrote again, "We are being used in an assembly line war."

15   "The young with the low I.Q.'s, the slow minds, and the afflicted are falling like flies with inadequate training sent into instant combat. You must do something Father, these men who love their Fatherland are seeing no loyalty from above. The Korps is not a land army—but the Army understands not the Korps—. This is a war for the souls of the little people—the poor Nam Bo peasants are the prize—not the geography; and there is a killing frenzy on the victim peasants, . . . and the child men."

16   And BolTer cried, and closed the letter,

17   "Father, I could not disgrace our Korps, but you must do something for these men who believe in the Korps. The King understands not the wasting of our brothers' flesh. . . I must close, . . Hu."

CHAPTER 3

1   "Much Wampum," said Injun to BolTer as they departed the special landing space near their air-conditioned quarters by the King's money projects.

2   And the Queen of Loot, the Duchess of Dough, and the High Sheriffs of Wall Street fed from the money caskets of arrogance and vanity from the fine little war.

3   And the young soldiers were enraged at the Father that allowed profiteers to reap unconsciously the shekels from their human sacrifice,

4   "Best war we got," responded BolTer sarcastically as he looked out the helo window as they flew down the narrow river to Holy Sea Forward Headquarters.

5   "Never seen so many ass holes in my life," commented InJun at the masses of Nam Bo village peasants with their pants down to their ankles sprattle-legged along the river banks taking the early morning defecation.

6   "Shit flows downhill," said Injun as the defiling, floating human excrement was easily visible on the river's surface gathered along side the helo landing dock as he piloted the helicopter onto the narrow river side landing space.

7   And InJun there met Cardinal-general Yu, the keeper of the western church, and also BolTer's father.

8   And the father and son of chinese ancestry embraced not but were stoic in each other's presence.

9   And it came to pass in the shadow of war that much was said, and much was said not.

10   "This is a misguided war," BolTer said to his father, "And we will lose."

11   The chinese face wearing identity lines of Marine Korps history across his brow responded, "Why do you think we will lose?"

12   "These Nam Bo leaders are corrupt, they sell drugs, they will be overthrown, it is only a question of time," BolTer looked at the man in whom he had only flickers of radon acquaintanceship for his father constantly left his mother and his brothers as he wandered the earth for the Korps, "And the good common people of this country are its prize, not its geography."

13   "Tell me how you know of this?" queried the man of much hard learning.

14   And BolTer responded, "It is a common secret, the government and its privies sell, trade, and exploit all the little people. Drugs, gambling, whores, and corruption are their trademarks. They are in the business of letting us make war for them. These are the corrupt rich; they give not of their sons to do battle nor of their money or land for the peasants. These leaders do not believe in the cause of freedom. I have seen dead enemy soldiers hanging from the wires who have died with smiles on their faces. The spirit of the people is not with these puppets. By joining with the outlaws, we have become the enemy of ourselves."

15   "War has given you much wisdom, my son," pridefully grinned the man of great power, "I am to meet with the Prince of Money, and perhaps talk with the King of Cash, what would you have me say to them."

16   "This is not our war," quietly but firmly came BolTer's words knowing that before he had come to Nam Bo he carried the blind dedication befitting ignorant youth.

17   "If we are to win," BolTer continued, "We have to give the common people hope, their land, and their dignity, . . . freedom . . . and get out of their lives leaving honest government . . . and you tell the Prince of Money that the soldier and his parents are beginning to see through the ignorance of this war."

18   Bolter paused, "Father, they are starting to wage a war of numbers . . . and you know we cannot win in a war of numbers."

19   The Cardinal-general answered, "We are soldiers, my son. Soldiers lives are committed for the simple asking. We can only follow orders. For now, the orders come from those who believe themselves infallible, who are misguided, and as you can see around you, they believe war can be taught in Harvard Business School with both profits and battles won in this jungle cost study marketplace. Nothing can be further from the truth, but we must follow orders, even if it means our wasted lives."

20   "But Father," respectfully hesitated BolTer, "We took an oath first to our Fatherland, to give it our allegiance first, what are you going to do if the King of Cash hides the truth of this war from our people? He is a profiteer!"

21   And the man of many wars had no answer for he knew that the Prince of Money and the King of Cash were hiding the truth from the people.

22   And the man of many wars knew that he would have to resign as a Cardinal from the High Church before he would be allowed to expose the many lies known to him, for he was then under a vow to his Majesty, the King.

23   "I am proud of you my son," said the old man to the parting helo driver, "And I shall carry the message of flawed equipment and useless death to the Prince of Money, and many other messages;"

24   And BolTer saluted his father and climbed aboard the helo, and he with InJun departed for Tru Lai.

CHAPTER 4

1   It came to pass across the earth that the Cardinal-general Yu jerked to himself and openly spat directly into his own face in the mirror; he was in the City of the Tabernacle of Power, not with his beloved Marines.

2   He was stressed by the lies; he hated the gluttony, the death-issuing ego, and the "I am the greatest" power whores.

3   God he loved, his Fatherland he loved, his Korps he loved; almighty God was present — but what had happened to the fundamentals, the principles of leadership.

4   The King would not admit error.

5   It wreaked of the military industrial complex.

6   "If I resign from the Priesthood, I'll be free to expose to the people the truth, but I will be branded a traitor — from which Marines will unnecessarily die, . . . for a yes cleric Priest lackey will follow me."

7   "If I continue, the lies will compound upon the lies while the war whores spit forth chess game death to child men flesh."

8   Cardinal-generals don't cry — but this one did.

9   Tarawa was good combat, for Tarawa allowed the enemy to deserve his vengeance, his skills.

10   Killing in the big war felt right. There you had an enemy who chose to pick the fight.

11   Killing in Nam Bo some how left you sick — it was overwhelming firepower against little brown men with ancestral weapons and antique cash support, but the war would be lost,

12   For the poor people fought for their homeland against a foreign enemy.

13   The Nam Bo peasants in Tekoa Wilderness loved the quiet one, the old George Washington hero of the North who said, "All men are created equal."

14   "Who to fuck is the Divinity of Defense kidding?" he whispered.

15   You cannot trade one life for a quota; you cannot win with an enemy of unending quota.

16   "I cannot serve two masters," the Cardinal-general stared into the looking glass. He read the Catechism book for Marines:

> You don't inherit the ability to lead Marines.
> Neither is it issued.
> You acquire that ability by taking an honest look at yourself.
> You see how you stack up against 14 well-known character traits of a Marine leader. These are:

> **INTEGRITY**
> **KNOWLEDGE**
> **COURAGE**
> **DECISIVENESS**
> **DEPENDABILITY**
> **INITIATIVE**
> **TACT**
> **JUSTICE**
> **ENTHUSIASM**
> **BEARING**
> **ENDURANCE**
> **UNSELFISHNESS**
> **LOYALTY**
> **JUDGMENT**

17   The dedicated warrior in search of soul took his cordite scarred finger and traced the homily meant to teach leadership. He read of unselfishness, loyalty and judgment.

CHAPTER 5

1 And of unselfishness, he read from the Marine scripture,

2 Unselfishness. Marine leaders don't pull the best rations from the case and leave the rest to their men. They get the best they can for all the men in their unit, all the time. A leader gets his own comforts, pleasures, and recreation only after his troops have been provided with theirs. Look at a chow line in the field. You'll see squad leaders at the end of the company. This is more than a tradition. It is leadership in action. It is unselfishness.

3 Share your men's hardships. Then the privileges that go with your rank will have been earned. Don't hesitate to accept them when the time is right, but until it is, let them be. When your men are wet, cold and hungry, you'd better be too. That's the price you pay for leadership. What it buys is well worth the cost. The dry clothes, warm bunk, and a full belly can come later.

4 Give credit where credit is due. Don't grab the glory for yourself. Recognize the hard work and good ideas of your subordinates and be grateful you have such men. Your leaders will look after you in the same way. They know the score, too.

5 And Cardinal-general Yu saw in his mind the air-conditioned leaders who fought battles from the cool and quiet high above the battle or back in the safety from the heat of jungles.

6 And Cardinal-general Yu saw the rows of officers eating from plate dishes, adopting habits of disgrace while their men were sacrificed.

7 And it was that the war profits of the King of Cash dishonored sacrificed flesh.

8 And it was that child men's lives were given so the Prince of Money would not have to mistake admit.

CHAPTER 6

1 And of loyalty, he read from the Marine scripture,

2 Loyalty. This is a two-way street. It goes all the way up and all the way down the chain of command. Marines live by it. They even quote latin for it — "Semper Fidelis." As a leader of Marines, every word, every action, must reflect your loyalty — up and down. Back your men when they're right. Correct them when they

are wrong. You are being loyal either way. Pass on orders as if they were your own idea, even when they are distasteful. To rely on the rank of the person who told you to do a job is to weaken you own position. Keep your personal problems and the private lives of your seniors to yourself. But help your men in their difficulties, when it is proper to do so. Never criticize your unit, your seniors, or your fellow leaders in the presence of subordinates. Make sure they don't do it either. If a deserving man gets into trouble, go to bat for him. He'll work harder when it's all over.

3   When it comes to spreading corruption, the proverbial rotten apple couldn't hold a candle to the damage that can be done by a disloyal leader. The Marine Korps has never had a problem in this area. Keep the record clean.

4   "The King of Cash could never be a Marine," thought the old Cardinal-general.

5   "Am I being disloyal not exposing the King's war profiteers," thought the now distraught Cardinal-general.

6   "Am I being disloyal by not exposing that Marine flesh is being given to protect men who are drug dealers, who are corrupt, who feel not the pain of the little people?"

7   And the man of Chinese mind whispered unto himself, "We must give unto the common people the greatest gift, freedom, it is the cause worthy of death."

8   "But the He-Whores of war seek access to power, to things to fuel more money."

CHAPTER 7

1   And of judgment, the Cardinal-general read from the scripture,

2   Judgment. This comes with experience. It is simply weighing all the facts in any situation, then making the best move. But until you acquire experience you may not know the best move. What, then, do you use for experienced judgment in the meantime? Well, there are about two hundred years' worth of experienced judgment on tap in the Marine Korps. Some of it is available to you at the next link in the chain of command. Ask and you will receive. Seek and you will find.

3   "Seek and you will find," he whispered aloud, "then I'll expose the bastards."

CHAPTER 8

1   The old man's eyes again began to tear.
2   Cardinal-generals don't cry,
3   But he searched his soul as the tears gather and trickled from the hands over his eyes.
4   His son had died — not in the glory of battle, but at the end of the political barrel of a manufacturing defect.
5   "The blood of my brothers shall not be shed for these whores,"
6   He slowly removed the priestly garments from his uniform with the quiet pride which placed them there.
7   An inner peace enraptured his soul not felt since he and Mac had shared the ten mile stares while marching one by one out of Chosen — frozen Chosen.
8   Tomorrow he would not fade away, the whores of Wall Street would have their money — but the victim Marines in Tekoa Province would have their rightful place above all other Marines — they had died not for the Fatherland, not for God, but in an inhumane dew of bitter-sweet honor,
9   Youth caught in the sugar trap of a King's Court mesmerized by easy money.
10   "I will fight capitalism's wars no more," he murmured to himself finding the mere words cast a new found comfort.
11   But it came to pass that the call of the Church of the Marine Korps beckoned the old man of the High Church,
12   And he elected his religion over his loyalty to the common child men Marines, and he pinned back on his High Priest rank.

CHAPTER 9

1   And it came to pass that the Cardinal-general of the West attempted to council the Prince of Money on the art of land warfare,
2   And the unwinning strategy of body exchange with an unending enemy,
3   But the Prince of Money believed himself of superior mind and knowledge,

4   For how could a small evergreen spot on the earth have a mightier nation than Sam Bo,

5   And how could this plain Chinese general understand things that the scholars knew not.

6   And the Prince of Money listened not to the tales of defective weapons,

7   And faulty equipment,

8   Nor to the shortage of bombs;

9   For the loss of flesh fit perfectly in the Prince's academic equation of war.

10   And the Prince of Money cared not that the Nam Bo common people were the victims of rape, pillage, and burn from the Nam Bo drug dealer leaders.

11   And the Prince of Money cared not that he protected men who sodomized children.

12   So it came to pass that the rejected Cardinal-general of the West obtained audience with the King of Cash,

13   But the King of Cash was an elephant, and the Cardinal-general was a pissant under King's feet.

14   The King told the Prince of Money, "I thought chinks could fight chinks, but this guy says our ally is crooked, that Bac Bo will just keep trading lives for lives, and we should give land to the peasants, and leadership to the common people — Hell, he wants to create a great zip society," and they laughed.

15   And the Cardinal-general of the West was much perplexed, for men who knew war not were wasting his congregation, the loyal child men Marines.

16   And blindness beget more blindness,

17   And great wealth gave greater wealth,

18   And the child men witnessed their Fatherland had donated them to Molech,

19   But the Marines believed in each other,

20   For only in each other could they have hope;

21   For Sam Bo was hopelessly harnessed to pocket-book thought and an elephant King's arrogance.·

22   And the child men Marines were pissants abandoned to die to protect their King's altar ego.

23   And the demons danced forth for the flesh was given by all the King's men in a smoke and mirrors war.

24   And in the King's ears they whispered, "Preach peace, practice war!"

CHAPTER 10

1   For BolTer, SnowWhite and the brotherhood of SnowFlight, there came a time of much death all around.

2   And the good soldiers on each side prayed the Angels of protection and the spirits of survival;

3   But the demons imprinting minds and souls puked forth messages of power, vanity, and greed,

4   For it was a time for harvesting the blood of ignorant youth cast into Molech's altar.

5   "Two or three of them for one of us is not victory," argued BolTer to SnowWhite on the intercom after seeing the field of blood with pits dug to bury the several hundred young enemy dead.

6   **THE DEAD KNOW NOT OF VICTORY**, were the words of SnowWhite in response to BolTer's question of winning.

7   And round-about men who loved their Fatherland refused to dishonor their homeland while leaders possessed by evil accepted the tide of human death and misery which emanated from the flicker of their away-from-the-war lips;

8   And round-about men who were loyal to their beloved Korps and refused to dishonor it died at the hands of the High Priests who hid the sins of the King and the King's yes men court.

9   And loyalty was given back not to the child men Marines;

10   And the child men became victims of honor;

11   And the child men Marines ached with abandonment for their fathers and mothers blindly knew not their children were being given unto Molech,

12   And the child men rebelled in the only way they knew, for they killed men, women, children, animals, and Priests.

13   And this the unleashed ego of the runaway hubris magnified itself over and over to the ever increasing ire of the people asked to donate their sons for the outstretched arms of a false god.

14   And there continued blind power of the misguided vanities of the milicrat mind,

15   For the job promotion opportunities of careerists who would speak out not for self-preservation sake;

16   So the young, innocent soldiers were left to give and did give all, so that the Fatherland could through time learn of the evils

and of the ignorance of allowing selfish leaders to steer the ship of the people through the seas of profits.

17   No greater price could be asked of the young men than to shed their life by a Fatherland that dishonored them,

18   And to convert their flesh to the cash pockets of derelicts who cared not at someone else's pain.

19   And the High Sheriff of Hubris cared not that child men died,

20   For death was the nature of war business.

21   And the children suffered great agonizing pain knowing that their flesh was to be burned at the altar of unworthy cause.

CHAPTER 11

1   And it was that BolTer returned to find that an Egg Beater helicopter had come apart right above the ground,

2   And it was that Hopper Honey was decapitated by the big blade spinning through the cockpit.

3   And BolTer was distraught at the defective helicopter slaughtering innocent child men while those responsible hid from view, and there also were those who worshipped money.

4   Then those of SnowFlight went forth and saluted Hopper Honey as the silver bird carried forth what had been the smiling flesh of life.

5   And SnowFlight sought counsel with SnowWhite, for they believed not that the children of Sam Bo would be so easily cast to the Idol of Easy Money.

6   And SnowWhite said, **A MAN KNOWS NOT HIS TIME: JUST LIKE THE FISH THAT ARE TAKEN IN A NET, AND AS THE BIRDS THAT ARE CAUGHT IN THE SNARE, SO ARE THE CHILD MEN SNARED WHEN IT FALLS SUDDENLY UPON THEM.**

7   **IT IS TIME TO LEAVE THIS PLACE.**

8   And it came to pass that SnowWhite told BolTer to gather round about cargo nets, for into the nets he would deliver food unto the orphans,

9   And BolTer believed not, for he knew of no food and believed not that SnowWhite could deliver food unto the orphan children of Nam Bo.

10   But SnowWhite gave unto BolTer secrets,

11   And BolTer smiled, for he saw in his mind what he believed not.

12   And it came to pass in the hours of departure of 777 unto the Island of the Floating Dragon, that there came the helicopters with cargo nets unto the palace of the Navy storage,

13   And the out-dated food of war was delivered to the soccer field of the orphanage.

14   And the little tan children waived,

15   And the women of non-war wearing the Catholic cloth of God waived,

16   For it was that little children and those of God knew that prayers were answered.

CHAPTER 12

1   It came to be that 777 left the Nam Bo war to the Island of the Floating Dragon for forty days and forty nights to meditate and train to return to the land of Nam Bo with fresh helicopters and new pilots.

2   And BolTer was a pilot's pilot, for unto him was flying knowledge unknown to the new child men pilot replacements destined for war.

3   Then there came days of wine bibbing, for the loud noises of non-war elevated the spirits and released the horrors homesteading the corners of BolTer's mind.

4   "Anyone who can't tap dance is a muther-fucker," SmegMa would yell in public drinking places,

5   And thereupon many pilots would jump up and start tap dancing on tables, on bar tops, and on walkways stomping quickly about in their black combat boots.

6   And laughter became contagious, and epidemic.

7   And when Vicar-major DingleBerry would come unto the drinking temple of the island church of the Korps, BolTer would yell, "Lets say hello to the Vicar-major,"

8   And the pilots would yell in unison, "Hello Ass Hole."

9   And amid the laughter, BolTer would yell, "Lets say hello to the Ass Hole,"

10   And the pilots would yell, "Hello Vicar-major DingleBerry."

11   And more laughter begat more laughter.

12   And there came a happy hour of happy hours, and the pilots sang a repeated song, which first came upon Dingle-Berry, and the song echoed forth,

Old DingleBerry used to own
    a grocery store,
In the evenin' he'd hang his
    meat upon the door
Little children comin' home
    from school would shout,
Hey DingleBerry your meat
    is hanging out
Hey DingleBerry your pork
    is dangling out.

13   And horrors of war were preempted by alcohol, silenced explosions, no sirens, and escape.

14   But it was that BolTer and TailWind sought out the deep sleep of MakeReady, and BolTer and TailWind would pop paper bags sending the snoring short man's mind into stark terror.

15   And it was also that in one night's middle, Injun and BolTer carried the naked MakeReady in his passed-out drunken sleep on his cot to the middle of a den of iniquity,

16   And there they dressed the passed out MakeReady maintenance troll in female undergarments; and painted his toe nails and finger nails with red polish.

17   And it came to pass on the Island of the Floating Dragon that the non-combat helo maintenance man awoke surrounded by singing and dancing only to realize he was clad in old women's nakedness,

18   And the pilot's yelled "get the fag, get the fag" as they chased the short pantyclad Marine out into the darkness.

19   And it was thereafter that MakeReady chained himself to a pipe each night in his quarters so that his body could not be stolen in the darkness and dressed "fit to fuck."

CHAPTER 13

1   It came to pass that SnowWhite lead the select pilots away from the ways of man to the mountains.

2   And it was that SnowFlight would fly during the day and in the coolness of the afternoons would meditate things that had been, that were, and that would be.

3   And there came to the place of thought a plain, small tan man who became known to the pilots of SnowFlight.

4   To the others, he was known as Lei'; but to BolTer, the weathered man with sparkling eyes became a friend.

5   "How do you know us," BolTer asked Lei'.

6   **BY YOUR PRESENCE**, said Lei', then smiled, **AND BY SNOWWHITE.**

7   "And how do you know SnowWhite," BolTer asked?

8   **IT IS A SMALL EARTH**, answered Lei', and continued, **IS IT NOT WITHIN YOU TO SENSE ALL ABOUT YOU?**

9   And it was that BolTer recognized in Lei another man who talked in funny riddles, but whose softness sterilized BolTer's thoughts of anger at a deceitful King,

10   And the disgrace of High Priests of the Marine Korps, including his father, who stopped not the wasted death,

11   Nor gave back ounces of loyalty to the child men Marines who gave lakes and rivers of tears unto the Korps' church,

12   And it was that the pilot called Lei' caressed the minds of SnowFlight with thoughts of wisdom, and with flickers of brothers chained to brothers by invisible bonds.

CHAPTER 14

1   And days passed, and it was in the night that BolTer came with perspiring dream, and sought out SmegMa.

2   "I dreamed I was a caged rooster," said BolTer, "and that the King of Cash blessed the Prince of Money as they ushered forth battle experiments with the High Priest helpers throwing us roosters into the Nam Bo game pen."

3   Then BolTer concentrated with emphasized speech, "And as the rooster fights continued, I wanted to fly away, and all I had to do is fly away for there were no bars, and there was no cage, but I

324   *The Revelation According to BOLTER*

stayed to fight, even as dead roosters were taken away, fresh roosters were cast into the fighting arena, what does it mean?"
4   "It means you are in need of a chicken, perhaps a laying hen," said SmegMa with instructions, "the next time you dream, throw in some young pullets, and a laying hen or two. There will be no fighting, just plain chicken fucking."
5   "Don't joust me," responded BolTer, "I'm scared."
6   "I know what it means," said SmegMa, "You need to go out and choke your chicken."
7   And it was that BolTer knew not what SmegMa the dream sayer, said not,
8   And it was that BolTer asked Chaplain Brother Hebert Hebert Head what choking a chicken meant.
9   And the Chaplain turned pale, for he believed that in a dream half way around the earth from his home that he had been discovered, for in his youth he had choked his chicken.

CHAPTER 15

1   Out of the night came the call for 777 to return from forty days and forty nights back to the war in the land of Nam Bo;
2   And there were many helicopters flying hither and yon in the capture of the child men Marines back to the ships of the sea;
3   And there were mighty boats carrying the mighty cargo into the holds of the mighty ships with the implements of war.
4   Then, out of the West came BirdMan, with the cargo of a simple golf cart,
5   And it had been quickly painted from blue to green and given the numbers of Marinedom,
6   And it was said that it was a flight line-item.
7   And BolTer flew the men of the sea from moving ship to ship casting flesh lots across the rolling waters;
8   And it came to pass that in the art of landing a helo on the moving ship on the rolling sea that the spinning helo blade winds blew a sailor man into the sea;
9   And it was that BolTer slipped aerially away quickly harvesting by cable hoist the human dot floating on the dark blue water taking a human soul away from the man eating fish that follow ships on the waters;

10 And it was that DingleBerry sought to give unto BolTer a rescue medal of war for saving the sailor flesh,

11 But BolTer sought not the badges of man given for simple good work,

12 But DingleBerry issued forth a letter for saving the sailor,

13 And SmegMa said it was a blow job that threw the sailor into the sea,

14 And RedLine said it was saving a draft dodger,

15 For to join the Navy was to dodge the draft.

16 And TailWind said it was only squid on a rope.

17 But unto the child men pilots of SnowFlight there was rejoice, for unto their skills were the gifts of rescue given.

CHAPTER 16

1 And it was that 777 came back unto the seas of Nam Bo where the high mountains and the sea's met on the wormwood shores;

2 And it came to pass that the child men Marines were sent unto the high mountains in search of men upon whom they could wage war,

3 For unto the bible of Marines it is written only to attack,

4 And words of retrograde are borrowed from the church of the Army.

5 There came an emergency call for unto the high mountain tops covered with clouds there were wounded child men.

6 And BolTer flew with SnowWhite on the impossible mission to rescue the injured who were smothered in clouds hidden among the folds of the constant jungle.

7 It was that in the blindness of the clouds others had tried to rescue the wounded but knew not, and could not,

8 And SnowWhite with BolTer flew unto the edge of where the high cliff rose up the mountains with the above clouds like a hat capturing the mountain top.

9 It was then that SnowWhite sought by radio the whereabouts of the wounded child men,

10 And it was said unto them that they were in the clouds at the top of the cliff,

11 Whereupon, SnowWhite stopped the helicopter in the air next to the cliff and then vertically rose next to the visible cliff wall up through the clouds to the top of the cliff,

12   And there was rejoice for unto the top of the cliff there was a rock upon which SnowWhite placed one wheel of the helicopter anchoring the flying craft in flight in the clouds with only one wheel touching the earth.

13   And the child men Marines were able to load the wounded Marines unto the cloud covered flying helicopter,

14   And when it was done, SnowWhite jumped the helo from the rock out into the white nothingness with an earth bound dive through the clouds,

15   And the helicopter sank through the clouds into the open air beneath, whereupon the wounded were delivered unto the field hospital.

16   And BolTer believed not what he saw, for unto his eyes behold, SnowWhite could fly with a grandeur unsurpassed.

17   And BolTer sought SnowWhite to teach his secrets,

18   And SnowWhite said unto BolTer, **YOU MUST BELIEVE.**

19   "But it is my nature to doubt," answered BolTer.

20   And SnowWhite smiled, and said, **UPON YOUR BOSOM SHALL BE GIVEN GREAT BELIEF**.

21   And it came to pass that SnowWhite and BolTer returned to the mountain cliff to rescue the other wounded,

22   And SnowWhite said unto BolTer, **TAKE US UP THE MOUNTAIN.**

23   And BolTer hovered the helicopter up the side of the cliff through the clouds to the rock of escape,

24   And BolTer recovered the wounded, then dove the helicopter into the white nothingness of the clouds.

25   And the doubting BolTer then did he believe.

CHAPTER 17

1   And it came to pass that 777 returned unto Tru Lai to make war on the enemy of unknown face and constant invisibleness.

2   It was written that unto the Nam Bo villages and peasantries, there was to be sent one Sam Bo pilot for interview unto the nature of helicopters,

3   And it came to pass that because of BolTer's ancestry, it was believed that BolTer should be cast to live among the common Nam Bo people,

4   But blindness begat blindness, for unto ancestral folklore the people of Nam Bo liked not the people of chinese.

5   Behold, the Nam Bo Prince of the Wilderness looked upon BolTer with crooked eye in the presence of the Sam Bo warriors in the Palace.

6   And it came to pass that BolTer was given time and space within the confines of the Nam Bo House of the Tetrarch of Tekoa,

7   And it was that BolTer witnessed the wonderful young Nam Bo girls kept in wire cages for the sexual use of the Prince and his men,

8   And it was that BolTer witnessed the small mountain boys of which the Prince partook in sodomy the evenings of a sick mind,

9   And it was that BolTer protested unto the High Priests, for the Nam Bo Prince tortured his people out of simple nothingness.

10   And it was that Sam Bo turned its head while the simple peasant peoples were given unto torture by the demons of darkness.

11   Then it was that BolTer wrote unto his father what he saw, and what he had heard,

12   And it was that BolTer did vomit for the child men Marines were being given unto unholy sacrifice to preserve the evil Prince.

13   And BolTer sought SnowWhite, for unto BolTer the horror was overwhelming.

14   And SnowWhite said unto BolTer, **WHERE YOUR TREASURE IS, YOUR HEART BE ALSO.**

15   **YOU HAVE WITNESSED THE PAIN OF DISBELIEF.**

CHAPTER 18

1   BolTer sought refuge in the hidden corners of the mind with much spirits in the Happy Hour.

2   And SmegMa yelled out into the singing crowd, "Anyone who can't tap dance is a muther-fucker," which brought about a room full of tap dancing combat boot clad pilots.

3   And BolTer sang, "You'll wonder where the yellow went, when the 'A' bomb hits the O-rient'."

4   And SmegMa licked the bald head of HalfRight, and proclaimed himself to Doc Baker that he was an amateur gynecologist.

5   And TailWind took bids but gambled not that he could fire forth a blue hue darter.

6   And DarkMoon showed unto Dingle-Berry the chitlin', which only was secretly a deep fried lamb skin from SmegMa.

7   And SmegMa told unto Chaplain Navy Brother Hebert Hebert Head that it was meant to eat pussy, for it looked like a taco.

8   And ShareCrop wagered the new boy with the first born moustache that child men could not drink a flaming hooker, which begat a fire faced child man in a learning curve challenge.

9   And TwoDogs challenged the Green Beret visitor that he could not throw his long survival knife high and catch it by the point, but unto the Injun's amazement, no blood flowed forth.

10   And there was much alcoholic escape, for unto their minds were the rows of 1369 body bags and the useless entrapment of child men in old men's ego fight.

CHAPTER 19

1   The child men of SnowFlight were angry, for they witnessed the money machine for the King and the King's Court,

2   The images of those who sought comfort in the god of greed,

3   And unto the clergy there were those who knew of the King's war profits.

4   And there were those who fed upon the kill.

5   And Injun said, "The god of money went West leaving a trail of tears."

6   And ShareCrop said, "The god of money went South, his priests were carpet-baggers."

7   And DarkMoon said, "My people were the money."

8   And TailWind said, "Its the price of gas."

9   And SmegMa said, "You can't get ten dollars for ninety-five cents worth of pussy."

10   And HalfRight said, "I could'nt even afford a daddy."

11   And StoneMan said, "War's Hell."

12   And RedLine said, "Only a frog's legs are edible."

13   And OverBoost said, "Are we unbaptized children condemned to wander through the air until we are judged?"

14   And BirdMan said, "Give me sky."

15   And BurnOut said, "The system's not bad, its always been this way."

16   And BolTer said back to BurnOut, "You Jews must be clothed in yellow."

17   So it was that the child men believed not in greed, in corruption, in high hubris, in selfishness,

18   For unto them it was seen that power begat blindness,

19   For unto them it was seen that rich men cast poor men as lots,

20   And unto them it was seen that the clergy of the High Church feared greatly the King of Cash and the loss of papal servitude,

21   Whereby the child men were given blindly unto Molech.

22   But it was also that the child men loved the Fatherland that loved them back not.

23   And the Fatherland disgraced the sons.

24   But it was that the sons became the Brotherhood.

CHAPTER 20

1   And it came to pass that war days became war weeks,

2   And war weeks became war months.

3   Thus, the things of war were hours of boredom with moments of stark terror.

4   There came the time that SnowWhite was sent to rescue two thieves in the place of the skull.

5   And he was thought dead until the third day when he escaped back to the Headquarters of the Holy Sea.

6   And there was the death of BurnOut who could take it not any more and jumped to his death from the helicopter high above the Aceldama OutPost.

7   And through time, StoneMan, RedLine, OverBoost, Two-Dogs, ShareCrop, DarkMoon, TailWind, SmegMa, HalfRight and BirdMan survived the war and were sent home to a new war of the mind.

8   Thus it was that the crevices of every day mind can be harnessed to war's horrors of long ago.

9   But forever there is the image of SnowWhite,

10   Who was the competent, leading the willing, to do the necessary to protect child men abandoned by their King.

CHAPTER 21

1   The disclosure of things seen which was shown unto BolTer on passage through the Island of the Floating Dragon returning home to the Land of Sam Bo.

2   To those who see and read, issue forth unto knowledge of those things that were, and those things which forth evil springs.

3   I, BolTer, the most doubtful, believe unto those things witnessed and shown unto me, and issue forth for future child men that they may bear witness to evil things that are done by men who bear the garments of self-righteousness,

4   And by men that succor not on the things that make men pure.

5   Draw near, and hear, for unto you I give secrets,

6   For unto you, I tell you of a mystery shown unto me.

7   You will hear the seventh angel with the seventh trumpet, for you carry forth in one hand the guidance of life,

8   And unto the other hand the witness of men.

9   Tarry not, for the time is not known,

10   And worship not the gods devised by man.

CHAPTER 22

1   The disclosure of Nowel White.

2   Speak kindly of those who draw near, and hear.

3   Honor, glory, and dignity issue forth to the church of the beloved Korps,

4   Grace to you and peace from him who is, and who was, and who is to come,

5   And from the seven spirits who are before the throne of everlasting life,

6   I, Hu U. Yu, son of many ancestors, was on the Island of the Floating Dragon on account of the Church, Marine Korps,

7   And from the visions of my mind in the hills of the tan man called Lei, there came unto me peals of manmade thunder and earthquakes like the carpet bombing called Arc Light.

8   And I turned to the voice of unknown and witnessed the huge nothingness as craters of the moon below blackness of the starry night.

9   And the craters were like unto bomb craters each filled with the colors of the rainbow,

10   For the blood in the seven craters was the scarlet of blood, and the one also was of blue of sapphire, and the yellow of sulphur, and the green of olive, with many pools and many hues.

11   And there in the midst thereof there were seven angels,

12   With hair and raiments white as snow.

13   And there among the seven pools of blood were the names of the seven congregations of the beloved Korps.

14   And the seventh angel with the seventh trumpet spoke to me in the seventh voice,

15   Remember what you see and hear, and go forth and write what is and what is to take place hereafter,

16   For unto you has been given vision of the seventh woe.

17   And there into the valleys, the mountains, the deltas, and the highlands, and the seas I saw many riders and many horses,

18   And the riders spirited forth on the black horses,

19   And the riders spirited forth on the red horses,

20   And a rider spirited forth on a pale horse,

21   And a rider of greatness spirited forth on the white horse,

22   And spirited horses of tiger stripe and camouflage awaited riders of the sacred word to make war on the last evil.

23   And out of the sky came forth a rider on a white horse whose mane was so white that it was silver-blue.

24   And the angels of the seven churches came forth on olive horses with the black tiger stripe markings smiling forth with infinity across the plains of war to the fretting demons.

25   And it was that there was war all around me, and I saw that the fallen and the elect were doing battle among the child men Marines.

26   And it was the church of the Marine Korps in its blindness did give greater slaughter to the child men Marines of its congregation.

27   And it was that the High Priests of the church of the Marine Korps did sing hymns unto the things that are of Kings of the Earth.

28   And those of High Blindness did give praise unto mammon's altar;

29   But the child men were sacrificed unto Molech while the High Priests gave rotten praise;

30   And it was that vegetable hearts made a Priestly stew.

CHAPTER 23

1   And the earth shook forth with the voice of a thousand bellowing canons,

2   YOUR WORKS AND YOUR TOILS ARE KNOWN; AND HOW YOU CANNOT BEAR WICKED MEN BUT HAVE TESTED THOSE WHO CALL THEMSELVES APOSTLES BUT ARE NOT, AND FOUND THEM TO BE FALSE;

3   YOU HAVE CARRIED THE BURDENS OF THE WOES OF MEN, AND YOU HAVE GROWN WEARY,

4   BUT IT IS AGAINST YOU THAT YOU HAVE ABANDONED THE LOVE YOU HAD AT FIRST,

5   REMEMBER THEN FROM WHAT YOU HAVE FALLEN.

6   YET THIS YOU HAVE, YOU LOATHE THE WORKS OF THE KING OF CASH, THE HARLOTS OF GREED, AND THE LESSER KINGS AND PRINCES WHO ROAM AND WEAVE THE TAPESTRIES OF EVIL WITH THE BLESSINGS OF THE DARK ANGEL AND THOSE OF THE ABYSS.

7   THE DEAD ARE DEAD, BUT THE LIVING MAKE THEIR WAY.

8   ARM YOURSELF WITH THE SWORD OF THE LORD.

9   BUT UNTO YOU IS GIVEN THE WEIGHT OF BLIND CHILD MEN,

10   AND IT SHALL BE THAT THE KING AND HIS COURT WEAR THE STAINS OF CHILD MEN BLOOD,

11   AND YOU HAVE WITNESSED THE AGONY OF HURTS.

CHAPTER 24

1   And it was that I was told to remember those things said and to be written;

2   AND TO THE GUARDIANS OF THE INNOCENT CHILD MEN,

3   THERE ARE PEOPLE THAT HAVE NOT SOILED THEIR GARMENTS; AND THEY SHALL WALK IN WHITE, FOR THEY ARE WORTHY.

4   HE WHO CONQUERS SHALL BE CLAD THUS IN

WHITE GARMENTS, AND HIS NAME SHALL SHOUT FORTH.

5 YOU, THE CHILD MEN, KNOW THE TRUTH, AND THAT NO LIE IS OF THE TRUTH.

6 YOU KNOW THAT YOU HAVE PASSED FROM BREATH OF LIVING HELL UNTO LIFE, BECAUSE YOU LOVE THE BRETHREN.

7 HE THAT LOVETH NOT HIS BROTHER ABIDETH IN DEATH.

8 NO GREATER LOVE CAN BE GIVEN THAN TO DIE FOR OTHERS,

9 YOU HAVE CARRIED THE BURDEN,

10 AND YOUR PAIN ROARS FORTH THE ECHOES OF GREAT WATERS.

11 REST PATIENTLY IN THE TABERNACLE OF YOUR HEART.

CHAPTER 25

1 Then it came unto me, Hu U. Yu, things doubtful, and things unknown,

2 For I could see demons laughing while child men killed the flesh of other child men,

3 And I could see demons frolicking at the merchants of the earth dispensing hardware of war and instruments of hate, exchanging child men lives for shekels of the mind and monies of the pocketbook.

4 And the seventh angel stood before me as I trembled at the unwritten woes sown for men who choose evil,

5 And there, written on the beast tromping on the nations of the craters of the rainbow among the dust clouds of blood at the beast's feet was one of the blasphemous words sang by the distraught crying child men, knowing Molech's altar.

6 And I fell to my face at such horror or horrors, for unto the child men Marines I saw that the demons of darkness directed innocent child men unto death through the grins of the he-whores of war,

7 And the meek, the innocent, the poor, and those who chose God were sent forth to kill the meek, the innocent, the poor, and those who chose God.

8   Then I saw men who proclaimed greatness chained and caged with ego, and the bars were called hubris, and egomania was upon their face.

9   And they puked forth lives of the child men as yellow and green vomit on the plains of time,

10   And such were the loves of the merchants of murder who harvested crops from the marketplace among child men flesh.

11   And the mothers of men hid from their eyes the donation of their sons to the ways of High Priests ministering Molech's altar;

12   And the mothers of men ached from the things other mothers' sons cast upon the earth.

13   But above the darkness, the light did shine,

14   And gushing sweet waters flowed cleansing my mind from the horrors old men dispense from self-righteous castles.

CHAPTER 26

1   Then it was that I heard the thousands of crying prayers shouting forth in the wilderness, like the peal of giant winds rising against the cliffs of the mind,

2   And the prayers were answered, for in the night of forgottenness, there came SnowWhite,

3   And SnowWhite was there.

4   And those who had eyes could see, and those who had ears could hear,

5   For SnowWhite was not of the flesh, but was of the glory of things told

6   And in my disbelief, I did disbelieve.

7   And I heard a voice saying, **BLESSED ARE THE DEAD WHO DIE IN THE LORD.**

8   And I knew that what I had not seen had become visible.

9   And I knew that unto the High Church of the Marine Korps there was the stainful shadow of a King guided by hubris,

10   And I knew that my brothers were my brothers.

11   And I knew that again the light would shine.

12   And I knew that unto love did the chains of the heart harness Marine to Marine.

13   And I felt the softness of SnowWhite into the night, and he smiled words heard unto me, **SEMPER FIDELIS.**

The Debriefing . . .

Lord,

Make me an instrument of your peace.
Where there is hatred, let me sow love
Where there is injury, pardon
Where there is doubt, faith
Where there is despair, hope
Where there is darkness, light
Where there is sadness, joy

O Divine Master,

Grant that I may seek not so much
To be consoled as to console
To be understood as to understand
To be loved as to love.

For it is in giving that we receive
For it is in pardoning that we are pardoned
And it is in dying,

That we are born to eternal life.

Saint Francis